Dr. London Wells, linguist and adventurer, has the unique ability to understand any language in the universe, including the languages left behind by the ancient dead races of the Lost Planets – making him an intergalactic celebrity. But London likes his privacy—and he always works alone. No assistants, no entourage. When he goes on expedition to a Lost Planet, it's just him, the memory of dead alien and the resident man-eating fauna. He's a self-sufficient sharp shooter whose insatiable curiosity can stand up to any danger.

Until he breaks his head falling from a cliff. That changes everything.

Now, after a long recovery, London is onto the greatest discovery of his life: a language to prove a connection between the Lost Planets. In order to investigate further, he'll need to travel to an unforgiving alien planet. But he can't go alone. That's his dean's last condition: either he travels with a research assistant, or not at all.

Unfortunately for London, graduate student Chas Chambers is not the only unexpected element on this trip...

Published by
NineStar Press
PO Box 91792
Albuquerque, New Mexico, 87199
www.ninestarpress.com

Warning: This book contains sexually explicit content which is only suitable for mature readers.

Print ISBN #978-1-9459-5238-8
Cover by Natasha Snow
Edited by Amanda Jean

THE SPIRES OF TURRIS

London Wells, Book 1

Christine Danse

DEDICATION

For Kathy, who set off on this crazy adventure with me. Crazier adventures yet to come. Turkey clap.

CHAPTER ZERO

It was a textbook ghost story.

Five researchers and their auxiliary crew landed on the planet Anemoi. The year was 2505, and they were the first humans to step foot on its soil. Their mission? To determine its habitability.

They searched three fertile valleys. Water was plentiful, plant life pervasive and well evolved. Weather patterns stable.

But the crew was spooked. All that water, all that flora. And not a single animal.

A simple survey mission meant to last one month stretched to three as the crew searched for anything resembling fauna.

No creepers, no crawlers. No creatures. Not an insect or a worm. Nothing with a digestive tract or more autonomous movement than a Venus flytrap. No fossils, even.

But in that last week, the crew stumbled across two parallel lines on a flat stretch of rock, a hand's-breadth apart. A neat series of marks appeared between them, marks that exhibited self-similarity, repetition, and pattern.

On a planet bearing no sign that animal life existed or ever had, they discovered language.

After a short, failed attempt to find more of the writing or its source, the research team packed up its camp and left. All nine members returned in perfect health and continued their explorations on other planets.

Of Anemoi and all of its fields, lakes, and fresh air, the final report read, "Favorable conditions, but unsupportive of animal life."

The single discovery of writing on Anemoi never went popular in the public. It went down in textbooks and became the stuff of academic ghost stories. Researchers and vanguards went to other, more exciting planets. Anemoi was rarely discussed, and when it was, a superstitious hush surrounded any conversation about the planet.

And so one of the greatest mysteries of all time had gone virtually unexplored.

☆☆☆

I was not superstitious.

I was many things, but not that. Insatiably curious. Tenacious. A sharp shooter.

And—quoth my sister, with no offense to our mother—"a stubborn, reckless son of a bitch."

Which was probably how I came to be wedged between the two walls of a narrow canyon on a planet that had been deemed, one hundred years before, "unsupportive of animal life."

Sunlight beamed down from high above with an amber cast typical of Anemoi afternoons. The whole planet was lit as if through a tinted lens, lending a gentle, dreamlike quality even to trying or awkward situations. Like this one.

I paused to give my calves a rest—and some other muscles I'd forgotten I had. Tiptoeing sideways through a narrow pass in the canyon for ten minutes had recalled me to them.

I propped my back in a hollow and took a swallow from my canteen. I still had water left, a fortunate thing. The canyon's smooth-sculpted sandstone walls suggested a river had once run through here, but that would have been more than several millenniums ago. Nothing now but dust. Dust and one small human scholar stuck like a bit of meat between two colossal molars.

There was a scrape like claws on stone, and a small avalanche of pebbles scratched down the walls. I ducked my head. A heartbeat later, the hail of grit hit the back of my neck.

"Hell," I said, and jammed the cap back onto my open canteen.

I shook my head and looked up. Nothing above but a thin slice of sky.

When I'd landed on Anemoi nearly two months ago, I still hadn't understood how five men of science could be spooked off a perfectly bright and verdant planet, like kids from a haunted house. But the crew had withheld one important piece of information from the official Anemoi records. Probably, they hadn't deemed it scientifically relevant.

Anemoi, though devoid of animal life, was not a still planet, and it wasn't quiet.

Winds moved its surface. After almost two months alone here, I'd begun to identify them, probably as the original crew had: The thin night wind that scratched against my tent in the cold hours before dawn. The brisk morning wind that woke me. The constant pushing wind that rolled over the plains. And this one—the sly wind that curled around the sides of cliffs to scurry down my back and drop showers of rock on my head.

In a temple I'd found twenty miles east of here, I'd discovered forty-two names for the gods of this planet's original residents, which really amounted to forty-two names for the wind and its every conceivable manifestation.

The names had no human pronunciation, so I'd translated them roughly into Basic, taking some creative liberties.

I called this one "The Prick."

It had followed me from the entrance of the canyon, at least a mile and thirty sweating minutes ago.

Something had followed me, and it had to be the wind.

There was no one and nothing else it could be.

A slap of air smacked me in the face and skipped up the high walls with a laughing shrill. I turned from another hail of dust.

Right.

I tossed my head, clipped the canteen to my belt, and continued my sideways journey.

Thanks to several lean and hungry weeks, I just squeezed through the narrowest of the pass by sucking in my chest, though my pack almost didn't make it. I hiked it over my head, through the somewhat wider gap above me. I winced as I tugged, feeling resistance as things inside scraped against stone and hoping they were nothing important. The expedition was virtually over, so theoretically I didn't need the equipment anymore, just the data that were in it. Still, I might need it one last time. That depended on what I found at the other end of this canyon.

At last I lowered the bag to my other side and squeezed out after it. I propped my knees against one wall and shoulders against the other and expanded my lungs. I wiped a layer of grit from the face of my watch to read the time.

I had fifteen hours until I needed to return to the ship and send out a confirmation communication, my little beacon back to the university that all was well on the Western front. It would be my final callback before I packed up and headed back. No more field quests after that. This expedition was officially over.

Or, almost. Only one matter remained: the white cliffs I'd seen from the wind temple two weeks ago. The distant stone had glinted alabaster even in the muted Anemoi sun, like no other formation I'd seen on this planet. They rose dramatically from the landscape as if built to catch my attention. And that, there, had piqued my interest. *Built.*

Through the binoculars, the cliffs had looked carved, their face flowing with whirls and curves as if winds had been frozen there. That could have been the work of time and natural forces, or it could have been the product of deliberate sentience, masterfully crafted to look like nature's creation. Alien architecture could be surprising in its subtlety—though there was nothing subtle about the cliffs, which by my estimation were three miles long and more than one thousand feet tall.

At last the canyon's walls opened, and I exited into a space maybe two shoulders wide. The wind fluted as it escaped the narrow confines behind me, its hollow voice rising and falling like the keen of a ghost.

Trembling red movement caught my attention. A small colony of rock plants bristled against the stone above. Their threads crisscrossed the wall between them, and more dangled loosely, shivering in the wind like feelers.

The absence of animal life on Anemoi should have been comforting, a good change from such niceties as two-headed snake bats and men-of-war that floated on the breeze. Even the plant life here posed no real threat to me, as it had never evolved the thorns, poison, or hair-trigger traps needed to wage war against animated threats.

Yet I paused to pull a tightly folded shoulder holster from my bag and secure my pistol in place.

The population of rock plants grew briefly more numerous as I walked on, all those tentacles waving, then thinned and disappeared. I had no idea where I stood in relation to the cliffs, but I had to be getting close. I hoped so. I felt the best I had in months, lean and efficient after weeks of hiking and climbing, full of fresh air and energized by the light of a true sun. Soon enough, I'd grow fat and slow again in the confines of a classroom. Still, a small part of me yearned for the soft mattress and hot food that awaited me on the ship.

That could be my age starting to show.

I rounded the last corner. I assumed it was the last. I couldn't actually see through the sudden blinding white glare.

"Jove's balls!"

I clapped a hand to my eyes. The wind, perhaps playing a last trick on me, whiplashed my backside and gave me a push.

I cracked my eyes. The wall before me filled my vision with bright white. It soared up and dazzled so painfully in the sunlight it seemed to disappear into the sky above.

I lowered my pack to the ground and spent several minutes dropping pieces of gravel into sample tubes. I wasn't responsible for the sample analysis. That would be the job of grad students and their undergrad minions at the college of the natural sciences. I snipped a couple specimens of orange grass as well. Something for the kids in the biology department to play with. I labeled the last tube, snapped shut the lid, and shook it to coat the grass with the preservative inside.

"Interesting geology," I said for my records. I took in a view of the tan canyon floor and then of the light-spangled white cliff. "It looks to be quartz—ouch, for crying out loud, that's bright—but where in damnation did it come from? Sandstone is the dominant form here. But this quartz is pure. Look at this." I ran my hand from the cliff wall to its base, where it met the tan stone of the ground at an almost perfect right angle. "Even the gravel here is sedimentary. No quartz. Look at that. Not a sparkle."

I didn't pretend to be a geologist, but I was fairly certain a flawless wall of stone didn't generate spontaneously from the landscape.

I tapped at the cliff with a chisel until it produced a small piece of quartz for me, dropped this into a sample tube, and zipped my pack up. I hiked the bag onto my shoulders with a restless, uneasy energy. I looked back at the way I'd come. Did I want to go back and give Sita a call, tell her I'd be a bit longer?

No. Not yet. Best to see what I could find here first before treading back to the ship and asking her to reschedule my return.

I walked along the base of the cliff. I found the whirling pattern in the stone interesting, but close up, I still couldn't discern its origin. The ridges and ripples flowed smoothly under my hand, intricate but random, the product of either nature's chaotic geometry or an alien aesthetic. But which was it?

I'd visited the White Cliffs of Dover a few times in sim. The first time, Dad had taken me to the World War II reenactment of the Battle of Britain to see the dogfights from Shakespeare Cliff. The aircraft had interested me, though not enough to distract my attention from the geology of the cliffs and the sheer beauty of them slicing down into the water.

"They're made of chalk," he'd said, crouching down next to me. The planes droned overhead. We thought nothing of leaning over the edge, the salt wind threatening to carry us away.

He teased a piece of the cliff rock free with his knife and held it up. "It's made of the shells of tiny sea creatures."

"It's impossible," I said.

"It's science. Nothing is impossible."

Actually, some things were. But I believed him about that for a long time. Not a belief easily shaken out of you, when it came from your dad.

Unlike the Dover Cliffs, the Anemoi cliffs were not made of chalk. No ancient sea creature sediment here. Just the white quartz sparking old memories.

A breeze, dispersed in the wider space, sifted over the orange grasses. Gravel crunched underfoot. In between these small sounds lay a profound silence, not an absence but a presence of its own, a watchful stillness.

I glanced up. I wasn't sure what caught my attention. It was one of those moments when you look up to find someone looking at you from across the room. Of course there was no one.

I did a double take and squinted another look.

Well, hello.

I looked at a vertical cleft in the cliff's face. It ran from the top of the wall to what I presumed was the bottom, although the base of the wall curved outward just enough to block my view of the lower half. I wouldn't have spotted the cleft if I hadn't looked up. More likely, I would have stopped right about here and turned back for my ship, missing the obvious in front of me.

I didn't believe in providence. But good fortune, I'd take.

I rounded the curve in the wall. The cleft did run all the way to the bottom, wider than it'd looked at first glance with remarkably straight sides, although that was hardly the most interesting feature.

No. That would be the stairwell inside.

The bottom few steps caught the sunlight and glowed. They'd been cut into the quartz of the wall and went up in a straight flight, deep into the stone.

"Exciting discovery," I muttered for my records, ignoring a chill. "We definitely had sentience at work here."

I mounted the steps. The way to the wind temple had not been as convenient. It'd taken three days to ascend that steep, rocky incline. Stairs were a treat in comparison.

I passed through the supernova of sunlit quartz and into the cool shadow of the walls, where the stone still held the chill of the night. A slipstream of mingled cold and warm air cut down the stairwell. It brought the pungent smell of drought-loving vegetation from above and an occasional *tick-tick-tick* of gravel bouncing down the stairs. I probably hadn't needed to bother taking samples for the geology folks. I just needed to shake off in their lab when I got home.

I followed the stairs to a landing, where they turned at a right angle and continued up another flight. Little sunlight reached down. The walls leaned toward each other like conspirators far above.

My steps echoed as in a cathedral. It sounded like someone walked behind me. Just a trick of the acoustics, of course.

I paused. The extra footsteps stopped, but not without continuing on their own for a moment, a ghostly *clap, clap, clap* of boots on stone.

Goosebumps rushed up my shoulders. I shook them off, allowed myself a look over my shoulder—nothing behind me except empty steps—and continued the climb.

I reached the next landing. I turned left to mount the next stairwell.

Well. There *had* been one, once upon a time. Two steps remained of that flight. Above them rose a mess of rubble that led in a general "up" direction.

Sunlight beamed down into the expanded space. It looked like a giant had swung its hammer through here. Maybe it'd gotten tired of carving each straight step and decided on a shortcut.

I considered the tops of the walls. There looked to be another 300 or so feet to go, which was a respectable height but no special challenge. I pulled my climbing shoes from the pack and also took the ropes just in case, although I'd climbed higher distances without them. Of course, never with a full field pack on my back. I considered leaving the fifty pounds of dead weight here for easier climbing. However, I rarely came down a mountain the same way I went up it.

I brought the bag for this reason, and not because I had the uneasy feeling it'd be gone when I returned. I shrugged off a crawling sensation between my shoulder blades.

I had my choice of rubble or vertical wall. On another day, I'd have scaled the wall. The vertical rock had broken in chunks, making for good holds. But a straight vertical climb would occupy my hands, and right now, I really wanted—needed—those free.

I didn't touch the pistol holstered at my shoulder, but my thoughts went to it. My palms itched.

I started up the mound of rubble that probably once had been stairs, and paused at the base of a boulder to take a deep breath. The sun had baked the cliff's vegetation and warmed the air with a scent like juniper, which—in a flash—made me think of Theo and the gang, and what kind of trouble they'd been getting in without me. I thought Antarctica had been slated for this month. Or that might have been last. Which would have been fine, since I didn't fancy the cold, simulated or otherwise. But I did miss my group in a keen way.

If that wasn't a clue I was ready for home, I didn't know what was. Never mind the staircase and where it led; what I wanted right then, just as badly, was a brandy and a smoke in the company of friends.

I gave the boulder a shove. I did that standing beside it, because if it fell, I didn't want to be on the unfortunate side of gravity.

It didn't budge. Grand.

I hoisted up and clung almost backward at first with the curve of the rock and the weight of my bag, but I crested the hump, and after that, made a leisurely climb to the top.

The breeze cooled the sweat on my face. Standing, I could almost see over the top of the wall a couple dozen feet away. Just a matter of crossing that gap and hoisting myself up a few feet.

I leaned my weight forward to peer over the side of the boulder for no other reason than to satisfy my curiosity. Maybe I just wanted a peek at my death, at the view I'd have as I plunged toward the jagged rocks below.

Maybe sooner than I realized.

The boulder shuddered under my feet. Deep below, something moved, like the root of the rock settling into an empty pocket. Stone scraped and groaned.

It began to fall.

I didn't have time to think about it. I just had the rope in my hands, the correct rope with the grapple attached. I'd had a lot of practice at this—too much, according to my mother and sister—and so my muscles remembered what to do, even as my brain flared with an SOS of adrenaline that spelled out *You asshole!*

My hand clutched the rope. It swung the grapple.

Beneath my feet, the boulder pitched backward. I stepped forward and let the grapple go. It flew and landed beyond the top of the wall. It slid.

The hooks snagged something solid and caught.

I pulled the rope taut. No more time than that to test its strength. I leaped and flew toward the wall.

I probably shouted. That was an unconscious thing. I curled in an attempt to control my point of impact and hit with my shoulder. I bounced like a lead ball and spun half a turn, gripping the rope in both hands like a lifeline, although I didn't need to. The carabiner at my belt had me.

Still in shock, I stuck my legs out and caught my feet against the wall. I could have used another moment to catch my senses, but in a moment, the boulder would crash down behind me, and it wouldn't take much of a vibration to knock me off. I pulled myself up, hand over hand.

I caught the edge of the top under my arms the same instant the grapple reached the end of its line and jerked. For a moment, I struggled with the fifty pounds of extra weight on my back and a slipping hold. Then I dragged myself up over the ledge.

I rolled onto my side, set my cheek on cold, solid stone, and stared at a magnificent peach sky.

My arms burned with scratches. My chest and shoulder smarted. I was weak with the shakes and winded, and knew tomorrow I'd discover all the muscles I'd pulled. But most of all, I felt like I could fly.

I laughed.

I pulled my arms out of the bag straps and left the field pack on the ground as I rose to my knees to take in the view.

It alone was worth the climb. Clouds had moved in and painted the distant sky with soft orange-pink lines like pulled cotton. Against that stood stunted silhouettes of windblown scrub bushes.

I pushed to my feet and approached the edge of the cliff. The wind coursed up its side, so it almost felt like I could spread my arms and tip over the edge and hang there, supported. I didn't. I did spread my arms to the wind's cold push and for a minute, at least in my mind, I soared over the land below.

The canyon looked almost small now beneath me, and beyond its trench spread a golden flatland. I saw the way I'd crossed, and the narrow pass in the canyon I'd squeezed through, and even the location of my ship in the distance—from here, just a short flight away.

Cold clean air chilled my face and filled my lungs. I might have laughed again. No matter how hard it tried, experience in sim would never match the adrenaline like ice in my veins and the sensation of expanding, becoming—for an instant—as big as the world.

I looked around the plateau I'd climbed onto and saw flat ground as far as the eye could reach, broken only by bushes and rocks. A couple heaps of rubble caught my attention. They might have been built structures originally, but on close inspection looked more like incidental piles of stone.

Here I stood at the top of the world. And at the top of the world was nothing but hunched pines and rock.

The lack of anything of interest didn't surprise me terribly. It was just the sort of paradox I'd come to expect on Anemoi. Evidence of sentient life, but no animals. A wind temple with no stairs. Stairs with no destination.

And like everything else about Anemoi, it got under my skin. The barren stretch of ground went on as far as the eye could see. The winds grew chill with the approach of evening, and I couldn't shake that feeling of being watched.

I collected only a couple samples of the tough, windswept vegetation. It was time to head back, especially if I wanted to make it through the narrow part of the canyon by dusk.

I followed the cliff's edge back in the direction of the stairs. Chunks of the edge were missing, making a jagged line—product of weather and the stone-drilling roots of the shrubs.

Ahead of me, the edge projected out in what almost looked like a narrow balcony—an effect heightened by the presence of a low rectangular stone atop it, like a plaque.

In fact...

As I approached, I became more and more certain of it. The rectangular stone was too regular in shape. Too planned.

Erosion had done its work here, too, removing sections of the "balcony's" edge. But obviously no accident of the elements had produced this projection of cliff.

Obviously, because symbols decorated the rectangle of stone stop it.

The ends of the stone were broken, so I couldn't tell if this piece had once been larger. For a moment, I thought the symbols were art. Crude and simple, like caveman paintings. But something struck me as strange about them. It took me a few seconds to realize what: These pictures represented animals of some kind. Also, they appeared with regularity.

I was looking at pictographs.

Pictographs that didn't match anything previously found on Anemoi. In fact, I'd never seen them before.

My mind was on this as I approached, and not on the brittleness of the stone ahead of me. Something alerted me at the last second, some scrap of survival instinct making me glance down and recognize the crack in the ground beneath me, even as I swung my foot forward to step on it.

Whoa.

My muscles locked mid-step, but my momentum and balance needed to go somewhere. And in that split instant of deciding where to drop my foot, I heard very distinctly the clap of running boots on stone behind me.

I whirled, foot slamming down for balance. I had my pistol drawn and pointed.

I glimpsed a ghost of movement, a suggestion of a human form, but before my finger could even twitch against the trigger, there came a tremendous crack, and the ground fell out from beneath me.

I was too startled to spread my arms. But despite my earlier fantasy of soaring, it probably wouldn't have done any good. I plunged through the wind and through the vast afternoon vista.

CHAPTER ONE

She waited for me in my office.

She looked like she'd gotten lost on her way to a date—slate-blue suit and hair pulled back in a tight ponytail. A single blonde lock curled over her temple, too perfect to have escaped on its own. She stared at the bookcase against the opposite wall with open-mouthed awe, so she didn't see me walk in.

I had no idea who she was.

I hooked my duster on the coatrack by the door and tried to place her. A current student? An ex-student?

"What can I do for you?"

Her eyes snapped to me and widened, like I was the next strangest thing in my office. Probably I was, although I'd attempted to dress moderately for class. Between me in my tweed vest and the office with its unlikely decor, she probably thought she'd wandered into a nineteenth-century Earth sim. The wall-to-wall wooden bookshelves, Oriental carpets, wainscoting, and brass chandelier had been an expression of my father's singular obsession with the British Empire and the Late English language. I'd inherited both the obsession and the office.

"Professor Wells?" she asked.

"Yes, that's me." I sat down in the desk chair and folded my hands over the studded leather armrests. Salvation awaited me in the thin desk drawer in the form of two small pills. I'd planned to slip in and grab them before my commute home to stem the pain that was just starting between my eyes. Now I was trying to figure out how this girl had gotten into my office.

She stared at me. "Are those real?"

"Beg pardon?"

"Your...glasses."

I looked at her over the tops of their frames. "No. I just wear them for decoration."

"Oh."

This one didn't have much sense of humor. Or possibly she wasn't all that bright, but her fine state of dress suggested she was a graduate student. In that case, the slightly clouded expression and lack of articulation were understandable—even forgivable. Once upon a time, I too had eaten air and slept between page turns.

"Can I help you?" I asked, resettling the glasses on my nose.

"I'm here to apply for the graduate assistantship."

"Which graduate assistantship?"

She blinked. "Yours."

I blinked back. "Mine?"

"Yes. I saw the email that went out last week. Are you still interviewing?"

That supposed I ever had been interviewing. The pain between my eyes crept behind my right socket and throbbed once in warning. My right hand edged toward the desk drawer and the two tablets waiting there. "What email do you mean? Whose name was on it?"

"Yours...I thought. Professor London Wells."

Hard to mistake that name for any other. A niggle of suspicion tickled at my skull—or that might have been the headache spreading. "Who sent the email?"

She looked confused, then blank. Then her mouth tugged into a frown as she fished up a memory and said, "Dean Tiwari."

I held my expression and my tongue. It wasn't becoming to curse the dean in front of a student.

"I'm sorry to inform you that I'm not looking for a graduate assistant."

Her eyes bugged. "Please? I need research hours for my practicum and every other professor in the department has an assistant already. If I want to graduate next semester, I have to finish 180 hours. And I *need* to graduate next semester."

And this had become my problem when?

I pressed my thumb into the hollow above my nose. "I'm sure not *every* professor already has an assistant." I'd heard grumblings at the last faculty meeting about the lack of good assistants.

"But they're not language experts. I brought my CV."

"I really don't have the time." I slid open the desk drawer and groped for the tablets.

Her cheeks reddened. It took me a moment to recognize the gleam in her eyes as welling tears through the blur of my own.

My hand paused in its blind search through pens and scraps of fiber paper. I went still as if I might avoid tripping the explosion.

"Please," she said, shamelessly deploying two fat drops. "I need to graduate next semester. The Institute of Human Language has offered me a position as archivist, but I need my master's first. They'll only hold the position for one more semester. After that, they'll list it again. I really, really need that job."

"All right, it's okay. Calm down." I squeezed my own watering eyes shut and tried to think. Samara had two assistants. Cortez had one. Drugal might be looking for one, but was Norn this girl's specialty?

"Why don't you tell me a little bit about yourself? How about we start with your name?"

"Albina Andropov. I'm in the Latin track."

"Do you have a focus language?"

"Portuguese."

"*Voca gosta da lingua?*"

Dawn broke over shadowed cheeks. "*Sim!*"

I stroked my temple. "And how about Italian?"

"*Il mio secondo preferito.*"

Fantastico. She watched with a mixture of fascination, doubt, and hope as I picked the slender telephone handset out of its cradle and put it to my ear. Another of my father's decorative touches, a working replica that connected to the university's communication system.

"Hi, London." Aelia sounded preoccupied.

"Madam Capra," I said in Italian. "Are you still seeking assistance with your research?"

"*Si,*" she said, voice sharpening with interest.

My eyes met the girl's and I smiled. "Good." I would have told her the girl's name, but I'd already forgotten. "I'll send her right over."

I replaced the handset. "Dr. Capra is a specialist in Italian. She's been looking for an assistant with her research. She'd love to see you."

"*The* Dr. Capra?" Her voice went up an octave.

"*The* Dr. Capra."

"Oh, thank you!"

"Don't mention it," I said as I ushered her out. I meant it.

I locked the door behind her, turned down the lights, and sat down at the desk to steeple my fingers at my forehead. I had the urge to search the office and see if anything had been moved or taken, but a glance around the room reassured me that she had probably done nothing more disreputable than welcome herself into an unlocked office and leer at my book collection. Which begged the question: what had my office door been doing unlocked?

I wanted nothing more than to go home, curl up with a cup of tea, and fall unconscious on the couch.

I found the pills in the drawer. I dusted the graphite powder and lint from them and swallowed them dry. Then I strode down the hall to the dean's suite and past her startled secretary to open the door with the artfully etched "S. Tiwari."

Sita didn't seem surprised by my abrupt and unannounced entrance. She looked up and smiled, slight behind the bulk of her desk, which in turn was just big enough for her larger-than-life presence. In burgundy lipstick and with her glossy black braid draped over her shoulder, she was as poised and enigmatic as a Hindu goddess. "Hello, London. Give me just a moment. Will you have a seat?"

"Nope, I'll stand, that's fine."

I tucked my hands into my pants pockets and waited patiently as her fingers flicked over the glassy surface of the desk, first typing and then arranging several files into a collection of folders. She worked calmly through the chattering of a monkey. The virtual window across from her desk opened onto a rainforest. Apparently my sudden appearance had startled the wildlife.

Her palm brushed the corner of the desk and the surface went black. She folded her hands over it. "How are you?"

"Good. Sita, I don't need an RA. I won't take an RA."

"She is more than qualified, London. She's a very good student."

"I'm sure she is. I sent her to Aelia. She needs and wants a research assistant."

"London, take a seat." She made it sound like an invitation, but I knew better than to decline. I sat.

"How are you feeling?" she asked.

"Good."

"Any episodes?"

"No. I'm not sure what this has to do with the current topic of conversation."

"This *is* the current topic of conversation. As long as I've known you, you've insisted on working alone. Why is that?"

"I haven't always worked alone." I sounded sullen even to myself.

"No. I suppose you worked briefly with Konnikov, didn't you? And I've always respected your autonomy, but maybe it's time to consider working with others."

With her beneficent smile and gentle voice, she made it sound like a mother's advice: *Maybe it's time to play with the other children.*

"Consider the students," she said. "Many of them would love working with you, Dr. London Wells himself. Is that why you avoid taking anyone on? I know you're shy of public appearance."

"No," I said, although she'd hit rather close to home. "I stand in front of a classroom of 150 students six times a week. Isn't that public enough?"

The monkey in the window began to scream.

"You know what I mean," she said, without blinking an eye. "I mean individually. You should be connecting with some students—and faculty—on an individual basis to share and develop your research."

"*Some* students. I have a responsibility to hundreds of students. How can it be to their benefit if I'm focusing all of my time and energy on a privileged few?"

"A research assistant would help you, London. You'll have more time, not less, if you learn how to delegate effectively and trust in another human being."

"And? You've had nearly fifteen years to thrust one upon me."

She spread her hands. "And I'm concerned about you. After your last trip, I don't think it's a very good idea for you to be working on your own. I think you should get into the habit of sharing some of your responsibilities and working with others. If you can learn to depend on someone in the office, you can know how to depend on someone in the field."

"I'm fine. Really. I am. It was an accident that would have happened whether someone else was there or not." At her expression, I said, "I was not pushed off the edge. No one else was there but me. I was delirious in the hospital. It's called head trauma."

"You seemed sure of yourself after being discharged."

"I was still worked up over the whole thing. I couldn't accept the fact that I'd made a mistake, so my unconscious mind concocted this elaborate fantasy that I was being followed. It takes time to heal from these things."

"Precisely the reason I think you need an assistant."

All right. So I'd blundered straight into that one. Maybe Sita was right and I did need help.

"I'm fine *now*. Back to working order."

Even better, now that the monkey had gone silent. I wondered if a snake had eaten it. Really, I didn't know how she worked with that thing running in the background. Maybe years of working with squealing students and headaches like me made her immune.

"London, please consider it."

"I will," I said, and it wasn't a lie. Would I take an assistant? Uhhh, no.

There. Considered.

Her black eyes gleamed and she shook her head slowly as I saw myself out. The desktop came back on, and she returned to her typing. I left her office and the sounds of distant parrots croaking.

I might have won this round with Sita, but I returned to my office in an even poorer mood than I'd left it.

I wish I'd kept my mouth shut about Anemoi. Of all the damage done by the fall, likely the worst was the way it'd unhinged my jaw. Apparently in the med complex I'd yapped to everyone—which, thank the Greek gods (or a little timely intervention from Sita to curtail visitors), had mostly been the medical staff. According to Sita, I'd been sharing my feelings for my dead father, my remote and complicated relationship with my mother, and sagas of old lovers.

I told Sita I didn't want to know what I'd said. Whatever I'd told her and the technicians could be buried with them.

A bit of gossip between the medical staff might have been the worst of it, but a journalist sneaked into my room one day. Sita happened to visit and discovered me telling the nice young woman all about my stalker on Anemoi who'd pushed me over the edge. Sita had the woman thrown out, university lawyers pressed the media company for invasion of privacy, and the story about my supposed escapades on Anemoi never leaked.

I didn't remember a bit of that encounter.

I did remember conversations with Sita near the end of my hospital stay involving me confirming that yes, I'd been followed on Anemoi.

Which was absurd. I'd been the first human being to step foot on its surface in over a century. After two months alone on the planet, my mind had been concocting sights and sounds.

I stopped in at my office only long enough to grab my duster. By then the headache had turned to a throb at the back of my skull. Perhaps I could make it home before the migraine hit full force.

☆☆☆

I didn't, of course.

I threw my duster onto the potted cactus just inside the front door, made straight for the bathroom, and dropped to my knees before the toilet fixture. There followed a long and compulsive prayer ritual that involved presenting the contents of my stomach to the gods of the water in order to appease the tortuous pain in my skull. Months before, when I'd made these sorts of visits to the restroom temple on a daily basis, I'd installed a plush rug in front of the porcelain offering bowl. Praying Catholics on ancient Earth couldn't have had it better.

Today I'd skipped lunch and had little in the way of sacrificial offerings. The gods could stuff it, anyway. No wonder they'd fallen out of favor. Only one thing that consistently killed a migraine, and it wasn't divine intervention.

It took me a few minutes of shuffling and fumbling around the apartment to find the first aid kit hidden on the ground next to the couch, where I'd probably left it the last time I used it. That would have been a little over a week ago. Not too long ago, I'd used it every day.

The room started to spin, and I rolled onto the couch. The bed was a better idea, but it was thirty feet away, and right now I'd trade the walk for a kink in my neck. The cushions accepted me like a cloud. I popped the top buttons of my shirt and found the port at my collarbone by feel. Even through my closed eyelids, the dim light of the flat pounded into me. I missed twice attempting to connect the kit's cord to the port, squeezed out a curse, then felt the tiny, satisfying click.

I relaxed back and held my breath tight, waiting for the kit to make its diagnosis. The process only took a few seconds, though it felt like an eternity every time. An almost bearable eternity, because I knew that in a few moments the migraine would melt and I'd drift off into blessed, blessed unconsciousness.

An expected unexpected giggle bubbled through me on the crest of an endorphin wave. Then I was swimming. This part I loved: pain and nausea relaxing their grip on my head, and every muscle in my body relaxing as euphoria replaced them.

"Command: lights off," I said. "Command: warmer by twenty-five percent."

The air in the room noticeably warmed. Cocooned and smiling, I slipped off.

CHAPTER TWO

I woke, damp with perspiration.

At some point during my drugged sleep, I'd rolled onto the med kit and so I came to with a kink in my back as well as my neck. I'd shoved my hand under my cheek in an attempt to pillow my head, and a trail of saliva was drying on my knuckles.

But the headache was gone.

"Command: cooler by ten percent," I slurred, sitting up. My fingers found the med kit's cord and disconnected it from my port. I dropped the kit to the floor where I'd found it. I pitied the future me who found it there.

I opened my eyes. The room was as dark as it had been with them closed, except for a single red point of light at the far end of the room. It blinked and blinked like the end of a needle jabbing, and finally I stood.

"Command: lights on."

I went to the control panel where the light blinked. Someone had called while I was out and left a message.

"Command: voice mail playback."

"You have one new message," soothed the female voice of the apartment, followed by a much deeper voice: "Lun, Mom and I are waiting at the cabin. Did you forget our date?"

I didn't recognize the voice, but I recognized the inflection and the unspoken "again" at the end of that sentence. And if those hadn't tipped me off, then the fluent Nahuatl the man spoke wouldn't have left any doubt. Victoria, with a new avatar.

"Shit," I said, and checked the time. My sister had left that message two hours ago.

"Command: wall cabin view," I said.

The living room wall sprang to life with a view into a rustic wooden cabin. Sunlight streamed in through the dormers high above, illuminating a large, open living space dominated by two couches. The couches were wood-framed hulks, wide enough to be rafts, with embroidered cushions and woolen throws woven into green, yellow, and red geometric patterns. They were very comfortable. The massive tiger draped across one of them shared the sentiment, if the boneless languor of its body was anything to go by. Its striped chest rose and fell in the steady rhythm of sleep. One paw hooked over the armrest, claws half-extended. It didn't seem to care that one whole haunch and back leg overflowed from the couch; this it propped on the coffee table, toes brushing an empty stone tea mug.

No humans present.

I left Switch the tiger to his afternoon nap and closed out the cabin. I rang Vic.

"You've reached Victoria," said a more familiar male voice in Basic. "Please leave a message and I will get back with you shortly. And if this is my brother, I expect pleas for forgiveness in no less than twenty-five languages, followed by a performance of the song, 'Wild Rover.' Translated into Basic, of course, so I can play it on pub night. Ta, darling."

I ended the call and stretched back on the couch with a twist of a smile. I wouldn't leave the pleas or the song, although she deserved both. I hadn't been a very good brother these last few months. Or son. Or friend.

I put a hand to my forehead. The migraine was gone but the memory of the pain shadowed my skull like an afterimage, and the fear lurked. It was a fear I'd never felt scaling mountainsides or running for my life from a pack of legs with teeth. A slow, cold fear that sat in my bones and seethed in all the places in between.

"Command: call Aelia," I said.

"London," she greeted, cordial this time. Probably home from the office. I imagined her in her plush living room with a glass of wine in her hand.

"Aelia. How did it work out? With the girl?"

"Albina? Wonderful, actually. She's an ace at interpretation. I think she's just what I need to get through all these translations. Kind of you to send her in my direction. That was thoughtful of you."

"The pleasure was all mine. She's doing all right, then?"

"I think she's happy to be at work, but then, she hasn't seen how thick this stack of documents is. But how are you? How's your head?"

"It's there. As hard as always."

"You do have a thick skull. Have you given serious thought to reinforcing it with rubber?"

"Now there," I said, "is a very nice suggestion."

We talked a little while about inconsequential things. University policies that had changed, the latest crop of students, professor politics. Teacher gossip.

"The Roman Empire, London. I am not jesting. He thought it ended in the nineteen hundreds. What are they teaching kids now?"

"What are they not?"

"Exactly. Exactly."

"Tell him it was obliterated in World War II. Then send him off to Drugal. He's teaching History of Germanic Languages next semester, isn't he?"

She laughed. She told me I was a bad person, and then said good-bye, it being dinner time for normal folks.

"And London?" she said. "It's nice to hear from you. I'm really glad you're doing all right."

I rose from the couch and went into the kitchen to make some dinner myself. I still wasn't hungry, but I remembered my empty stomach and keyed in a meal of cucumber sandwiches. I ate them standing at the counter.

My thoughts returned to the conversation with Sita earlier. The headache treatments always left me feeling mellow, so I couldn't drum up any anger at her now, just weary annoyance.

And a nagging question. I took a cup of tea to the table. It was scattered with three months of notes I'd collected on vellum as I'd convalesced, most of them not very good. Sad that the worst passages I remembered agonizing over the most. I piled the sheets into short stacks and went through them, trashing the worst and sending the work that didn't quite make me cringe into my Scraps file on the main server.

Finally, near the bottom of the mess, I found what I searched for. A plain notebook, cover slightly bent, powdery with a layer of rock dust. "Ai 5" it read in small characters. Anemoi, fifth excursion.

I held it in my hands and stared at it. There was a reason I'd avoided going through the mess on the dining table, and this was it. Buried under three months of tortured notes—my grasping attempts to break through the pain and mash together a coherent thought—was the only available record of what had happened before my fall.

It had taken the rescue party a week to arrive at Anemoi. Apparently, after the fall I'd walked back to my ship, where I'd sent out a distress signal and passed out on my own berth. There I'd lain, more or less unconscious, until my rescuers had found me. They said I must have gotten up to drink water, because I'd been in remarkably good shape—no dehydration. Just a cracked skull.

When they had found me, I'd opened my eyes and said, "There you are." Then I'd closed them and hadn't open them again.

So they told me. My recollection of the whole thing existed as a long blank, broken by a beer-froth of fuzzy impressions that popped if I examined them too closely. I'd been walking through the canyon. I remembered that. The cliff in the distance hadn't looked quite like a cliff and a little more like something built. I'd found only the single wind temple, which was a remarkable discovery in its own right, but disappointing in its isolation. I wanted to get one last look in before I took off back to the university.

My first clear memory was of sitting in a hospital bed.

I keyed in the journal's passcode and flipped open the cover with a dense anticipation.

I started with my entry on the wind temple. The short, excited narrative jarred me. I'd just finished my climb to the top of the mountain when I jotted these paragraphs, high on adrenaline. I couldn't identify with the man who'd written them. But as I read, memories came back to me.

The temple, almost hidden in the lee side of a mountain peak, its walls carved by the wind, or carved by skillful hands to look like it had been shaped by the wind into those graceful, sanded curves. The garden of desiccated puff flowers that tangled over curving terraces at its foot. That slicing sunbeam of elation that split through me as I rounded the corner and slipped through the hidden threshold into that airy open room.

The room had been a room only in the loosest sense. Wide windows that ran nearly from floor to ceiling, with only a couple of feet of wall between them, made it into more of an arcade. It was backed by a single solid wall, which was the mountainside. The temple's builders had designed it in such a way that the architecture broke the constant barrage of wind at the mountain's top and redirected it to flow through the space in caressing swirls as light as bird wings.

Writing covered the room's single solid wall, the same language identified by the original researchers. There was more than enough of it here for me to translate. The lines of writing were a devotional to the wind gods, dedicating the temple to them and calling down their favor. Nothing exciting and nothing surprising. A prayer. The Lost language scripts usually were.

I flipped through pages of photographs, technical notes, and little rough pebbles of poetry, past descriptions of plant life and speculations about the lack of fauna. (Had my wind-loving aliens been some kind of mobile sentient flora?)

The journal ended abruptly, at the end of three interpretations of the temple's text and a picture-set of rocks that, apparently, had interested me at the time. They were just rocks.

And that was it. Nothing about my discovery of cliffs in the distance. No record, in fact, of ever leaving the top of the temple.

Well, hell.

Had I even made it down from the temple?

I tossed the journal onto the table and dropped my head in my hands. If I concentrated hard enough, or relaxed enough to let the images come on their own, I could just remember the squeeze of canyon walls.

We only assumed I'd cracked my skull falling from the top of a cliff based on my memories. My broken, mostly missing memories.

Did I honestly believe I'd fallen from a cliff, picked myself up, and walked miles back to my ship?

Maybe. Maybe not. But that left the question: How *had* I broken my skull? Tripping up the steps into the ship?

Had someone knocked me in the back of the head?

The thought sat like a lead slug in my chest. I shook my arms and ran both hands through my hair.

That was the sickness thinking, not me.

I stood and paced the living room, a circuit well traveled these past several weeks. Before then, I'd been mostly limited to the couch, as evidenced by the buildup of detritus at its foot. Blankets, an overstuffed pillow, a couple of mugs, a plastic basin, and a few stiff, dried washcloths. It looked like someone's bad idea of a good time.

I scooped up the lot and dumped it into the recycler, minus the med kit, which I toed under the couch. Aelia had offered to come in and clean the apartment for me, but I'd declined, too embarrassed by the mess.

Now it finally looked good enough to invite her over—which meant I was well enough to clean my own damned apartment.

Although with the mess of papers cleared away, along with the evidence of my one-man sleepover, there was little left to clean. I didn't keep much. My only irreplaceable items fit onto one shelf in the living room, and they weren't much to look at. An assortment of river rocks, a pinned carapace, the plaster cast of a worm burrow, a set of eye bones mounted with wire, and the dried knobs of pneumatophores. My hunting trophies, so to speak, and the largest collection of Lost Planet samples outside a museum or lab. I had a rule when on expedition: I took no artifacts, and nothing I couldn't hold in one hand. The latter was more about practicality than ethics. I had to be able to carry the thing.

I picked up a small glass vial, latest addition to the collection. It held three pieces of dirty-white gravel, none larger than my pinky nail. I'd recovered them from my field bag, which according to my rescuers I'd still been wearing when they found me on Anemoi. Whatever had happened to me, I'd broken more than my skull. Rattling around with the wreckage of equipment inside the bag had been a dusting of broken glass, sand, dried vegetation, and the same sort of tiny rocks that never failed to find their way into my boots and make hiking a living hell. I guessed these were samples I took. After removing the smashed wreckage of my equipment, I'd left the rest for the natural sciences department to sort out—minus these three bits of rock.

Rocks generally weren't my favorite. I could usually find something more interesting for display on my trophy shelf, but these had caught my eye first, and I hadn't felt like rummaging through the broken glass.

I rolled the vial between thumb and forefinger. The stones winked as light reflected from crystalline facets on their surface, too small to see otherwise. That was one of the interesting properties of stone. Whereas organic matter lost its identity when broken small—a femur became bone shards, and good luck reconstructing the whole from the pieces—rock remained rock, no matter how small the bits. For the most part.

I held the vial up to the dining room light and turned it in my hand. The effect resembled sunlight glinting from high, cold mountaintop rocks. I frowned.

I sat down in front of the journal with the vial of gravel in one hand and scrolled back through the entries. I'd taken plenty of pictures of the wind temple and the surrounding environ, which included a lot of geology—stunning displays of boulders, arches, and outcroppings. Some looked like figures trapped in stone, witches caught by the sun or maybe adventurers arrested on the summit by the view and carved by time and elements into abstract sculpture.

I'd taken more photos of geological features than usual, for sure, probably because some of them might have been architecture. I couldn't tell. The pages were filled with pictures of boulders molded into forms too graceful for nature and temple pillars too rough to have been shaped by hand.

But these photos were all gray granite—mountaintop and temple all formed of dark, weathered stone. In all these pictures, not a glint of white.

I shook the gravel in its bottle. A mystery. Not a very big one, but then, I couldn't resist an enigma of any size.

This wasn't a mystery of the usual sort, though. I knew I knew where I'd collected the quartz pieces. I just couldn't recall the knowledge. The enigma was my memory. It frustrated me more because I had the distinct impression the elusive memory wasn't even a distant one. I'd seen this kind of stone recently. Today, even.

Of course.

I skipped through the rest of the journal to the bottom of the last page and its three unlabeled photographs. Random rocks. What had I seen in them at the time? Maybe nothing. They looked like accidental shots. The tip of my boot appeared in one of them. Another showed a stone ledge in silhouette against a bright sky. The third presented the same ledge in better color, but with details smeared by movement.

I removed my glasses and examined the photograph of my boot. Difficult to tell by the brightness of the picture, but the stone looked white. Of course, to be that bright, the stone under my foot almost *had* to be white.

"Hang on," I said.

I stood. I had a brief flashback of brilliant open sky and wide vista, of elation and fear.

I sent the three photographs to the main server with a flick of my fingers and called them up on the wall. The photo with my boot made my eyes ache, so I sent it away. The stone of the third photo was definitely white. I couldn't make any details out of the blurriness, but I had the gut feeling I looked at the same kind of stone as my three pieces of gravel.

I closed the blurred picture out. That left the one clear photograph with the poor contrast. Expanded to take up most of my living room wall, it looked like a scene I could walk out onto. The thought made me uneasy.

I played with the contrast until the stone ledge approached something like the white color it should have been. I couldn't get the sky right, though—until, with a jolt, I realized the bright orange *was* the right color.

And there I was, standing near the edge of a stark white cliff, looking out at the late-afternoon sky. It was still in my apartment, but I knew the winds would have been streaming around me. I'd been here before.

I had not taken this picture by accident. Now that I'd fixed the color, I recognized an intention to it. My gaze drew to a low rectangle of rock at the far end of the ledge, the center and apparent focus of the photograph. I squinted.

No, I didn't imagine them. Symbols lined the rock, too small for me to make out details.

I rocked forward to paw through the pile of blankets and electronics at the foot of the couch—the pile I'd just cleared away. My hand landed on empty ground. Drat.

I hadn't left the thing I needed there, anyway. In fact, I'd never actually used it before. I went into my room and groped around the shelf above my clothes and found the memory extraction unit tucked neatly into a wooden box. I'd fabricated it just before Anemoi, planning to use it when I returned. I peeled away the protective coating and opened the bag of electrodes, then shook them into my hand.

I stood in front of the mirror and placed the electrodes on my forehead and temples. One kept falling off. I licked it and finally it stuck.

I sat on the couch to fiddle with the unit's controls. My fingers pressed all the wrong buttons. I was no stranger to memory extraction, but I'd never performed one on myself before. A technician usually did this part; my only job was to sit back and close my eyes. I didn't think the controls could be too hard to figure out, but it took me a few minutes to play with them. By then I was wondering why I'd thought ordering a home unit would be more convenient than scheduling an appointment with the lab and sitting in their hard molded chair.

I scrubbed my forehead and remembered the electrodes only as they came off in my hands.

"Bloody damnation—"

But at last I had it set and the little pads in place and lay back.

The electrodes grew warm against my skin. There was the usual blackness behind my lids, then it swam into a static gray. I dropped down into a half-place between consciousness and sleep. A thought came to me as I sank back. What if I hadn't set the device correctly? What if I was lost here for hours without someone to monitor me? But then it dissolved, like all thoughts dissolved and slid and swirled in this space.

And then I was climbing back out of it. Someone gasped. Lungs expanded and breath entered.

I came to, sweating. The memory extraction unit was still warm in my hand.

I struggled up out of the pillows and threw my legs over the side. I picked the electrodes from my forehead. I'd just been feeling better from that headache. Now I felt washed-out like a long night out at the pub, except without the pub.

I splashed water on my face, drank a tall cup of juice, and paced to get my energy back up while the computer chewed through my memories.

"Simulation complete," the computer said.

I probably had about 200 hours of sim time racked up after several months of nonuse. I dropped the net over my head and called up the simulation, and then I felt the familiar rush of diving as the world flip-flopped.

I appeared in the wind temple. Fine grit ground under my boots as I turned. The familiar dancing winds eddied around me. It was all here: the tall, wide windows looking out on an open vista of mountains and plains, the wall of prayers, and here—yes, if I moved this stone in the corner, I found a bit of script hidden behind it.

I stood from a crouch, hair whipping in the breeze.

"Command: transport me to the cliff top."

The scene blurred. I had the slight sensation of soaring.

I stood in a high, bright open place. I shielded my eyes with a hand, but that didn't help much. The light reflected off of the white rock below.

"Command: eliminate glare effect."

The cliff top became a matte-white landscape stretching off in both directions. The details were off, but I couldn't say how, because I couldn't remember how this place should look. It had that feeling of a dream—a cliff that went on and on with indistinct features that the computer had filled in, so it looked real enough, but generic. More computer guesswork than reconstruction of memory.

I had the vague notion to walk right, so I followed the feeling. The landscape took on more detail as I neared the cliff edge, just as I began to suspect I'd entered a memory of the photograph and not a place I'd ever been.

I avoided the edge itself as I walked parallel to it. The wind pushed against me the whole way, but I didn't bother to eliminate it.

I saw the ledge coming up on my left. Something about that felt wrong, and I had the impression that I should be approaching from the other side.

I stopped as I got close. I had the urge to look over my shoulder, but I saw nothing save the bland computer-generated landscape. I looked down. My "body" in sim didn't register the same jolts of adrenaline and other thrilling hormones as it did in real life, but I experienced as close to a jolt of surprise as I could when I recognized the image of my boots against white stone.

It took me a moment to step forward to the ledge. The hesitation was at least partly anticipation. I could tell even from here that the symbols on the rectangle of stone at the far end of the ledge did not represent the same script I'd found on the walls of the wind temple. This was something different.

I walked forward, out into the sky. The wind shrilled as I crouched in front of the stone. The symbols were pictographs of some kind, distinct stylized images of birds and plants and animals. If they represented written language, there wasn't enough of it here that I could translate it, though I doubted it was art. The symbols were arranged in too-neat rows, and two of them—a winged creature and something like an insect with too many legs—repeated like words.

I recognized them. They didn't belong to any language in my vast store of languages, but I'd seen them. I knew them. I'd stood on this ledge and taken this picture. But I'd also encountered them before that. Some older memory stirred, not one of the recent blanked memories but one lost in the normal way to time and age.

I'd been looking at this before my fall. I hadn't imagined the cliff. I'd made it to the top, and this was what waited for me there.

But what did it mean?

I stood and scanned the cliff top behind me, the computer's place marker for what I couldn't remember, or had no memory of to begin with. I knew with certainty I would discover nothing else here. Also, I'd had enough of high places for the afternoon.

"Command: transport to cabin and delete previous sim."

The world flew away from me as if the computer snatched the cliff out from under my feet. Then I stood in the dark hush of the cabin, between one of the massive sofas and the long, wide coffee table. The clock ticked from the fireplace mantel. Switch the tiger was nowhere to be seen.

Night had fallen in this sim. A low fire burned red in the fireplace. The room smelled like cedar and tiger musk and the cold night air coming in through the window. I lifted a scrap of thick, felt-like paper from a drawer in the desk near the hall and scratched out a message: "Mom and Vic—sorry to miss you today. Vic, regarding the song: Are you attempting to punish me, or your poor pub friends?"

I left the note under an old horseshoe on the coffee table. The fire popped from its nest of logs. The window curtain flapped and fluttered in that single, never-ending breeze.

The cold made me shiver. Right. Well. Speaking of pubs.

"Command: transport to Old London."

I closed my eyes. At an exhalation of steam and a clatter of horse hooves, I opened them. The dim cabin interior had been replaced by sepia-tinted sunlight, gray cobblestones, the rusty brick walls of an alleyway. A newspaper lay limply on the ground, half in a puddle. "Gazette" read the dry corner, with the numbers "1887" beneath it. Voices heckled and hallooed from the street beyond.

Better.

I touched my hands to lapel and forehead, and found my duster and top hat in order. I felt my jaw. Too smooth for my mood right now.

"Command: beard growth twenty percent more."

With a day's worth of stubble, and some mud added to the hem of the duster and my boots, I looked a bit more the way I felt. I pulled a pipe from my coat pocket, tamped some tobacco inside, and lit it.

The world-weary gentleman adventurer set off in search of a pint and a crowded counter to drink it at. He had some thinking to do.

Chapter Three

I didn't find any answers at the bottom of a virtual beer mug. They found me at seven o'clock in the morning.

My eyes popped open. "It's in the bloody book." I threw the blankets aside, rolled onto my feet, knew a moment of dizziness and steadied myself against the bed. My hand found my glasses on the nightstand, and I jammed them on.

"Lights on," I ordered the computer, and hop-tripped over the pile of homework at my bedside—one mess I couldn't just toss, despite my wishes.

I knew I'd seen those pictographs from Anemoi before. They'd been in a book, a real printed book that I'd held in my hands.

But which one?

The bookcase in my room was nothing as grand as the one in my office, but still stuffed with volumes—mostly Late English literature. I pulled titles out, swiped them open, and snapped them shut again to add to the mess of paperwork on the floor. Arthur Conan Doyle, Henry Rider Haggard, and H. G. Wells were not what I was looking for.

I had as much luck in the living room. Less than a handful of books had survived last night's cleaning rampage, and nothing relevant to my search. If the book I needed had been out here, I'd thrown it into the recycler. No lasting loss. I'd have it archived on the main server. The problem was I didn't know what I was looking for, and I had hundreds of titles in my catalog. I called them up on the wall screen and scrolled through them.

"Fie," I said. I pulled on the sim net and entered the library simulation. Bookcases towered around me like gorge walls. Here, my collection of Earth geography. There, my travel journals. And there, my collection about the Lost Planets. The gleaming floors echoed as I walked to that case. I gazed up its thirty-foot height.

"Command: narrow collection to titles that have illustrations."

About a quarter of the spines disappeared. That improved matters somewhat.

I let out a noisy exhale and reached for a volume just above my head. Something about that action snapped a memory into place.

Of course. The book wasn't here. It was on the shelf in the office. I'd read it when Dad was alive. I had a sudden recollection of him sitting at the desk as I'd slouched in the wingback chair, one leg hooked over the armrest, that book propped on my stomach. It must have been shortly before I'd run off on my first expedition.

I couldn't remember the title of the book or even precisely what it had been about, but it had something to do with the Lost Planets, and it was one of the books that'd inspired me to go on that first crazy quest. The other was good old Allan Quatermain in *King Solomon's Mines*. Sometimes I wondered if Dad had nurtured my interest in Lost Planet research because otherwise I might have moved to Earth, plugged in to the mainframe, and disappeared into a sim of the nineteenth-century African bush to hunt big game and lost treasure.

I didn't think even he'd expected me to charter a ship, fly to Oblitus, and disappear into the alien wilderness.

I checked the time. Seven thirty. Just enough time to make it to class in an hour, with a little rendezvous at my office beforehand.

I took a speed shower and ordered an English muffin from the dispenser while still buttoning my dress shirt.

The usual crowd crammed the tube that morning, plus a pair of women who stared around with the open curiosity of tourists. They bent together in murmuring conversation. It wasn't Basic, and it wasn't one of the Classical languages. One of the Diaspora, then, maybe from an inner planet. It sounded faintly Germanic. I recognized something like Dutch in there, but with influence from Basic and what sounded a little...tribal. It took me a minute to catch on, and when I did, the taller of the two was sharing how she'd finally confronted the hotel staff about the terrible taste, only to be told that "you weren't supposed to drink it."

"He had the audacity to look affronted at me," she said. "Did you know what that box next to sink is supposed to do? It doesn't even have a faucet. He said—"

A tall man stepped between us to lean into a neighboring woman, narrowly missing me with his leather bag. His gaze was fixed to a piece of vellum he held. He swore.

"Look at this," he said, looping his arm around her shoulder so she could read.

I could just make out the text of the title. "Mi'hani government executes new immigration regulations." Nothing too surprising there. A lot of the inhabited planets were toughening their borders, especially the more prosperous ones, likely taking a cue from Earth. But there had been mutterings about Mi'hani in particular lately, mostly to do with tightening laws and economic growth and some kind of heavy technology advancements, and pockets of anarchists unhappy with the developments.

None of it meant anything to me. Saraswati University was an unincorporated space station, a law unto its own. But a lot of the students came from the planets or planned for careers on them, so I witnessed a lot of cross-chatter. Usually I found it vaguely interesting, in an anthropological way. Today the subjects crowded too close.

The train braked and the doors opened, and the man and woman flowed out with the current. I hopped off one station later. "Hopped" was a bad word. "Shoved" and "jostled" were slightly more appropriate, especially if used in conjunction with the noun and verb forms of "crush." Nine fifteen ante meridiem found me squeezing through the terminal with every language and written arts student on their way to morning class.

"Hey, Dr. Wells!" said one of the faces. I couldn't identify which one. "Are you collecting that reflective analysis today?"

I didn't have the oxygen to respond. That was being sucked in by the two hundred twenty-somethings all shouting to be heard over one another.

I ducked through an opening between two sets of shoulders and took the long way around the back garden that, at this time of morning, was the short way. As I took my detour past carefully tended beds of foxglove and marigolds, I reflected that there were things I missed about home while off on expedition, but throngs of humanity were not among them.

The Humanities building was one of the two largest compounds in the university. I made my way through the literary rose garden toward the Languages wing. A bronze rabbit in a waistcoat checked its pocket watch under a drooping cluster of tiny pink buds. Around a hedge, in its own little green alcove, a plaque stood under a trellis of red blooms. Shakespeare's "A rose is a rose by any other name..." A bust of the Poet himself stared flatly and, I thought, a little dourly from its post. No doubt remembering all of the times I'd leaned against its marble side as a twelve-year-old, reading twenty-first-century smut in the shade of the roses.

All up the height of the Languages wing, lights were on in the windows. A few of the windows had been thrown open to the sweeter air of the garden.

On the other side of a reflective pond, the neighboring wing stood silent and dark. Until seven years ago, that had housed the Social Sciences, a department that had been ping-ponging between Sciences and Humanities for several decades, until the university finally swept it into its own building halfway between, where—last I heard—the department heads were petitioning to rejoin Sciences.

I entered the back entrance and took one of the lesser-trafficked hallways past the utilities office and the housekeeping lounge. I cut past the mural painted by the classical arts class that had graduated five years ago and then I came to my own hall, blessedly empty.

No unexpected guests this morning. I found my office door closed and locked with the lights off, just as I'd left them.

I went in and turned them on. Before passing away, my dad had been one of the big earners for the department, pulling in a lot of sponsor money with his work reconstructing Late Britain for the sims. He'd declined appointment as dean—twice—but I think he'd enjoyed his status in the department as a sort of beneficent Father Professor, and he hadn't been shy about requesting resources for a plush office. The chandelier cast a warm gaslit glow over the rich wood paneling and Persian rugs. The whole thing had the effect of making you want to curl up and open a book.

And there were a lot of books. Twelve foot by fifteen of them—the height and length of the entire opposite wall. My eyes skimmed over the shelves, zigzagging up. And there it was, just what I was looking for, right where I remembered it: blue-spined and slightly taller than the other books. On the very top shelf.

"Hell," I said.

In that moment, I cursed my dad and his eccentric fondness for very tall bookcases. Never mind that as a kid, I'd loved climbing up and down the ladder to fetch him volumes. I'd thought it was great sport. It occurred to me now that he'd probably never had to bother climbing the thing himself, with a monkey for a son.

I found the ladder pushed up against the corner wall. A layer of dust had formed on its steps, and its little wheels creaked in their tracks as I slid it to the center of the bookcase.

My stomach knotted at the sound. I locked the ladder in place and looked up its height, then down again.

"Twelve feet," I said. "Not even twelve feet. Six feet, and the rest is more or less you."

I wanted that book. I wanted that book with a burning in my gut.

I glanced at my watch. Eight fifteen. I had ten minutes to face this monster. I gripped the sides of the ladder and breathed.

"Right," I said. "Pull yourself together. We're doing this."

I fit my booted toe onto the first rung and stepped up. Nothing to it, actually. Just like stepping up a curb. I climbed up the next two rungs the same way—just a couple of steps, nothing at all.

Indeed: nothing. Not even a wobble, not even the merest dip in my stomach. Hope flared through me. The migraines had improved, so why not this?

I took the fourth step with more confidence—and that was when the world fell over. Like a ship capsizing under a high wave, reality rolled out from under me, sending my head spinning one way and my guts diving in another.

I flung my arms around the ladder and pressed my forehead to a rung while the ship swooped and swooped.

Breathe, I told myself. *Just breathe. You are completely motionless. It's all in your head. It's all in your cracked and bloody head.*

A cold sweat beaded down my temples. The world righted itself in increments until it came to a stop, leaning dangerously on its keel.

I opened my eyes and stared straight ahead at the shadowed books in front of me. I wanted to tear out the lot of them and pitch them across the room.

Regroup. I tilted my gaze up. The blue-spined book was there, just a few feet out of my reach. Two or three more steps and it would be mine, if I could stretch an arm up.

I took one step, then another, then clutched the ladder hard and very deliberately did not look down.

One more step. I climbed it and then spent a minute clinging hungrily to the ladder while I stared at my book.

There it was. *Beira, Temples in the Ice.* I could almost remember the page with the picture I wanted. About halfway through the book, not quite to the middle crease: a black-and-white plate of an inscription found in one of the blue caves.

I slid the book out, inch by inch, until I had the full weight of it in my hand. It was a beautiful volume bound in soft blue leather, probably one of my Dad's original watermarked texts. The picture of an ice cave had been stamped into the leather of the cover. Aging had darkened the lines and details of the image. Only the barest shelf wear softened the bottom corners. This book had known nothing but loving hands.

I stared at this gorgeous piece of art now weighing my arm and wondered how the hell I'd climb down with it.

Not all of the books in Dad's collection were watermarked handcrafted originals. More than half had come out of a fabricator. One of those I could drop to the ground, and to hell with it.

I opened the book one-handed and managed to prop it against the shelf. I was jostling the cover with my fingers, trying to tease the pages open to the list of plates, when someone said, "Dr. Wells?"

I yelped and snapped the book shut.

"Professor?"

The voice was deep, male, laced with concern.

I set my forehead against the rung. "Yes?"

"Are you all right?"

"Yes."

I realized I still had the book in my hand. That was the good news, at least. But now I found myself in a different kind of bind. I had an audience.

"Can I help you?" I asked the book spines in front of me.

There was a pause, then: "I can come back if this is a bad time."

I almost laughed out loud, but that would have upset my delicate balance.

"I have class soon," I said.

My wrist began to ache with the awkward weight of the book. I moved it slowly, felt the leather slipping slowly in my sweaty fingers.

Feet shuffled below me, but there were no receding footsteps. My back itched with the weight of a gaze.

I made the mistake of taking a look over my shoulder and caught a glimpse of my office door wide open and a startled face—thick dark eyebrows, eyes wide and light-colored. The ground dipped toward me. I shouted and jerked my arm back to grab the ladder, slamming the book against the rungs.

"Whoa! Do you need help?"

"Perfectly. Okay."

Somehow, he was still below me. This meant I was still at the top of the ladder. That was the good news—and the bad.

I had to climb down, or there would be a scene. The thought of security officers and all those clanging portable ladders swinging through the office and Sita scurrying through it all, lashing everyone with her rare, high angry voice, gave me the strength to lower one foot, then another. My hands followed, one at a time, clutching ladder and book both. I looked up at the empty space in the shelf now out of reach and realized that I should have put it back.

I might have tossed it to the wingback chair, but my unsolicited gentleman caller stood below me. While I could do without the audience, I didn't fancy explaining an unconscious body with a book-shaped bruise to Sita.

I ventured another step. The book began to slip in my numb fingers. I fumbled it and loosened my grip on the ladder. My balance slipped away from me completely. I scrabbled for a second and kept from falling mostly by plastering myself to the rungs. I smelled dust and sweat on them.

"Hold on!" said my audience. "Don't go another step. Hand that book to me."

I was in no position to refuse. Grateful, relieved, and more than a little annoyed, I lowered the book. From the corner of my eye, I could just see the top of his shaved, dark head as he positioned himself below. He raised a hand. It was a big one, with strong fingers stretched.

"All right," he said. "I've got it."

I let it go. My hand recoiled to clutch the ladder. By this point, I was almost beyond embarrassed. I just wanted down, and this person gone, and a few minutes to lie prostrate on the ground.

Blast. And I still had class.

"All right," he said. "You're good. I'm right behind you. Just take it slow."

I gritted my teeth. I might have clung on out of stubbornness, but my guts, not wanting to be left out of the action, started to slosh. I couldn't—I would not—cover the book collection with the contents of my stomach. I took a step, then another.

"Almost there," he murmured, voice closer.

My toe reached for the next rung. My fists were all knuckle as I clutched the side of the ladder. "Would you...kindly...leave me—the—"

I gasped. My foot didn't quite meet the next step.

I had a moment to register that this time, I was falling in truth and then I hit something solid and warm that was most certainly not the floor.

Two arms closed around me. For a brief moment, a wall of muscled chest held me firm. My audience smelled like leather and alcohol. Trim beard rasped against my cheek.

I nearly emptied my breakfast onto that hard, pleasant-scented shoulder. I pushed away and staggered against the ladder. Dragged in a breath of air.

He gave a nervous chuckle. "Well, that was quite an introduction."

I glanced up at him over my glasses. I straightened. We were the same height, but he was lean and muscled in a way that made him seem taller. His close-fitting olive shirt did double duty, molding to every curve of his arms and bringing out the green in his hazel eyes. I wondered how much of him was original. The little cleft at the end of his straight nose? The lush dark lips? The smooth light-brown complexion was too perfect, for sure.

I didn't know why the thought of his modifying his body should irritate me. I pushed a hand through my own brown hair, which was a 100 percent Mom-and-Dad DNA original and probably in need of a cut. I suddenly felt pasty under the lights. The warm tan I'd acquired on Anemoi had been sucked out of me by months of convalescence.

"You were here because...?" I stroked a hand over my chin. In my rush out the door, I'd forgotten to shave.

His expression sobered. "I came to interview for the research assistantship."

I'd been bending to retrieve the book off of the footstool where he'd set it down. I froze. Straightening, I went to the ladder and pushed it back to its spot in the corner. "I'm not taking interviews."

"Oh. You're done, then?"

"No. I never started." I turned to him and saw disappointment and confusion in his beautiful eyes.

"So, you haven't started yet."

"And I won't be. The dean made a mistake."

"Oh."

He didn't move. I hoped he wouldn't break into tears like the girl.

But no, the expression on his face was different than that. The gleam of his eyes wasn't the flat sheen of welling tears.

My neck heated. The book that held my very interesting mystery sat on the footstool just beside me, but I couldn't seem to move for it.

"I have class now," I prompted.

"Right. Yeah. Sorry about that. You probably already have enough assistants. I didn't— But if you—"

I bent to take the book. And now I would have no time at all for it, even to peek.

"I apologize about the mix-up," I said as I went to my desk and slipped the book into a drawer. Closed it. Locked it—against myself.

I glanced at the half-cluttered surface of the desk and for a moment couldn't remember what class I had this morning, or what I needed to bring with me.

The man hovered. "Well, thank you anyway. And it was a pleasure to meet you."

He held out his hand. I looked at it. If there was any mockery in his tone, I couldn't sense it. I shook his hand. It was surprisingly cool and a little damp, although that might have been my own sweaty palm.

"You, too," I said. "Sorry again." *Another time*, I almost said.

I could still feel the press of his hand after I'd closed the door behind him and was sorting over my desk again—doing circles around the drawer with the book in it, I thought—when the phone rang. Probably a student, calling to remind me to come to class.

"London," said the dean.

I shot a glance at my watch. Only five minutes late for class. Hardly severe enough for the dean to be calling me. For heaven's sake—was she monitoring me now?

"Sita," I said.

"I thought I'd find you there." She sounded smug, if anything. Pleased and indulgent.

I moved the receiver from my mouth and blew out a breath. Then: "You caught me. I was just leaving now."

"Good. Meet me after class."

"With pleasure," I said.

CHAPTER FOUR

The class I taught that morning was Advanced Language Theory. The students catcalled me through the open door as I ran past down the hallway, kindly recalling me to this. I backpedaled, entered the brightly lit lecture hall, and went to the podium.

"Thank you," I said into the microphone, and tamped the pages someone else had left on the lectern. "I think I was off on another expedition."

Scattered chuckles.

"Right," I said. "Pop quiz."

Sighs and groans.

"Extra credit."

Piqued interest. Attentive shuffling.

While they wrote three paragraphs about the relationship between language and cognition, I sat down and collected myself. I found the notes I'd scribbled for the day's lecture in my Profess folder. Someone had left a closed bottle of water on the table. I cracked it open and drank.

Teaching class calmed me. Unlike my undergraduate students, my graduates had a real interest in the subject matter—as well as a bit of a clue. Usually I let the students carry the discussion with only a little guidance. It was a lot better than lecturing for four hours. The students agreed, perhaps a little too emphatically for my ego. But then, my ego had never had to drone to seventy post-adolescents in an after-lunch slump.

We'd covered the ancient, middle, and late classical languages of Earth and today began the topic many of them had been waiting for: the languages of the Lost Planets. It pleased me to see the class full today, no absentees.

"There's no reason to study the Lost languages together," I said. "The only relation they have to each other is their similar backgrounds. They were all created by nonhuman species, now extinct, and were all preserved in a written format on structures similar to those built by ancient human societies. Stone temples, caves, halls of etched tiles.

"We have no way to know if these languages were spoken or how they sounded, or if any of them—or none of them, or all of them—were designed specifically for religious or governmental use. They have only ever been recovered from buildings designed for official use. If they recorded any other form of text—poetry or fiction or accounts of personal life—it's been lost to the ages."

A young man, Joby, flicked his fingers in what passed for a hand-raise in grad courses. "Did you decipher *all* of the Lost languages?"

It was the inevitable question, but I never failed to hesitate. Technically, I had. I hated to think some misplaced loyalty to Felix stayed my tongue, but still I offered the polite version of the truth.

"I was involved with the deciphering of each of the languages, yes."

I didn't know why I just didn't say it. *I was robbed.* Of more than just my academic work, or even my good sense. That was probably the hardest to admit. My sister sometimes accused me of missing a heart, which was true enough, though not in the way she meant.

I waited for the next question, the one that had been shining in their eyes all semester.

"Is it true that you can understand any language?"

I'd been standing. I hooked the stool to me and took a seat. "Every language that I've come across, yes."

The class was effectively derailed at this point as every face lit up, feverish with unasked questions.

It wasn't a mod, no, I answered one girl. Another asked if I knew instantaneously. That was also a no. I needed time to listen or to study the written word. I couldn't explain the process any more than I could explain intuition. It wasn't an ability I'd been trained in. I'd been born with it.

That inspired its own discussion. They wanted to know, as everyone did, why researchers didn't just study my brain and come up with a mod so that anyone could understand any language. The short answer: They had. They couldn't find the reason.

This baffled the students. Surely, researchers could figure anything out.

"There may be mysteries left in the world," I said. "Take, for instance, the Lost Planets..."

I took this chance to segue back into the topic gratefully.

Despite many studies, researchers still did not know why the Lost Planets were empty and might never know. Less than a handful of the planets were being actively studied. A lot of that had to do with funding and interest; really, it had to do with the funding that followed interest. Earth had little interest in external affairs, and the other human-colonized planets were of course busy with their own matters: building infrastructure, establishing—or abolishing—budding class systems, developing their economies. The independent research institutions, like this one, had finite resources. Though many people believed it was important to understand the mysteries of the Lost Planets, there just weren't enough resources for the kind of full-scale multi-planet project that might have a chance at cracking the puzzle.

"Now, as I've said, we only discuss the planets together for convenience. But what if they shared something other than their mysterious emptiness? What if there were some connection between them?"

"But they were completely different species," said one girl. Dark hair. Front row. Always with the skeptical remarks.

"Do we know that?"

She struggled for a moment. "No. They never found any hard evidence, like skeletons. But some of the ruins were found in totally different environments. The underwater shrines."

"Humans live in very different environments."

"But we adapt with technology."

"Very true. And is it so impossible that our aliens had technology?"

She thought about this. "We never found evidence of it." But she sounded doubtful.

"Never. Found. Evidence. No homes, no pottery, no games. No bodies? No evidence at all. How do we know they existed?"

Uncomfortable silence.

"Well," I said. "We have their temples and their government buildings. We have their words. *We* certainly didn't put them there—at least nothing in our science can explain how we could have put them there millenniums ago, so we can safely rule that out. So we have to assume they existed, these mysterious absent aliens, and that they developed to a level of sentience and science sufficient to create language and build monuments. But ancient humans could do that well before space flight—well before instant communication across continents, even. Advanced technology was not necessary to create the monuments the Lost species left behind. So. And we haven't discovered any remains that are indicative of a higher level of technology. Nor have we found a shared language that might have linked our space-faring, planet-colonizing aliens, if they even existed."

I came to a dead stop. I had an urgent impulse to turn, leave class, and dig the book out of the drawer. I stared at the students. They stared back.

I picked the talk up where I'd left off only because I'd given it so many times, I could recite it in my cups. More or less. "Never mind that some existed thousands of years apart." What was the next bit? Right. The grand finale. "But then, this all assumes that the link connecting these planets is a similar ancestry. What if the link is something external—an as-yet-unknown enemy race? Something that wiped all of the planets out.

"There's one good reason to crack the Lost Planet mystery: we could be next."

☆☆☆

An hour later, I stood in the dean's suite. I would have forgotten if the phone hadn't rung as I opened the door to my office. I don't know why I picked it up, what with my book waiting in the desk drawer, practically screaming for me to open it. Sita greeted me. I left the book and went to her office.

"You look well," she said, in the act of pulling her shining coil of black hair into a bun. Gold bangles clinked under the cuffs of her charcoal jacket.

I thought about this. I did feel well, considering. I chalked it up to a good class.

"I'd be even better if you stopped foisting potential assistants my way," I said.

Her face squeezed into something between a grimace and a puzzled scowl. "I retracted that posting."

"Tell that to Tall, Dark, and Handsome who stopped by earlier."

"London, I can't erase that announcement from the heads of students who already saw it."

"Technically, you can." Now I was just baiting her.

She gave me a look that said she wasn't having any of it. "No, I can't. Not unless you'd like to pay six years of schooling for me and find a replacement dean."

I met her raised eyebrows with a steady expression. She'd been trying to groom me for the position for years, and like my father, I'd been dodging.

We both managed not to grin.

She leaned forward, propping her elbows on the koi pond that currently decorated the surface of her desk. I realized then that the rainforest wall screen was blank. Blessedly so.

"So there's another reason I asked you here," she said. "You know the annual student-faculty mixer is tomorrow night. I didn't notice your name on the RSVP list."

Fancy that.

"I must have forgotten," I said, and rubbed at my forehead.

She set her chin on her hand. She smiled a little, always a dangerous thing. "I know a lot's been going on for you and you're just getting back into the swing of things, but I think that's why it will be good for you to go to this. Good to get back in contact with your colleagues, and with the students—your future colleagues. You didn't go to last year's."

In other words: your sick leave is officially up.

"Last year, I was getting ready for Anemoi."

"I know. And that's why I didn't insist you attend that one. But I'm insisting you attend this one."

I could plead migraines. Family emergency. Head cold?

She pointed a finger at me. "Don't. You're going. It's two hours long, there will be cocktails, and you will be wearing a suit and will sustain conversation with other faculty and with the students you've been turning down for a research assistantship."

I couldn't help it: I groaned aloud.

"No," she said.

I groaned louder, probably making what my sister called my petulant face. Apparently my inner child was alive and well—and a brat.

The dean watched me with an expression that said, *Are you quite done?*

"Yeah," I said. "All right."

She smiled. "Good." She swiped her hand over the desk and the fish disappeared. Her fingers typed swiftly. Most likely my name on the RSVP list. Or it might have been my obituary. "1800," she reminded me.

"Be there with bells on."
"That's the spirit."

Back at my office at last with the door locked and the shade over its little window drawn, I pulled the book out and placed it on the desk. It looked no worse for its morning adventure, maybe a small indentation where I'd slammed it against the ladder. One look inside the cover told me I needn't worry. No watermark, which meant this gorgeous thing had been spat out by a fabricator. I could have thrown it across the room, torn out the pages, made a flock of paper swans, and printed out another copy that evening at home. Not that I would have done that to a book from Dad's collection, but it meant I could have avoided that entire scene with the ladder by waiting long enough to print my own.

I set my hand on the title page. My thumb and pinky just touched the edges, palm covering an image like the one embossed on the front cover, one of the blue caves. I thought of my student from class with her reasonable explanation for why the Lost races could not have been in communication. I thought of the high cliffs of Anemoi and the underwater caves of Beira, and suddenly I couldn't bring myself to turn the pages. Either I'd find disappointment or a discovery that would explode the world. I wasn't sure I was ready for either.

I took the tube home before the afternoon rush. I sat with the book on my lap while watching a landscape of cafes, manicured gardens, and dormitories roll past. A small crowd had gathered around a couple of sketch artists—students practicing for midterms.

The comm was chiming in my apartment when I arrived home. I could hear it through my closed door as I keyed in the lock code.

"You have impeccable timing," I groused in English, accepting the call and standing in front of the couch.

The living room wall came alive with a view of the cabin and Victoria sitting on the arm of one of the sofas. Today she looked like herself. Dirty-blonde hair, blue eyes, flannel shirt, corduroy pants, breasts.

"You just getting home?" she responded in Basic.

"Yeah." I sat down, rested the book next to me, and began to undo my boots. I couldn't remember the last time I'd seen my sister looking like herself. I had a sudden flash of her leaning over Dad's desk, braid draped over her shoulder, consulting with him about some notes she'd taken in class. Two tawny heads, two hands propped on the desk's surface.

"What's up with the avatar?"

She looked down. "Don't you mean the lack of one? Anti-costume party at Becker's."

"That's original."

I tugged off the second boot and dropped it next to the first. Victoria silently regarded herself. She even had Dad's way of standing, one foot cocked and knee slightly bent, like she'd been standing in front of a class for three hours and was giving it a rest.

She shifted feet. "You know, I can't remember the last time I wore my original skin. I think I'd begun to forget what I looked like."

"Strange not to have a dick?"

She shot me a look part humor, part danger. I braced myself for a comeback—"you'd know" seemed in order—but she said, "How are you feeling?"

"Been better." I stretched out on the couch. "Where's Mom?"

"Learning how to shrink heads." At my look, she said, "No, really."

"I have a feeling I don't want to know."

"Probably not. So, are you just going to stay in there? You're not going to visit?" And then: "What is that?"

I glanced up. "It's a book. It has words in it that you read."

"Asshole. What book is it?"

"One of Dad's." I slowly flipped through the introduction. There were pictures here—of sculptures in ice, of research submarines, of the first inscriptions in the Beiran language—but none were what I wanted. If I remembered correctly, I'd find that farther along in the book, closer to the middle. I set the book aside and put a hand to my head, squeezing my temples.

"Headache?"

"Just some tension behind my eyes."

"You know what helps that."

"Oh?"

"London, don't be an asshole."

I gave a short laugh. "Fine. You're right. I'll be right there." I found the sim net on the end table and shook it open. "I need your help with a wardrobe question."

I sat back and dropped the net over my head. A moment later, I breathed in the fragrant woody smell of the cabin. As Vic had suggested, the headache was gone. Discomfort didn't translate into simulation. If I were lucky, by the time I logged out and returned to physical life, my body would have relaxed enough for the headache to disappear.

"You have my attention," Victoria said, leaning forward like a hawk that had just heard a rustle in the grass.

I told her about the faculty-student mixer and the dean's insistence I attend. "And she wants me in a suit."

"Poor baby. Did she specify what kind?"

"No. That's what I wanted to ask you. Any ideas?"

She stroked her chin and regarded me. "Do you have a theme in mind, or do you just want me to go crazy?"

"Not too crazy," I said, although I did want Sita to regret roping me into this, just a little. As Vic walked around me, predatory grin on her face, I thought to add, "I don't want to embarrass myself."

"It'll have to be black, to go with your hair and bring out the bronze in your eyes." She'd labeled my hair "sable" and insisted my brown eyes had streaks of green-gold. She pulled at her lip. "I'm thinking something long and Victorian, with a dark-gold silk vest to match. I'm not sure about the tie. Here." She pulled up a window and began to scroll through pictures of somber-faced men in frockcoats and vests.

An hour later, she had me outfitted in a suit and pants that would have made me look at home in a gentleman's club in Old London. In fact, I'd once worn something similar for just that occasion, but never with quite this eye for detail. I usually did something brown and a little plain. She was right; the black and gold did bring out my eyes and complement my hair. I looked dapper.

She showed me how to put the suit on. I would have to do it myself tomorrow, after I exited the sim. I didn't ask how she knew more about putting on a Victorian men's suit than I did, although that mystified me. In simulation, you didn't need to dress yourself. You changed your outfit with a word.

She expressed some dismay that I couldn't get the tie the first couple of tries. It'd been a long time since I'd donned one.

"You call me if you have any trouble," she said.

"I'd rather you fabricate a family emergency so that I can skip the whole thing."

"Unfortunately for you, there are no family emergencies on this side of the circuit board. That's all you, baby brother."

Chapter Five

A night, and a morning, and another afternoon passed before I admitted I was avoiding the book.

It perched on the back of the couch where I'd left it before visiting Victoria. I lay curled on the cushions beneath it, drifting in that sort of strung-out, displaced funk I often experienced after spending a day in simulation. With no classes to teach that day, I'd decided to work from home and had spent the morning and afternoon seeing students in my virtual office. Working via sim was generally discouraged but allowable. The hours didn't count toward the max number of sim hours granted each week, but even so, the university kept an eye on how much time we spent online.

Eventually I peeled myself from the upholstery and limped to the kitchen. Bent and stiff, I leaned against the counter while the food dispenser spat out a bowl of chicken and rice. I ate it standing. I followed this with a salad—a nod to Mom—and a beer, necessary muscle relaxant. Fortified and slightly less stiff, I took a shower and pulled Victoria's creation from the printer. The suit and pants had that crisp smell of ozone that clung to newly minted items. I hung them from one of the ceiling panels in the living room to air out. The outfit looked like a headless ghost hanging in the middle of the room, flat and helpless.

"You and me both, old chap," I muttered to it.

I drank another beer. The world started to come into focus around me, losing the surreal post-sim dullness. It was probably a good thing I'd been roped into attending the mixer, because the blank white walls were starting to get under my skin. I couldn't remember the last time I'd spent so long in simulation. My impulse was to jump right back in again, to immerse myself in the clarity and chaos of Old London, haunt my old haunts, hunt down familiar faces. The net lay on the floor at the foot of the couch. I could just visit for an hour. It'd make me feel better. I could hop off just in time to get dressed and make it to the mixer, where the crowds and noise would bring me back to myself. By the time I made it home that night, I'd be fully grounded.

Thus spake the addict's mind.

My gaze lifted to the book sitting a few feet away. What the hell. I had to open it sooner or later, and it would keep me occupied.

I could have skimmed for the pictographs. I didn't. I leafed through the book from the beginning, page by page, lingering on every picture, reading the headings, the captions—trying to recall the wonder I'd felt when I'd discovered this book for the first time. There was a full-page plate of a wall inscription at the beginning of the first chapter. As a teen, I was almost—almost—able to make out what it said. If there had only been a few more paragraphs of text, I might have been able to decipher it right then and there in Dad's office, legs folded, head bent. I'd tried. Now I ran my finger over the symbols and knew them; this was a directory of deities, a description of which underwater chamber belonged to the worship of which god. But at the time, I'd felt like the alien words held some secret for me, and I knew right then that I wanted to decipher them all—every Lost language, that this was my life's work.

"Well, you did it," I said, and turned the page. Historical perspectives, biography, research methods, equipment. Planetary features, geography, flora, fauna, weather.

I reached the full-color plates. My hand paused and hovered over the glossy insert at the center of the book, flipped the first page to reveal haunting deep-blue landscapes of caverns filled with water so clear they could have been filled with air. There was the research team, flushed and grinning from the cockpit of the submarine. There, the double jaws of a shark-like creature with an exoskeleton. Below that, the full-color detail Beiran inscriptions.

And then—last page—there they were. My pictographs. They decorated a panel set into the floor of a Beiran tunnel, half-hidden near the crease where wall met ground. The researchers had found them by accident when scanning for a way into what seemed like a caved-in hallway. They'd never found a way into the hall, and the inscription—only a few symbols long—might not have made it into the book, except they were the only example of unique artwork. The researchers had never found a match for them.

But I had.

☆☆☆

I appeared at the Humanities ballroom at 1800 sharp with everything but literal bells on. The suit fit snugly. A folded piece of vellum was tucked into my vest pocket.

Small knots of people stood scattered around the bright antechamber. The yellow and blue crystals of the chandelier threw geometric patterns of light around the room. A student waved from one of the corners.

I waved back and strolled to the double doors of the ballroom. The sound of chamber music drifted out with the din of voices and a sweet smell, like champagne.

I scanned the drifting mass of bodies but didn't see Sita. There seemed to be a pretty clear path around the wall; I could make a quick circuit around the room to find her before I collected a glass of bubbly and started the tribal ritual of bumping elbows with students and fellow faculty.

The student waved again, vigorously, from the corner of my vision. I realized she stood next to a research poster. Damn, and she'd already caught my eye. I smiled and approached.

It was Aelia who saved me, three student posters and twenty minutes later.

"London!"

I glanced back to spot her approaching in a slim red dress, waving at me with a champagne flute already half-emptied.

"Please excuse me," I said to the undergrad who had been telling me about Tuvan time orientation. I turned and bowed. "Doctora Capra."

She flushed. "Dr. Wells, you're looking...dashing." Her dark eyes traveled up and down the length of me. "Look at your shoulders in that suit."

"And you look extraordinarily stunning, my lady." An Italian beauty, with olive skin and a cascade of mahogany curls. I'd've been head over heels. If. Her red lips quirked, like she knew it too. I offered her my elbow. She took it, and we walked arm in arm toward the ballroom.

"A top hat and everything," she said. Her eyes danced at me.

"Do you like it?"

"It is very you. Very...Victorian gentleman."

"I'll take that as a compliment," I said, and touched the brim.

We grinned. Then we pressed into the sea of sound and bodies through the ballroom doors. I bent my head to her ear. "Have you seen the dean?"

"Somewhere around here," she half shouted. "Don't worry. I'll vouch that you were here."

"Very kind of you." I patted her hand. "Hey, I think that's her. I hope you will excuse me, my lady." I raised her fingers, kissed them, exchanged a wink with her.

Sita, if that had been her, had already disappeared into the crowd when I turned. I wove through, hoping to catch sight of where she'd turned. I froze.

I thought perhaps I was just seeing things, the Ghost of Faculty Mixers Past, but then he turned his white smile to someone next to him and I caught an unmistakable look at his profile. The Roman nose and the square chin that, on another person, might have looked like a caricature artist's joke. He made it imperious.

Felix Mata.

He began to look up, and I pushed back through the crowd. My heart banged—but not in anger, as it should. Ridiculous. *He* should have been the one running, not me.

This wasn't "running," though. This was tact. If I collided with Mata tonight, I wasn't sure I could control my expression or my mouth. I was here for Sita.

"Dr. Wells? Would you like a glass?"

I realized I stood next to the champagne bar. An ex-student watched me hopefully and expectantly, waiting to place her own order. Half a dozen other people watched me, too. They probably thought I'd skipped the line. I touched my hat in silent apology and said, "The asti, please." I could use it.

The student dazzled me a smile and repeated the order to the bartender. A minute later, drink in hand, I was safely ensconced in a group of students with my back to the wall and no Felix in sight. Also, no dean, but I could be patient, especially now that Mata had already shaved the edge of immediacy from my excitement. None of the students asked me about research assistantship, certainly a plus.

I drank, nodded to the conversation, and kept an eye on the crowd. Felix Mata. What would he be doing at a faculty mixer? The first and obvious answer was too distressing to consider. Of course, I might have been mistaken, as I'd only caught a flash of him. But a flash was all I needed to recognize that aristocratic profile and black mane of hair. He still wore it down and unbound. He must be near fifty now. What self-respecting man of fifty wore his hair down like some twenty-year-old Don Juan? There was a shot of gray in it. I wanted to feel smug about that, but the fact was, the color suited him. Everything suited him.

I drained the last of my champagne. I realized the small circle of students had gone silent and stared at me. Someone had asked a question.

"I'm sorry," I said.

"Will you be offering another section of Advanced Lost Languages next semester?"

"You'll have to ask the dean. And tell your friends to ask, too. Courses are offered if enough people show interest in them. If you'll excuse me."

I ducked out and skulked for the doors to catch a breath of fresh air and regroup. I was sweating under the suit, and the edges of a headache threatened.

Out in the antechamber, the din of voices dropped back like a curtain. Once there, I knew I'd be calling it a night. I'd made my appearance, and I could show Sita my discovery tomorrow.

"London, there you are."

And there was the dean now, parting the crowd with her slight form. She looked handsome in a classic black dress, hair twisted into a slick bun. I thought she'd scold me for leaving early, but she smiled with glossy maroon lips.

I'd tucked my top hat under my arm to make myself less of a target in the crowd, an attempt not to be noticed by Felix. As I turned to meet her, I placed it back on with a twirl of my wrist.

She held out her hand. "I've been looking for you, London."

I squeezed her fingers. "Dean Tiwari. Afraid I would bow out?"

"Never, if you know what's good for you. Look at you. You look like you stepped right out of a Victorian sim."

I bowed low at the waist and kissed her knuckles. She smelled of sandalwood and cardamom. The piece of vellum in my breast pocket burned a hole there. I straightened, lips parting to ask if we could move somewhere quiet to speak. My gaze rose to the man standing at her elbow and the words died.

Sita's smile widened. "London, I'd like you to meet someone. Chas Chambers. He's a master's student in Language Studies. Chas, this is Dr. Wells."

Suddenly I felt a fool in my costume, a big kid playing dress up. My hand went to my hat. I removed it.

"Chas," I said, taking the big hand he proffered me. This time, it was dry and warm. My all-too-helpful gentleman caller from yesterday cleaned up well in a charcoal suit. Its sharp angles accentuated his high cheekbones and trim waist. Almost alarmingly trim, under the broad chest and arms. The suit contained him neatly, but just. He looked powerful but sophisticated. In short: classy. He smiled at me, and a trace of the self-consciousness remained, but there was confidence in his demeanor this time. His other hand was tucked into his pants pocket.

"We had the pleasure of meeting just the other day," I said with a nod to Sita, as if he hadn't walked in on me nearly toppling from a ladder. "Language Studies, huh? You're a new student, then."

"This is my third semester," he said.

That would put him nearly halfway through the program. I did the math. He must have begun the program the same semester I set out for Anemoi and had completed nearly half of it since then. It hit me then just how much time had passed. It also hit me, in a strange way, how expendable I was. I was director of Language Studies; in my absence Sita must have admitted him herself. Life went on without me. The wheels continued to turn.

Into my own dumb silence, I said, "Well. And what's your focus?"

"The Lost languages." Then, in carefully clipped Oblitian, he said, "This is my favorite of the languages. I fell in love with it while reading *Words in the Wilderness.*"

It was the first time I'd ever heard anyone else speak a full statement in the language. Sita smiled, not because she understood Chas' words, but because she understood the expression on my face.

"You know it well," I responded in the same language.

He nodded. "I admire your work."

Right. Well. "Thank you."

Sita looked between the two of us, her smile quizzical.

In Basic, I said, "Good luck with your continuing studies."

"Thank you. It's really good to meet you. Properly, this time."

Now why did I feel like such a chump for turning him down for a research assistantship that had never existed?

"London," said Sita. "Would you meet me in my office in an hour? There was something I wanted to talk to you about."

My hand went to my vest pocket. "I wanted to talk to you, too."

"It's a date, then."

☆☆☆

Sita's face was bright when she found me in her office an hour and twenty minutes later, and her mouth parted as if she might say something. Then she saw what I'd done and her smile froze.

"What's this?" she asked, gaze skipping over the surface of her desk. I'd commandeered her desktop, though I'd had the deference to sit in one of the guest seats and not in her own desk chair.

"Tell me what you see," I said.

She approached the desk slowly, studying the pictures I'd called up onto it—one from my notes and one from the book on Beira, both enlarged to show detail. She placed her fingers on the glass and rotated them, slowly. "Pictographs?"

"They might be."

"Cheeky. Where are they from?"

"This one—" I tapped the desk. "—is from Anemoi." I actually paused to be sure. Side by side, digitally touched up, and enlarged to the same size, they looked nearly identical. Which, of course, was the point.

She gave me a look that said *and?*

"And this...is not from Anemoi."

She leaned over the desktop and shrunk them, rearranged them. I recognized the hunch in her shoulders that meant she was thinking. She stuck the knuckle of one thumb between her teeth.

"This one I found on Anemoi," I said. "I recorded it in my travel log. It's different than the language previously discovered." I brought up a sample of the Anemoi script to illustrate. "This other one came from a book in my father's collection. This photograph was taken in an underwater tunnel on Beira."

She continued to study them. I said, "The book was published before Anemoi was discovered."

"London—" Her comm rang then, cutting her off. She leaned over the desk to see who it was. She swore. "I have to take this, and it's going to be a long call." She pointed a finger at me. "See me tomorrow. I have news that will excite you."

Excite me? I made my way out of her office with the distinct impression that she hadn't understood what I'd just shown her.

CHAPTER SIX

The next morning found me in one of my undergraduate classes. I could barely think, much less lecture, so I gave the students a group project and cut them loose. To the background noise of three score voices talking, I thought through all of the planets I'd been on, all of the Lost languages, all of the ruins, trying to connect pictures and find similarities. Were Anemoi and Beira in close proximity? They weren't as far away from each other as some of the others. But then, there were other planets closer to each of them.

I stopped by my office after class. It was only for a moment before seeing Sita, but a knock came at the door.

Blast.

The knock came again. I opened the door and my mouth to ask whoever it was to blow off—in a polite manner, of course. My jaw snapped shut again, and I very nearly snapped the door shut too.

"Hi, London," said Felix.

Last night, seeing him across the ballroom, I'd felt a stab of panic and anger. Sane and reasonable responses. But faced with the reality of him two feet away, my immediate reaction was visceral longing. He looked the same. Gray in his hair now, as I'd observed last night, but not as much as I'd thought. Somehow it made his black eyes darker and even more sincere-looking under the straight dark eyebrows. His upper lip still had the same little dip, the one that made me think of the boy he must have been. The little patch of beard at his chin only served to make his lips look even smoother.

Eleven years, and he still devastated me.

Not appropriate. Not fair. Not acceptable.

"Dr. Mata."

His eyebrows raised at this use of his professional handle, as if I hadn't called him Felix and even Fee for almost two years. "You look..." A funny smile. "Different, actually. You look good. And still with the glasses, I see."

"Can I help you? I was just leaving." I stood filling the doorway with one arm propped against the doorframe. No entry.

"I apologize. I'll come by later, then."

Which was exactly the thing I didn't need—for him to show up when I actually had the time. I dropped my arm. "No, no. I have five minutes."

I perched on the corner of my desk and flipped through my inbox, not looking for anything in particular but to keep my eyes off of him.

He moved into the room. Hands in pockets, he turned slowly in place, taking in the whole of the office. Book cases packed with hand-annotated volumes, end tables piled with sketchbooks. I followed his gaze, trying to see what he saw, not because I wanted to see it through his eyes but because I wanted to see if there was anything that might catch his interest, anything he might catalog for later. Anything he could take.

"Wow. It feels like your father is still here. I'm really sorry about him."

I grunted. "It was five years ago." A not-so-subtle reminder of how long ago it had been over between *us*.

"I know." His eyes scanned the shelves. He picked a book off the wingback armchair and flipped to the title page.

Four minutes now, I almost said. I took a calming breath and studied him. Besides the gray hairs, his features were a little craggier, and a little softer too. Gently worn. A decade had passed since I'd last seen him in person. That was a long time in the metric of a natural human lifespan. Really, there was no reason to be angry at him still. I'd traveled much farther with my career than he ever would with his. My certificates and medallions of recognition lined the wall for him to see. Books with my name in them filled their own little bookcase. I had the translation of eight Lost languages to my credit. He had one.

"How are things with the museum?" I asked, mildly enough. There was a reason he was here. Was the museum not happy with a Lost language expert who couldn't put out good research on his own?

"Well enough," he said. "I've been heading up the language workshops these last few years. We're expanding remarkably."

"Oh?"

"Yeah. You've inspired a new generation. We keep a stack of your memoir in the shop that we have to replenish regularly."

"That's nice." I hoped he choked on the pages. I wondered how it pained him to see that book tucked under young arms. I wondered if he ever sold copies of it himself, handed it over with that charming smile and a recommendation. No, I really had no reason to be mad at him anymore. I rarely even remembered him, except when I taught Kandam. Meanwhile, his reminders of me came daily.

"And you?" he said. His eyes made a pass of the office, traveled over my awards and certificates. "Your father would be proud of you. Director of Language Studies. I'm sure Sita is grooming you for dean." The edge of his mouth twitched up, then down. "But how do you feel? I heard what happened on your last adventure."

"I'm fine. Just a bump. Completely back to new." I fished the watch from my coat pocket and looked at its face.

"London, I stopped by for a reason."

"Did you?"

"As I said, the museum is expanding its language program. How many Lost language students do you have here?"

Chas Chambers. My one dedicated Lost language graduate. I also had the students in Advanced Language Theory, if you could count them. The memory of Chas' voice speaking Oblitian purred in my mind.

Felix's mouth stretched into a flat smile. "We currently have nineteen students in our Lost language series, and six more enrolling next term." He let that sink in. "Our exhibit on the planets spans an entire level. We have a rock course that replicates your famous climb on Oblitus and a sim lab with eighty hookups."

"Oh yeah?"

I tried not to look staggered by the number of students they had. Sometimes, encouraging students to take up Lost Planet studies felt like hustling. Nobody wanted the Lost Planets. Oh, they wanted them. They wanted to explore them, wanted the romance and thrill of adventuring on them in sim, of standing in the alien temples. But nobody wanted to study their written words. They wanted Earth—Late English and Late Mandarin, Classic Japanese and Egyptian hieroglyphics and Koptic. They wanted novels and films, theater and poetry. The Lost Planets were ghost towns—interesting to visit, but ultimately they were husks, stage sets without actors.

But what were those students learning at the museum? What was the quality of education? The museum wasn't a dedicated research institution. It was an institution of entertainment and dissemination of popular knowledge. They regurgitated and, in order to bring the past and the unknown to life, they fabricated. I'd seen pictures of the rock course, and it was a cartoon of the terrain I'd climbed on Oblitus—a scaled-down, plastic movie set from a twentieth-century film. And most of the museum's Lost Planet sims would be, at best, as accurate as my makeshift sim from Anemoi. I knew, because most of the Lost Planet sims in circulation—the accurate ones, in any case—had been fabricated from my own memories. At best, they were filled with holes. So, much of the exhibit had to be fiction—human and computer imagination. And the only reason any of it was possible was because of research done by this university.

"But you know," Felix said. "There's one thing we don't have."

Originality? Tact? Intelligence?

"You."

I laughed. "Me?"

"Yes, you. The museum would like you to teach the Lost language series. And that's all. You wouldn't have to supervise, you wouldn't have to manage. You could just focus on teaching—and maybe writing."

"Because you're already director, is that it?"

He frowned. "Is that what you want?"

I shook my head. "No. I mean, no."

"No? But why not? You won't even think about it?"

"No. I'm *happy* with my job. I'm happy with what I do at the university." How could he even look me in the eye and offer such a position? "You know I wouldn't leave."

He set his jaw. He looked like he wanted to say something else. I beat him to it: "So is that why you showed up here after all these years? To recruit me?"

"No. As it turns out, I'm returning to adjunct." He glanced at his wrist. "Looks like my five minutes are up."

He made for the doorway and paused to look back at me. "You really are looking well, London. Congratulations on everything."

☆☆☆

He wore the same cologne.

I tried but failed to think of anything else on the ride home. Who the hell wore the same cologne for fifteen years?

My comm chimed as I unlocked my apartment door. "Son of a—" I answered the call. "Yeah?"

"London?" Sita's voice sounded uncharacteristically unsure on the other end.

"Yes?"

"Did you forget our meeting?"

I covered my face. "Oh hell. I'm sorry, Sita. I just got home. And I'm really tired." More like slightly sick and in a bear of a mood. "Can we reschedule for tomorrow?"

She said yes, and we ended the call. I'd intended to update the slide show for an upcoming lecture but ended up perusing old photographs on my local hard drive. A lot of pictures of me in my early twenties, face slimmer and eyes brighter, but otherwise eerily the same with my short-clipped brown hair and wire-rimmed glasses. Only, smiling.

My dad was in many of the photos. Striking, how closely we resembled each other, in features if not colors, although he was noticeably unsmiling. I think he liked to imitate the old Victorian daguerreotypes of straight-faced men, but the humor was there in his eyes. I stopped at one of him in a striped bathing suit and boater hat from a faculty costume party years back. I'd forgotten about that. Mom and Vic would have been around still, but none of us were in the photo, probably steering well clear of the embarrassment. The sight of his crinkling eyes leveraged a familiar pain under my chest bone. Familiar, but always alarming in its intensity. I closed out the photo.

Pain. There were the kinds you couldn't help but stew in, that satisfied some basic need for self-destruction, and then there were the kinds you locked away and never loosed, or they would crush you.

I moved through the other pictures. Dad, and Mom, and Victoria, in her days of Roman sandals and elaborate French braids. And there, in a folder in a folder, Felix. Felix surrounded by research papers at his desk, looking up with a quirked eyebrow. At the lectern, addressing a class of hundreds. In a three-piece suit, with me at his elbow. I looked eager in my brown jacket and wide grin, maybe even a little starstruck. We didn't touch in that photograph, but the magnetic pull was so obvious, it was almost painful to look at. So much for keeping us a secret. Sita had to have known. The whole department. We should have walked hand in hand down the halls, crooning Shakespearean endearments. That would have been less conspicuous.

I scrolled through more photographs, past the dignified shots captured at awards ceremonies and student mixers to the other photographs of Felix. The bare shoulders, the tousled hair and strong, curled hands. His taut bow of a back. His eyes staring across the flat plane of a stomach. Mine.

There were more. Pictures I'd forgotten I'd taken. Pictures I should have deleted centuries ago.

I closed the photographs and went to the kitchen to order a bowl of rice and beef and a cup of tea. I tried working on the lecture slides but couldn't stop seeing Felix. Couldn't stop remembering the feel and taste of him, like something dark with a splash of brandy. Memories long buried, unearthed by a whiff of cologne and the subtle bouquet of pheromones.

Cripes. Mata, teaching adjunct. That meant I'd be passing him in the hallways and bumping elbows in the faculty lounge. Even if I completely avoided university functions and snuck to class through back hallways, just the knowledge of him crawling all over the space station got under my skin.

The problem was, my body remembered Mata even better than I did. It didn't care about the intervening years or a betrayal or two. It also remembered that I hadn't been with a real flesh-and-blood man in...longer than I cared to admit.

And I'd been perfectly all right with that until Mata showed up. Perfectly, completely, and absolutely all right.

Safety. Heat. Sleep. Passion. I'd associated a lot of deeply comforting sensations with Felix before the bad, impressed into my cell memory. He'd wound me up down to my double helices.

Or maybe he'd just conditioned me like Pavlov's dogs. Felix. Sex.

Love.

Well, I could always retire and move to Earth. Mom and Vic would be happy with that.

And I couldn't believe I'd just had that thought.

So, the man activated outdated circuitry. I'd adjust. And if I ever needed a check back to reality, I only had to flip open one book. I went to the shelf and pulled it down. *Kandam, the Script and the Language of a Lost Planet* by Felix Mata.

I was satisfied and relieved at the ice that stilled my blood upon seeing *my* words, my sweat and hours of work, between two covers with Mata's name.

Every night spent in his arms. Every whispered endearment.

"I can't believe I lived without you," he'd purred in Portuguese.

Yeah, I bet he couldn't.

I felt a pulse of hurt and longing. The ice thawed as quickly as it'd frozen, leaving an echo of my old pained confusion. Confusion that someone I trusted so deeply would use me so completely.

The comm rang. I put the book away and answered it. I thought it would be Sita again. But a man's voice answered on the other end.

"Dr. Wells?"

For a confused second, I thought it was Felix or maybe even Victoria, but neither would greet me with that deference. Or uncertainty.

"Yes?"

"Hi. It's Chas. Chas Chambers."

Chas. Right. I recognized the deep voice now. My stomach did a funny flip, probably confusion because I'd been thinking about Felix. Not that Chas sounded anything like him, except for the rich depth.

"Hi, Chas."

"Hi. I'm sorry for bothering you. I was just wanting to ask..."

I found myself holding my breath in anticipation of his next words.

"Well, you know what," he said. "Never mind. It's something I can ask the dean. Sorry. It was nice to see you at the mixer."

"Nice to see you, too." Suddenly I was grumpy and remembered I was supposed to be getting over an unwanted Felix flashback. "Can I help you with anything else?"

"No. That was it."

"Great."

☆☆☆

"London!" Sita said when I stepped into her office the next afternoon. "Have you eaten yet?"

"How are you, Sita? No, I haven't."

"Good. Stay right there. We'll go down to the cafeteria together."

"You, take a break for lunch?"

"Stranger things happen." She leaned over her desk, hands doing their dance over its surface. "All right. Let's go." She tucked a folio under one arm and offered me the crooked elbow of the other. Arm in arm we went down the hall, her in her pantsuit, me in my duster.

"I miss your suit," she said. "I was glad to see you mixing last night."

"It was all right. I met some students who showed interest in the Lost languages. Can you believe one student came just to ask me questions about a paper due tomorrow?"

I didn't mention Mata. I still carried a sick pit in my stomach, and maybe a part of me was sore at her for taking him back on faculty. Irrational, of course.

My gaze swept over faces as we walked, but I didn't see him. We passed through the lobby and down a short hallway. I smelled food and wash water. We took up trays at the entrance of the cafeteria and got into line, which had backed up. I didn't understand the holdup until I caught sight of the wall screens at the far side of the room. The panoramic shot of an explosion splashed across them. As usual, the footage was on mute—fortunate when you didn't care to hear it, frustrating when there was a piece of news you wanted to catch—but text in the bottom right corner of the screens read, "Three dead in Mi'hani prison break. 'Shaper' extremist group implicated."

The grim-faced announcer came on screen, mouth moving silently. The food line moved forward. Sita and I slid our trays onto the counter and pushed down to two neighboring dispensers. We pressed buttons and waited for our food to appear. It was all very calm and normal. Difficult to believe that at this very moment, somewhere else in the universe, cinders smoldered in the wreckage of a prison and three graves hadn't even been dug yet.

"Chas is a good student," Sita said as she collected her meal. "I think it's a pity he started when you were out."

"He's something else." I picked up my tray and followed her across the dining room. I wondered what he'd wanted to ask her last evening. "So did you have to rope him into the Lost languages? Or did he come preset?"

She laughed. "Preset, preprogrammed, and preloaded. He was already halfway to understanding Oblitus when he started."

"That's impressive."

"It is."

We sat at a corner table far from the wall screens and their larger-than-life images of crying children. Sita navigated a beef-and-cheese wrap too big for both hands. She wiped strings of dairy from her mouth and said, "How are you feeling today?"

"Well enough. No bad allergic reaction from last night." Attentive crowds triggered my immune system.

"Exposure makes you invulnerable," she said.

"No. It *sensitizes* you." And stumbling across old lovers added extra injury. I picked through my salad, waiting for her punchline. Last night, I'd thought for sure her exciting news had something to do with the Lost Planets. Now I feared it had something to do with Mata.

She worked steadily at the burrito, approaching it from different angles like a puzzle. She knew I was squirming to hear her news. She had fun making me wait.

I decided to broach the issue myself. "So Dr. Mata is returning to adjunct."

"He is."

I tried to read her. "Is he filling in for Fundamentals of Symbolic Communication?" We'd been passing that class around the department like a deflated ball. I rather liked the idea of it being pitched to him.

"Actually, yes. And a couple other things." She finally put down The Beast to use a napkin and take a drink. She didn't meet my eye.

"Oh yeah?" I asked with forced casualness. Sita had been covering a lot of my duties as Director of Language Studies while I'd been out. I should have been thankful she hadn't replaced me. But the liberties she'd taken without even consulting me still hit me wrong. Admitting and advising Chas Chambers? All right; if I were doing my job correctly, that wouldn't have slipped past me. But taking Mata on for a full schedule of courses?

She said, "English Evolution and Introduction to Language Theory."

My hand dropped to the table. "Those are my classes."

"Well, they're not *yours*," she said, stretching the napkin in her hands and dabbing her clean mouth. "They're classes. Anyone can teach them."

"I designed the theory curricula. English Evolution was Dad's. We wrote those classes." Someone from a neighboring table glanced over. I leaned forward and lowered my voice. "No one else teaches them."

"It's okay, London. It's not set in stone yet. It depends."

"On what?"

"On you."

I sat back. All of the humor had gone from Sita's face. Fine, grim lines spider-webbed the corners of her eyes.

"What...are you saying?"

"I'm saying if you don't teach those classes next semester, he'll cover."

"But of course I'm going to teach them. I'm perfectly fine."

"Are you?"

Was this what all of her nudging, hovering, nagging, and wheedling had been about lately? Had she been building up towards something? Testing me, supervising my performance? The betrayal and indignation stung. So did the fear.

"Yes! Of course I am! I'm teaching a full load of classes. I keep regular office hours. I've reapplied to the review board of the journal. I interviewed the new applicants. I'm writing..." My stomach sank at her expression. "Did the students complain?" I recalled my lateness to class the day before, the meetings I'd missed with students because of migraines, the general fog that had clouded my thinking until a month ago. But all of that was getting better. I was getting better.

Sita pushed aside her burrito and produced the folio from beneath the table. I'd forgotten she'd brought that. Her fingers shuffled through several sheets of vellum. "Students are always complaining, London. Here. Look at this."

She passed one sheet to me. I stared at it blankly, not sure what I was seeing. I'd expected some kind of evaluation sheet or an organized collection of student feedback. This was a solid block of technical text. I didn't even see my name. "I don't understand."

"Just read it."

I scrolled through the text, only skimming at first until several words caught my attention and I swiped back to the top of the page to start at the beginning again. This had nothing to do with students, me, or even the university. It was a report on Turris, the fifth Lost Planet. The university had been running a few survey scouts there, but otherwise, little research had been done on it. The ruins on the planet were badly preserved, broken to rubble by the wildlife and the elements. This was one of the survey reports, dry and difficult to follow, really just figures strung together into sentences.

"Keep going," Sita said as I moved slowly through the text. There was an unmistakable smile in her voice.

I began to skim again, eyes darting over sentences, picking up key words. I paused over several pictures of tall and brittle-looking spires, eerie rock formations, and a turquoise pool of water that could have been painted. I almost felt Sita's effort not to reach over and commandeer the sheet. She leaned forward on her elbows and watched me with an open smile.

"What is it?" I asked, giving up. The document was more than a hundred pages long.

"Here." She pulled the sheet flat to the table and flicked her finger over it. Text and pictures scrolled by in a blur.

Her finger jabbed down, stopping the page. She flicked backward and paused at a picture, enlarged it. "This."

"It's..." I removed my glasses and brought the sheet closer to my face. "Blast and damnation."

Pictographs. I was looking at pictographs carved into the rock. Only a few of them, because the rest were buried under rubble. Quite familiar symbols, and they weren't Turrian. In fact, if the page didn't have "Turris" marked at the top, I would have said they came from Anemoi or Beira.

I looked at Sita.

"That's all there were," she said. "That's the last transmission. We could send another drone. Or..." She raised an eyebrow. "Are you *sure* you will be teaching classes next semester?"

CHAPTER SEVEN

"You want something," Victoria said.

She wore a male sim today as per usual, skin and hair an albino white and eyes as blue as the ice throne she sat on. I'd dubbed it her Ice Prince avatar. Amused by the name, she'd designed the decor to match.

"Why do you say that?" I asked. The sim was cold, but not as cold as some of the environments I'd been in. A cartoon kind of cold, not quite real. A nip, like walking into an ice box.

"Because you called me here instead of your apartment. You never drop the net without coercion."

"I like being in sim."

"I didn't say you disliked it. I was just stating an observation. And it's true, isn't it? How did the suit work out?"

"What? Oh. Good. Sita liked it."

"Good." She folded her hands and looked at me with an expression patient and cool, her Ice-Prince-entertaining-visiting-serfs expression.

I pulled my mouth flat. "Okay. Yes. I do want something."

She nodded regally.

"I'm going to see the doctor tomorrow and need your friend to delete some data from the first aid kit." At her raised eyebrow, I added, "Just a few headaches. Not even that many."

She sat back and steepled her fingers. "I haven't seen Oliver in a few days." She lowered her hands to the armrests and regarded me with narrowed eyes. "Just a few headaches?"

I nodded.

"What does it matter then? Is the dean on your case?"

I looked up at the ice stalactites. "Can we go somewhere warmer? With drinks?"

She pursed her lips. Then she snapped her fingers.

We sat at the bar of a tiki hut. Heat bounced off the sand below and warmed my skin, made perspiration pearl on the glass of pink liquid on the counter in front of me. I pushed up on the brim of my sudden straw hat and plucked the paper umbrella from the drink. "Really, Vic?"

"What? It's warm, and there are drinks."

I shook my head and took a drink of a perfectly sweet mai tai. I ran my finger over the perspiration and watched the droplets run together and down the glass. "Do you think this is what it was really like?" I removed the hat and dropped it to the stool next to me. "I mean, this all seems kind of...ridiculous."

"Historical research, London. You should know. And probably a bit of imagination. So why do you need to delete medical information?"

"I'm feeling one hundred percent better. The doctor doesn't need to know that I have occasional headaches. It would give the wrong impression."

"Oh, would it?"

"Everyone gets headaches, Vic."

"Really!"

"Everyone who doesn't live in a computer."

She twirled her drinking straw in her pale fingers and regarded me with cold blue eyes. I ignored the look. I plucked my straw out and downed the mai tai. A flush crept up my cheeks as if it were real alcohol. Half the power of sim came from imagination.

I set the glass down and toyed with its base, debating. What the hell, I thought. I told Victoria what Sita had shared with me, and her proposition: that I could explore the ruins, but only if I were completely recovered.

"That means a brain reprogramming," I said.

"I don't understand. You've been suffering for months. Get the reprogramming."

I felt a flare of heat. It might have been the imaginary alcohol. "Absolutely not."

"No? Great. I have a better idea: don't go. It'd be *better* if you stayed. Are you really going to consider this? When the hell is enough enough?"

"When hell sings and the fat lady freezes over. Vic, I'm asking for a favor, not a guilt trip."

"No, you go on enough trips. You don't need mine. No, London. I will not contact Oliver for you. I will not in any way help you to dodge your physician. I don't know what the hell Sita was thinking showing you that report. You're like a compulsive child when it comes to those things. But she's right about one thing. Whether you go or stay, you need the procedure. I never understood how you can live like that."

"Carefully and with a lot of endorphins."

"You're going to die, Lun. Just like Dad: from plain, idiotic stubbornness."

"Not now, Vic." I put my head into my hand.

"No, not ever. Stubborn. Good luck with the doc. Be sure to ask her how long humans live naturally in the wild."

"Not as long as in captivity." I lifted the straw hat and tipped it at her.

She curled her lip in an expression that wasn't quite a smile. On her slender male face, it looked almost feral. With a cue I didn't catch, she disappeared.

Blast and damnation. I exited the sim with a vocal command and took a moment to let reality right itself before I got up.

I stared down at the first aid kit on the ground. My savior and my snitch. I could "accidentally" break the thing, and all the history of my headaches would break with it. Oliver had done one previous favor for me: he had made it so that the kit would not communicate with the med servers—a "glitch" in the firmware that wouldn't be detected and fixed until I saw the doctor. It had taken a lot to persuade Vic to ask Oliver for that favor. It kept Sita from breathing down my neck any more than she already was; she was bad enough without reports from my med kit keeping her apprised of my every burp and hangnail. Victoria could at least understand my need for privacy. It wasn't as if I'd asked Oliver to actually tamper with the data—just delay their delivery to the doc.

And now it was time to deliver.

☆☆☆

The Explorer's Club had never existed in real life but was based on a creative interpretation of Victorian Era gentlemen's clubs, an austere red-bricked building with two floors and a basement level, furnished in self-important mahogany, brass, and gleaming leather. The decorations edged the line between rich and ridiculous. A stuffed bear reared in the corner of the roomy antechamber, its mouth frozen in a display of teeth. A red fez perched on its head. Members of the club called the bear "Melvin."

Voices and laughter spilled from the cracked door of one of the card parlors. The allure of tobacco wafted from the smoke room down the hall from it. On another day, I might have taken the pipe from my breast pocket and helped myself to a new flavor of tobacco from its selection of glass jars. It'd been a long time since I sampled its offerings—a pleasure I indulged only in sim.

Instead, I turned to the metal cage of the lift opposite it and tipped my hat to the operator. He looked bovine in nature with a broad jaw and wide-set eyes. He chewed a plug of tobacco with somber dignity. A long time ago, I'd figured him for a computer-controlled individual. But then, I had my doubts. I worked with a couple people at the university with less personality. I always treated him politely.

He transferred the cud to the other side of his mouth. "Floor?"

"Lower ground," I said, and stepped onto the lift.

The cage door rattled shut and the operator pulled the lever. It descended with a jolt.

The halls and rooms of the lower ground floor were kept dim, lamps turned low and a haze of indeterminable smoke in the air, scentless and tasteless. They were noisy with loud voices and raucous laughter, the clink of glasses, the clack of dice hitting felt-covered wood. Here were the twin lounges, the darker, drunker card room, and the cocktail bar.

I stepped into the bar. Tiffany lamps hovered low over round tables to the right. Men sat around these with their tumblers of brandy and their serious expressions. I gave these only a quick scan. My real attention went to the stretch of bar itself.

I spotted the familiar vest and narrow set of shoulders. There like clockwork on a Wednesday evening. Good to know things on this side of the circuit board hadn't changed during my absence.

I slid onto the stool next to him and set my elbows on the counter. "They still let drunkards like you in here?"

Theodore's ruddy face cracked in a grin. "Rider!"

It was good to hear my sim handle. Comfortable, like slipping into an old coat. I found myself standing as Theodore sprang to his feet. We clasped hands and thumped backs.

He laughed loudly. "I was beginning to think I'd never see you again, man!"

"I thought you chaps had had enough of me for a while."

Theodore spluttered an incredulous noise and waved the bartender over. "A cognac for my friend."

The bartender pressed his mouth flat in what passed for a smile. It was probably the most pleased he'd ever looked to see me. Really, the most pleased he'd ever looked, period.

"God, it feels like years," Theo said. "What the devil have you been up to? How's the noggin'?"

"Patched up and good as new. No more cracked than it was before the fall."

He laughed. "You had a real crack to match the one in your brain, eh?"

"Something like that, yeah." I grinned. I accepted the snifter from the bartender and swirled the deep-amber liquid before taking a drink. A sweet, dry bite. I'd missed this. I'd forgotten just how much.

Theodore watched me drink with open delight. I swallowed and then muttered something inarticulate and heartfelt. He chuckled and took a pull on his stout.

I ran my tongue around my mouth. "So how has the club been getting on?"

He shook his head. "Not the same without you, for sure. We just finished a tour of the Great Wall of China a week ago. Of course, Horace had to orchestrate the entire thing."

I grimaced and made an appropriately sympathetic sound.

"So when can we expect you back in the field?"

"Probably not for a while yet," I said. "I may be going out on another dig."

His expression flickered disappointment. "Well, that's quick. That is, long for *you*, and long for us, certainly. But quick to be running out there again, don't you think?"

Theodore was one of the few people in sim who knew my real identity. I still wasn't sure how he'd managed to crack it. We'd done a sim trip to Oblitus a few years back, not long before he guessed the truth. The sim had been based on my own trip, and I'd put a lot of effort into seeming as new to the environment as the rest of our adventure group had been. Maybe perhaps too much effort. Theodore fancied himself a bit of a Sherlock Holmes, deerstalker cap and all. When I'd asked him what had tipped him off, he had demurred. I suspected a small amount of hacking had been involved. This should have disturbed me, but it all seemed to be a game to Theo, harmless fun. He'd never held the information above me or made any mention to the others. No hints, no slips. It pleased him to be the only one to know who I was, and I had to admit, it was nice to have someone to break character with.

"What do the others think of my absence, anyway?" I asked.

He slanted me a look. "They've all figured you for an off-worlder a long time back. Wife, children, work." He turned his glass with his fingers. "It's a bit of a sport for them. Speculating, you know."

I choked on a mouthful of cognac. I wiped my mouth. "You're not serious."

"Oh, I am." His dark eyes twinkled. "We've got you figured for two children and a recent new addition. A university librarian. Married, mind you, to a scholar." He laughed at my expression. "Whoever you're married to would have to be busy herself, to put up with how much time you spend in sim."

"But I have three kids," I pointed out.

"And that's the reason for your long absences with us. You can't keep a nanny, you see, because your children are mischievous little demons. They take after their father."

I shook my head.

"I told them they were wrong, of course," he said. "You're a vanguard on long assignments. Of course you don't have a wife and kids. As soon as you get your pay at the end of an assignment, you spend it all gambling and plying the brothels—a real proper seaman—and when you've spent it all, in every possible way, you come back to us. You've a sympathetic family member with a net, a couch, and sim hours to spare. Am I right?"

I snorted.

Vanguard. Actually, that wasn't far off the mark. I'd briefly considered joining them. Back when I was a teen, the intergalactic military's scouts had seemed like the closest thing to Allan Quatermain to me. Explorers of unknown worlds, pioneers of habitable planets. Breaking the hearts of mothers everywhere.

"I thought you'd like that," Theo said. He chuckled and finished his beer. "So, just back for a visit? Making sure the old place is still holding together in your absence?"

"I'm surprised how well," I said. I clicked the bottom of my snifter against the counter, watching the last little bit of richly colored liquid dance in the glass. "Actually, there is some—"

In a flash of movement, a small, lithe form pounced onto Theodore's back, swung onto his shoulder, and squatted there. Two black beads stared at me.

Theodore chuckled and raised a hand to scratch the chin of his pet marmoset, Drusilla. "I seem to have a monkey on my back."

"Don't so many of us," I said, and cringed as the little demon leaped the distance to my shoulder. One tiny cold hand grabbed my earlobe. "Nice monkey. Yeah, I missed you too."

Actually, I'd hoped Theodore had finally tired of the little monster. Tiny feet scampered over my shoulders. Fingers like slivers of ice scraped through my hair. The faint but unmistakable sound of clockwork whirred in my ear as its limbs worked, an eerily disturbing noise—although that was almost comforting compared to the shriek it let out as Theodore extracted it from my shoulder.

"Now, Dru," he said. His voice dripped indulgent affection.

For an instant, the gremlin face stared into mine, mouth yawning open in anger. Then Theo returned the creature to his back. It skittered to his opposite shoulder, turned, and had the nerve to chitter at *me*.

Theo canted it a look and threatened to let some of the tension out of its springs if it didn't behave itself. It let out a final sharp bark and then hunkered down, glaring at me with glittering black eyes.

Theodore cleared his throat. "Sorry about that. She's just excited to see you and a little upset you've been gone so long."

I grunted and combed back my hair.

"You were saying?"

"Right," I said. "While I was convalescing, I decided to rearrange the old office. Probably not the best of ideas. I had a bit of a misstep and took a plunge."

Actually, not too far from the truth, was it? I had a sudden recollection of strong arms catching me—Chas Chambers—and felt an uncomfortable pang of embarrassment.

I scowled at that and waved my fingers at Theodore's muttered exclamation. "I'm fine. No more cracked than before. But a piece from my dad's collection, a cut crystal vase, shattered. It was an original. I thought you might know someone who can put it back together for me."

I found myself tilting the snifter so sharply the brandy almost spilled out. I set it down. There was another reason I didn't lose sleep over Theodore prying into my identity: I knew something about him, too. A little tit for tat. Like that he lived on Earth—no surprise there, as most full-time sim users like my mom and sister resided in stasis on Earth—but also that he hadn't spent all of his life there, or even much of it. He'd hinted as much. Vic's pet hacker, Oliver, had corroborated the information and even filled in the picture for me. Theo had been a mechanical engineer, and his work had brought him to some interesting outposts.

One of his longest stays had been on a small planet near the center of the universe that had gone from impoverished backwater to a center of technological advancement over the course of a generation. Mi'hani. Theo had been there almost forty years before, around the time the planet's name became a household word. A lot of his files from that period were blanked out, but I suspected he'd been a part of the team that built the reality engines that transformed the planet from Wild West to boom town.

In his time there, Theo had also made acquaintances with a number of...nongovernmental individuals. The kind you didn't meet at the pub for drinks.

Technically, I wasn't supposed to know this. I might have been crossing a line. But then, we'd been playing this game for years. Theo had made the first move years ago when revealing his knowledge of my true identity. My turn to advance the game piece.

"I don't know any antiques repairmen," he said. "That's the kind of specialist you'd find at a university."

"Not a repairman."

He stroked his chin thoughtfully. Dru, the marmoset, stared at me with round sober little eyes, its tiny hands working through Theodore's hair, petting him slowly as it stared at me. "In that case, you could have a fabricator recreate it."

"I don't want a copy. I want to fix what belonged to my father."

He gave me a long considering look. "If you're asking what I think you're asking, I know someone who might be able to help. Of course, you'd have to send the piece via transport. It'll lose its watermark. You'd just as well recreate it."

"It's the sentimental value that matters. I'll at least know it's the same piece."

"Not the *same*..."

"Strictly speaking, no. Have you transported?"

"I'm afraid I've had the pleasure."

My grin was sour. "You're not the same man who went into the transport. You're a recreation, yourself."

"We're none of us the same men, Rider my buy," he said gruffly. "We're none of us the same." He patted his breast pocket, eyebrows drawn together as with some private trouble. Finding it flat, he opened his jacket and searched both inner pockets.

Dru the marmoset chirped sharply, leaped to the bar top, and picked up the black pipe sitting near the empty beer glass.

"Ah!" He broke into a smile. He plucked the pipe from its tiny hands, produced a bag of tobacco from his coat pocket, and offered the bag to me. I held up a hand.

He shrugged and pinched tobacco into the bowl. "So tell me about this new dig. It must be something special."

Now why in damnation had I even mentioned the expedition to him? I could have given him any explanation for my continued absence from the group, feigned a longer convalescence—though strictly speaking, I wouldn't have been feigning.

Maybe I hadn't wanted to admit the other truth—that I could barely tolerate sim any longer, and feared I never would again, what with the disturbing hangovers I'd been experiencing afterward. And maybe I felt I owed Theodore the truth about the expedition. Maybe, even, I was lonelier than I'd realized.

It occurred to me Theodore was my only real friend outside my colleagues and family. I had other friends—sim friends, like the other members of our adventuring group. But then, they weren't mine. Strictly speaking, they were friends of Rider, nineteenth-century British explorer and crack shot. Theodore was friend of London Wells, twenty-sixth-century xenoarchaeologist and crackpot.

"It is something special," I said slowly. "Actually, I can't really talk about it."

"This is exciting! Is it Sahara? No? Asura?"

"You think you're going to wheedle a confession from me."

"No, no... Just— It isn't Asura, is it?"

I snorted. "Are you going to smoke that thing, or just hold it?"

He appeared puzzled. Then he looked at the pipe in his hand, laughed, lit it, and puffed. "You'll have to excuse my enthusiasm. I live vicariously, you know."

"I'm told it's the safest way to live." I reached for my own pipe. "You know what, let me see some of that after all."

CHAPTER EIGHT

Theodore parted with the promise to get in touch with his friend for me. "Friend" was his word, not mine. The use of it surprised me. I'd never considered shapers people to be friends with. Acquaintances, yes. Contacts, surely. "Friend" seemed too familiar a term. Was that prejudice on my part?

I didn't expect Theodore's call the next day. I'd have thought a week, at least. But he rang while I was scrolling through the morning news and told me his friend could speak with me as early as next week. Nero Calwin was his name. Mr. Calwin didn't have a sim connection, Theodore warned me, so we'd have to make our transaction through comm. Theo and I worked out a date and time, and I ended the call with a creeping feeling.

Four days later, I arrived at the Blue Communications Room with the first aid kit in my pocket and a nervous kink in my neck. The Blue Room was no smaller than my own office but had a claustrophobic feel. Bare, off-white walls, no screens to play outdoor scenes, no color to give it depth and warmth. Only five doors: the one I came through, and four leading into small, even more claustrophobic booths. It was the janitor's closet of the communications offices, half-forgotten by most of the university. Which is precisely why I'd chosen it.

There was no one else in the comm room besides myself and the operator, but I spoke in a hushed tone anyway. He listened without a word, hunched in his chair. Smudges under his eyes gave him a haunted look. It was the same kind of face that had stared back at me from the mirror for three months.

When I was done talking, he said, "The university keeps a strict record of every call made from this office. What you're asking is against policy."

"Just one call," I said, holding up a finger. Then I corrected myself. "Two. Two calls and two transports off the record."

Sweat prickled on my brow, and I hoped he didn't notice it. I half expected him to ring security. It was true I hadn't had physical relations with a live man in eight years, but I wouldn't exactly describe my response to the thought of being wrestled out of here by someone bigger and stronger than myself as *anticipation*.

The operator studied me with a severe expression. "We might be able to work something out."

"That's all right, it was inappropriate of me to— What?"

He said, "I have a friend who designs sims."

I put pieces together. "So you'd like me to consult." I felt something like relief. Consulting wouldn't be bad.

He shook his head. "Memories."

"Ah." I waited, with a sinking feeling, for him to go on.

"He wants a more complete Oblitus."

"That planet was huge. I didn't explore every inch of it. I couldn't."

"No, but you've seen more than you've shared. We want an official, sanctioned, newly updated sim based on real memory. No computer reconstruction."

I had my reasons for not offering up full versions of my memories for public consumption. Not least of which was: they were mine. To disseminate discoveries was part of the thrill of going on expedition, but I put limits on what I'd share. I liked to think at least some corners of my life remained mine alone. That there were some things about me you couldn't call up on a database.

In other words, I liked my privacy.

A light flashed on over one of the cubicle doors. The door opened, and Chas Chambers stepped out. He looked as surprised to see me as I was him.

"Professor Wells," he said.

"Chas. Good to see you."

A strange moment passed as we stared at each other. He looked subtly different today wearing a loose gray shirt and a guarded expression. I waited, every muscle tense, as he exchanged a brief word of thanks with the operator, bid me good-bye, and exited. Tense, because I thought the operator and I had been alone in the office. I rewound our conversation in my head. How much had he heard? Nothing. The doors were soundproof. Neither of us had even been aware the other was here.

The operator looked at me.

"Right," I said. "Yes. Memories of Oblitus. All of what I have, minus the very personal bits."

His mouth stretched in a very thin imitation of a smile.

He led me into the same cubicle Chas had just come out of. My mind still spun with the decision I'd just made. All of Oblitus. All of Oblitus for the world to see.

Then I realized the screen in the room was the solid green color that indicated an open line.

"It's still connected," I said.

"No reason to disconnect. Going to the same place."

I sat down on the worn upholstered chair, still warm from Chas. Although I might have been connected, my contact had not yet arrived, so when the operator closed the door behind me, all I had was the blank green screen and silence.

Now this was interesting. Chas had been communicating with someone on Mi'hani. That shouldn't have been startling. It was a densely populated planet. But I had never seen him so put out. He'd looked almost...guilty.

Criminally guilty, even.

Now I was just projecting my own shame and apprehension.

The green screen turned black, and then I was staring at the tan face of an exceedingly normal-looking man. He sat in a bare, gray-walled room much like my own. He was clean-shaven and dark-eyed. Possibly his one noteworthy characteristic was the hair he wore down to his shoulders, as straight and black as Sita's. I'd never met anyone from Mi'hani, much less one of their wizards. I didn't know what I'd expected a shaper to look like, but it wasn't this slender man in a black shirt.

"Nero Calwin?"

My surprise must have been evident, because his voice had a dry note: "Dr. Wells?"

Oh, brilliant form, London. I cleared my throat. "I appreciate you taking the time to meet with me in such short order."

He nodded, expression utterly serious. A hint of wariness dulled his eyes and the corners of his mouth. Hard to imagine this man as the friend of cheerful Theodore, unless Theo had used the term loosely.

Since I had no idea just what Theo had told him, I started delicately. "Theodore may have told you about my problem with a shattered family heirloom."

"He told me about a vase."

"Right." This was awkward. "It wasn't a vase."

More like the last of my good sense.

"It's something else, actually," I said. "A, uh, more discreet matter."

Not a blink from him. I received the distinct impression he'd been expecting this.

I pushed on. "I'm not sure what you'd like in return, but I'm willing to barter. For your services, and for your...discretion." My face heated. Did I think I was in a mafia sim?

"There's nothing I need right now," he said.

Well. I didn't know quite what to say to that.

He continued to regard me with that unreadable expression. He could have been considering turning me over to the university authorities for attempted illegal activity, or he could have been planning lunch.

"You've been to the Lost Planets, correct?" he said.

Uh-oh. It was my turn to be wary. I nodded.

"I've heard that you translate. Translate what?"

"Anything."

"Anything?"

"Any language that exists. If I can read it or listen to it. Yes."

"No shit."

"No shit," I agreed.

"And you teach at a university?"

I nodded again.

"I don't need anything now, but I might in the future. If I accept your request, those are my terms: a future favor that I deem of comparable value."

Good gods. I had the feeling that by the end of the day, I'd be out my memories, my soul, and the deed to my apartment. Would I throw in my spleen for good measure?

"You might consider my right kidney of comparable value," I joked tensely.

He shook his head. "No personal resources."

I almost laughed at that. Then I realized he was being completely serious. The image of a fireball rolling through the night came to me, crying faces and a grim newscaster. The news piece about the Mi'hani shaper extremist group took on reality. What was I getting myself into?

But this was a friend of Theo's, and I'd been the one to ask for this.

I pulled in a breath. What the hell, right? "Okay. I accept your terms."

The wariness in his eyes gave way to a shrewd gleam. He leaned forward, settling down for business.

No going back now. I pulled the first aid kit from the pocket of my duster and placed it on the table in front of me.

"Med kit?" he asked, after giving it a long look.

I nodded. "I need information cleared off of it. Records of headaches."

He waited as if for more. When more was not forthcoming, he said, "And that's it?"

"And that's it."

He sat back, gave a disbelieving shake of his head.

Was he put off by the mildness of the request? Disappointed, maybe, that he wouldn't be able to get much of a return favor this? I wondered what exactly he'd had in mind for me.

But apparently, I misinterpreted.

"Information is hard to shape," he said. "It takes certain skill and ability. I can do this. I'll need three days."

Three days? It couldn't truly take that long. He was bluffing to make me think it took him more effort than it did. He'd have it done in ten minutes and gathering dust on his shelf.

Of course, what did I know about shaping? My knowledge of the subject came from textbooks and conjecture. At the center of the universe, reality was fluid, and any person could manipulate the world with a thought. The farther you traveled from the center, the more stable reality became. Mi'hani was the closest planet to the center of the universe that had ever been inhabited. It was just stable enough to support life, but also just close enough that a small population of individuals could shape their environment. Maybe talent, maybe genetics, the evidence was still up in the air. I assumed they exercised their ability as easily as a person at the center of the universe, using a thought to effect instant change.

But then, I knew better than to assume.

"Do you want all of the files deleted?" Nero said.

"Not all of them."

I'd already considered this. I couldn't clear all of the headaches on record from the device. That would be too suspicious. I told him what I wanted deleted, and thought myself pretty clever. The migraines wouldn't have disappeared overnight, of course. They'd have tapered off, resulting in the last three weeks being blissfully—believably—pain free.

We made plans to meet again three days. I tucked the kit back into my pocket and left the little cubicle. I met the operator's eyes. He stood and led me a short way down the hallway to a transport room. The machine dominating the center of the space looked something like a metal filing cabinet with two very large drawers. I placed the first aid kit inside the drawer helpfully labeled "In" and closed it.

The operator and I stepped behind a partition and the machine thrummed to life. Inside the drawer, a series of sensors would be analyzing the kit, mapping every centimeter, every atom, and committing it to memory. Like anything, the kit was—at its essence—information. Every particle and wave of its three-dimensional being was a data point that could be stored on a two-dimensional plane. It was difficult to send an entire house across a vast distance, and a waste of resources; more efficient to send the blueprint instead and build the house at its destination. The same went for the kit. It was far quicker and easier to send its blueprint across the vast reaches of space.

Somewhere on Mi'hani, a few minutes from now, Nero Calwin would be standing next to a transporter much like this one. The computer would send my kit's blueprint to the transporter's printer, which would create a replica, particle for particle. For a brief span of a few breaths, two identical first aid kits would exist in the world. Then, inside the very large drawer marked "In," our transporter would destroy the original kit. In essence, evaporating it.

Human transportation worked in exactly the same way. Something fun to think about on rainy days.

As I left the comm room with two light pockets, it occurred to me I was now without the thing that had made my life livable for months. Certainly, I didn't need it anymore. Even I, in my vast and incredible idiocy—of which I was reminded often by family and friends—would not consider launching on an expedition to an as-yet-unexplored Lost Planet if I were still medically unstable and dependent on the timely interventions of a battery-powered box. Besides, I had pills.

Despite this, a sick, cold feeling clutched at my chest. Maybe this was what made me extra jumpy as I navigated the hallways. They had the dingy, cramped atmosphere common to most of the university's original structures. I passed door after identical closed door. An occasional socket studded the long blank stretches of wall, as if screens had once hung there. I passed an empty waiting room, turned a corner, and went down a dim set of stairs.

I paused on the steps, and the sound of my footsteps stopped with me. I looked up, past spiral after spiral of stairway, to the ceiling. A person could fall from that height and die on impact against the ground still two floors below me.

I didn't look down. I continued my descent, unsure of why I'd taken the stairwell at all—only that something about the elevator and its single shut, metallic door had deterred me. I'd needed to keep moving.

The ground floor hall was deserted. I glanced behind myself at the stairway door as it shut, but the little window showed only an empty stairwell.

I emerged into the yard. Far above, the space station's ceiling projected the pink hues of late evening. Somewhere off in the distance, where people gathered after work, voices talked and laughed. I avoided these, though there was no real point in trying to hide my exit from the building. I could have been there for any sort of business.

I walked back through a deserted rock garden. An uneasy, distinctly familiar feeling crawled between my shoulder blades.

I glanced behind but saw nothing save hedges and the path itself, curving out of sight.

Oh, not this. Not after I'd just sat in Sita's office and told her it had all been in my head. It *had* been in my head.

I continued at an even pace. I glanced into a pool as I passed. My own reflection rippled on the surface, pale face and dark head of hair. Eyes and glasses resolved into clarity for an instant before dissolving into shimmers.

Another face gazed with me. I had the impression of nose, mouth, hair of an indistinguishable shade, and eyes that met mine.

My heart slammed. My gaze jerked up, but there was no one there.

I abandoned the garden path for a more direct route back to the Humanities building. I'd originally planned to return home for the evening, but right then I wanted to position myself behind the first locked door I could find, and my office was closer than my apartment.

I cut across a wide common area and spied, with relief, the hedges of the Humanities garden. I snaked through the roses, past the disapproving stare of the old Poet, and went through the back door of the building.

The old familiar halls of the Humanities building were also vacant this time of the evening, but in a comfortable, hushed way. The screens on the walls announced theatrical productions and debate tournaments. Someone had doodled a cartoon panda bear that trundled along the lower edge of the screen, grabbing stray announcements and munching them. I turned the corner just as the panda squatted and began to pass a stream of words.

I unlocked my office and went inside. Closed the door. Locked it, pulled the drape on the window, and stood there in the leather-scented quiet.

I covered my face with a hand and laughed. The Great London Wells, Leaper of Shadows. I deserved every bit of flak I got from Sita. I shrugged out of my hot coat and loosened my shirt, unbuttoning the cuffs. Well, might as well do something useful while I was there and tackle the pile of student papers on my desk.

A knock at the door sent me halfway to the ceiling. I landed on two feet, clutching my hair.

Good gods. It was just a door. Any hint of habitation was like an open invitation to students, never mind the closed door and pulled curtain.

"Yes?" I called.

A pause, then a muffled male voice asked, "Dr. Wells?"

I released a breath and went to the door. I cracked it. "Can I help you?"

The man smiled and leaned a little to peer at me. "It is Dr. Wells, right? It's a pleasure to meet you. Forgive me for interrupting you, but I happened to be on the station and hoped you might sign a copy of *Words in the Wilderness* for me." He held the book up, tilting it so the title was just visible through the narrow opening in the door.

Right. I stifled an uncomplimentary sound and stepped back, swinging the door open to a less paranoid width. The man's smile also widened, and he held his hand out, and we shook. Something about this was both awkward and familiar. It made me uncomfortable.

It was something about the man, I decided. I'd seen him somewhere before.

He proffered the memoir. I took it. "Come inside," I said, remembering some of my social manners. I brought the book to my desk and opened it. I bent to fish a pen out of the drawer, and when I looked up, the man stood gazing around the office.

I cleared my throat. "Who should I make this out to?"

"Hm? Coeus."

When he offered no surname, I signed the book to just Coeus. *All the best in your endeavors. —London.*

I heard a sharp intake of breath, and my pen hand jumped, scratching a line of ink. The man strode across the room to the bookshelf.

"Forgive me," he said, "but is this an original *War of the Worlds*?"

I closed the signed memoir and straightened. "Yes."

He looked back at me with a plea. "May I?"

I nodded. I was used to the kind of attention Dad's collection brought. I took a seat at the desk and sorted through the student papers. Typically, I might have entertained a visitor, but he had come in out of office hours—way out of office hours—and I wasn't in the condition, much less the mood, to be gracious.

In fact, I completely forgot he was in the room until I heard a book close. I started and looked up to see the man slide the volume back into place on the shelf. He stepped back and appraised the wall of shelves. "Absolutely amazing," he said. "Are they all watermarked?"

"Many of them." Despite myself I felt a stirring of pride. Not that I'd had much of a hand in amassing the collection.

"Just incredible," he said. He didn't seem ready to leave anytime soon. Strangely, I didn't half mind. He was quiet and unobtrusive. I returned to grading.

After a time, he said, "Thank you kindly."

I startled again, muttered a distracted "you're welcome," and plugged another comment into a student's paper. When I looked up again, the office was empty and the door stood open. A chill stole over me. I distinctly remembered closing and locking it when I'd ducked into my office a few minutes earlier.

I stood and went to it slowly, but my office was empty and so was the hallway outside. I ducked back in, closed the door, locked and double-checked the lock. My hand shook a little as I pulled it away. I shoved it into my pocket.

On the way back to my desk, I spotted a copy of my memoir lying on the corner. I was sure I didn't remember leaving it there. It lay open to the first page, and there was an inscription in my handwriting. *To Coeus. All the best in your endeavors. —London.*

I returned it to the bookcase, next to my other two copies.

I glanced around the office. The feeling of being watched had passed, although I had another feeling, a whisper of an impression, like I'd forgotten something but couldn't for the life of me remember what.

CHAPTER NINE

Cordially, I invited Doctor Felix Mata into my office. Cheerfully, even.

"Take a seat, Felix," I said with a sweep of my hand. Twelve years ago, he would have been the one inviting me in with a self-satisfied grin. Twelve years ago, I would have been the one sitting down on the other side of the desk and fidgeting quietly while he finished work on his desktop, waiting like a hound for the moment he turned the heat of his attention on me. Now I spent an extra couple of minutes poring over a student email that could have waited till later.

Leather and wood creaked as Felix shifted in his chair. I sensed him searching for somewhere to place his gaze—anywhere but at the top of my head or the casual way my arms propped against the desk as I leaned over my work.

I'd seen a lot of Felix's crown and shoulders when I'd been in his place, and not always when it was a desk he leaned over. I hoped he drew on similar memories of me as he waited.

I closed out of the email and slid two sheets of vellum to him. "Introduction to Language Theory," I said, tapping one. I tapped the other and said, "English Evolution."

English wasn't Felix's primary language of study—that would be Portuguese—but I knew he was competent with it. And he'd taught Language Theory before. I'd been his teaching assistant in that. Technically, he knew both classes well enough to teach without my notes. I was only too happy to spend the next hour going over them with him in detail, anyway.

All the while, the knowledge was taut between us—the knowledge that I would be leaving on a university-funded Lost Planet expedition while he stayed behind to teach my students. Because I was going. The doctor had cleared me, and Sita had given the Turris project the go-ahead.

It had been a strange month, mostly filled with a fretful kind of waiting. Waiting for the first aid kit to be returned, to see the doctor, to receive my results. The kit came back a week later as promised and worked exactly as I'd asked the shaper. The physician congratulated me that the headaches had decreased in incidence, asked me a few questions, and ran a panel of tests which showed that, physically, I was back to my old self. Nothing so much as a thread of scar tissue. Another three weeks passed after that as, elsewhere in the university, a creaking group of admins deliberated over the expedition proposal Sita brought them.

Then: The green light. And here I sat.

Felix listened to my lecture with a sort of subdued acquiescence. It both satisfied and disappointed me. I'd been half-prepared for a fight. There were several points in the curricula I knew he would disagree with on principle, and I was prepared to sharply and cheerfully assert my authority, but he accepted these without word or expression.

"That's it?" he said, when I'd come to the end of the notes for both courses.

"That's it. Thank you. You can take those." I indicated the sheets of vellum.

He scooped them up, tapped them together against the desk, and stood. I opened my email again.

He hesitated. I felt it like the weight of hands on my shoulders.

"London?"

I looked up. Impatience must have been evident on my face, because he paused and the puzzled expression on his face deepened.

"Is there some sort of...animosity you feel toward me?"

I held his gaze, unblinking.

His eyebrows furrowed. "I sense some sort of...anger. Is that just me?"

"Thank you for meeting with me today, Dr. Mata. I'm sure you'll take good care of my classes in my absence."

"There is! Where is this coming from, London? Is this something to do with— You don't still hold a *grudge*, do you? That was a decade ago."

"What was a decade ago?"

His face reddened. "Now you're playing games. You know very well what I mean. Us, London. We happened. And if you'll remember correctly, it was not me who ended things."

I stared, then nearly laughed. Nearly stood up and choked him. Instead I shook my head. "Thank you, Felix. Now if you'll please, I have work to return to. Good day."

We leered at each other like hackling dogs.

"Unbelievable," he said at last, though I never learned what he found so unbelievable because he turned and shut the door very softly behind himself. Maybe it was the fact I no longer sucked in the smoke he blew.

Pressure squeezed my eyes. I shook out a few pain pills from a bottle in my desk. The good news was I'd passed the physician's inspection. The bad news was my first aid kit was back to working order and would communicate all activity directly to the doctor. If a migraine hit before I left for the expedition, I'd have to ride it out on my own.

I went to the break room to fetch a strong cup of coffee for my head. The caffeine stemmed the pain, though the bitterness was hell on my stomach. Felix's words wouldn't leave me, nor his expression. It was the rawest response I could remember getting from him. There'd been nothing polished, suave, or sexy about his anger. And what the hell was he even angry about? He'd made his choice. It was bound in embossed leather; a copy of it sat on my shelf.

I should have felt a sense of satisfaction from seeing Felix unraveling over the topic of our relationship, some vindication for all the pain I felt, knowing that he'd experienced a measure of it too. But I only felt ill. Though that might have been the coffee. I dumped the rest down the drain.

I had the rest of my afternoon free. I didn't want to go home to the sickly pall of my apartment. Victoria was ignoring me. Conspicuously. She still hadn't forgiven me for agreeing on the expedition. She left souvenirs all around the cabin so I'd know just how much fun she was having without me on dinosaur digs, train rides, and ice cave spelunking trips, if I were to guess from her gifts.

I returned to my office to pull on my duster, locked the door behind me, and went for a walk. Thoughts of Felix, Victoria, and the expedition weighed on me. And, weirdly, Chas Chambers, though in his case not a formed thought so much as a fleeting awareness.

I didn't realize where I was heading until I came to a stop and recognized the door of the shooting range.

The attendant inside looked surprised to see me, which made me realized just how long it'd been since my last visit. I took a pair of goggles and a weapon down to the farthest stall and warmed up with a few practice rounds. I'd grown rusty during my extended leave.

As I fell into my stance and sighted down the gun, I finally put form to something that had been bothering me. Was I actually going on this expedition just in response to Felix?

I pulled the trigger and the kickback punched me in the shoulder.

"Ow. *Shit.*"

I rubbed my arm and glared at the target. The energy round had tagged the wall far above it.

The thought disturbed me. It was just like me to take one look at Felix's face and fly off on an expedition to prove I was stronger, braver, and smarter. And that I absolutely did not need him.

I lifted the gun and took sight again. I breathed. This time I clipped the shoulder of the target, and not my own. Still piss-awful shooting.

Whatever my motivation for going on this trip, I sorely needed to start training.

I crouched into position and pulled all my focus together. I put Mata out of my mind and drew my attention into the straightness of my arms, the bunched muscles of my shoulders, and the curl of my fingers. I breathed. Became the target.

My shooting improved almost immediately, but I didn't need to see the bright-red marks on the targets to know that. I could feel it. All my thoughts came together to a point.

Out in the field, I existed in a different state. I became an elemental thing of wits and strength. When your entire world narrowed down to survival and discovery, you could be that.

I took another series of shots and almost slipped into that zone. Amazing how quickly I'd forgotten what it was like to be myself. In a handful of months, I'd come to identify with the cranky, reclusive, helpless convalescent London. How could I have forgotten this?

I knew then I needed this trip to Turris. Not out of anger at Felix, not for my research career, but for myself, to pull out of this...funk, this rut, whatever this was. I needed it to be alive again.

Chapter Ten

Sita called me in the next day.

"Oh, it's you," she said when I arrived, cracking open her office door. She glanced over my shoulder, then opened the door an inch more and ushered me inside. I squeezed through and looked back just as she shut it.

"What was that all about?" The waiting room had been a ghost town and the secretary, who never gave me a glance, had put a finger to his lips and gestured with a fist that I should knock. Sita never locked her door. But now I watched her throw the bolt.

She put a finger to her lips and fast-toed to her desk, where she froze in a pose of listening. I had no idea what for. The beat of a different drummer, rats in the walls, the whisper of personal voices. Demons, maybe. In that quiet, I heard my own inhalation.

"All right," she whispered a minute later. "Come here."

I stood at the edge of her desk while her hands worked over its surface. She'd completely cleared it. A stack of papers sat on the floor against the wall with a pen holder, a potted plant, and the carving of an elephant.

An image appeared on the desk. Mostly beige, bordered with spots of color; here and there, a speckling of pinkish white and black ripples. A map.

"That's Turris," I said.

She put the finger to her lips. I glanced over my shoulder, but we were alone in the office.

She touched the finger to the center of the beige area. "You'll be landing here. On this plain, away from the spires and the mountains. You don't want to get too close to those. Electrical storms. From here, it's a straight trip to the entrance of the ruins—here. There's some kind of subterranean network, but what you want shouldn't be too far below the surface. And they are just below the mountains, not in them, so you should be safe from the storms."

"Hold on," I said, and edged behind the desk next to her. I leaned over the map. Turris was a low-gravity planet. The race that lived there had been airborne, probably living and working in the forests of spires that covered large swathes of the planet's land mass. Those would be the speckled pinkish-white areas framing the beige plain in the center of the map. The black ripples at the top of the image would be mountains. I pointed to the place she'd indicated at the bottom of them. "The site is here?"

Sita nodded. Since dropping the news about the Turris discovery onto my lap—or my lunch plate, as it were—she'd been incredibly cagey about the details. Now for the first time I stared at my destination.

"It's underground? But the race flew."

She raised her eyebrows.

"So this is flat land. Grass land? I can land here, make camp, and..." I slid my finger north, to Sita's little red marker at the base of the mountains. "Go in here."

She nodded.

"And that's it?"

No climbing, leaping, or athletics. Just a stroll through a sunny field. And it suddenly made sense why Sita had no qualms sending me on this trip. Likely the most important discovery of my lifetime would be a walk in the park.

Sita smiled.

☆☆☆

We spent a few more minutes reviewing the map, but there wasn't much to go over. It was all exceedingly simple.

"The problem won't be the terrain," Sita said. "It's the fauna."

She showed me the picture of a gigantic flying creature, something like one of the prehistoric winged reptiles of Earth.

"I've seen this before," I said. "My mother wore a face like this the first time I ever told her I was going on an expedition." I took another look at the numerous teeth. "What's the scale on these things?"

She manipulated the picture. A moment later, the silhouette of a person appeared next to one of the thing's legs. Two of the little men could have fit inside the long bill.

"Brilliant," I said.

"But you shouldn't really have to worry about them. The majority of the animal population is concentrated around the spires, miles in either direction from your landing position."

I was sure I'd sleep soundly at night.

She wouldn't let me take a copy of the map, but she did give me access to the rough Turris sim she'd compiled from available survey data. The sim was stored on an encrypted server, the kind used for top-secret projects, of which I'd only heard rumors.

Arriving home, I found my mailbox stuffed with messages regarding an assignment due in two days, but I ignored these and loaded the Turris sim.

I appeared at the base of the mountains. Sita's research site was somewhere to the east, probably hidden in the rocks. Much of this landscape was computer guesswork based on photographs and numbers. Even so, I wanted to see what it had made of the ruins.

The sight of a tall cliff arrested me. Beautiful for climbing, full of shelves and vertical fissures I could almost wedge my entire body into. So perfect, Sita might have placed it here to tempt me.

And it did tempt me. Since returning to health, I hadn't tried a climb even in sim. Did it make a difference? The doctors had all said there was nothing wrong physically with my head any longer, that whatever lingering effects were in my mind. So how did that translate in sim?

I sized up the cliff and mapped out the easiest route. No need to push it. Just perform a casual experiment. And if I fell, big deal. I wouldn't break any virtual bones, and it was a low-gravity environment anyway. I'd see how high I bounced.

I started up it. Hesitantly at first, and then with increasing confidence. It was hard not to. With the low gravity, I could practically jump from shelf to shelf like a monkey. I leaped one gap across a fissure. Empty air and sky flashed by, and I landed on the other side, powering into another jump. It was madness. I would never dream of climbing—climbing! more like acrobatics—like this in real life. But here in sim, what the hell?

I crested the top of the cliff, flipped over the edge, and landed on my back. I stared up at the alien sky. I laughed.

It was all in my mind. The vertigo, the fear. Of course it was all in my mind—a phobia—and I had found the cure.

I could do this. I could get myself back in perfect working order before this trip.

☆☆☆

Easier said than done.

I stared up the height of beige wall. The climbing harness creaked with my weight, as nervous as I about the prospects. I'd been practicing virtually as much as my time and sim ration would allow over the past week, but standing here now in the university's rock climbing gym, I was reminded of the difference between sim and real life. The rock course was no match for the cliffs I'd been scaling in sim; the red and blue and green handholds could have been scaled by a child. Even so. My heartbeat escaped from me.

Damnation. Fear.

I was afraid of that fear more than anything. My fear of fear. Here in my real body, I was prey to several million years of evolved physical processes that took one look at that height and released a cocktail of chemicals. My breathing quickened. My palms sweat on the rope. I hadn't even begun climbing yet, and I'd already fallen.

"That's a little taller than your bookshelves," said a deep voice behind me.

I turned. Chas Chambers leaned against the wall, arms crossed at his chest. This morning he wore a simple black tank and shorts, which showed off impressive brown calves.

"What are you doing here?" It came out an accusation. My heart, already juiced with nervous adrenaline, was suddenly pounding beneath my ribcage.

He pushed off from the wall with a nudge of his muscled shoulder. "Good morning, Dr. Wells. Sorry. I didn't mean to interrupt you."

Interrupt? There had been nothing for him *to* interrupt. I'd been staring at the cliff face for at least ten minutes. How long had he been standing there?

I wanted to say something clever and collected but was rattled by how hard my heart had taken off. I managed a frosty "Can I help you?"

He looked a little thrown. "I'm here to climb. Do you mind if I join you?"

"Sure. Why not? Be my guest."

I could pretend I'd just finished a climb, but I didn't know how long he'd been standing there. Being caught in that lie would be humiliating.

I busied myself with checking my harness, though I'd already done that several times. He stepped up to prepare one of the other climbing rigs. His large hands picked nimbly at the straps.

"So," I said. "You climb often?"

He flashed me a smile. "Not recently, but I used to."

"Of course. You had to make time for cramming Lost languages."

He gave me a less certain look. "Actually, yeah."

I had a sudden image of this broad-shouldered creature leaned over a desk, hand to his forehead, straining to decipher Oblitus at two o'clock in the morning by the light of a single desk lamp. Because of course not everyone could just look at some words and understand them.

Right.

I diverted my attention back to the climb course, as if it were a puzzle and if I stared at it long enough I could figure it out. But the puzzle wasn't there. The puzzle was inside me.

It was all in my mind. If I could climb in sim, I could climb in real life. I just had to get over myself and I could do it.

And I would never get over myself with all my attention being diverted to six feet of testosterone crowding the gym.

Chas executed a deep stretch routine. Then, with a grunt and a squeak of harness, he leaped straight up. He bared his teeth in a grin, hanging casually from one hand like he'd been raised in the rain forest with Tarzan and his monkeys.

I'd never understood the male need to show off physical prowess. I'd never understood the drive to compete. I didn't climb to satisfy some sense of ego. I climbed because my life's work was on the Lost Planets, and you didn't stroll on them. You climbed, and crawled, and sometimes you sprinted for your life.

But something clicked in me then, and I didn't need to think. I measured the distance above me, shoved my foot into a toehold, and vaulted upward.

I landed next to Chas, who said, "Not bad." The unspoken seemed to be, *For a man who couldn't scale the ladder in his own office.*

And that was it. I took off.

Chas raced beside me, hand over hand in a graceful economy of movement. We reached the top at roughly the same time. He wiped a hand over his shaved head. His face gleamed with a healthy sheen of sweat, and I was satisfied to see I wasn't the only one panting.

"Not bad," I said, probably grinning like an idiot between drips of perspiration. I'd forgotten how good this was, real endorphins, the kind you worked for, your pulse pounding.

"Not bad," he conceded and laughed between breaths. His hazel eyes were fever bright, almost glowing next to his bronzed skin and the black of his eyebrows and neatly edged beard.

And just like that, I was on top of the world. All it had taken was a little click in my brain to break the feedback loop. I was myself again.

Until I looked down.

"Hey, you okay?" Chas said.

There was movement at the periphery of my vision as he reached toward me. His fist closed around the cord that hooked into my harness, and even that little movement, the shiver of tension that went through the line, jolted my nerves, and flipped my stomach.

I stared at the gray matte surface in front of me. "Yeah."

I closed my eyes, aware then of my grip on the handholds. I was 170 pounds of bones, fat, and muscle poised on fingers and tiptoes on a cliff face, thirty feet from the floor. If I dropped from this height onto hard ground, I'd bounce and break. Or break and bounce. Or just break.

A dizzy wave of hysteria skirled through me.

But I had the harness. And, strangely enough, once Chas' hand went still on my line, I felt safer for that touch.

Inexplicably, that angered me.

"Dr. Wells?"

I'd set my forehead against my fist, and my eyes were still closed. I opened them. "I'm fine. Been a while since I climbed. Out of shape." The lie was automatic. I heard the shape of it as it sunk between us, but surprisingly, Chas didn't call me on it.

He leaned in. His voice lowered. "Yeah, me too. We'll take it down slow, all right?"

I looked at him, met his gaze, and barked a laugh. Then I took my line in my hand and leaped from the wall. I caught the flash of surprise on his face before the world rushed past. I wasn't sure who was more startled, him or me.

It was a controlled fall, but the impact still jolted my ankles. My brain took a moment to catch up—catch down—with my body and register I'd come to a stop.

Chas landed nearby with a springy grace, putting those considerable calves to use. "Or we could do it the quick way."

I flashed him a wooden grin and fumbled with my harness straps. The world swam around me. If I just concentrated on my two feet planted firmly on the floor, I'd be okay.

Chas watched me with his light eyes. I read concern there, and wariness. Maybe something else, but I didn't want to know. "That it for you?" he asked.

"Yeah." I pulled the harness off and took an experimental step without its embrace. My legs were steadier than I expected, like stiff rubber.

"You won't build stamina only one climb at a time," Chas said.

"Yeah?" I returned the harness to its housing. "Is that something Confucius said? Or is that your own hard-won wisdom?"

He gave me an unsure look, and seemed about ready to ask the question.

Oh, gods. Don't ask. Do not ask.

He didn't. I turned for the door and made a dignified exit, as dignified as I could make it while I felt like I walked through low gravity and pressure built at the bottom of my throat. On the way out of the leisure and exercise complex, I stopped at the restroom and dropped to my knees in a stall.

☆☆☆

My body was a mess of soreness the next morning. I woke on the same side I'd gone to sleep on, face mashed in the pillow, to discover my arms, legs, and torso had been replaced with mismatched slabs of aged beef. I liked beef. I didn't much like empathizing with it.

I rolled from the bed and stumped to the bathroom to glare at the disheveled man in the mirror. A minute of climbing hadn't been enough for him yesterday. After scraping his knees from the bathroom floor and refilling his stomach with coffee, he'd had the bright idea to go on a run—leaving me with this Frankenstein's monster. A crease like a suture line split my cheek. I shambled into the kitchen on a long moan.

Well, my exploits the day before had revealed to me what kind of shape I was *not* in. Forget the vertigo. If I couldn't sustain a few minutes of running on Turris without coming apart, I was in deep trouble. Among my responsibilities on expedition, "running for my life" ranked near the top for importance. Sita had said the toothed flying nightmares kept away from the plain. That was nice.

I decided to start a daily training regime.

I began after breakfast. Just stretches and walking to start, working my stiff muscles loose. Then, because my arms were about the only thing that didn't hurt on me, I dropped into a battery of push-ups. I reached forty before I flipped onto my back and languished like an overturned turtle.

So Chas climbed. Of course he did. Along with pole vaulting and throwing javelins. How else would he stay in shape? I imagined he ate raw meat for breakfast before a daily ten-mile sprint, then came home and learned a Lost language over a cup of tea.

What rock had Sita found this kid under?

I squinted at the ceiling. Where the devil *had* he come from?

I probably should have worried myself with more professional concerns, like why I hadn't involved myself in his education. Though I was back to teaching and advising, I'd hardly seen him. And Sita hadn't even called me to task about it. Shouldn't I have been bothered that Sita had admitted and was supervising a student through *my* program?

I climbed to my feet and called the school database up on the wall, telling myself it was for completely work-related reasons. "Chas Chambers," I instructed the computer. This was something I should have done a long time ago—something I would have done upon admitting him, if I'd been around to do it.

Chas Chambers. Twenty-five years old—a tad older than I'd guessed. He was the age I had been at the height of my own arrogance and angst. At twenty-five, you thought you knew it all. It had been a nice wind while it lasted. How hard the fall.

Born on one of the younger colonized planets, attended college at a regional on-world institution. Three Forks Continental College. Never heard of it. Decently high marks, although he seemed to have focused more of his attention on varsity sports than academics. Track. Paddling. A couple of games I'd never heard of.

Nothing about Mi'hani, I noticed. In fact, he'd never been off-planet until a year ago.

I flipped through some of his work for the directed independent study courses. Good marks. Consistent improvement. There was absolutely nothing of note about Chas. He was a good jock, and a good student.

I had a few months before I left for Turris. If I wanted to, I could take Chas' supervision over until then. As Director of Language Studies, I had the right.

But why would I even consider that? Just to piss on my territory? *My program, my student.*

Hell no. The last thing I needed was him calling into my office on a regular basis, exuding vitality and clean male sweat. Anyway, it'd be childish to take him back for a few months near the end of his program, just to bunt him back to Sita when I shipped off on expedition.

What Sita had said about interacting with students came back to me.

"Well, you can't have it both ways," I said to the wall as I closed out of the database. "Can't scold me for spending time away from the students and then send me off the station for months at a time. And sir, you're talking to yourself. Evidence it's time to do something more productive with your day."

CHAPTER ELEVEN

Mom called the next evening, startling me from a doze. I'd lapsed into a dream about boating down a river with the knowledge that some unseen presence followed me. I wasn't alone in the boat. Chas Chambers was with me. He'd surprised me by revealing he was a hunter among his people. I was still puzzling over who his people were—somehow, this demanded my attention more urgently than the danger that tracked us down the river—when Mom rang.

I entered the cabin sim and found her tucked in the corner of the couch, one hand petting Switch's massive orange head. It was the first time I'd seen her in over a month, and I had a hard time guessing what she'd been up to from her appearance. Unlike Victoria, who had an avatar for every occasion and rarely wore her own skin, Mom always appeared as herself when at home in the cabin.

Her expression bore an uncanny resemblance to the tiger's this evening, a sphinx-like coolness. She wore her brown hair twisted up in a bun, loose strands falling around her face. She appeared younger than I remembered her when she left the university. A fit early forties. Unsettling to think I'd be reaching her apparent age soon. She could have been my sister.

The room smelled, as always, of wood and wool, the musk of tiger, and the snap of sweet grass that blew in through the open windows.

"Hey, Mom," I said, and stepped around the coffee table to kiss her cheek. Had it been just as soft and cool in real life?

With a pang, I missed her. Which was pretty pointless, because here she sat, smiling and pecking my cheek in return. I straightened and backed up to sit in one of the adjacent chairs. The experience was as good as real. But I missed her just the same, sitting three feet away from her. Three feet and 220 miles.

"How was your trip?" I asked. "Vic mentioned something about shrunken heads."

"Did she?" An enigmatic smile. Her fingers stroked the tiger's fur into tufts. "I had a good time."

Mom was Dad's opposite, really. He would go on a weeklong trip and blather on about it for a year. Mom didn't say a word, but might write a book about it and slip the book into a drawer. Through my childhood and young adulthood, I'd figured I'd inherited my personality in equal parts from both of them. As I got older, I thought rather that I'd taken after Mom, and Vic after Dad.

"Vicky tells me you're leaving for another expedition."

I almost replied, *Did she*? "That's interesting," I said. "We haven't talked in weeks."

"I wonder where she got that from, then." She rubbed Switch's ear, and the big cat leaned into the caress, yellow eyes closing to slits.

I sat back. "I am going. I just hadn't made that decision the last time we talked. What did she tell you?"

"Very little." She shrugged. "That there's been another discovery, this one more important than the others, just like all the others, and of course you have to go."

I bit back my immediate retort. "Yes," I said. "I do have to go. This is the connection I've been looking for between the Lost Planets. I've been waiting for this for ten years."

My life's work.

She considered this silently. "And you falsified the evidence to pass the physical exam?"

If I hadn't been in sim, which muted mental-physical responses, I might have gone blind with the surge of wordless fury that roared through me. Vic and I had always held each other in confidence, a pact from our time as kids. We'd learned quickly we could achieve far more mischief, both together and separately, if we just didn't tell on each other. As we grew older and got put through life's ringer, the agreement became important for other reasons; we unloaded our guts onto each other's laps, and it wasn't good decorum to slop those messes onto our parents' feet. The vow of silence was not something we needed to invoke.

"She *told* you that?"

Mom's eyes glittered triumph. "She told me the dean had given you an ultimatum. I know you wouldn't consider reprogramming. Neither would you consider not going. Last I saw you, you were suffering three migraines a week. That kind of damage doesn't heal itself over night. I could draw my own educated guess."

And I, glorious self-righteous fool, had just confirmed it.

She shook her head and said, "You really are just like your father," negating my idea I'd taken fully after her. She made it sound like a personal failing. I wasn't sure how to respond to this. She continued to stroke the tiger's ears. Almost casually, she said, "I told Vic not to go to the dean. Oh, she quite seriously told me she'd tell Sita."

Sometimes I didn't know this woman who was my mother. I could almost feel my neck muscles stiffening somewhere on the other side of the circuit board, back in real life. "And why did you stop her?"

"*Because* you're just like your father. You'll get your way, just like he did. Meanwhile, the entire world will hear my son's a criminal."

"I'm not a criminal," I muttered, absorbing her words. Was she more worried about her reputation, or mine? But that wasn't what really caught my attention. "What do you mean about Dad?"

"Just what I said. He always insisted on getting his way, no matter the cost."

"He didn't insist on having a *heart attack.*"

"Of course he did. He ignored the symptoms for months. He refused to see the doctor, even at my insistence. Of course he didn't give a care what I said." She gave me a baleful glare that included me in this accusation. "If he'd have just come to Earth like I asked, it never would have happened."

I held my face in my hands and stared at her.

She brushed a thumb over the tiger's nose and continued in an almost conversational tone, "I *told* your dad that I wanted to move to Earth. The university was fun to work at, to live in, while we were young. We wanted to have children. But you and Victoria were all grown up, and your father and I weren't getting any younger. The ideals of youth wouldn't keep us alive forever. Your dad, of course, wouldn't consider it. He just couldn't see the university was as fake as the simulations, everything perfectly maintained, everyone pursuing tasks that are exercises in self-indulgence."

I barked a strangled laugh. "You're kidding me," I said, but the cool expression she turned on me was anything but kidding. "Dad drove himself into the ground for you. He worked himself into a heart attack so he could finish up his work and return to *you.*"

She made a sharp "tsk!" but averted her eyes. "Don't be ridiculous. I don't know what he told you. I don't know what he told himself. But he never had any true intention of coming to Earth."

"Of course he did! Why else would he have sent you ahead? He had the tickets, for Jove's sake!"

She gave me a disgusted look.

I covered my face. "All right. Mom. I don't want to talk about Dad anymore."

"I miss him, too."

"*Mom.*"

A hinge creaked. I looked up, half expecting to find Vic there. But it was just one of the doors down the hall, pushed by the breeze.

"Anyway," Mom said, just a little delicately. "I didn't call you to talk about your dad. I can't change the past, and I've made peace with that."

Like hell. "But you know history repeats itself."

"I didn't call you here to try to talk you out of it, either. I'd be wasting my breath."

"So what is this special occasion?"

"I wanted to see you before you go off and get yourself killed."

"Mom."

She shrugged. "It's the truth."

I stared at her—at the unforgiving brown eyes and the set, thin mouth uncannily like my own, the same mouth that had once smiled at kid me—and then I laughed. A painful kind of laugh, and absurd at the same time. Mom's mouth twitched down, but then she grinned. For a second, sporting that sarcastic expression, she looked like Victoria.

"Hell," I said, and rubbed my forehead. "Let's go get a beer."

☆☆☆

I returned to the climbing course late that night. I began training again as if from scratch, a kid in the jungle gym. Just minor, repetitious exercises at first, relearning my body. Amazing how I'd forgotten to communicate with it in a few months. I needed to build back up my strength and my confidence in my body's power and balance.

I returned to the gym every night after that. It was good to know myself again. I'd always taken my strong relationship and trust with my body for granted.

I spent a while with the exercises before I made another attempt at climbing. And when I did, I started small. The doctors had to have missed something—some damage in my skull, some misalignment of brain cells. The vertigo could not be psychological. But I could overcome it in degrees by acquainting myself with the way it felt and how my body and mind reacted.

By the time three weeks had passed, I could have given a lecture on balance. I became an expert on dizziness, an authority on lightheadedness. I couldn't fight it, but I could collect myself and push through. And wasn't that life?

CHAPTER TWELVE

Amazing, the worries the mind could concoct at ten o'clock the night before liftoff.

I lay in bed and imagined the most elaborate situations that could go wrong. That my ship, being an unscheduled takeoff, had not been fueled. That the media would get wind of the expedition and mob me as I boarded. That Sita would discover my deception with the first aid kit and pull the plug.

I pulled the pillow over my head and counted sheep. I made it to six before the sheep became items from my supply list. Boots. Hat. Rope. Recording equipment. Backpack. Knives. Rope. Twine. Stove. Fire starter. Recording equipment. Sunglasses. Canteen. Stove. Rope.

Blast. I sat up, scrubbed my face, and turned on the lights.

Under the LEDs, my bed was a wreck of rucked sheets and flattened pillows. It looked like the scene of a violent crime. I left it and went out into the living room where things were calm and in place, an organized spread of research documents and notes on the table, the kitchen counters clean, the couch empty.

I found my sim net on the end table next to the couch, dropped in, and went to the cabin. It was early morning there. New light came in through the east-facing dormers. Switch the tiger opened his eyes at my arrival and twitched his tail in annoyance or welcome, I couldn't tell.

Neither Mom nor Vic were there, which didn't surprise me. I checked the two bedrooms just in case but found them empty and neatly made.

Back in the living room, I bent to leave a note and noticed a scrap of paper on the coffee table.

Don't fucking fall on your head again, read Victoria's neat hand.

Love you, too, I wrote on another scrap. My handwriting was not as neat.

I considered sending a note to Theodore, but it wasn't like I'd ever gone out of my way to keep in touch with him before. We'd only really ever socialized in the context of the adventuring club, even if he was my only "real" friend in sim. I'd never bothered to send him a "hello" or a "good-bye" when I went on expedition.

Should I have?

I signed out before I really began to worry myself over that, made a cup of strong tea with cream, and stood in the kitchen, reviewing all of the responsibilities I needed to check off my list before leaving. Final grades were in for my classes. I'd dealt with the small avalanche of student concerns and otherwise survived the last week of the semester—one of the longest, and shortest, I'd ever endured.

I hadn't seen Chas in a while. I'd gotten used to seeing him around, usually in passing on my way back from the track or in the Humanities halls, but I didn't remember seeing him at all this last week or two. How had he fared in his classes? Probably well. Sita knew how to choose and groom students.

A small case of ammunition sat on the table. And here would be an example of why I never could sleep the night before takeoff. Too many small things would slide through the cracks if I weren't awake to obsess over details.

I pulled on my running jacket, scooped up the case, and went out into the midnight halls. Might as well take the case down to the ship and see if I'd forgotten anything else.

I passed few people on the way, students winding their way home from end-of-semester parties. Instructors, too. I made my way behind apartment complexes with checkerboards of dark and light windows. A window on the ground floor went out as I passed. The university was lying down to sleep. Meanwhile, my own day was ending and beginning.

My ship waited in one of the main hangars. This one saw so much traffic that one extra ship taking off at an early time would not be noticed. I entered the passcode and went into the bay. The vast space was dim under yellow security lights, shut down for the night. Strange to think that in a few short hours, it would just be waking up again, and I'd be flying out of here.

I walked between the neat lines of parked ships. My ship would be a small, slender model near the end of the aisle. I'd visited a couple of times for prep and stocking, always at odd hours, so I was used to the emptiness and quiet. But something made me slow as I approached the ship, to shift my weight to the edges of my feet.

The fuselage door stood open. Dim light came from inside and limned the threshold.

Part of the hangar crew? No. Not so late, and they'd have every light on in the ship as they banged and laughed around. Anyway, checks had already been performed.

I lowered the case of ammunition to the ground. In the official records, my ship was not set to launch for another two days, and even then, it wasn't in my own name—although tomorrow's launch had to be down in someone's book, unless Sita planned to launch me herself. So it was possible for someone to have found me out.

I doubted outright sabotage or even theft—not of physical objects, in any case. Theft of ideas, maybe. Theft of information. Media reporter, planting a camera?

I'd left one of the pistols in with the ammunition. Quietly I loaded this, though I didn't need to. An empty weapon would have sent the same message.

I unfolded from my crouch and went up the gangplank like Switch on the hunt. I'd worn my running shoes and not my boots, which gave me the advantage of rounder, more flexible soles.

The light came from deeper inside the ship. I flattened against one side of the ship's door and peered around the corner. No movement from inside and no noise.

I stepped into the hall and inched down it. Peeked into the cockpit. No one there.

The galley light was on. The dispenser had the red light that indicated hibernation, so no one had used it in at least several hours. But one chair was pulled out, sitting at an off angle to the table.

A foot scuffed behind me. I whirled and raised my gun.

At the face of Chas Chambers.

Speaking of chambers, I almost unloaded the pistol's out of pure surprise.

Wisely, Chas didn't say anything. Just kept his hands up while we stared and I tried to work my rage and surprise into words.

"What the hell are you doing here?"

"Dr. Wells. I can explain."

"You'd better," I said.

He lowered his hands as I lowered my gun. What *had* possessed me to take a loaded weapon onto the ship? Right then, I was too tempted to use it. He said, "Dean Tiwari asked me to come as your assistant. That's it. I'm just here loading my things."

I heard the words. I even understood what they meant. But I had trouble processing their implications. I was still working through my shock of finding him here, filling the hall with his shoulders and earnest intentions.

I shook my head. "No. You're not."

Chas looked uncomfortable. That was probably because I still held the pistol with two fists. I opened it, shook out the magazine, and shut it again with a loud clack. I slipped the pistol into one pocket and the magazine into the other.

"You're not loading your things," I said, keeping my voice even. "You're taking them with you and vacating this ship."

I wasn't angry at him. No. This was all Sita. Of all the things she had done, of all the lines she had crossed, this was the most unforgivable.

But yes. I was angry at him. Strangely, I'd trusted him. I hadn't really known him, but I'd trusted him. It was there in his face: guilt. Sita might have put him up to this, but he'd known it was wrong.

I turned before I said something—did something—I'd regret.

I imagined Chas standing there, hands still slightly lifted. The charged silence followed me down the gangplank and down the lane of silent ships. I closed the hangar door on it firmly.

I marched. I didn't care now who saw me. I cut across one of the public lanes and made for one of the apartment buildings on the other side of Humanities.

Sita lived on the third floor of a building fashioned after Moorish architecture. I followed the paved walkway to a foyer decorated with tiles, carved soapstone, and stained glass. Night light shone through the glass and made weak dappled color on the ground. I didn't appreciate the beauty. I jabbed the button for the lift and waited, hating all of it.

Sita's apartment was at the end of the hall. She opened the door after the second round of pounding. Her hand clasped her silk robe closed. She did not look surprised to see me. Her hair lay in a mussed braid. She met my gaze, grim and wary.

For once in my life, I used my greater height to my advantage. I pulled myself tall and looked down at her. "No," I said.

She glanced around my shoulder and lifted her free hand in a wave. I couldn't help myself. I glanced behind to see an older gentleman peering out his apartment door down the hall. At Sita's gesture, he retreated like the nose of a turtle.

Sita stepped back and gave me a look that clearly said, *Come in, you asshole, before you wake all of my neighbors.* I didn't want to come in. I wanted to confront her here in the middle ground of her apartment door, where I had the advantage of a full set of clothes and a potential audience. But I had the distinct impression she would swing the door shut on me, so I passed inside, into her sanctum.

As orderly and bare as Sita's office was, her apartment was a crowded wonder house of leather-and-gold-bound books, Persian vases, thick rugs, carved finches in birdcages, tea tins, and elephants—elephant bronze statues, stuffed toys, pewter figurines, paintings, pillows.

Sita went around me and flipped on the kitchen light. "Warm milk?"

"No." I struggled not to add *Thank you.*

She came back half a minute later with two steaming mugs anyway. She left one on the crowded kitchen bar and sat down with the other at a glass coffee table. She took a sip and regarded me over the rim of her mug. I crossed my arms.

"I refuse," I said. "You have grossly violated my trust, and I just refuse."

She took another long drink and set the mug down. She licked a line of milk from her lip. "If Chas doesn't go, neither do you." She clasped her hands over her knee. "So think about what you're refusing."

Neither of us blinked.

"You really mean that, don't you?" There was a note of incredulous wonder in my voice.

"I do."

Her lips were thin. Usually elegant, she was lined and frumpy with sleep. But that didn't take anything from the strength of her presence.

I could have howled at her. I could have fallen onto the ground in a kicking tantrum.

I sat down on the barstool.

She watched me. Across the room, behind her, thick embroidered curtains covered the wide window that looked out onto the courtyard. The only other light on was a black lacquer lamp with a paper shade. A clock ticked.

"How long were you planning this? From the beginning?"

"It sounds like you already know the answer," she said. "I don't think you really need my response."

Her comm chimed. She rose and took up the handheld receiver.

"Hi Chas," she said. Her eyes met mine. "No, don't worry. I wasn't sleeping. Uh-huh. Uh-huh. I know. Don't worry, you're fine. He'll be all right. You can just finish loading and be ready to leave at six. I'll let you know if that changes. Thank you so much. You, too."

She replaced the receiver.

"Blast it all to hell," I said. I picked up the warm mug of milk and drank. "Does he even have experience? Did he train?" As I asked, I remembered those ropey muscles and the nimble way he climbed and realized physical training wouldn't be a problem.

"He's prepared," she said. She might have meant for Turris, or she might have meant for me.

The poor bastard.

"I want one thing clear for the record," I said. "It wasn't my call to bring him. If something happens to the kid, it's not my responsibility. My conscience is clear."

Sita raised her mug. I raised mine. We drank.

☆☆☆

The alarm clock blared at three thirty and dragged me up out of a deep hole of unconsciousness. I came to my senses with my face smashed in my pillow and the lights in my room fading on.

Ironic I'd take most of the night to fall asleep and then not be able to get up. I couldn't wait for the hours to pass. Now I wished for a few extra.

I dangled at the edge of the bed. The pair of painkillers I'd taken at one thirty had mostly done the trick of stemming the headache that started at Sita's. I hadn't stopped at the ship again. I didn't want to chance seeing Chas. I expected I'd be seeing too much of him for the next couple of months.

Weeks of waiting, and it came down to this: coaxing a cup of coffee and a breakfast pastry from the dispenser, dressing, and giving my checklist one last review. Calling the cabin up on the wall screen and finding it empty. Taking a long, quiet walk through the predawn dark.

The ship was closed and dark when I arrived. Well, there was something. At least I'd have this.

I went inside and turned on the lights, room by room. This was my ritual before takeoff: arrive before the preflight crew to sit and meditate with the ship. Here I was, on the cusp of one of my greatest adventures. I sat in the pilot chair with my hand on the controls, alone and on the edge of discovery.

I toyed with the idea of taking off then.

A short-lived fantasy. I'd hardly caressed the controls when I heard footsteps outside. They paused at the open door and came slowly up the ramp.

Chas peeked around the door. "Morning, Dr. Wells. Peace offering?" He held up a cup of coffee.

He could have looked guiltier. In fact, despite the late hour he'd kept last night, I'd have called him "bright-eyed." I understood why when he rounded the corner. He held a second coffee cup in his other hand, this one half-empty. They were not small cups.

I suddenly had a headache again.

I waved him in and stood from the chair. He'd freshened since I'd seen him a few hours before, hair buzzed to a suggestion of stubble over his skull and his jaw shaved smooth. He brought with him a wave of coffee smell and woody aftershave.

"I really do apologize," he said as I considered him. "Dean Tiwari told me to keep it a secret from everyone, including you."

Well, if he'd been as discreet with everyone else about the mission as he had with me, I would have no worries about media leaks. I could have shaken Sita with my anger, but I did trust her judgment, so I knew I should be able to trust Chas. She wouldn't have sent someone I couldn't count on. Still.

"I might have shot you," I said.

"Yeah. I'm really appreciative you didn't."

Strangely, so was I. But that was mostly because I hated press.

The headache moved to the ridges of my eyes. I accepted the cup of coffee from him, assessed the heat of its contents, and after deeming it a reasonably sane temperature, tossed it down.

"Right," I said, meeting his wide-eyed look. I handed him back the empty cup. "You can make sure everything is securely stowed. I'm going to prep for launch."

Sita had given me the coordinates for Turris on a scrap piece of fiber paper. Normally the ship would have been loaded with all of the navigation information a week before launch. I entered it now. I tried not to be conscious of Chas on the ship, looking at things, touching things. Taking up space. Leaving scent trails of aftershave.

The computer ran through its calculations. It would be at it for a few minutes. I stood and went down the hall, past the galley—its light had already been turned on—to the living suite. The door to the head stood open and dark. To the left, my own room was closed. I opened the door to my office, to the right.

And stopped.

Chas looked over his shoulder at me, paused in the act of changing his shirt. Shoulder blades sharp as axes glided under smooth brown skin.

"Hi," he said.

I backed out of the room and closed the door. For a moment, I had no coherent thought. The afterimage of his sleek waist and back muscles—*back muscles?*—burned my retinas.

Then: *What the hell is he doing in my office?*

I rewound the scene. He'd been crouched in front of a bag I hadn't recognized. The desk had been folded up, and the berth pulled out.

Of course, where else did I think Chas would be staying? It was the only other sleeping quarters in the ship.

So, all right. I should have expected that.

My own room held only my things. One of the bags was secured in a strap I knew I hadn't left it in. I took a deep breath. I had told him to secure the ship, after all. I fought the juvenile urge to re-stow the bag.

I flipped off an unnecessary hall light—a light *I* hadn't turned on—as I passed back to the galley. What I needed was a cup of black tea. And possibly a lobotomy.

I saw Chas had already made himself at home here, too. An empty cup sat on the counter with a drip of coffee in the bottom. Not the same cup he'd been drinking from earlier. I wondered just how much caffeine swirled in his blood. I probably didn't want to know.

I pressed buttons for tea. I took a sip of the resulting liquid and immediately spat it back into the sink.

I stared into the cup. The liquid looked like black tea, and now that my taste buds had a moment to sort out what had just hit them, I could say it even tasted like tea, if the tea had been over-steeped, squirted with lemon, and then sweetened so heavily I was surprised not to see crystals dusting the bottom of the cup. Someone had doctored the parameters for tea, and that someone had not been me.

I put a hand over my face.

The sound of footsteps coming up the ramp brought me back from the brink of meltdown.

"There you are," Sita said, looking in.

"Here I am." I dumped the tea.

Like Chas, she looked far more awake than she had any right to look. Bags and creases had disappeared. Her shining hair was pulled into a coil.

She held up a cup. "Coffee?"

"No, thanks."

Chas appeared and she said, "Coffee?"

"Absolutely."

CHAPTER THIRTEEN

Miraculously, the launch went without a hitch. Sita gave us her little pre-trip pep talk, and I smiled to show her I was playing nicely. She left us to the care of the preflight crew, who did a final check on the ship's systems and navigated us to the gate. I closed the ramp behind them. We launched.

The moment of takeoff was my favorite part of the trip. Nothing beat the first push into space, not even the first sighting of the planet or the first discovery of ruins. All of the waiting, all of the preparation culminated in that squeeze of acceleration, the view of stars expanding in the windshield: a field of bright possibilities and black unknown.

Chas sat silent in the copilot chair. He might have been nervous or he might have just been enjoying the experience, like I. It probably would have been the kind thing, the right thing, to ask him. For all I knew, this was his second-ever trip into space. He hadn't spoken since Sita left, just stood back and watched the preflight crew and me go about our business, and I counted that in his favor.

I was just beginning to think this might be an okay trip after all when the acceleration decreased and the computer chimed that it was safe to move about the ship. Then everywhere I turned, he was there, being helpful.

I went into the galley to fiddle the tea parameters back to default and he was pulling a cup from the dispenser. He turned and nearly swung it into my chest. "Oh! For you. It's black."

I went into my room to sit on the bunk and gather my wits before transport, and he was stacking my equipment. He looked up. "Sorry. I thought these were secure."

I returned to the cockpit to check the trajectory and found him leaning over the dashboard, drawing code. "We were pulling off course—"

"That's fine," I snapped. "I've got it. Just...sit down."

He hesitated. "I was in the middle of—"

"Sit *down.*" I brushed past him to scrawl a Cancel code on the dash, aborting his command. I ran a quick diagnostic and surveyed the situation. He was right; we were off course from the way station. It looked like a minor change in the station's position the computer hadn't accounted for. I paused a moment, trying to remember the command to fix it. Chas hovered.

"Get the hell off my back," I snarled.

In the silence that followed, I watched his reflection in the dash pause, wide-eyed. He turned away and left the cockpit.

Brilliant. Now I couldn't think over the echo of my own shout. I squeezed my temples. The symbols wouldn't come to me, only the image of Chas' startled face.

I slashed a sequence of code onto the dash, seeing if my hands would remember what my head wouldn't, and miraculously the ship began to right itself. Six hours until we arrived at the way station.

Chas returned a few minutes later. He sat in the copilot seat with a glass of water and gazed out the window.

"Sorry," I said, gruffly, after a minute. "I'm just not used to another person—" I almost said *underfoot.* "Around."

He grimaced, chagrined. "I know."

"Oh, do you?"

"Yeah. All of your excursions have been solo." He paused a beat. "That is public knowledge, isn't it?"

"Yes, I guess it is. And you can probably see why. Why I fly solo, I mean."

He smiled at me over the rim of the cup.

"Given up on the caffeine?" I said.

He looked surprised. Glanced at the water. Gave a chuckle.

Things were a little easier after that. It helped that there wasn't much to do. I only had to wait for six hours and try not to think about my nerves. It'd been almost a year since I'd last transported. While awake and aware, anyway. The actual last time I'd transported, I'd been cold unconscious. That was just after the accident. They'd stabilized me by the time they'd taken me through the way station, but I'd still had a cracked head. Sometimes I wondered if that was what had screwed me up, if some glitch had occurred in the programming during transportation, a minor miscalculation due to the injury, and some of my code was just a little out of place, causing lingering neurological effects.

"Do you want to catch a nap?" Chas asked, and I realized I'd been staring at the ceiling. He asked tentatively, as if unsure how helpful he should try being now. "I can keep an eye on the ship," he added.

Now that I thought about it, the command of his I'd canceled just before inputting my own had looked similar. Maybe identical, if a little neater than mine. I looked at him like a puzzle I'd just discovered. "Where'd you pick that up?"

I meant the piloting, but he smiled and shrugged and said, "I figured one of us might as well get some rest, and it isn't going to be me." His gaze fell pointedly onto his cup.

"It's not going to be me, either." And hours of tense silence didn't seem promising. I shifted in my seat. "So what did Sita tell you, anyway?" Might as well make use of the time, and I would need to know where to start with him.

"Nothing."

"Nothing?"

He frowned, bemused, and shook his head. "Not much, anyway. I know we're headed to Turris. I know generally where we'll be landing, and the terrain to expect. Flora and fauna."

"And the ruins—you know *why* we're going, right?"

A touch of amusement. "No." At my dubious look, he said, "Dean Tiwari told me the excursion is under your direction and you'd tell me as much as I needed to know after launch." He gave me a long look. "She...didn't tell you."

"No." I put my chin on my fist and absorbed this. Sita was a devil for details. I'd thought for sure she'd fully briefed him for the expedition. She didn't do things halfway. Which meant she'd purposefully sent him on the trip with limited knowledge. The queer thing was, that actually made me feel better. Tension went out of my shoulders I hadn't realized was there.

Here I'd imagined Sita planning this for months, talking with Chas in parallel to me, telling him everything she'd told me in confidence, showing him the photographs, explaining the implications of the research. That thought had bothered me as much as her springing an assistant on me.

Poor kid. We'd both been thrown into this. Just what had she told him to rope him into this crazy scheme?

Actually, probably not much. Just "Will you go with Dr. Wells on a trip?" might have done the trick. That sort of regard still mystified me.

Tell me as much as I need to know. Effectively, that didn't need to be much. I could tell him a bit about the ruins, enough to navigate and be useful taking pictures and field notes. But it was nothing I couldn't tell him in a couple of hours, and nothing he needed to know right now.

I sat back. "So tell me about your qualifications. Tell me why you're right for this job."

Disappointment flashed across Chas' face, but only fleeting.

"Well..." he said. "I can carry eighty pounds on my back."

For a few beats I just looked at him, and he looked at me, and then we both grinned.

☆☆☆

I did take him up on the offer for a nap, if only for an excuse to be alone in my cabin. That, and if this trip were going to be successful, I'd have to have some trust. Or at least show some.

Not that I actually expected to get any sleep, not with the way station approaching in less than five hours. But I stretched out on my bunk and folded my hands over my chest and stared up at the ceiling, trying for calm.

Lying by myself in the cabin was the closest I felt to being back on expedition. Here I could almost imagine it was just me and the infinite field of space.

There was definitely a difference between being alone at the university and being alone in space. Out here with no people around, I existed in an absolute kind of solitude. A clear and pure solitude, not at all like the expectant, guilty kind of feeling that pressed in on me at the university, the kind of loneliness that came from knowing thousands of other people existed within seconds of me, and that I probably should be engaging with one or more of them at that moment.

Chas was here this time. That gave the solitude an even different quality. I distracted myself from my agitated nerves by trying to feel it out. It wasn't the heavy loneliness of being in my apartment, but it wasn't the clean solitude of striking off into space on my own.

Actually, it was disturbingly intimate. Context was everything. Surrounded by millions of empty miles, the few feet between us were like nothing. The walls were a courtesy. I was practically standing next to Chas. Lying next to. We were breathing the same air.

Had he told Sita anything about our encounter at the climbing course? Or my performance on the ladder, for that matter? Not likely, if Sita hadn't confronted me about it.

Now that was interesting.

During our chat in the cockpit, neither Chas nor I had mentioned our various run-ins around the university. In listing his skills to me, he had matter-of-factly cited his ability to climb, and just as matter-of-factly I nodded, as I'd nodded to each of his other credentials: preparation in field research, specialization in Lost languages, track training, and resistance to sleep deprivation.

"That," I said, "may very well be your most important skill."

Not that I was a very good at exhibiting this skill myself. Somewhere between thoughts about Chas and worries about the way station, I must have fallen asleep, because the next thing I knew, an alarm was pealing through the ship. I swung my legs from the bed just as I registered that no, it wasn't an alarm. It was a notification. A warning, but not the emergency kind.

Chas rapped at the door. "Dr. Wells?"

I grimaced. I'd have to talk to him about that. I couldn't do two months of being called "Dr. Wells." I tolerated it at the university from my students, but I still had to stifle the impulse to look over my shoulder for my father half the time. Or my mom.

"I'm up," I said, raking a hand through my hair.

"We're approaching the way station."

I resisted the urge to remind him I'd been doing this for eleven years. "Strap in."

Silence after that. I went to my bags, forgot what I might be looking for, clamped an arm over my stomach, and dropped onto the bunk again. A keen ache began in the center of my head behind the point between my eyes. I pressed a thumb there. "Gods. Please. No." Not a headache. Not now.

I'd have liked nothing more than to curl up on the bunk, pull the blanket over my head, and ride the transportation out like a nightmare. Instead I walked out, stopped at the mess for a cup of water—better to have that in your stomach to dilute the acid—and went into the cockpit.

Chas had already strapped himself into the copilot seat. He looked up, face lit with excitement. Had he ever transported before? Supposedly some people got a kick out of it.

The way station loomed larger in the screen, a giant ring that existed solely to copy, create, and destroy. Maybe it supported life somewhere in its hull, a contingent of workers to supervise its functioning, but it seemed like a dead thing, a metal monument floating in the void of space. I gave it a passing glance on my way to the pilot's seat. I sat down on lumps, remembered the seat belts, jerked them out from underneath me, and began to buckle them with trembling hands.

I was going to be all right. No need to be more nervous than usual. Breathe.

I had trouble making the ends of the buckles meet, and it occurred to me how profoundly unready I was for this. How fragile my recovery. I could walk, I could talk, but tap on me and I began to crack.

Chas didn't stare outright, but I felt his curious attention on me and had a fresh pang of resentment for Sita. "Was that the ten minute or five?" I said, gaze fixed on my chest as I worked the last buckle. My hands jammed it twice before it snicked home.

Right on cue, a second warning pealed. That would be the five. Chas chuckled, and maybe I was projecting, but it had a touch of nervousness.

I tested the snugness of the belts and was comforted by their pressure over my chest, lap, and legs. I settled back. Glanced at Chas. "You ever transport?"

"Plenty of times."

That could have been matter-of-factness or arrogance. I couldn't tell right then, although something about that easy admission struck me. It wasn't something I had any mind to investigate at that moment. I wiped my damp palms on my pant legs. "You ever been on one of those?"

"What?"

I chucked my chin toward the screen. "The stations."

He looked at the ring of the way station. Parts of it now disappeared beyond the edges of the screen. "Once."

"No shit?"

He smirked. It might have been self-deprecating. "Emergency docking. My ship was in the hangar for four days."

"So there are actually people on there?" My surprise was bald, almost comical. Nerves made me exaggerate.

His smile widened. "Not like the university, but yeah."

We both fell quiet, watching the ring slowly disappear beyond the edges of the screen until we couldn't see it at all, only the open space beyond.

I closed my eyes when the last warning went out, the thirty-second bell. I gripped the armrests hard enough to numb my fingers. Part of me wanted to snap off a droll remark, but I couldn't have gotten it past my dry throat even if I could find the words.

It was nice knowing you.

Chas asked me a question. I didn't register his meaning, because in that moment, I came apart.

I never could figure out if that was me dying or being reconstructed. It was brief, not even enough time for my breath to catch in my throat—and then I was back again, heaving against the chest belt like a man jolting out of a nightmare. Or into one.

My hands shot to the buckles, scrabbling to undo them. I bruised a finger in my haste. The first buckle fell away, and I went onto the next. I could just make out Chas' distant "Dr. Wells?" over the roar in my head. I really did need to tell him to call me something else.

A strangled noise escaped me. The last buckle came free, and I jerked out of the seat, making blindly for the hall.

The ship ripped slantways; my stomach squeezed through my throat. I grasped the corner of the wall to steady myself. Of course, the ship was perfectly steady. It was my own skull that was imploding.

I stumbled into the head and dropped to the floor in front of the toilet. Unfortunately, only a too-familiar position for me. I vomited the water I'd drunk just before, fouled with bile. I gagged until tears ran down my cheeks and clung to the cold bowl a while after.

Chas hung in the doorway. I didn't look at him, but I could feel him just outside of my sight, watching. "Dr. Wells?"

"Call me London," I rasped.

He paused. "London. Are you all right?"

I blinked tears out of my eyelashes and reached up to flush the toilet. "Fabulous." I stood. I stepped up to the sink and washed my hands without looking at him. "I'm glad you could share that with me." I rinsed my mouth. Removed my glasses and wiped my eyes with my wrist. Dried the tears that flecked the lenses.

"Is that why you travel alone?"

"What?" That surprised me into looking up.

A little sweat shone on his own forehead. "Is this... Do you go alone on expeditions because you don't want people to see your reaction? This is from the transportation, right?"

I dried my hands and my mouth on the towel. I would have smiled, if I could remember how just then. "No. I mean, yes, this is how I always react. But that's not why I travel by myself. I have absolutely no qualms about turning my stomach inside out while someone watches."

Did his complexion grow darker? "I am so sorry. I thought..."

"It's fine. Nothing to worry about."

And, blessedly, it really wasn't something to worry about. The pain was already abating, and the ship had more or less straightened out and steadied itself around me. No migraine, even. Most importantly, no damage.

I stepped past Chas and went into my room to shuck my shirt and pull on a fresh one.

I found Chas in the mess cradling another mug. More coffee? I felt a pang of annoyance, as if he were doing me a personal grievance by mainlining stimulants.

Maybe it showed on my face, because he said, "It's hot chocolate. Would you like some?"

"Hot chocolate?"

"Yeah." His smile was a tad sheepish. "I always drink a cup after transportation. Kind of a tradition."

"Yeah? Whose?"

"Mine." He set his mug down and turned to the food dispenser. "Here."

I wasn't a fan of chocolate, but I took the mug he proffered. I sniffed the steam delicately, bracing for a squeeze of nausea, but nothing. It even smelled good—sweet and dark—so I took a sip.

The chocolate chased away the sour remnants of sickness and left a trail of heat straight down to my stomach, where it warmed my guts. My fingers tingled. The tension in my head released.

"Yeah?" he asked, a hopeful smile in his voice.

I peered at the dark liquid. "Is this spiked?"

"No." His chuckle was rich and velvety, like the hot chocolate. "Just milk and cocoa. And a lot of sugar. A touch of vanilla."

I could have sworn out loud in appreciative surprise. I took another sip instead.

Chas lifted his mug and raised it in salute. "Cheers," he said in English. He sipped, looked into the mug, swirled the contents, and said, "I don't know what it is, but the chocolate steadies my nerves after a jump."

I had to agree. By the time I tipped back the dregs of chocolate, I felt almost like a real person again. I dropped the mug into the recycler and said, "How'd you ever come to that?"

He gave that sheepish smile again. "My mother used to make me a cup before school when I was nervous. It worked."

We went into the cockpit. A fresh landscape of blackness and stars filled the screen. I called up the ship's rearview and got a picture of our receiving way station shrinking from view behind us. It looked largely like the station that had sent us, though this one might have been just a bit slimmer, maybe a newer model. That, and the absence of the Sol system planets, provided visual verification we had arrived in a different place.

I switched back to forward view and set about charting our location on the dash. The codes were coming back to me. I scrawled them in quick strokes.

"So maybe I shouldn't ask," Chas said. "But, you never got fixed for transportation?"

"I wasn't under the impression I was broken."

"Well, reprogrammed. You travel a lot. I was just surprised."

I finished a command and turned. "No, I never did."

He looked part surprised, part horrified. Although transportation technically made no changes to your makeup—it effectively copied, destroyed, and recreated you at a distant site, down to the last atom—it triggered a violent neurological reaction commonly known as "jump sickness," which I had just enacted. In some individuals, it caused blackouts. In others, hallucinations. In most, disorientation, pain, and nausea. Neurologists attributed it to a "fault" in a human's natural mental wiring, which could be fixed with a simple reprogramming procedure.

"I don't do reprogramming," I said. "I never have."

"Never?"

"No."

"But...why?"

Because the same kind of operation that fixed you of jump sickness could be used to fix you of homosexuality, if you wanted. I had problems with technology that could make you into someone else. I leaned the small of my back against the dash and chose my words. "Because I don't want to risk the consequences if they screw up."

He looked dubious.

"You know I'm an automatic polylinguist." Really, what I was was an anomaly. It still amused me they'd actually come up with a term for me.

He nodded, still doubtful. "But jump sickness isn't related to language ability. The reprogramming wouldn't touch that."

"They don't know what causes my ability. They haven't been able to pinpoint it to any one section of the brain. No one knows how it works, so there's a good chance that even the best reprogrammer could screw it up."

He frowned, considering this. "I'm sorry."

"Why?"

"Jump sickness is rough."

I shrugged. "You get used to it." Like you got used to hangovers, or twisting your ankle.

I returned my attention to the screen. "We have nine days of travel before we enter the Turris system. Enjoy your hot cocoa while you can."

CHAPTER FOURTEEN

Through sheer force of will, and propped up on nothing save dignity, I made it through a few more hours in the cockpit. Chas gazed through the screen. The silence was a balm. Maybe he thought I still suffered the effects of jump sickness, but truthfully, I was just tired. Transportation usually took it out of me, but not like this. The bones had been knocked from my body. Weights, tied to my shoulders. Every few minutes, I straightened for fear of falling into a slump I wouldn't have been able to pull myself out of. I imagined sliding from my seat into a heap on the floor.

At length, I muttered an excuse to Chas and shuffled to my berth. I didn't remember undressing or rolling into bed, but I must have managed both, because I woke on the hard mattress in my briefs. My head was on the pillow, so I'd even crawled in on the correct side.

I blinked and sat up, assessing. I seemed to have my bones back, and the blurry grogginess felt like something the shower could wash away. I glanced at the time and did a double take. One o'clock in the morning. I'd slept ten hours.

I went into the hall expecting dimmed lights and a deserted ship. But the light was on in the mess, splashing out into the hallway. That pinged irritation. I was already preparing a lecture on energy conservation and the importance of turning off lights when the smell of coffee registered; I turned into the mess to find Chas sitting at a side table, one hand curled through the handle of a mug, the other flicking slowly through the contents of a sheet of vellum.

Here was a Chas I'd never seen. The bend of his head and the lean of his shoulders softened him and deemphasized his musculature. He looked as at ease sitting at the table as he did hooking up at the climbing course. And for an instant, I couldn't imagine they were the same man.

Chas looked up at my entrance and smiled. "Morning. Get some good sleep?"

I grunted and went to the dispenser. At this hour, I hadn't anticipated interpersonal communication. Parts of my brain were still firing up. My speech centers blinked one lazy light in standby.

Chas returned to his paper. He'd changed into a loose white shirt and had a contained, wakeful energy that drained me just to look at. One o'clock was an abysmal time to be up—I'd set my sleeping schedule all askew—but the thought of sleeping anymore that night was impossible. I leaned against the counter, hands cradling a mug hot from the dispenser. I didn't drink the coffee so much as pour it slowly into my mouth like fuel. The liquid loosened up my inner workings, while the caffeine sent a signal to my brain. *Awake. Full activation. Engage for morning interaction.*

"What are you reading?" I asked, testing my voice. Rusty, but coherent.

"Your essays on Turrian."

"Oh."

He looked chagrined. "It's always given me trouble."

In Turrian, I said, "You find it challenging?"

His expression registered no understanding. He shook his head and sat back. "You see, you make it seem so natural. Makes me wonder what the hell I'm doing wrong."

I snorted. "Nothing. It's a difficult language. Only a handful of people know it." I hooked a seat across from him and sat down, leaning heavily on my elbows. I slid the sheet of vellum around and tapped through the text. "It's not logic-based like Basic. It's based on conditionals. Every word can only be understood in context." I found the passage I was looking for, planted my finger on it, and slid the page back to him. "Here. See? The same word for 'sky' can mean 'ceiling' or the transcendent intellect or spirit of the race, depending on the modifiers attached to it."

He bent over the sheet, cheek propped on the heel of his hand. His eyes tracked the text. He had particularly long lashes. Soft and dark. "Elegant" was the word for them. They had the somewhat paradoxical effect of accentuating his otherwise cut, masculine features.

His gaze flicked up and met mine, that startling light hazel. One eyebrow raised in wry amusement. "That doesn't exactly help. There could be endless number of meanings for one word."

"Yes. And no. Look." I commandeered the vellum again. After opening a fresh document, I drew in a few sentences. "You have to think like the Turrian. Not just their grammar, but their philosophy. To them, all of creation is a reflection of the sky. So to them, everything is made of air. Air is in constant flux, and so everything in the world is, too. It's all one kind of thing, moving into different shapes. That's mirrored in their language. Few words, moving around, representing their entire world. It's not just that the context tells you which concept the word represents in that specific instance, it tells you how that word is moving, how it is manifesting." Chas frowned, and I struggled for imagery. "We call a bird a bird whether it is sleeping or flying or dead. We recognize that it is still a bird, but the rest of the context tells us what state the bird is in, how to picture the bird. The Turrian saw all things as one thing, so as far as they are concerned the sky and the collective soul of the race are the same. It is not one word that represents many concepts; it is one concept that takes on many forms."

I moved the words around in the sentences, changing their position, their context, their meaning. I went through several examples like this. I saw the moment when the light came on for Chas. It flashed over his face, and I sat forward. "You see it?"

"Yeah..." His face twisted into a funny expression, pleased and doubtful at the same time. "I think I do."

He looked up with shining eyes and opened his mouth to say something else, which was remarkable timing, because at that moment my stomach broke out in a whale song that would have impressed a cetologist. Even better, his jaw snapped shut as the sound died out.

Chas threw back his head and laughed. It was deep, warm, unselfconscious.

He wiped a tear from his eye. "It was trying," he said, "but it didn't sound much better than me." At that, he spoke a sentence in Turrian—badly, and in a slow, singsong voice.

"Oh, no," I groaned. "Stop. Stop."

He grinned at me and wiped the heel of his hand over his cheek. "I'm so sorry to keep you from breakfast. What would you like?" He stood.

"Uh, anything."

"Hot or cold?"

"Cold," I said, though a little doubtfully because there was an odd glint in his eye. Mischievous.

I stared at his backside as he did something at the dispenser, and the image of his trim, naked torso came back to me. As I watched the white shirt bunch and stretch with his movements, it occurred to me a hot breakfast would be nice. Something lean and salty, with bones. And a side of fraternization.

I scrubbed my eyes.

The sweet smell of coconut came to me a moment before Chas' "Dr. Wells?"

"London," I reminded him, and pulled my hand from my face. He slid a dish in front of me. I stared down at three white logs the length of my palm. They looked naggingly familiar, like sushi rice with the piece of fish peeled away. Except no sushi rice I'd ever seen had little brown and green bits mixed in with it. "What is this?"

"Just try it."

I wasn't sure I trusted the smile on his face, but it was probably in his best interest not to make me sick. Or kill me. So I took a hesitant bite.

I stared at the sticky residue it'd left on my fingers as I chewed it. "What *is* this?" I said in a thick voice. "Is this breakfast or candy?"

"Breakfast," he assured me.

I swallowed and dug a single finger into the other half of the log. "What's in it?"

"Rice. Condensed milk. Coconut. Dates. Nuts—pistachios, almonds." He paused in thought, then added, "Honey."

"Really?" I asked, dryly.

He nodded. The smile flickered out of his eyes and he asked, "Do you like it?"

His earnestness was endearing. "Yeah." I rolled the residue between my fingers. "Maybe too much. Do people actually eat this for breakfast?"

The smile returned. "Yeah. It's traditional on Xindi. It's farmer food. They pack them after dinner and chill them overnight so they have something to eat early the next morning. It's high energy because they're out in the fields all day. I thought you could use a pick-me-up after yesterday."

"This'll do," I agreed. I chewed stickily through the other half of the log. "So is that where you're from? Xindi?" I knew it wasn't from his student record, but it wouldn't hurt to play ignorant.

Surprise flickered over his face. He shook his head. "Nah. I just have this kind of hobby. I like to recreate traditional foods. Name any planet and any meal. Breakfast, lunch, dinner. Dessert. Snack."

Now, why hadn't *I* thought of that? I'd never tried coaxing anything but standard fare and Late English staples out of the dispensers.

Maybe he interpreted my expression as dubious, because he added, "It was something to kill the boredom in undergrad. It got me away from the books. And everyone wanted me at their party because I could conjure some pretty wild hors d'oeuvres." He raised his eyebrows.

"I bet." I finished the other two logs. He was right. The sugar perked me up. I almost felt like a living thing again.

"So…" I said. "I've gotten all the sleep I'm going to get tonight. I don't know about you." But he was already nodding. "Then how about we reconvene in a few hours. We'll go over Turrian, and then you can make me lunch."

"It's a date."

I was beginning to like that smile of his. Maybe a little too much.

☆☆☆

Three hours later, I found Chas waiting for me in the galley. He dazzled that gorgeous smile at me and thanked me, quite clearly in Turrian, for honoring him by making him my pupil. I could imagine him practicing it in front of the mirror. That solved the mystery of what he'd been doing in the bathroom for half an hour. And here I'd been suspecting culinary experimentation gone wrong.

He infected me with his enthusiasm for learning. Though, for the sake of fairness, it didn't take much to excite me. About teaching, that was. I *liked* teaching languages. In fact, I'd forgotten just how much I loved one-on-one tutoring. Something inside me roused and woke for the first time since the accident.

Chas looked up from the page. "You're smiling. I think this is the first time I've seen you really smile."

To my surprise and chagrin, I was.

Later, lying on my bunk, I wondered if this was really why Sita had sent him with me. Bless and damn her, she was right. I'd been holed up in my own version of hell for so long, I'd forgotten how to connect with students. I'd forgotten *to* connect.

And Chas was a star pupil. Who knew all that muscle could sit still so long? He was waiting in the mess the next morning with his books, two cups of coffee, and breakfast. Breakfast turned to lunch, and then I finally needed to peel myself away to check our course.

His enthusiasm didn't flag. Morning and night, if he wasn't in the cockpit babysitting the autopilot, he was in the mess with his book and a cup of coffee.

"Is there something wrong with your berth?" I asked on the third evening.

He looked up. I could read lines of text in his eyes. "Huh?"

"I was wondering if everything is okay with your room. You don't seem to use it much."

"Oh. I just don't like to spend a lot of time in the same place I sleep."

And apparently he didn't sleep much.

"Am I in your way here?" he asked, raising his arms to gather his things. "I'll move if you want me to."

"What? No. I just wanted to make sure you were comfortable." I was sorry I had said anything. The galley was the only casual communal space in this hat box. Who was I to call him out for spending time here?

He smiled. "I'm fine."

I considered him over my cup of tea. I put it down and crossed my arms. "So why the Lost languages?"

Something like alarm crossed his face, but I might have been wrong, because an instant later he was carefree again. He shrugged. "They're interesting. They're not human. We don't know anything about the things that spoke them, but we know how they spoke. Or how they wrote, anyway."

"But not what they spoke *about*," I said.

He smiled the smile of a man who knew your secret. "No great works of fiction, no news pieces, no epic poetry."

"If only. Only signs, and the driest semireligious passages."

"That is pretty strange," he said. "If a human planet suddenly had to be evacuated, something would be left behind."

"Not if everything was digital. If Earth were destroyed tomorrow, I bet there wouldn't be a scrap of literature to be found." I paused and rocked my head in thought. "Maybe you'd find remains of the computers it was stored in."

"But there is no indication of advanced technology on any of the Lost Planets."

"Ah," I said, tapping my finger in the air. "And that's the rub."

Chas looked at me with a fervent expression close to reverence, and sudden heat spread over my neck. I turned to retrieve my tea and busied myself taking a drink.

"And that would be the reason for the unpopularity of the languages," I said. "No one cares about words if there's nothing of interest to read."

"Except us."

"Except us," I said, and weirdly, if felt good to say that out loud. Two packages of meat in a metal can floating in space, the only souls in the vast stretches of the galaxy who gave a damn about a bunch of dead languages and the nonexistent aliens who may have spoken them.

CHAPTER FIFTEEN

The next week passed in sameness. I spent time reviewing maps and notes on a makeshift desk I'd made up in my cabin. It was the only place I was sure to be alone. Not that I didn't like Chas' company. It's just I had started to like it too much. Even in our long stretches of silence, I was comfortable to the point of forgetting he was there. Awkward, when I looked up from picking my back tooth to find him watching me.

Tutoring took up about three hours a day, the amount of time Chas could stay attentive and absorb new information before starting to fade. After that, I left him to study on his own. Mealtimes were interesting. Chas brought the galley alive with smells and sights I'd never encountered before—including a few I hoped I never would again.

We spent most of the hours between study and meals preparing for landfall. That began promising enough. We'd already established Chas' abilities. In addition to his physical capabilities, he had a full complement of field research skills, which we reviewed in depth. Sita hadn't sent a slacker.

Still. As we went over the plans for Turris, I found myself wishing for simulations and training facilities—tools we'd had back at the university. I kicked myself now for being so stubborn with Sita. I could have had months to train Chas. I still didn't know what would happen once we landed. The kid could unpack and assemble field equipment, and he could climb a rock face, but that told me nothing about how he'd perform in the field.

Chas didn't appear to share any of my misgivings. He listened attentively as I reviewed information on Turris using the text and pictures we had available to us, so I couldn't place why I felt put off. Maybe it was the fact that Chas never asked a question.

"Nope, I got it," he'd say.

Flora, fauna, terrain, weather, route, data-collection methods: "I got it," with a sure smile.

The cool confidence worried me. I didn't realize just how much until I stood in the galley the night before our arrival, facing the dispenser. I'd been staring at the buttons for ten minutes, deciding between Mildly Unnerved and Silent Panic. Both gave me indigestion. I realized part of the apprehension had to do with my own personal misgivings. It had been easy enough to push them away for the last few weeks while I dove into research and preparation, but with landfall less than twenty-four hours away, all the doubts and fears came gnawing back. I'd lied to pass the physical. So, I could run a few laps on an atmosphere-controlled track. What did that mean? I still had deep psychological damage from the last trip. I could deny it all I wanted, but I knew it to be true. I had no idea how I would respond on land. Added to that was Chas, another unknown variable. So quietly assured, I could only think that he didn't understand all of what we'd face.

"Are you all right?"

I leaped and spun to see Chas standing in the doorway of the galley.

"Just fine." My heart pounded against my ribcage. I wasn't sure what bothered me more: that he'd caught me brooding, invaded my private moment, or sneaked up on me.

He took a step inside. "Excited about landing?" he asked, with a ghost of sarcasm.

"That's it exactly."

Chas grinned and leaned back against the doorframe. He'd changed out of his day clothes into the soft flannel pants and sleeveless shirt he wore at night.

"Since this is our last night on the ship, I thought we could celebrate."

And why was it that my heart should suddenly skip a beat? That my stomach should jostle? I couldn't manage a word in response, but raised my eyebrows.

"Well," he said. "We have use of the dispenser for one more night. Everything's ready for landing, so there's nothing else for us to do. So I thought I'd show you a few of my favorite drinks."

Challenge gleamed in his eyes, and maybe something else. Hope?

I did not drink with students. Most importantly, I knew better than to drink with *this* student. But he wasn't just a student now, was he? He was a colleague.

And there was something in that challenge I couldn't resist—something of a stag brandishing its antlers.

"Well, this should be good," I said.

I leaned against the counter while Chas did his magic with the dispenser. I took the glass he offered and inspected the pale-green liquid with some suspicion and an inkling.

Chas swirled his own glass. "Yes. It is."

"It can't be real, though. The dispenser wouldn't make it."

"Why not? It's alcohol and herbs. It doesn't actually make you hallucinate. That's just a story."

"It smells like a cat voided licorice."

"Yeah. It is pretty strong."

I watched him take a small drink. I knew about absinthe, of course. Damned if I knew why I'd never tried it, at least in sim. It'd always just been a background detail, something the men at the Explorer's Club mentioned occasionally but never actually drank. Taking a sip, I could understand why.

The sharp tang of licorice went up my nose and numbed my tongue. "Good God," I said.

Chas laughed.

I held up the glass. "Why in God's name would anyone drink this if it doesn't actually do anything? Why not pour grain spirits down your throat? You like this?"

"It doesn't do 'nothing.' I said it doesn't make you hallucinate. But it does have a really nice buzz. You'll see."

"I think perhaps not." I peered into the glass. The single sip had already warmed my stomach.

"Sorry. It was just a thought. I knew you liked nineteenth-century England."

"There's probably a reason absinthe died with that century," I said. It looked gently radioactive, like something Dr. Jekyll might have mixed up—a potion with dangerous possibilities. What manner of creature would it transform me into? Probably something dangerous, with Chas leaning there in his pajama bottoms.

But what the hell. I tossed down the rest.

A bad idea. I knew this as the drink hit my gut and exploded. A good thing I was leaning against the counter. The alcohol filled me with heat that buoyed me up like a balloon. Chas' surprised expression floated into my view, exactly as I imagined the face of those witnesses of the first hot air balloon—the awe and horror for one who has defied the laws of reality.

I waited for the muzziness to hit, that smothering, stupefying effect of alcohol, but nothing yet. Only the gently floating feeling, and an uncanny clarity.

Chas watched me. "Feel good?"

Two beautiful words from a beautiful mouth. "Ask me in a minute."

Chas grinned and drained his own glass. "In the meantime, I'll refill us."

I accepted the next glass from Chas, and the next. It was so easy to take them while bobbing several feet from the floor on a warm pillow of air. Every movement felt surreal and graceful, executed in slow motion, although I remained lucid in a way I did not with other kinds of alcohol. Chas' second absinthe creation was mixed with raspberry liquor, and the third with sweet vermouth, a drink so potently herbal I could have been standing in a Ye Olde Apothecary Shoppe.

"Now I see what you *really* do with your time off," I drawled.

Chas' eyes met mine over the edge of his cup, and he smiled. It may have been my imagination, or my strange heightened awareness, but he seemed to put care into that sip. His throat rippled, once, as he swallowed.

"I don't indulge often," he said in perfect Late English, to my surprise. I hadn't been aware he spoke the language. "I really do spend most of my time studying."

The sound I made was too inelegant to be a snort. More of a splutter.

"You think I lie."

"No. Of course not," I said, and raised my glass in salute before draining the last of the herbal liquid. I almost didn't notice the burn anymore. I quite liked it, in fact.

When I offered the glass back for a refill, Chas gave me a look. "Are you sure?"

I affected mock outrage. "Of course I am. I was having my first drinking parties when you were still pulling juice from a kid cup." I exaggerated only slightly. Chas, in fact, wasn't so much terribly younger than I.

He gave me a look of *yeah, right,* apparently having the same thought. Then he took my glass and filled it with a red creation. This one tasted bitter and fruity.

We were both smiling by now. I had reached that level of inebriation at which the decision to drink seemed like a very good one. I congratulated myself on loosening up enough to enjoy my last night aboard the ship. There was, after all, cause for celebration. A grand future awaited us. Us. Because I'd be able to share the moment of discovery with another human being. That the human being was Chas Chambers seemed right.

I realized I had been staring at him, and he had been staring back. He cocked his head. "Is it strange to say that you are nothing what I expected, but everything?"

"That is strange," I agreed.

"You've got this incredible mind," he said. "And you're like this larger-than-life figure, but you're also so approachable. Like, just this nice guy everyone thinks is this recluse."

Until that moment, I'd been admiring Chas in my drifting absinthe glow. I could have just...strode across the galley and kissed his grinning mouth, never mind if the mouth wanted to be kissed or not. I could be persuasive. But that statement jolted me back to reality.

"What?" I asked.

Chas froze. I could see him mentally rewinding. His smile fell. "Please forget I said that."

"No. That's important. 'Everyone' who?"

He grimaced. "The students. They say how reclusive you are. Not in a bad way, just..." He seemed to decide it was better not to continue, but then seeing my expression, he put in, "It's only been since your last trip. A lot of them thought you were worse off than anyone would admit." He pulled a face, catching himself again.

I stood there holding my drink aloft like a big, dumb, blind fool. Of course they would talk. It just hadn't occurred to me. No. I'd been too busy dealing with myself to wonder what other people would think or say. I looked down at the half-gone glass of absinthe.

"I've got a really big mouth," Chas said. "If I flap it long enough, something stupid is bound to come out."

The chagrin was endearing. All that tough muscle and bone, and he looked like he could just melt into the cabinetry.

Actually, in two strides, I could make him do just that.

I eyed the red liquid in my glass. "This stuff should be illegal. I can't believe the dispenser makes it." I set the glass down. "Wait right here. I'll be back."

Chas followed my command to a T. I found him in the same place when I returned a minute later.

I pulled a chair out at the table and gestured for him to join me.

"Here, look at this," I said, and pushed a sheet of vellum toward him.

He studied it a long moment, leaning heavily on his elbows. He smelled of spicy soap and something darkly sweet I couldn't identify but reminded me of the maple trees in Old London, maybe with a splash of brandy.

"What is it?" he asked.

"What's it look like?"

"Maybe a language. I've never seen it before. I'm guessing Lost Planet, because you're showing me. Is this from Turris?"

"Hold on." I repossessed the vellum and opened another picture. "*This* is from Turris."

I waited for the inevitable look of puzzlement as he took in this second photograph. I reached under his gaze, close enough to feel his breath on my hand, and flipped back to the first picture, pinching to zoom out. I'd attached the photograph to a map. Chas' eyebrows furrowed as the picture disappeared, giving way to rocky mountainous terrain, to green fields, to a continent.

"That isn't Turris," he said.

I put my chin in my hand and gazed at Chas as he stared at the map. His eyes rose to meet mine.

"This can't be what I think it is."

I quirked both brows.

"No shit."

I closed my eyes and smiled.

Chas leaned back, gripping the table edge with both hands. He spoke slowly. "You're telling me you found a connection between Anemoi and Turris, and we're going to investigate."

My smile grew. I folded my arms on the table and said, "And no one knows but me, the dean...and you."

☆☆☆

I woke with a headache. *Cripes.* It simmered somewhere between my brain and my skull. Probably not a migraine. This was usually good news, although the hangover wasn't much of an improvement.

I turned my head on the pillow. I sat up. No nausea accompanied the movement. My mouth was dry and bitter. I scowled at nothing and reached to put my glasses on, only to realize I'd left them on while sleeping.

Without turning the light on, I groped through my bag for pain pills and swallowed these down with the last dregs of water from a cup, then lay down again while the pain congealed in my skull. What I really needed for this to go away were food and water, once I could think of either without inducing symptoms of physical and psychological distress.

After an indeterminable amount of time, I rolled out of bed and cracked open the door. The hall lights were blessedly dimmed. The light in the galley was on, though. I squinted my way toward it. I thought I heard a male voice.

Chas stood at the far counter, his back to the door. He didn't turn at my entrance—apparently, too engaged in conversation.

Anger split my skull and for a moment, I couldn't see. "Who the hell are you talking to?"

Chas whirled, eyes wide. A red light shone in his eye. He raised a hand to his temple. "Recording, end."

"What the hell do you think you're doing?" I snarled. My mind pitched like a ship on storm waves. Chas hadn't been talking to someone—he'd been recording—recording what? The information I'd shared with him last night.

"Just a video log," he said. "A personal log. I made a bowl of adobo and was just talking about it."

Through a haze, I became aware of the plate of food sitting on the counter next to the dispenser, where Chas had been facing. My stomach turned over, reacting to the meaty smell I hadn't noticed until that moment. I smelled pepper and vinegar. It was hard to think through my pounding head.

"I can't write very well," Chas said, making a face. "So I vlog instead."

I went to the dispenser and pushed the button to call up a cup of coffee. My neck and the tips of my ears were hot. I was aware of Chas hovering near my elbow, nervous. I blew on the coffee, sending up a bitter steam. Took a cautious sip.

"What else do you vlog about?"

He paused. "About Turrian, the language. Food. Personal thoughts. Mostly food." He watched me. "Nothing confidential."

I should have been withering with shame, but I was just in more pain. So I blundered on. "You can't post anything until we return."

Surprise. "I know."

Of course. He *couldn't* post anything until we got back. But still, I was uncomfortable with this. It rode up my shoulders and made my temples throb.

"I can show you them, if you'd like," Chas said. "I don't even make many of them public. Most of them are just for me."

I grimaced. The only thing that made me more uncomfortable than the idea of Chas making video logs of our trip together was the idea of watching them. "That's all right."

We shared a few moments of conciliatory silence. An apology was probably in order, but the thought of one just now sent a spike of pain through my speech centers.

Chas stirred his stew, thick chunks of meat in a brown sauce. "Would you like a taste?"

The sauce had an oil sheen. Some of the fat had separated into a thin film of yellow. "No, thanks. I'm still enjoying last night."

"Oh." There was apology in that word.

I flashed him a sour glance. Then I asked the dispenser for toast with honey and a glass of coconut water and took them to my room. I ate and drank gingerly, then cleaned up in the shower and returned to my room to unpack my field bag, take inventory, and repack. The headache had mostly gone away by that time but remained a kind of nagging, vague distraction. My hands were not completely steady as I re-stowed the field bag for landing—pre-landing jitters made worse by lingering alcohol and a lack of protein.

I stood and continued to stare at the bag as if checking off a mental inventory list. But I wasn't thinking about the supplies. I was hearing the echo of my own voice in the galley. That had been a complete faux pas, an outburst triggered by nerves. Of course Chas would be keeping a personal log. I'd have been surprised if he wasn't.

If we were to have a successful trip, I'd have to check myself against projecting past betrayals onto him. If Sita trusted him, I would too. I wasn't cheerful about it, though.

Chas glanced at me briefly as I entered the cockpit. Turris, which had been growing steadily larger and more discernible, now dominated the screen. Chas turned his attention back to it.

"Enjoying the view?" I asked.

"It's unreal to see it from above, and to know we'll be on it in a few hours."

"It's real," I said. I went to the controls. I wished there was more to do, but we were all on course. The computer told me the weather at the landing site was clear for landing—unnecessary, because I could make out our target continent and its pattern of wispy, benign clouds myself.

I made myself sit.

"I apologize for my outburst earlier," I said at length.

"It's okay," Chas said in a too-casual voice. "It's a highly confidential trip. And I did serve you copious amounts of alcohol last night."

I shook my head. "It's nothing to do with you." I almost said more, which I would have regretted—because really, we were here to discuss the planet's past history, not my own.

Blessedly, Chas didn't probe.

Together, we watched the land masses grow and take shape in the view screen. My body hummed with an uneasy cocktail of anticipation and apprehension. I'd been born on the university, so I would never know the experience of approaching one's own home world. To say each Lost Planet landing was a homecoming for me would have been poetic, but not true. Every terrain was foreign—solid ground that welcomed but never claimed me. Maybe my drive to explore the Lost Planets was an unconscious search for home, a need to have soil to call my own.

Next to me, Chas didn't move. What was this like for him? Was he watching Turris, or was he seeing the memory of his own approaching world? I wondered if any part of him looked at the alien terrain and thought, *Home.*

Chas asked, "What do you think it means?"

"What do I think what means?"

"The symbols that appear on Anemoi and Turris. What do you think the connection is?"

"It could mean anything. It could mean absolutely nothing. I could be crazy. I'm sure that's something else the students say about me." I meant it to be teasing, but the tightness in my stomach made the words come out curt.

Chas looked surprised. Poor kid. If he survived this trip with me, he'd have his own stories about moody Professor Wells to tell. I tried to smile to smooth it over—only I wouldn't be smoothing much of anything with the stiff grimace I managed.

"They don't say you're crazy," Chas said a quiet moment later. "Eccentric, but not crazy. The ones who know your work well say you have vision, but no one else wants to see."

My turn to be surprised. I stared at Chas with absolutely no idea what to say. He returned my gaze with a slight lilt of one eyebrow, but I didn't have time to consider that expression—was that a faint, self-mocking smile on his lips?—because at that moment, an alarm blared.

The ship jolted. I hadn't anticipated needing to be buckled yet. I was knocked onto my feet and made a flying start to the controls. I swore as I hit the console. The computer had halted the ship's course—or so the flashing note at the corner of the dash informed me, in case I hadn't noticed my body pitching through the view screen. The question was, why? All conditions looked fine for landing. I checked and double-checked the coordinates against the view of the continent below. Our plain was broad and flat. The area's clouds looked like stretched tufts of wool.

It could only be a problem with the ship. I ran the diagnostics, then ran them again, because I didn't quite understand what they were telling me: nothing was wrong with the ship. According to the computer, the reason it couldn't land on a wide, empty, flat plain was because something obstructed the area.

I roared my frustration. I slashed out a command to override, but the ship wouldn't allow it. Safety mechanisms had kicked in.

The ship jolted again. A yellow blinking symbol informed me we'd just gotten snagged by the planet's gravitational pull. We'd either power our way out of its grip, or we were about to take a plunge, with or without the blessing of the ship's computer.

The dash flashed as the ship recalculated its path. Symbols scrolled across the screen, looping and looping like a dog that had lost sight of its tail. Blast it. I killed the ship's autopilot. It'd been a long time since I'd cold-landed one of these things, but the conditions were good, and I had a better chance of getting us down now while positioned over the landing site rather than situating us in orbit and browsing for another place to bring us down—especially if something were wrong with the ship.

"Wait," said Chas. I'd completely forgotten he was even there. "Hold on. Look."

The lights on the dashed stuttered and strobed, the computer gone utterly mad. Above them, the image on the view screen flickered and broke apart in pixels. Went dark.

The alarm stopped. Neither of us made a sound.

The dash lights stammered and evened out. Like that, the view screen popped back on, and there was Turris again, in clear, bright, steady colors.

A city had bloomed beneath us. For an instant, I thought we had changed course—that somehow, in the short seconds the screen had been off, we'd shifted locations dramatically—but then I recognized the shallow bowl created by the ridge of mountains at the north and the frame of forest to the east and west. Only, what had been an empty plain was now covered in an organized pattern of round and square structures that at first glance looked exactly like buildings and the streets between them.

Chas shouldered in next to me. "Give me the controls. I'll land us."

I snapped out of my surprised stare. "What?"

The ship jolted then as it hit atmosphere. I slammed into Chas, and he pushed me back to my feet.

"We don't have time. Move over."

I couldn't have protested even if my life depended on it, which it probably did. My stomach tried to squeeze into the spaces between my chest organs. The room spun and pitched. With no thought to dignity, I lowered to my knees and braced against the control bank. We were doomed if I tried to land us, anyway. I should have been mortified Chas could see that so clearly: we had a better chance with a rookie college kid. But I felt no shame. I was too busy holding on as my guts leapfrogged my skull.

"Get buckled," Chas said, and made for his chair.

I staggered toward my own, grabbed it, and buckled in. On the screen, the zoomed picture of the city had been replaced with a picture of our immediate view of ragged clouds and rapidly approaching topography.

We were going to die. Just like this, we were going to die. I wondered what it would be like to hit. Would I have time to feel the pain of impact, or would it be too quick to register?

I looked at Chas, and was surprised to see another man sitting there in Chas' body. His expression had shifted into something set and hard, nothing like the smiling, mocking grad student. He gripped both piloting sticks and pulled hard on them. Muscles and tendons stood out on his arms. His light brown skin had gone ashen.

I put my head back and clutched at the arm rests as the ship began to pull and push and veer. An unseen hand pressed me hard into my seat, only to yank me out of it again. I became a doll trapped between chair and harness, a smear of thought over the floor and walls of the ship. The more pertinent question wasn't if I'd feel the pain of impact, but if I'd even notice it over the intense vertigo.

It was a very long drop. Probably the torture of the experience made the seconds drag on, but still, it was a very long drop. I almost began to wish we'd hit already.

I peeled my eyes open. I couldn't make sense of the chaos on the screen over the chaos in my head. I closed my eyes, opened them again. I made out a sliver of sky at the top of the screen, and tall spikes appearing—an entire forest of them.

We were falling sideways?

"Hold on," Chas reassured in a low, tight voice.

The spire tops loomed large in the screen. The ship jostled and jounced. I gave myself over to the misery.

I'd be falling. Falling forever. My punishment for trying to steal fire from the heavens.

We hit the top of our first spire—more of a brush than a solid impact, but it sent us reeling. We clipped another, and that set us back on course. "On course" being straight through the forest. I had the surreal impression of descending into a jungle of gigantic white asparagus. I closed my eyes, only to open them because I couldn't not watch. The experience took on a surreal, out-of-body quality. What a memory this would make. Too bad it would die with me.

And then: One of the spires zoomed toward us in the screen. This was it—and I knew then I absolutely did not want to die. I opened my mouth, and I might have yelled. The ship dropped. My stomach slapped the roof.

With an impact that threw me against the harness—red-hot pain exploded in my shoulder, which dismayed me, but then I remembered that I was going to die, so it didn't matter—we hit.

CHAPTER SIXTEEN

A lot of noise accompanied the explosion in my shoulder. Alarms blared and metal groaned and my innards slammed against my ribcage, all of it compressed into one screaming sensation. We were falling. We were rising. We were ripping apart.

Going still.

Listening to the silence.

I sagged against the harness like a dead weight, but was not in fact dead. It took me a few moments to realize this, and a few more to realize we had come more or less to a full stop and the ship had not blown up.

Opening my eyes was a mistake. The image on the view screen showed me the diagonal lines of a crazed white-and-gray abstract painting. I closed my eyes again and just breathed, reacquainting myself with the idea that we had not—were likely not going to—die in this landing. I didn't know how this was possible. Likely it was beyond my capacity for comprehension at the moment. I was still relearning how to breathe.

"Dr. Wells?"

Chas' voice came to me from another plane of existence. I marked it with relief and surprise. Deep and solid, his voice, like a hand reaching through to grasp mine.

"Dr. Wells? London?"

His concern—and rising volume—grated against my raw nerves. "I'm alive," I said.

"Oh thank God."

Buckles clicked as Chas released himself, and the scrape of metal on metal brought me around to myself. I raised my hands to my own harness and let myself free.

"I'm fine," I said to Chas, who was sitting forward in his own chair, ready to spring to my rescue should I go toppling.

"Good," he said, and stood. The entire ship swayed. I gripped the chair arms.

"Don't. Do that."

A long quiet followed. Chas stood still, arms and legs spread. Slowly he lowered his arms. "We're going to have to get out of here."

I was glad one of us was aware of the obvious and could be decisive about it, because I'd left most of my own wits spread over the ceiling. Or that might have been the remnants of toast with honey. I vaguely wished I hadn't drunk the coffee, because now my hands trembled finely. I'd never had this reaction to caffeine before.

Chas was looking at me. Waiting for a response, I realized.

Right.

I couldn't quite bring myself to look at the view screen yet. From the corner of my vision, I made out forms like white pillars, large with closeness. I tallied this up with the gentle sway of the ship. "We're high up, aren't we?"

"Yeah."

I took a long breath. I had the bad feeling in my gut we'd survived a fall from space only to perish in our fall from a spire a few hundred feet up.

Oddly, the thought brought me back to myself.

"Okay then," I said. "We need our things, and rope. Time to put your hobby to work."

I stood and braced myself. All was fine for a moment, and then the ship began a slow roll to starboard. Chas and I stared at each other with mirrored expressions of alarm. I had the fleeting thought of flinging myself across the room to distribute weight in the opposite direction—but then the descent accelerated. I grabbed for the back of the chair.

The ship met resistance. Came to a stop. Settled.

Neither of us moved.

I ventured forth a foot, then another. The ship had shifted and settled more securely into its perch, but I didn't trust it to last long.

Chas looked me a question. I nodded.

We'd survived a crash landing more or less intact, and just exchanged our first silent communication. In less than five minutes on the planet, we had consummated our relationship as a team.

I turned toward my room. Despite the nausea and pain riding shotgun in my skull, an excitement kindled under my breastbone. I passed the galley on the way down the hall, the dispenser quiet in the corner, waiting to deliver one last meal. Good-bye to comfort and the known. Good-bye to the tin can.

Despite having lodged more securely into its landing place, the ship still swayed gently bow to aft as Chas went about his business in the other rooms. I could only assume we'd landed in the arms of one of the spires. From what I remembered, these were not particularly thick, and who knew how sturdy. I tried not to wonder about this as crawled about on my knees, trying to find where in damnation my pills had flown off to. I found them in the corner under my bunk and popped one for motion sickness and another for pain.

In the cockpit, Chas leaned over the controls, looking a little too at ease.

He glanced over his shoulder. "I've run a preliminary. They're Mi'hani. One large camp of them."

For a moment, I had no idea what he was talking about and then I remembered the city that had arrested our landing. *That* camp.

I crossed gingerly to the dash and looked down at the small diagnostics screen, shifting the coil of rope I held to the other arm so I could lean in.

"Here," he said, and brought the image up on the windshield view screen. I opened my mouth to protest because without a view of the spires outside, it felt even more like being trapped in a tin can. But Chas was already moving through the pictures.

"One main settlement here, on our plain. The dwellings don't look permanent. I'm thinking a camp. There is some scattered activity here and here, at the base of the mountains."

"Excavation." I pointed. "That's a digger."

There had been one incandescent moment as we dove when I'd thought we'd actually stumbled across a living Lost race. In that instant I'd grasped the importance of that discovery the way one grasped the wordless beauty and grand design of a sunbeam piercing the clouds—a discovery I had been sure would die with me in the crash.

But this was no Lost race.

Chas said, "Looks like your secret isn't a secret."

"Damn and damn." I watched tiny points of activity crawl over the map. For some uncanny reason, Felix Mata and the museum came to mind. Not that I'd told Mata where I was going or what I'd be doing, but the man wasn't an idiot and, after all, he'd been a little too acquiescent in accepting my classes. "Are you sure it's Mi'hani? How do you know?"

"The design of these structures, here. And look at the ships. That's Mi'hani Republic."

That would rule out Felix, or at least the museum.

"But how could they know?" I said.

Chas took my question for rhetorical. We stared at the screen in silence. Sita and I had been so careful. Of course, that didn't preclude the Mi'hani from sending their own scout, but since when were they interested in the Lost Planets? And even if they had employed their own scout, what would make them interested in Turris specifically? As far as anyone else should be concerned, there was nothing notable about the unidentified symbols at Turris. Sita and I were the only ones who had made the connection between them and those found on Anemoi and Beira.

Ice crept up my back. I remembered a face in the garden pond, the scuff of footsteps behind me, and the weight of being followed...

"I'm transferring the data to our handhelds," Chas said. "I'm going to take advantage of the ship's instruments to run some more investigations first. I've got our route from here plotted."

All things I should have—would have—been doing. "You seem comfortable with the computer," I said, suddenly nettled.

Chas looked at me with surprise. "I'm sorry. Shouldn't I?"

I smoothed my feathers down. "No. You should. See if you can find a route that will take us farthest from the camp. Those excavations, where are they in relation to our destination?"

Tension went out of Chas. "Here." He brought up another dot on the map. "The scout took the image here. The entrance to the caves is here."

"They're digging in the wrong place!" An unexpected blessing. I thought fast. "We need to get word to Sita. The university has the only sanction to excavate on Turris."

"We can't," Chas said with a firmness I'd never heard from him. At my look, he said, "If they don't already know we're here, if we attempt communication they will. And they'll know our location. It will take at least a week for anyone to reach us. That's more than enough time for them to dispose of us before packing up their operation and leaving the planet."

I gaped at him. "I'm surprised at such paranoia from you."

"This may be the single most important discovery in human existence," Chas said quietly.

His gaze held mine. The ship creaked in the silence that followed.

I swallowed. "We have to. We send out a message now. That will give us just enough time to find our evidence. Away from the ship, they won't be able to track us easily. They could destroy the ship, but that won't matter if another is coming for us. In the meantime, they can't spend too much energy looking for us, if they need to pack up before our reinforcements arrive."

Chas considered this. Before he could reply, the ship rocked. Neither of us had moved. The ship drifted gently, and then there was a *crack-crack-crack*, like a very big tree branch snapping under stress.

"We go now," I said. My hands flew over the dash. The red light of a distress signal flashed on.

Chas was already moving toward the door. I went after him but halted at the blast of cool, dry air and the smell of foreign flora and the view of spires and sky.

"Watch out." I dropped the heavy coil of rope. Not the smartest move, I realized as its weight hit the floor. I braced myself for the ship to sway, but the only things that jolted were my kidneys as they squirted off a fresh shot of adrenaline.

I held one end of the rope and faced the door. "Shit."

The ship hadn't been designed to anchor rope descents. I looped the rope through a hand grip in the doorway and hoped it would hold our combined weight. I regretted the sweets we'd eaten on this trip, from the hot chocolate to Chas' exotic confections. Next time, more tea and push-ups.

My hands tied the knots they knew so well. Good thing. My mind had already flown off with the wind.

I almost asked Chas if he'd ever abseiled, then remembered who I was talking to. He'd already buckled his harness and hooked up his hardware and watched me load the rope to mine.

"Simultaneous?" he asked.

"Yes." We didn't have time to set up two ropes. We'd take the one, jump together, and pray hard.

He took the other side of the rope. His fingers made quick sure work feeding the belay device. A comfort.

I reached to make the next knot. The ship tilted. I dropped what I was doing.

"Let's go," I said. Chas shot me a surprised look, and I pointed at the hand grip I'd looped the rope through. "We need to hit the ground before this ship does."

His eyes widened. Yes. Brilliant me, anchoring us to a ship about to fall.

"Let me just finish…" he said, hands tying a quick knot to brake his fall if he lost his grip.

Cripes. I knew I'd forgotten something. To hell with it. I threw the rope over the side in two coils.

"Ready?" I said.

"Yes."

Shoulder to shoulder, we stood with our backs to the boundless Turris sky. My gorge rose. I closed my eyes.

"We'll go at the same time," he said.

I nodded.

"One. Two." The ship dipped. He didn't say "three." We stepped off.

I threw my arm out and plunged, incandescent, like a falling star. Rope sang. I didn't pause to see how quickly Chas followed, trusting he'd match my speed. Like ripping off an adhesive bandage, I wanted this over before the distress signals reached my brain.

From somewhere close by, I heard Chas' muffled "whoop!" laced with laughter. Something inside me nearly smiled.

Vertigo seized me.

I braked myself with a quick movement of my arm and jerked to a stop.

"You all right?" Chas called. His voice came from a little above me.

I pressed my cheek against the rope. The crisp breeze pushed me a little so I spun like a pocket watch at the end of its chain. The air smelled weird, like burned plastic. I had a death grip on the rope, and sharply regretted not tying the autoblock. Only two bands of muscle and tendon saved me from a drop of several hundred feet.

The rope shivered as Chas lowered a few more feet.

"Stop!" I hissed.

"Hey. Okay."

I swallowed down my heart.

"We're okay for a minute," Chas said. "I think the ship is stable again."

Good. Right. Just catch your breath. With my eyes closed, my senses expanded to encompass the sky, the rope, and ground. I experienced this kind of expansion on a good climb and usually, paradoxically, it made me feel bigger, a small part of something truly huge.

Right now I just felt small.

I opened my eyes to slits. We were about midway down the height of the spires. They were the thickness of ancient sequoia trees, if sequoias had been the smooth, pasty white of a deep sea creature. Near the tips, they bifurcated into two or three branches, with heads that reminded me again of asparagus. If I survived this trip, I'd never eat the vegetable again.

I became aware of a low muttering above me. Chas. The horror of Chas looking down right now, witnessing my panic, hit me harder than the vertigo.

I looked up. His soft muttering continued. I couldn't make out the words, because he didn't address them to me. He gazed up, speaking to someone else.

"*Chas.*"

He shot a look over his shoulder. A red light shone in his eye.

"Don't record!" I snarled.

His eyes blew open in surprise. At that moment, the ship groaned and shuddered. I had the experience of dropping through the air despite my grip on the rope. In my alarm, I let go—and then I was truly dropping. Dropping, dropping with no brake to stop me. Chas gave a shout above me.

After that, neither of us made a noise. The fall was almost surreal. The ship shrank above me. The spires rose, thrusting upward like spears. I caught a glance of Chas' small form sailing downward.

Impact was almost a surprise. I hit and bounced and landed on my side, stunned that I was still conscious. And alive. Then panic and urgent need blinded me. I rolled onto all fours.

Back in the ship, I'd thought of taking a last meal from the dispenser. My last good meal, maybe for weeks. A voice in the back of my mind had warned me it would be in vain.

Having christened the alien soil, I rested, propped on my elbows.

Something just about came back to me then. A vivid impression of stone slipping beneath my hands, of landing and staring up at a sky. And something else. A knowledge I wasn't alone.

As quickly as it had come over me, the memory snapped, and I was just here on Turris, flat on the ground as the world circled and circled to a stop. I remembered having gotten blind drunk a few times just for the novelty of it and sitting there in wonder while the room spun like an amusement ride. Felix had been a part of one of those rides, and that had certainly been amusing—our first wild night together, spinning and looping, and not all just from drink. Felix Mata. I didn't know why he popped into my thoughts just then. It angered me, especially that the man had invaded my thoughts here, on this planet, at this moment, while I unmanned myself on the ground—and that, of all things, it was our first drunken coupling that came to me.

In the silence following my own tortured sounds, I heard another: a scraping, a gasping.

"Chas?" I rasped, and wiped my wet mouth with my wrist. I turned. Chas lay on his back, one leg steepled and the other straight out, face turned up and arms spread, like he'd given himself up to the sky. He didn't blink.

My heart flipped. "Chas?"

I scrabbled closer. His head turned, light eyes meeting mine. I grabbed his upturned hand and squeezed. "You're all right." A reassurance and a question both.

He nodded and squeezed back. At his touch, I remembered myself and withdrew.

Chas grimaced and pushed up on his elbows. The peculiar white sand of the ground dusted his skin and gave him an ashen cast. I had the overwhelming and absolutely unprofessional impulse to brush it away.

He blinked owlishly and gave his head a shake. Flattened his other leg to the ground. Looked up.

I refused to look up yet, not with my stomach in a delicate state of recovery. And I wasn't sure yet I wouldn't faint. The memory of Anemoi rested just beneath my temples.

My hands went to my shoulders. The backpack was still there. Of course, I'd tightened and retightened it enough on the ship. I probably would've stood a greater chance of losing my arms than that bag. I shrugged it off and found one of my canteens. I offered it to Chas. His own pack sat in the dust next to him, looking reasonably un-squashed.

Chas tipped back a drink, swallowed, gasped. "Well, that was the quick way," he said with strained humor. "But I wouldn't suggest that on the other planets."

I accepted back the canteen and rinsed the sour dregs of acid from my mouth. Right. On most other planets, we'd be in chunks over the countryside.

I stood and found that, besides a bruised backside, I was fine. So fine, I underestimated my own strength and went up like a shot. No sim training in low gravity could quite prepare me for the real thing.

When the blood had returned to my head, I went over to the reeking puddle I'd left on the ground and scuffed dirt onto it.

I risked a look up. It was a dizzying height to the ship, which I took moment to locate in the spire tops. I'd lost all sight of the rope.

Chas hadn't moved from his spot on the ground. Still stunned, from the look of it. "Did you hit your head?" I only realized what I was asking as the words left my mouth.

Chas missed the irony. He shook his head.

Well, that was a relief. All we needed was two brain-addled fools on this trip. I squatted next to my pack and went through the contents, making sure our supplies had fared as well as his skull. The handheld was all right, cushioned by clothing. I flipped it on.

"We'll need to head this way," I said once it had processed our position—slowly, as if it, too, were stunned. "We landed far enough away from the camp that we can circle around it entirely. Are you all right?"

Chas' face was tight. Slowly, he was bending his left leg, the one that hadn't before been steepled. It folded well enough at the knee, but when he began to circle his ankle, he jerked and choked back a cry. He grasped his calf, expelled a shaking breath.

I dropped the handheld and crabbed to his side. "What's wrong? Is it broken?"

Veins stood out on his dusky forehead. He visibly composed himself and said, "Likely."

"Put it down. No, don't move it. I mean, move it, but down. Like that." I turned back to the bag and plundered it for the med kit. Like an ass, I'd buried it at the bottom. My hands moved quicker than my thoughts. I had half the pack on the ground before remembering I had in fact put it in one of the side pockets for easy access.

Kit finally in hand, I looked up to find Chas watching me with a sort of bemused expression.

"Do you need pain medication?"

Chas shook his head. Of course, how could I forget? He ate iron ore for breakfast and spat out tacks.

I laid out the med tools. I glanced at the handheld a couple of times and up at the sky, but no activity showed. Far above, the ship swayed with the movement of the spires but did not budge from its perch. It occurred to me then it was only dumb luck the ship hadn't tumbled down after us. It still could.

"You ever had a brace on before?" I asked.

Chas had drawn the other knee up and clasped his hands over its top, watching the setup as I laid it out. "Yeah. I broke my arm when I was a kid."

"So you know there's going to be a sharp pain while it sets the bone, and then you can't put a lot of impact on it, probably for a few days. Maybe a week."

A silence as we absorbed the implications.

"Sorry about the recording," Chas said as I fit the last of the brace together. They made these things incredibly light and compact, which made them convenient to pack and a pain to set up.

I shook my head, negating Chas' need to apologize. "Although, I don't understand why you don't just do memory extraction."

I scooted closer to Chas and opened the brace, preparing to apply it. I looked up to see his twisted smile, and couldn't for the life of me interpret the expression. "What?"

"Not everyone is a worlds-famous archaxenologist. Who would pay to extract my memories?"

I had no idea what to say to that. I'd always taken it for granted people would vie for the privilege of mining my memories.

I blinked. "Right. Well. Not everyone crash-lands a ship on a Lost Planet like a fly on a head of asparagus and then survives a three-hundred-foot fall to the ground with the worlds-famous archaxenologist."

Chas did not reply, though the tiniest of smug smiles tugged at the corner of his mouth. The smile disappeared as I slipped one hand under his calf and slid the brace underneath. His leg weighed in my hand like a meat bone. I rolled up the cuff, lowered his leg to the brace, and closed it. Lights flashed on. The device exhaled a clicking sound, and Chas flinched. The brace ran through its full diagnostics and then powered down into sleep.

"All right?" I said.

"Unless you have a brace for my pride, as well."

"Ha. We could all use one."

I glanced up at the ship. The tall spire leaned with its weight, but otherwise it hadn't moved.

In my rush to find the med kit, I'd scattered my things across half the forest. I lifted a pair of pants from the ground four feet away, powdered with white dust. I shook these free and bundled them into the bottom of the pack, along with the rest of my clothes. I settled the recording equipment and the field ration dispenser atop these. The ammunition, I placed at the top for easiest access. The last thing I needed was to be disgorging my pack in another emergency. Our survival would depend on expediency.

I glanced at Chas as he carefully folded his pant leg down over the brace.

Hells.

But...it wasn't his fault. Not even my fault. Just an extra challenge. A need to be more careful.

I found my extra gun behind me, filmed with chalk. Curses. I wiped it free and dismantled it. Damnation. To hell with Turris and the Mi'hani and every cursed grain of dust on this planet. It had even gotten into the chamber.

"Dr. Wells?"

Something wet landed on my shoulder. I touched a hand to it. Rain? But the glob of moisture was too big for a rain drop, and viscous.

"London!"

I glanced at a swift-moving form, and then I was thrown backward. In the low gravity, I flew. Hit the ground with a large weight atop me. Bounced.

I recognized Chas' scent. He caged me, his forehead nearly touching mine, his lips close enough that I felt the puff of his breath.

Then he lifted an arm and glanced behind himself, opening my line of sight.

"What the hell..." I breathed.

At the base of the spire, not far from my pack, a gooey mass—like a grub—peeled the rest of the way from the spire and plopped to the ground. It settled, then squirmed, lifted one of its ends, and rooted around. Then brandishing a hundred needle legs—it walked.

Chas flipped away from me. "*Jesus* Christ!"

But the thing wasn't after us. After waving its head around, it aimed for the spire. It spent a couple minutes with its head against the smooth pale trunk, and I couldn't tell if it was resting, or tasting it, or dead.

Just as I began to relax, the thing undulated and—heaving itself erect—scuttled up the trunk. It stopped ten feet up and plunged its double complement of needle legs into the stalk. Sap oozed out and rolled over it. In moments, it was encased in a gelatinous shell.

I swallowed. I looked up and down the spires, noticing the little bulbous growths I'd thought were just part of the stalks. The hairs on my arms raised.

"That has got to be one of the top five creepiest things I have ever seen," Chas said.

I grunted. With the handheld, I scanned the liquid on the ground. Mostly water, with sugars and a mild toxin, maybe an agent to keep the stalk from healing itself.

"You'd get a better reading if you held the scanner closer," Chas said with a grin from his spot safe on the ground half a dozen feet away.

The other life-forms in the area included the spires themselves—not white, I realized, but a pale purple—another, smaller parasite that flew, and fungi-like growths. None posed an immediate threat, but that's when I remembered Sita's pterodactyls—the ones that wouldn't be a threat, because they haunted the spire forests.

Better and better.

At a scuffing sound behind me, I whirled. Chas had stood, favoring his injured leg.

I bent to pick up his pack. "Can you walk?"

He hopped a couple steps, misjudged the gravity, and pitched forward. I leaped to catch him.

"I'm fine," he said, starting to pull away.

"I'm sure you are. But we have thirty miles to travel."

He relented, but only after I agreed to let him carry his own pack.

"There's nothing wrong with my back," he said, close to my ear as he leaned against me.

With my arm linked around his back, I had to admit that no, there was nothing wrong with it. It was a strong and fine back indeed.

We set off through the spires.

CHAPTER SEVENTEEN

We traveled steadily through an unchanging landscape eerily akin to a redwood forest stripped of branches. The spires created no canopy, but they cast long, wide shadows. The sun shone between in bright patches.

I was exquisitely aware of Chas at my side—of every twinge of pain and the small, sharp inhales that accompanied them, of the exhaustion that curled his spine and the raw resolve in his tight muscles. I suggested breaks, but he shook his head. Finally, I complained of my own aching shoulder and called for a rest. We stopped in the shade of a large stalk, and I knelt to check his brace. Despite the abuse, it had held up.

Afternoon heat gathered even in the shade, but we didn't sweat. The air was too dry. We'd passed no bodies of water, but the spire stalks were covered in life-forms and filled with water, so I surmised these tapped deep into the ground and brought water up for the other organisms to draw from. I was aware of water wicking out of my own body. We would need to replenish our supply before long. To this effect, I tried cutting into one of the stalks, but found the skin too hard for my knife.

"We could tap the grubs," Chas said, a thought I'd had as well but hadn't voiced.

"Later," I said. "I'll feel better when we've gotten a little farther."

I ignored the amused lift of Chas' eyebrows.

We passed a small herd of very tall insectoids like giraffes with long tusks that were not, in fact, tusks. They were pincer mouthparts that chewed at the air. The creatures used these to extract the tick grubs from the spires, then unrolled trunk-like proboscises to suck the sap oozing out.

Like the spires and the ticks, the insect giraffes had a pasty, almost semitransparent cast to their skin. Milky solid masses nestled in their stomachs. The white line of a spine curved up their bodies.

And like the spires, they had a purple tinge to their skin darkest at their back—good for blending in.

"Maybe they harbor symbiotic microbes that convert energy from the sun into food," Chas murmured as we watched them from the safety of a spire a couple hundred feet away. "Interesting they'd make them the same color as the spires. They might even get them from the spires." He glanced at my expression. "What, you're not interested in biology?"

Actually I was, and I found the idea intriguing. But I said, "Show me a stilt-mite that talks and I'll be interested."

Chas snorted. What I didn't say was that I worried because the presence of camouflage suggested something to camouflage against. And the stilt-walkers were not small animals. Not compared to us.

I glanced up often.

Not long after we'd left the herd behind, a shadow slid over us. Chas grunted as I slammed him against the trunk of a spire, but it wasn't one of Sita's pterodactyls. It was a ship.

Its shadow rippled through the shadows of the spires. It flew a straight path, turned, and made another pass at an angle.

"They're scanning for life," Chas muttered.

"And finding a lot of it."

Chas flashed a smile. That smile, which curved inches from my own mouth, made me aware I'd braced myself over him, effectively shielding his body against the spire. With the ship still making sweeps, I dared not move. I tried to pretend I couldn't hear him breathing as I hovered inches from him.

The ship moved on. We moved on.

We walked until the sun sat on the horizon. Despite everything, we'd made it far—eighteen miles—and that had mostly been at Chas' insistence we keep moving. I'd gotten accustomed to his weight against my shoulder. I could feel him wearying, and we needed to set up camp before dark. With ships sweeping the area, we wouldn't be able to risk turning on any kind of light to aid us.

The stilt-walkers seemed peaceful enough—or in any case, preoccupied enough with their life thirty-something feet in the air to pay us no mind—but the appearance of another herd pushed us closer to the edge of the spires out of caution. An evening breeze washed over us as warm air from the clearing beyond rushed into the cooler spires, bringing a bitter and chalky smell.

I sat Chas down atop an unfolded thermal blanket and checked the progress of his ankle. After the care we'd taken and all of his leaning, the ankle had still taken stress and its healing had been slowed. Hopefully a few hours of sleep would help.

"You know," I said, even as I wondered how I could suggest it, "it might be safer for you to stay here in the forest while..."

I stopped as Chas shook his head. "No way."

I had my own reservations about leaving Chas, but hearing his refusal kindled annoyance. He would hold me up. Especially with the Mi'hani circling like vultures, he was a liability. It was true, now more than ever: I was stuck with the kid.

"I'll be better in the morning," he said, because my expression must have flared like a match striking in the dry air. "After a few hours of rest, I'll be okay. I won't hold you back. You'll see."

I met his determined gaze. And I realized I'd been a real prat, thinking of Chas as a burden from the moment he stepped onto the ship. Because he wasn't; he was a man, with a man's pride. More than that, he was my partner in this.

"Of course you will," I said. In a voice that sounded less like I was strangling, I made myself add, "We'll make it there together."

Chas' mouth tugged back in a smile. In answer to the self-mocking humor there, I said, "We do make a pair."

We put up the tents. While Chas fiddled with the field ration dispenser, I took my knife to one of the tick grubs. It wouldn't have been quite so bad if a film of ooze didn't slime my hand and make the blade slip. The thing had burrowed deep enough its body wasn't visible under the shell of mucilage. Chas watched me struggle and slip and stab from his reclined position next to the dispenser. I perceived him only as a lighter form against the shadows of the tents, but I could see humor in the cant of his head.

"Would *you* like to try?"

"Not really. I'm enjoying this."

Finally, I remembered the first tick had fallen off after our crash landing, and surmised we'd stunned it on our descent. After that realization, it only took a few well-aimed blows to knock one free, releasing a gush of viscous fluid. I captured a pitcher's worth of sap before the flow stopped. While the water purifier played with that, I scanned the dead grub using my handheld. The results informed me that, basically, the grub was a bag of water, protein, fat, and sugar.

"Dinner," Chas suggested.

Gods help me. "If we run out of rations." And shoe leather.

Before I disposed of the grub, Chas asked to look at it. He also asked my permission to video log, which embarrassed and annoyed me—mostly at myself for reacting as I had earlier to his logging. Dusk hung a long time, like the world holding its breath. By its light I could just make out the slick glisten of the grub's body and the lift and fall of Chas' shoulder. He had a good speaking voice and the easy humor of one accustomed to using it. He summarized the observations we'd made about the plant and animal life that day, with some interesting ideas about the ecology he hadn't shared before: We were traveling through a desert landscape with a keystone species, the spire, supporting a delicate ecosystem that in fact had no plants, all animals. Photosynthesis was provided by microorganisms like algae that lived in the animals, a total symbiosis because they needed the moisture provided by their hosts.

Despite the gloom, Chas was careful not to look at me. The red light never pointed in my direction. He paused the recording twice to ask if he could share certain pieces of information. I said yes. At this point, I almost told him to record whatever he bloody well pleased and ignore me. I would probably end up selling most of these memories anyway, and much of what Chas shared with the camera would eventually be public knowledge. Maybe, if Sita had her way, there would even be another memoir one day. Sita was right. There was nothing private about my life, no matter how much I wished and pretended. Not even my vertigo, with Chas as my witness. Not a thing was safe.

Except my fears. Those alone were mine.

Once Chas was done with the grub, I tossed it well away from camp, not wanting to attract any unwanted dinner guests. Who might, after all, want seconds. And dessert.

Chas served us our own dinner, a field meal of bulgar wheat, textured protein, and minced unidentified greens. It went down well with the metallic water from the purifier. Nothing would have completed it better than a bit of that shoe leather.

Silence hung between the spires, probably the same silence that'd been there all day—for thousands of years—only made more apparent by the darkness. The sole light came from the spires themselves, which glowed ever so softly.

I said, "Probably not what you expected."

"Hm? Oh. I guess. I mean, it's an expedition on a Lost Planet. I was ready to expect anything. It's you who was probably caught off guard."

Surprised, I considered his words. Yes. I'd definitely been caught off guard. Another expedition marked by crashing and falling; that rattled me. And to be on expedition not only with an unexpected partner, but with possible hostile parties?

I might have been the so-called expert in my field, but in our current venture, I was as new as Chas. Humbling that he recognized this.

"Yeah," I said eventually, because he wouldn't have been able to see my expression in the dark. "I guess I was."

Something settled between us, a presence like a veil floating to the ground. Or maybe it was just the immense silence of the spire forest pulled to the earth by its own gravity.

"Have you been practicing your lessons?" I asked in Turrian.

He paused, maybe surprised by a pop quiz in the wilderness, and then said, "Honored teacher, I have been practicing. Now I am here in this beautiful place, I can begin to understand the Turrian mind."

"Perhaps," I said, with warm teasing, "you can furnish us with the first poetry written in Turrian known to mankind."

"This is a worthy idea. I will start with a ballad about our magnificent descent from the heavens."

☆☆☆

I retired to my sleeping bag but couldn't actually sleep. Chas rustled and turned over in his own tent. I wondered if he needed pain medication. The brace had a mechanism for quelling pain, though I knew from experience some still broke through.

I almost asked, but the silence was a thick presence. I had the heavy, almost superstitious impression it'd bleed if I cut it.

After a few minutes, Chas quieted.

Usually I had trouble sleeping on a planet, which also usually wasn't a problem. I was good at subsisting on rations and excitement on these trips. But this wasn't the usual restlessness. A deep uncertainty sat in my marrow.

When things sounded quiet from Chas' quarter, I emerged from my tent to look up at the stars. They streaked the sky in two pearly belts like lines of diamond dust over black velvet. The heavenly hand that had placed them hadn't been exact, and scattered grains glinted between the lines over the black backdrop.

At the university, the night ceiling projected a facsimile of stars, and if you were a kid with a big imagination, it almost did the trick. That was, if you ignored the occasional safety light or square black patch of a broken ceiling panel. Also, if you'd never been on an actual planet and experienced the depth of open skies and the erratic, hard glint of light thousands of years old.

"Having trouble sleeping?"

In the low gravity, I did literally jump a foot off the ground. If Chas noticed, I couldn't see his expression well enough to tell. In the soft almost-light from the spires, I could just make out his shoulders and head sticking out from the tent.

"I always do," I said, after I'd recovered my breath. "When I'm on a planet."

"Too excited?" he said. He crawled out and sat before the doorway.

"Yeah."

For a time, we looked up at the stars.

Chas said, "Somehow it's different to see them in real life, compared to sim."

"Yes, that's really them up there, not just code."

"Well."

"Because, after all," I said, finishing his thought, "everything is information."

So the scientists told us. Reality was the manifestation of coded information. All matter, all energy, the product of some great heavenly meta-program. Hell, maybe we were all the product of a simulation on someone else's computer. Out there somewhere, beyond our universe, some god with razor rash and a chipped tooth was having us on.

"Still," said Chas, "it's different."

Yes. To see real stars was different than seeing the simulated kind, even if the difference was just in our imaginations. Of all the things I loved about visiting the Lost Planets, stargazing might have been my favorite. To sit, for hours sometimes, and trace constellations no human had ever set eyes on.

"We aren't the first ones to look at these stars," Chas said. For an instant, I had the impression the night's blackness dissolved barriers and my thoughts were as transparent as the sky. A queer feeling flickered through me, not quite a shiver.

"Yeah," I said. "The Mi'hani got to these."

"No. I mean the ancients, the aliens. I'm just sitting here wondering if they made constellations, and what shapes those would take. Did they name the stars? Did they connect them with supernatural powers, associate them with gods...?"

A long, otherworldly cry split the night's quiet like a knife blade.

I jolted a glance at the handheld, but it showed nothing. No nearby movement and no flying forms, living or mechanical.

I breathed tight and shallow in the ensuing silence. I rubbed my arms and pretended it was the chill of the air that put the gooseflesh there. The night had cooled significantly, typical of deserts. I was grateful for the coat I'd packed, even if it had weighed down my bag during the day's hot trek.

"You know," I said. "This kind of reminds me of one of my first nights on Oblitus..." I paused, testing the effect of those words. Chas didn't move, didn't say a thing. Didn't take a breath, even. I smiled. Nothing like a captivated, not to mention captive, audience. "I came to the edge of the forest, which was completely different there. The canopy blocked out the sky almost entirely, so I'd been walking through twilight all day, but then I came to edge just in time for the most brilliant sunset, blazing pink across the sky. I'd never seen anything like it, not in any sim. I set up camp on a hill and watched the colors change for hours. That's one of the defining moments in my life."

My first sunset on a Lost Planet. My first sunset on any planet.

"*Then* the ground beneath my tent started to shake. I thought it was an earthquake. I woke up to the floor giving out beneath me and debris falling all over the tent. The ground was falling, the sky was falling, and then I realized the debris wasn't falling on my tent, it was crawling up the walls and ceiling."

"No."

"Uh-huh. The hill I'd planted my tent on wasn't a hill at all. It was a mound. An entire army of spiders swarmed the tent, as big as rats. I grabbed my gun and leaped out as if the tent were on fire. So there I was in my underwear shooting at the swarm, or what I could see of it in the dark. It was like shooting shadows."

Chas laughed. "No way. You didn't put that in your memoirs."

"Hell no. I finally dragged my tent free, but I'd shot it full of holes. I was lucky I hadn't shot my equipment. After that, I learned to sleep with my handheld on alarm if anything came near. And you'll be damned sure

I checked where I set up camp after that. It rained the next night, I'll have you know."

He was still chuckling when my handheld pinged.

His shoulders straightened. "What was that?"

I scooped it up.

"Ship," I said. "Heading straight for us."

But it couldn't be coming for us. How could it? We were surrounded by complex life-forms and had lit no fires, no lamps.

"It's the handheld," Chas said, at the same moment I came to that realization myself. They'd tracked the power. I nearly dropped the unit.

I powered it down and sprang toward the tent. Suddenly, the faint glow from the spires was bright enough to see by. I dove inside, grabbed my bedding, and wadded it into my bag. Pulled the bag out. Tore down the tent.

Chas dismantled his own tent. A good thing they folded and unfolded on their own. My instincts screamed at me to run, but we couldn't leave our gear. That would be certain death.

Chas wrestled the tent into his bag. I gave it a push and held the edges of the bag together while he yanked up the zippers. I scooped an arm under his back. We fled.

Or we tried. Chas tucked up his bad leg and ran along on one leg like a pogo stick, using me as his crutch. He was remarkably graceful, like a three-legged cheetah. Our strides stretched long in the low gravity. We moved in a way we hadn't moved earlier. Fast.

But not fast enough. In fact, no run would be fast enough to escape the patrol. They had coordinates on our last known location. From there, they would systematically search until they found us. Even if we outran and out-hid them now, we could only last so long without turning on a piece of technology.

A stitch needled my side. The cold, dry air scraped my lungs raw. Over the sound of our breaths and our footsteps, I could just make out the approaching drone of engines.

"Wait," I gasped. I stopped, and Chas stumbled to a halt with me. "Here." I slung my bag to the ground, and then, realizing I needed at least some of my supplies if my plan were to work, dropped next to it to paw at them. The tent and bedding stayed, but the ration dispenser needed to go, the med kit, a set of clothes, one of the canteens.

"What are you doing?" Chas demanded. "We need to run."

"No," I said, shoving the tent and bedding back into the bag. "You're going to run. I'm going to go back."

"What? No!"

"Yes." I emphasized the word by yanking the bag closed. Much easier this time, with half the contents gone. Much lighter, too.

"Listen to me," I said. "It won't take the Mi'hani long to figure out who I am, if they haven't already. They'll expect me to be alone. We've sent out the SOS. If you escape, you'll be here when they arrive and can tell them what happened. Take these things—the ration dispenser is the most important. Don't turn it on for at least a day. Leave your handheld off. Try to make it back to the ship, so backup can find you."

Chas watched me quietly as I stood, the outline of his body tense.

"Good luck," I said.

We grasped arms. Something about that contact made the moment real. I was reminded of the first time we met, and my world flipped over at that hit of déjà vu.

Then, we broke contact.

I ran for edge of the spires, back the way we'd come. As I ran, I flipped on the handheld. This would be the most painful part. I thumbed through the files and selected all the data related to the research site. I trashed them. I was tempted to erase the entire memory, but that would be too suspicious. After a moment's hesitation, I decided to leave a couple of correspondences from Sita and a document with her instructions for landing and heading north toward the site. It'd be enough for the Mi'hani to gloat over, until they realized it was useless. Without coordinates—now gone—it was all useless.

I reached the last of the spires. The sound of the ship grew louder. I saw no sweep of lights but knew they'd be searching with a spectrum unseen by human eyes. Against every screaming instinct, I ran out into the field. Because of my time in the Turris sim, I had the impression I'd been here before, although the dark made the landscape of stick-like grass strange and unfamiliar. I glanced up. The ship was a shape of deeper black against the star-speckled night.

I came to a stop and, like the complete fool I was, jumped up and down waving my arms. The rush of adrenaline allowed me to play the part of a stranded scholar spotting salvation convincingly.

The engines grew louder. The ship didn't seem to be slowing. Had they somehow sensed Chas? Would they simply rush past me to the forest?

An unnatural wind unrolled over me. Dust and dried matter blew at my face. The ship circled like a vulture, spending its momentum in a sharp turn, and swept to the ground. I lowered my arms. I had my weapons with me, although they wouldn't do me much good against the ship or whoever came off it. And for all I knew they just wanted to talk. In the middle of the night. With their lights off.

Would Chas be able to make it? He should. I had to believe that. As long as he kept his devices off, they'd have no reason to suspect his presence. Still, with my back to the spires, I felt like I stood before a wide-open door, trying to hide what was blatantly visible in the other room.

The ship lights still hadn't gone on. The engines powered down. I jogged toward it, waving. I came to a stop some thirty feet away and dropped my pack to the ground. I bent over with a show of being out of breath that was only part act.

The ship stood still and silent. If I were truly stranded and needed rescue, I'd be faint with anticipation. Instead I was just sick. A charged air sat around the ship. I caught a whiff of something metallic.

The door hissed open. A rectangle of light appeared. I straightened, swung the bag onto my shoulders, and tightened the straps. Automatically, I felt for the security of my gun. It felt snug in its holster, solid. I patted it but did not take it in hand, despite my instinct.

"Halloo!" I hailed, cupping a hand to my mouth. "Hallo! I'm one man! I'm unarmed! I won't hurt you!"

Ridiculous, because they had enough artillery to blast a small city out of existence. But I prattled out the first things that came to mind, hoping to sound as doltish as I felt right then.

"Please!" I said, just as feet flashed at the top of the stairs and a face ducked down.

Five of them descended, one in a white uniform flanked by four in black.

"Oh, thank all the gods," I said, with real relief. I'd begun to think they were debating what level of stun they'd use and which of the turrets they'd use to deliver the shot.

Perhaps—I would later think, pondering my idiocy as I watched the faintly glowing spires slide past through a thick window from high above—falling to my knees was a bit melodramatic, but right then my knees were weak enough to buckle convincingly. And because of the low gravity, it was an awkward fall, all the more believable.

"Oh, thank the gods. I thought I was lost out here for sure," I babbled, and babbled some more, channeling my very real fear into the act.

The man in white watched my performance dispassionately.

At last I petered out of words. The man's expression had a shark's flat malice. He didn't blink.

Then he knelt and scooped up the handheld which had fallen from my slack grip. He scrolled through it. The screen illuminated his face and made his eyes gleam like glass.

I didn't move. If I were really what I pretended to be, I'd have said something by now, wouldn't I? I'd have demanded to know what the man was doing, would have shown indignation. But I couldn't have said a word. I could barely breathe.

Still. Deep inside, I felt a hysterical little flutter of glee as he searched and searched, and found nothing.

His eyes flickered. "Bastard."

He gave me little more than a glance before standing. He strode toward the ship.

"Get him inside," he said.

I jumped to my feet, nearly launching into orbit, but the men in black were already on me. One big paw closed on my shoulder and another clamped my arm.

"Unhand me!" I cried. "There's no reason for this!"

In my rising fear and anger, I reached into myself, and what I pulled out was my Rider personality from sim. I was surprised I didn't yell the words in Late English. My captors should have been laughing. But they didn't twitch so much as an eyelid as they dragged me toward the ship.

That was when I knew I was in deep trouble.

My heels scraped the stairs. I had a blinding impression of bright lights and cold white ceiling panels, and then I was being dropped onto a cushioned bench. "Cushioned" was a lush word for the thinly upholstered seat. My friend the man in white sat on the bench opposite, measuring me with half-hooded eyes, mouth pinched with contempt.

Two of the black-uniformed guards sat down on either side of me, while—at little more than a look and flick of fingers from White—the other two moved off. The door hadn't yet closed. The ship's engines hummed at idle. They'd left me my pack. I could bolt now. But of course it was pointless—it was at least a couple hundred feet to the cover of the spires, and their guns had a range of at least five hundred.

I straightened in my seat and looked back at White.

The ship vibrated as the door closed. The quality of the engine hum changed. The ship tilted, lifted. We rose, and then the direction of the momentum changed. We were flying off.

White nodded to one of the men in black. "Search him."

They divested me of my bag and went through it with ruthless efficiency. The gun came out first. The man held it up for White to see, then deftly fingered the safety, pried it open, and ejected the ammunition. He tossed the ammunition over my head to his partner and pocketed the gun. He then emptied the rest of the bag, item by item, finally turning it over and dumping every last, loose item that had settled to the corners of the bag. This included a chitinous chip from one of the spire ticks and a pair of nail clippers I'd lost.

What would Allan Quatermain, my nineteenth-century adventuring hero, be doing? Talking his way out of this mess. He'd have something charming to say. No. He'd be here with his companions, and *they* would make some fortunate mistake that would save their hides. Quatermain didn't travel alone, didn't get into trouble alone, and certainly never got out of it alone.

"That's it, sir," said one of my guards. "Just the field supplies and weapon. No maps. No notes." He turned the bag inside out as he spoke, running his hand over the fabric and the seams. He gave a shake of his head.

White regarded me with those contemptuous eyes. "That was a stupid move, Dr. London Wells. A desperate, stupid move."

I wasn't sure which one he meant, but I was forced to agree.

CHAPTER EIGHTEEN

The rest of the trip passed in grim, ugly silence. I could see past my guard's face to the window. Through it, the faint glow of the spire forest gave way to black sky. My faint reflection lay atop it, mussed and hollow-eyed.

The ship turned. A distant glimmer of lights on the horizon slid in and out of view.

When next I saw the lights, the ship was circling for a landing. It tilted steeply, affording a good view of the camp through the window, though "camp" was an understatement. "City" would better describe the bright, organized sprawl. How long had they been in operation?

The ship rocked as it settled to the ground. I tensed, but I wouldn't be making my escape. Before the door opened, the guard beside me grabbed my wrists and snapped them into cuffs. He gave them a hard tug and then shoved me up. White held my eye. He didn't smile, but didn't have to.

My guard led me down the plank. I went with dignity.

The ground, once covered in the peculiar grass-like organism, had been trampled flat and dry. A wind moved through the compound, unchecked by the spires as it had been in the forest. The feel of moving air laden with the smells of alien life and dust reminded me uneasily of Anemoi.

But that was where the similarity ended. The sight that greeted me was not of an empty planet, but a military base.

We'd landed alongside a row of ships that stretched a quarter mile or more, all parked in a perfect line, like sharp, silent soldiers.

And in the direction we walked: a low, sprawling compound of buildings. It was hard to focus on it—it was dark and seemed to blur up into the sky—and I realized this was the intent of the structure, to trick the eye. The impression I did get was of a thickly armored crab squat to the ground with long offshoots.

People in uniform milled like ants. Huge cannons pointed skyward. A good thing Chas had landed us where he had, far from their sights.

A hair-raising cry tore the air, not unlike the call Chas and I had heard at camp—only, much closer. I looked up. Flood lamps lit the bellies of hazy clouds. Somehow, that light made the night seem all the more closed and dark. Nothing moved in the sky.

I had the satisfaction of feeling my guard skip a footstep, but his grip remained firm on my wrist. We pressed on. The cry raised again, closer, rousing a chill response from my lizard brain.

From the threshold of one of the storage outbuildings gleamed an array of glinting lenses. A chain-link gate had been pulled down in lieu of a doorway, showing a form like a ship in a bay.

Not lenses. Eyes.

And not a ship, but—

The creature opened its sectioned jaws and issued another cry. It slammed the bars of its cage.

My first thought was this was some kind of Mi'hani shaper monster, brought here for a twisted purpose unimaginable to me. Then the jaws closed. It fixed me with its mad eyes. It was one of Sita's pterodactyls.

Nearby on the trampled dirt another of the creatures lay spread on the ground. A corpse. The dust and floodlight sucked the colors from it, made it into a dry thing that had never been alive.

Suddenly, the cannons made sense. I was incensed with wordless rage. Chas and I had gone the entire day without seeing the creatures. I'd been thanking my luck we hadn't encountered any. But it hadn't been luck. It'd been artillery.

I was no biologist, and I hated carnivorous flora and fauna as much as the next man. I didn't care about the life cycles of giant slimes. What I cared about was getting around the things to access the artifacts beyond. If one attacked, I defended myself.

But this was something else. This was destruction for no reason, the casual decimation of an ecological system. I strangled on the arrogance.

We left the creature behind, shouting increasingly hoarse cries of anger. The creature. Not us. Although I did feel like shouting.

My eyes hurt as we approached the sprawling, crab-like compound. It resisted any attempt to look at it directly. It scrambled my gaze. My eyes crossed and slid away.

It had some kind of cloaking. Given the pterodactyls we'd just passed, that (and the building's lowness) made sense as a kind of defense. Or it would, if not for the cannons. A lot of effort had been put into hiding from something they were just going to raze from the sky.

We entered one of the crab's long legs through a double door. Men passed in various stages of dress. The air was stuffy with the smells of sweat and soap. I recognized the charged atmosphere of a barracks.

Half a dozen men watched a friendly wrestling match near the water dispenser. A couple looked up to watch us pass.

I lost track of how many times we turned, like an old English hedge maze. When we stopped finally, I surmised we'd reached the center of the building.

We'd scraped most of my honor party on the way. White, my guard, and another were all that entered a small room with me. The room had exactly three chairs, but none of us sat while White disappeared through the room's other door. I heard the suggestion of voices, but couldn't make out the words. Next to the door sat a single potted plant. I didn't recognize the kind.

The door opened, and White came out looking more displeased than he had going in. Gone was the haughty air. He threw a look at my guard and gave his head a savage jerk toward the door.

I was pushed inside. The door closed firmly behind me, leaving me in a room as lush as the other was empty. Images covered the walls—maps and bird's eye views of Turris. On one wall was a window to the outside, disabusing me of the idea we'd traveled to the center of the building. As my eyes skated over it, the view changed to another location in the encampment. Wall screen, then. Another screen looked out on a completely different view—a cityscape I realized must be on Mi'hani.

A single large desk sat in the center of the room, surrounded by a garden of potted plants, all alien. All, I suspected, Mi'hani in origin. The desk itself was black and stark in its neatness.

A man sat behind it, husky and middle-aged, with thinning hair. He had neither the dramatic features of White nor the military harshness of the guards. His hands were folded on the desktop. He watched me with the remote, keen look of a hunting cat that had eaten but might make the effort to catch dessert. He made no move to switch off the maps of Turris on the walls, including one map that'd been outlined and dotted. I noted how far south and out of the way some of the red dots were.

On a table in the corner of the room was a personal food dispenser. Next to that, a decanter of clear liquid and a short stack of glasses. It took an effort not to stare at the decanter.

"Please," he said. "Take a seat. I think there might have been a misunderstanding."

I could have refused as a token resistance, but that seemed childish, not to mention futile. So I sat. I was interested to know what kind of "misunderstanding" there had been.

The man offered his hand to me, palm up. The gesture reminded me of the handshakes we offered in Old London, and so I grasped his flat hand. Apparently the wrong response. He gave me an odd look.

"My name is Stafford Myall," he said, recovering his hand. "I am chief officer of this operation. And you are the venerable Dr. Wells."

Thoughtful of him to introduce me. I'd begun to doubt myself, what with all the falling and blundering into captivity.

Before I could formulate a reply, he said—with dangerous cheer—"You'd better not deny it. I've seen enough videos and simulations to know who you are. I'm a very big fan of your work, Dr. Wells."

Thanks?

I spread my hands on the desk. "You...flatter me."

Mr. Myall shook his head. "No, I speak the truth. I say there was a misunderstanding. My captain mistook his orders to retrieve you and I'm afraid that as a result you were mishandled."

That was a lot of misses, all around.

He said, "We witnessed your ship crash and I feared you'd perished in the crash."

No, he'd hoped I'd perished.

"Can I get you something to drink? Something to eat? A brandy?"

I should have been touched, or maybe afraid, that he knew my drink preference. Although what I preferred at the moment was water. But that seemed somehow like a weakness, which I didn't want to admit. I nodded to the brandy.

He poured two glasses of amber liquid from a small, cut glass bottle and returned its crystal stopper with a clink. A prop meant to suggest luxury and class. A fabricator had probably spat it out in thirty seconds.

He placed both glasses on the desk and bid me take my choice. I slid the one on the right toward me. He picked up the other and took a sip, assessing me with eyes crinkled in a way that wasn't quite smiling.

He set the glass down. "I'll be straightforward with you. I think you're here for the same reason we are. As you can see, we haven't had much luck on our own. But I think we could both benefit from working together. A little partnership. We could use a mind of your distinction, and you could use access to our resources."

Which were obviously plentiful.

"And what have you come looking for?" Knowing they wanted something from me restored a little of my confidence.

"The answer to a mystery," he said. He flicked a finger, and the blank of his desktop came to life with an image I recognized instantly, although I'd never seen this exact photograph before. The wall of unfamiliar Turris symbols, including a few I hadn't seen before, as if this picture had been taken from a different angle than the one Sita had shown me.

"I've never seen it before." Too nonchalant, I knew as I said the words. Nonchalance was never my response to a new discovery.

"Maybe this, then?" he said, and brought up another picture.

A jolt went through me at the sight of a familiar cliff's edge on Anemoi. Again, I recognized the site but not the photograph. This image had been taken from farther back than the one I'd snapped, taking in some of the ledge and the sky beyond. It was the first time I'd seen a full photograph of the site where I'd fallen. I'd begun to think I'd made the place up.

Something wasn't quite right, though. I blinked. A chunk of the ledge was missing, I realized—and with it, part of the stone tablet.

My skin tightened.

Myall watched me narrowly. He sat back and twirled his fingers slowly over his desktop, turning the pictures while he considered them.

"Remarkable," he said. "Two planets, one script."

His words echoed distantly and then stuck. *Two planets.* So he didn't know about the connection to Beira?

I lifted the glass of brandy and swirled the liquid. "Where were these taken?" I said. My voice sounded dry. I moistened my lips with the brandy. His eyes noted my movement with predatory satisfaction.

"That's not public information," he said. He reached forward to close the pictures with one movement of his fist.

Of course it wasn't public information yet. Which was exactly my point.

I set the glass down. "So is that what you want my help with? You want me to crack this new language? If you bring them back up, I can take a look at them."

"Just like that? Just a few lines of text, and you could decipher an entire language?" His eyebrow arched with his voice.

I scoffed. "How do you think I was able to crack the other Lost languages?"

THE SPIRES OF TURRIS | - 180 - | CHRISTINE DANSE

His face changed. He leaned forward. What I'd mistaken for middle-aged surety and arrogance shifted into something vicious. "By hunting them down. By picking through the bones of the planet to find what they'd left behind." He called up the pictures with a clawed swipe of his hand. "You can't know what these say, because there isn't enough script here. You need at least twice as much as what's written here. And that is precisely why you are here."

I turned my gaze to the pictures as if casually considering them, taking a moment to regroup.

"I work for Saraswati University," I said. "They don't take kindly to sharing. And I don't take kindly to collaborating. There's a reason I work alone."

His face hardened and flushed red. His mouth twitched, ready to make some response.

A bell rang.

He snorted and reared like a bull interrupted from a charge. "Come in."

White entered. "We found the ship."

Mr. Myall's face, already red, darkened to a shade of purple.

"We found it in the spires to the southeast, where we last detected a signal. Our initial sweeps didn't yield results because we were looking for an intact ship. The salvage crew has been sent to extract what's left, which won't be much. By now, it's been largely digested." He looked at me. "Nothing left by chunks of melted metal."

He must have enjoyed watching the blood drain from my face. It all came together at that moment: the glistening tops of the spires, the way they'd seemed to spread their branching tips heavenward. The proliferation of the spires in nutrient-poor soil.

Always good to understand the local flora and fauna, because you never knew what would try to eat you, or the tin can you flew in on, or the hope it represented in the form of communication devices and the ever-important beacon for help.

"Tell the crew not to worry about it," said Mr. Myall. "There will be nothing left to salvage, and we can't lose another ship to those damned things."

White nodded sharply, spared one last glance at me, then closed the door behind himself.

"So you see," Mr. Myall said, "you need our help. You need our resources."

I registered his words from a long way away. My face burned. I found myself shaking my head, more of an automatic, dumb movement at first—then purposeful.

"No," I said. "No, I don't need your resources. But I thank you for the offer. The university is sending a backup."

He leaned forward and lowered his head like a cobra. "And they will find scrap metal on an empty planet. Professor London Wells is no more. You will give up your secrets, either willingly or because I pull them from your skull. There are scientists on my planet who would bid for the privilege of dissecting your mind." He paused briefly and eased back an inch. "When they're done, there might be something left. We could even send you back to the university. With some facial alterations, a tweaking of the vocal chords. I think your career as a linguist would be over, but I'm sure they could find some other work for a half-wit with no personality."

A stony coldness went through me. I held his stare, unblinking, unmoving.

Rider, my adventuresome alter-ego, would pull out a hidden gun now. Pow. Point-blank.

Behind Myall's head, a point of light curved through the black sky of the Mi'hani cityscape. The blue leaf of one potted plant trembled in a breeze from the air vent. The brandy sat on the table in front of me, casting a single sliver of amber onto the tabletop. I itched to tip back the rest of it.

"You're digging in the wrong place," I said.

I stood. Mr. Myall's hand flinched in the beginnings of a short command, and I raised my eyebrows at him as I strode past the desk to the map of dig sites on the wall.

"I take it you've been here," I said, circling the red areas with my finger. "The ruins aren't at the edge of the mountains; they're in them." I glanced over my shoulder to see how he took this lie. He'd pushed back from the desk and watched me with evident wariness.

"The mountains are dotted with cave openings," I said. This was true enough. I remembered this from a conversation with Sita. "The Turrians were a flying race. We are almost certain of that. We think they lived with the spires in a kind of symbiotic relationship, although now we've had a taste of what that could have been like, so maybe we're wrong about that. But then, they wouldn't have been the only species living symbiotically with the spires. There are still all kinds of fauna that live in an interconnected way with the spires. The spires eat flying creatures, but the Turrians would have been smart enough to bypass the stalks, or maybe they had some kind of smell, some kind of cue, to keep the stalks from digesting them."

I was surprised at how the theory came together as I talked. It could have really been like this.

"They might have pollinated the stalks," I said. "They would have hunted beneath them for the prey the large flyers couldn't get to without landing in the spires, and they could have also hunted the large predators from beneath the protection of the stalks. They would have been lords of the forests."

"And what does this have to do with their language, and with caves in mountains?"

I jolted back to awareness. For a moment, I'd been back in class, lecturing.

In the quiet tone I reserved for disruptive students, I said, "Because the Turrians wouldn't have kept the seat of their civilization here in the forests. The stalks were too unsteady and dangerous. They would have lived here, but they would have kept their shrines and tablets here in the mountains, where they could truly fortify them, and where important historical documents wouldn't be accidentally digested."

If I hadn't known the ruins were nowhere near the place I pointed on the map, I would have believed it myself.

In fact...

The ruins weren't far from where I pointed, buried in a cave at the base of the mountains. I stared at the map in wonder. I might have just pulled the best theory for the Turrian ruins out of thin air.

"I wonder if you lecture better than you lie," Mr. Myall said. He flicked a finger toward the map. "Those mountains are covered in electrical storms. If they'd stored their priceless artifacts there, they'd have been safe even from themselves."

Electrical storms. I could curse myself. How had I forgotten?

"There are tunnels," I said, blithely.

"Tunnels."

"Tunnels," I agreed. I returned his look steadily. Admittedly, it was a little easier to assume an air of authority standing while he sat.

He leaned back. "What was on that handheld that you erased?"

I paused. That might have been fatal—and by the glint in his eye, he knew I knew. One slip.

"I erased the location of the tunnel that leads into the mountain," I said.

He considered this in silence. "You're lying."

I lifted a shoulder in a shrug. Actually, it was close enough to the truth. "Maybe so. But what have you got to lose, if I am?"

"Time," he said. "You're buying time, hoping your university will arrive. They will, eventually. Even if your SOS hadn't gone out, when you don't contact them they'll come sniffing for you. I'm surprised they sent you out at all after your little accident, much less alone."

"The university employs me. It doesn't keep me," I said. I didn't have to feign the heat in my voice.

Meanwhile his words echoed in my mind. *Little accident...*

"But it will come for you," Mr. Myall said. "In the meantime, we'll chase your ghosts around the mountains."

I shook my head, as much to myself as to him. "It looks like you've already been chasing your tail around." I picked a place on the map that was a respectable distance from the red already on the screen, but not so far as to be unbelievable. "The ruins are here, deep in the mountains. The opening here probably provided light and ventilation, but the site would have been primarily accessible through a tunnel that probably led from here."

I trailed my finger down to the base of the mountain, an arbitrary location. But as my finger came to a stop and I realized where it rested, ice prickled over my shoulders. I pointed almost exactly at the real location of the ruins.

Realizing I was in danger of staring, I retracted my finger and turned to meet Mr. Myall's gaze.

With a casual hand gesture, he opened the map on his desktop. A bold white line had appeared on the map where my traitorous finger had traced a path. He turned away from me to look down at it, unconcerned about leaving his shoulder and head vulnerable to me.

The derringer itched in its thigh holster. I hated how I hesitated. A few months ago, I would have pulled it. I had the advantage, after all: They wouldn't want to kill me or seriously harm me. Not yet. They needed me alive and functional. But I hesitated. Something had changed inside me. I couldn't even put thoughts to it.

I paused a few seconds too long. He glanced up at me. "We've lost three planes to the electric storms already," he told me calmly.

"That's too bad," I heard myself say. I looked at the map again. "That must have been here, and here."

"I take it you'd be able to locate the place by sight, since you've so conveniently erased the information from your handheld?"

I swallowed down the little leap of hope. "I might. I might recognize landmarks if I see them."

He smiled but did not meet my eyes. He was occupied studying the map.

My brain raced. I knew what to expect now from the Mi'hani. There would probably be a few guards again, and my hands would likely be bound. But they wouldn't risk more than one ship on such a trip, so that meant no more than five captors. Alone with them, away from the encampment and its layers of security—close to the caves and to the ruins—I'd have a chance of escaping and hiding.

His hand flashed. "Security," he said.

A guard stepped in.

Mr. Myall said, "Take Dr. Wells to the room that's been prepared for him and make ready a ship for Mi'hani tomorrow. Make sure one of the rooms on it is appointed for our guest comfortably but securely." Here, he glanced at me. "Then have one of the planes provisioned for an excursion. Stock it for digging and blasting."

The guard nodded assent.

Mr. Myall looked at me. "It's been a pleasure spending time with you, Dr. London Wells. Your theories about Turris are certainly intriguing. I hope they can be proved. We'll know for certain soon enough. I'm confident that with your help, we'll find the site. And when we do, you'll crack the code for us. It'll be a brilliant partnership. You'll love working with us."

CHAPTER NINETEEN

A pair of guards ushered me down the hall. "Firmly, but not roughly," Mr. Myall told them. "Dr. Wells is an eminent scholar. We want to treat him professionally."

They treated me to a professional pat down. They spread me against the wall of a small, bare room. Their hands moved over my arms, torso, and thighs in a thorough search.

"Well, this is an unexpected pleasure," I said. I could barely hear myself under the pounding of my heart. My face pressed against the cold wall.

One hand swept up my inner thigh and lit on the derringer. An instant later, they had my pants at my ankles and the holster unbuckled. They didn't say a word. The sound of ammunition being ejected broke the silence.

After a second search—this one more rough than firm, despite Mr. Myall's directions—they left me alone in the room.

I picked up my pants and re-buttoned them.

There wasn't much to the room. A bed. The single door I'd come through. No window, no view screen. No table or chair.

I was an idiot.

But they'd left me my boots, which meant I had one trick left.

I lay stomach-down on the bed with my face in the pillow. They'd send me to Mi'hani tomorrow while they pursued my fake lead—maybe straight to the real ruins. Meanwhile they'd scrape every greasy morsel out of my brain. Maybe they'd leave nothing but my intellect, a machine to decode languages. Or maybe they'd craft me into a willing tool. I didn't know which chilled me more.

I jumped from the bed and paced. Stopped midstride. Glanced around the room.

Just because I couldn't see the cameras didn't mean they didn't exist.

So I made a show of skimming my hands over the flat seam of the door where it nearly disappeared into the rest of the wall and of looking through each corner of the room, discovering every nook and cranny. There weren't many. Then I sat on the bed with my head in my hands. I wasn't sure myself if it was an act.

After a time, food and drank came. The woman who brought it left it on the ground. A thick cut of prime rib with red juice running to the edge of the plate, glistening green beans, a thick pile of red-skinned mashed potatoes. A glass of red wine. A tiny wrapped mint.

I put my head back in my hands.

After a time, pride and spite gave way to reason—or hunger—and I ate it.

Finally, I lay down again. I pulled the sheet and thin blanket over my head. There was no way to turn off the light. It was probably meant to rattle me.

I drew my knees up to my chest. Under the blanket, I smelled like dry dust and boot leather, and for an instant I was back at camp rustling out of the tent to look up at the stars. I resisted the urge to reach down and tug loose my laces. The bottom of my feet itched with my last hope. Some hope it was. Two thin blades hidden in the soles. I could give my captors shaves.

Dr. London Wells, explorer of five alien planets, climber of mountains, scholar of 1,000 languages. Sitting duck.

Still, they hadn't thought to take my boots, which meant they didn't see me as much of a threat. Possibly my one advantage.

I lay under the yellow-tinted dimness beneath the covers and strategized. My ship was destroyed. If the university did come, they'd find it in pieces. If that. They wouldn't think me missing; they'd take me for dead. Which meant the Mi'hani could do whatever they wanted with me, up to and including dismantling me and shaping the pieces back together. I was theirs. In that case, I was better off dead—and the means of my death rested under my sweating feet.

If I accepted death as an acceptable, even preferable, outcome, that opened other possibilities to me, like a suicidal rampage in a last attempt to escape. The only problem with that: They wouldn't kill me. They'd only incapacitate me and take away my toys.

But Chas. The university would find him when they came. They'd know I wasn't dead from the crash, but kidnapped. Chas. How was he doing? He wouldn't get far with that brace, and he likely hadn't been outside a town or the university before. But from what I'd seen, he was resourceful, and he'd be safe under those spires—as long as he was smart about not using the electronics. I could picture him clearly, stumping along, eating rations, listening to the sounds of the alien wild. Night would fall again. He'd be alone.

That wouldn't be so bad though, really. I smiled a little. I remembered my own first nights on Oblitus. That had probably been a more dangerous environment.

But then, I'd had the confidence that came with youthful ignorance and bravado, and I'd had full use of my body, and my only threats had been the flora and fauna, not people with ships and guns and agendas.

It was easier to worry about Chas than my own predicament. Would he know that the spires had eaten the ship? Would he be able to locate the remains? Had enough of a signal been sent out before the ship's communication unit had been...digested? Hopefully even if it hadn't, it wouldn't be too long before the university sent backup when they didn't hear from us. But we weren't due to send our first check-in for another two days. And after that, it could be another week or more before they arrived. Chas didn't have rations for that long—not without letting the dispenser go through a calibration and charging cycle, which would pop up on Mi'hani sensors if they were watching for that kind of activity.

Damn Sita for sending him with me. If she hadn't, he wouldn't be in this mess, and at least I'd have some kind of intellectual heir to take up teaching the Lost languages... My throat closed weirdly at the thought. It'd be a shame to lose him. Brilliant and beautiful—all that enthusiasm wasted. And that smile. That unassuming personality, almost goofy at times, which made the moments of deep insight all the more surprising.

I was startled to realize that, somewhere along the way, I'd honestly come to *like* Chas.

I turned in bed—from side to stomach to back to side, like meat turning slowly on a spit—until another meal was brought. Roast chicken, caramel brown and glistening. Tucking into that felt vaguely like cannibalism. I briefly considered going on a hunger strike, but decided I wouldn't like it when they stuck a tube down my throat. And I needed to keep my strength up, because what the hell. Miracles.

They hadn't left me any utensils save a single spoon made from unbreakable plastic, so I tore the meat with my hands and wiped my fingers in the bed sheets when I was done.

Remarkably little sound penetrated the walls. I had no idea how much time passed and couldn't hear a thing going on save the thoughts rattling in my skull. I considered what weapons I could make out of the dishes, but they hadn't provided me with anything that could do more than leave a small bruise or a paper cut—and probably hurt me in the process.

I lay down once more. Despite it all, I slept.

I paced. I jogged. And after a while, I lay down to stare at the wall.

Despite everything, I was bored. You could only think about your doom for so long before you became numb to it.

So I drifted. I thought about Chas' food creations and his impeccable Late English. I thought about the Explorer's Club and Theo. How would Theo feel when the news reported me dead? What would the rest of the adventuring group think when I never showed up again? And Mom and Vic...I hated to prove them right. I should have taken their advice and just moved to Earth and plugged into the mainframe with them. What discovery was worth immortal life?

I thought about Aelia, and Sita. I hoped Chas made it back to her safely.

My chest tightened and I closed my eyes against a warm salt block of useless emotion.

That, there, was the first crack. Which meant it was all over now. Just tap me once, and I'd fracture to pieces.

The mattress trembled beneath me. But not, as I first thought, with the impact of my spirit breaking.

I stopped breathing and went still. I felt it again: the rumble of a deep, distant tremor.

I sat up and cocked my ear. I couldn't hear a thing.

I swung out of bed and stretched on the floor. I pressed my ear to the ground, which was cold against the side of my face and smelled faintly of sweat.

Nothing.

Then another vibration. And another.

I pushed to my feet. The entire room rumbled with an almost rhythmic thundering. Through the thick walls, I could just make out raised voices. I put my ear to the door. Yes. People shouting.

It was the cannons, I realized. The cannons were firing.

The next impact staggered me. The walls shook like loose window panes. That wasn't just the cannons going off. We were being shot at.

Shot at? But who—

The university.

Oh, thank every god ever conceived by man and alien. The rescue ship had arrived.

But that couldn't be right. A week hadn't yet passed. My time in the cell had disoriented me, but not that badly.

For all I knew, though, the ship had already been in the vicinity. Sita might have even sent an escort after us. And why did the thought make me angry? I should have wanted to kiss her. Damn her, bless her.

The floor shuddered beneath my feet, and I sat hard on the bed. I had no window, no sense of what transpired outside. Nothing to do except wait. I crossed my ankle on my knee and unlaced the boot. It took a few moments to work the sole out and fish out the paper-thin blade beneath.

I wasn't sure what I was going to do with that, but when the door clicked and began to slide open, I dropped the shoe, dashed across the room, and pressed to the wall beside it. Maybe it was a friend, but if so, it was an awfully quick rescue.

The door opened. I pressed the back of the knife to the person's gut. It was remarkably flat and hard under several layers of fabric—not the starched black of the Mi'hani uniforms, but a dirty and wrinkled beige.

The man went stiff. Startled hazel eyes met mine.

"Chas!"

"Dr. Wells, you are a dangerous man to surprise."

I withdrew the blade. He smiled, a smear of white dust standing out against his brown complexion. The top of his shirt was torn. He'd seen better days. He was the best thing I'd ever seen.

A question formed on my lips, but before I could voice it, Chas looked down and said, "What happened to your shoe?"

I sheathed the knife and slipped it into my pocket. "Nothing," I said, and retrieved the boot.

Chas glanced over his shoulder. "All right. You ready? I passed a group on their way here. You're a popular guy, Doc."

I made an unpleasant sound.

Despite my supposed popularity, the hall was empty. I suspected my captors were engaged with more pressing matters. I wondered what had happened to the group Chas passed. I was about to ask when another explosion rattled the building and threw me into him.

We pulled apart. "This way," he said, and cut down another hall. This led us back to the main section of the building, but beyond that, I had no idea where we were. I'd noted my surroundings as I was led to my cell, but things looked different now. A few explosions had that effect.

This apparently did not faze Chas, who'd probably passed through here since the impromptu renovations. We circled around a fallen ceiling panel.

It was good to see Chas. I wasn't sure what relieved me more: my own release, or Chas alive and well.

"How did they get here so fast?" I said.

He tossed me a look. "The Mi'hani?"

"Whoever's out there. Is it the university?"

He sent me another brief, puzzled glance. "The university? No. That'd be nice."

"Then what—"

We rounded a corner, almost straight into a group of guards. Chas lifted his gun and felled the four of them before I could even lift my knife.

Which would explain what had happened to the first group Chas had encountered.

"Where the hell did you get that?" I said, staring at the gun I'd somehow not noticed.

"Off a guard. Here." He dropped to a crouch beside one of the bodies—my conscience hoped it was still alive—and divested it of gun and weapon belt. He tossed these to me.

I caught the firearm in both hands and checked the safety and power level. I set it to Stun and buckled up as we moved down the hall. We stayed close to the wall where we could trail a hand for support. The ground shook beneath us. Another explosion hit, this time contacting the building, and the ceiling rippled. A light panel crashed to the floor.

I glanced up after the rain of glass and spotted another trio of guards. "Here," I said, and grabbed the back of Chas' pants. I hauled him into a closet with me.

The door swung shut and closed us in muffled blackness. We braced against the walls, breathing heavily. The room smelled like sharp chemicals, sweat, and dust.

A sliver of light illuminated Chas' eye and cheek as he peeked through the door. "Now's the time," he said, and we dashed from the closet to the end of the hall fifty feet away, where the door stood open to the outside.

We exited into a chaos of running guards, gun flashes, and falling debris. A large shape swooped overhead and I ducked, but when I glanced up it was gone.

Chas led us around the side of the building. We nearly ran into a pair of men, and this time I was the one to take them down—not to be shown up by my own research assistant.

We paused over the bodies to catch our breaths and get our bearings. I cringed as more shapes swept overhead. I recognized the roaring of an animal, which I'd originally taken as part of the noise from the cannons.

Those weren't all ships above us. Some of the shapes flapped their wings, and I recognized them as pterodactyls. One of them caught a ship midair and ripped it open, bits of metal—and a body or two—spraying to the ground.

While I gaped, another blast hit nearby. Something small stung my cheek as I dove to the ground.

"What the hell?" That had come from one of the Mi'hani's own cannons. "Can these guys not aim?"

"The guns are on autopilot, which is apparently broken. They've been firing randomly. Let's go."

I went after him, and that was when it hit me: There was no rescue ship. No university. Only Chas and this barrage of shots coming from the cannons.

We scuttled along, hugging the wall. We ducked from debris but didn't bother to hide from the guards. They were all too busy to give us a glance.

We passed the cage where the pterodactyl had been kept. The door had been ripped open, the thick metal grate burst and bent like wire mesh.

The situation started to come together for me. A group of pterodactyls must have attacked the compound, triggering defensive fire from the cannons, which had malfunctioned, blasting the situation into general pandemonium.

"Did you do this?" I asked, incredulous.

"What?"

I flapped a hand at the cage and the cannons.

"That? No. But it's good cover."

"Yeah," I said. "If we don't get covered."

He flashed me a crazed grin and I felt an answering bubble of elation, probably hysteria, rising in my own chest.

We made our way to the back of the compound and jogged between storage sheds, moving quicker because there was less activity here. The pterodactyls seemed to be focusing their attentions on the ships and cannons out front. By my hasty counts, there were four of them. I suspected one of them was the escapee. If I wasn't mistaken, the cannons weren't targeting them.

One of the storage sheds stood open. I glanced in as we passed and saw big slabs of rock in piles and leaning stacks. Masonry, for building more permanent buildings?

I did a double take and jogged backward. No, I hadn't been mistaken. The *masonry* was carved with Turrian script. The Mi'hani weren't collecting building blocks. They were collecting artifacts. What looked like an entire tower temple had been dismantled and stacked in the shed, as neat as lumbar in a warehouse.

Just how long had they been here, and why hadn't our drones picked up on the activity?

The answer to that was probably related to another mystery. Why, exactly, had our drones stopped sending transmissions?

The Mi'hani hadn't even done a neat job of cutting the stone. Some uneducated goons with energy saws had sliced it in same-sized rectangles, probably to fit the bed of their ship. The script was cut off mid-symbol in places. It would take a week and a fleet of heavy machinery to reassemble these stones, and then, where had they even come from? I hadn't seen anything like this in Sita's files. Had these stones come from the mountains, or had they come from some built structure, representing previously unknown masonry skills of the Turrian race? Taken out of context, these slabs told us almost nothing. A photograph of this carved wall, when still whole and continuous, would have been more useful.

This was worse than looting. This was a crime. How many of the sheds back here were filled like this?

"Dr. Wells," Chas prompted.

I shook my head.

"Hey!" cried a voice—not Chas, this time.

Chas and I looked up to see one man drop to his knee and take sight down the barrel of his rifle while a female companion pointed a pistol. If I wasn't angry enough before, I was raging now. I lifted my own pilfered weapon and sent both guards to the ground. Then I grabbed Chas' arm.

We went at a jog. The sheds gave way to hills of trash and a hazard of half-buried pipes, then nothing—just a flat plain and a mountainous horizon. The compound had no fence, because apparently the threats on Turris came from above, not from the ground.

Chas ran a little ahead, leading us. I guessed we were headed in a northwest direction, straight into the foothills. I'd explored the area enough in sim. Even with the unexpected and unfamiliar landmark of the compound sprawling over the plain, I had a pretty good handle on where we were.

The sounds of fighting continued behind us. I glanced back in time to see a plume of fire roll into a black cloud above the camp. The next time I saw it—if I ever saw it again—it might be ashes. I didn't know how I felt about that. On the one hand, the Mi'hani deserved it. On the other, they represented the only outpost of civilization on this planet—and a fleet of ships that could get us off of it.

Speak of the devil: A dark shadow passed over us. A ship making a run for it. I watched, fascinated, as one of the pterodactyls spun off from the camp to pursue it. The ship fired at the creature, and whoever manned the gun turrets had no idea what they were doing, because shots went in every direction. Or maybe that was the tactic. Fire enough, and one was bound to hit—a law in artillery and male reproductive biology.

A bolt clipped the ptero's wing. It screeched and fell away, floundering in the air.

The pterodactyl spotted us and deemed us better targets for its wrath. It screamed and dove. So did Chas.

I dropped to my knees in a slide and brought my gun to bear. It didn't fire. Shit. I popped the energy cell, grabbed a replacement from the belt, and ratcheted it into place. Looked up. Four jaws spread wide, revealing rows of curving needles and a black tube tongue, close enough to see the string of saliva stretching across.

I took aim. Fired. The four jaws spasmed; the thing shrieked and spun away. It crashed hard in the dust.

Nearby, Chas scrabbled to his hands and knees. He let out an alarmed sound and looked at me with wide eyes.

"What?" I said. "Did you think I just shoot like that in stories?"

I didn't feel guilty about killing the creature. Out here in the wild, it was kill or be killed. But I didn't feel proud, either, especially since I'd just downed a sort of unwitting ally.

Meanwhile, the ship escaped off toward the mountains. I hoped the dumb bastards flew right into a lightning storm.

We took off again. More booms sounded behind us, although the earth no longer shook with the blasts and they sounded a little more controlled. Glancing back, I saw at least some of the fires had been put out.

We continued to run. After a couple minutes, it became obvious the cannons were back under control and the pterodactyls had all been downed. It even looked like the bulk of the compound still stood. Too bad.

Then I thought about Mr. Myall standing in his office with the ceiling caved in and his fussy crystal brandy bottle in shards on the ground, and felt some grim satisfaction.

We reached the first outcropping of stone that would eventually become the foothills and dropped, panting, into its shadow. We'd run a long way with bounding steps through the low-gravity landscape, although with the thinner atmosphere it took a long time to catch our breaths. A very long time, in my case. I crouched to the ground, heaving and heaving, with the strangling panic I'd never catch my breath. I was going to hyperventilate and pass out. I pulled my shirt collar over my nose and breathed into the fabric. Finally, my breathing slowed.

Nearby, Chas sat with his back to the rock, legs stretched out in front of him, his chest heaving.

That was when it occurred to me he'd been sprinting without a hitch. And not only that: he wasn't wearing the brace.

"What"—gasp—"the hell?" Gasp. "What"—gasp—"about your leg?"

Chas shook his head—more of a rolling back and forth against the rock—and said, "It's fine." Before I could find the breath to say more, he added, "We should get closer to the caves before night," and pushed to his feet.

CHAPTER TWENTY

We continued at a loping jog, which was a little easier to sustain. Twice, ships passed overhead. They headed back in the direction of the Mi'hani compound. Returning after receiving an all clear, I suspected.

Chas pressed on like a wolf through hostile territory. We made an erratic path through the grasses, pausing only for ragged breaths and to check our progress against the distant ridge of mountains. I had no idea what resources or fauna waited for us there, but we could lose ourselves in the many caves, and the electrical storms might deter the Mi'hani.

We'd emerged into late afternoon. By the time we reached the foothills, the sun was just disappearing over their tops. Dust and sweat grimed my face. I pressed a hand to the stitch in my side.

"We should make camp here," I said, indicating a flat stretch of ground between two rocky prominences. A shelf of rock jutted over it at an angle, providing cover—at least from natural sight. It was our safest bet till morning, when we'd make our last dash to the mountains.

"Uh-uh," Chas said, and shook his head. He continued on.

Bemused, I followed him through the odd landscape of standing stones and rocky ridges, a garden of abstract statuary. He ducked past some other decent candidates for camp sites that offered partial protection from the elements and airborne threats, and finally came to a stop in a hollow between hills with a lumpy ground and a full view of the sky.

"Here," he said, and slung his bag to the ground. He went on one knee and tugged the zipper open. He glanced up, saw my incredulous expression, and pointed. "Look there."

I looked, but wasn't precisely sure at what. Smooth, round stones covered the ground. They had a grayer cast than the rest of the rocky ground—or so it seemed in the failing light—and they were perfectly circular. Rather curious, geologically. I couldn't imagine sleeping on this.

"They're life-forms," said Chas.

Oh.

Oh.

"Right," I said. That would take care of the life scans, if a ship came patrolling for us. Although, knowing these squat gray stones were living made the prospect of sleeping on them even less appealing.

We chose the flattest space and put up the tent. One tent, since my things were gone. That loss rankled me deeply—more deeply than it should have, considering I'd transferred all the essentials to Chas. This would be the first expedition I'd lost my supplies.

Also: one tent. I eyed that none too happily.

Chas reassembled the food dispenser and the water purifier.

"I wouldn't advise that," I said, and glanced up. I saw no ship lights in the sky, only the stationary stars, but that didn't mean they weren't out there.

Chas followed my gaze. "I really doubt it. They're going to need every hand to clean up that mess."

I shook my head. "Now's the best time. They can catch us before we hit the mountains. They can spare a two- or three-man crew for that. They're dead without me."

I recounted for Chas what had happened since I'd left him in the spires. My chest and throat tightened as I told him they'd been preparing to ship me out to Mi'hani for a memory scrape.

The sun went down completely, leaving only the deep blue of lingering dusk. Chas was a motionless black shape a few feet away.

"I've heard they could do that," he said quietly. He knocked food from the dispenser into two bowls and offered one over, setting it on a narrow sliver of ground between two of the stone creatures. So far, I'd stepped on them, rapped them with my knuckles, and now sat on one. I figured that if they hadn't retaliated by now, we were probably safe for the night.

I took the bowl and spooned salty stew into my mouth with trembling hands. Shock, only hitting me now.

"Well, at least we know we're on the right track," Chas muttered, echoing my thoughts from earlier. Then—delicately, as if wanting to break the news gently—he said, "Although, I'm not sure help will be coming anytime soon. I saw ships flying toward the crash. They've probably stripped the hard drives and killed the communications. That's another reason I don't think they'll be coming for us right away. They have what they need to find the site without you."

It took me a moment to realize Chas didn't know what had happened to our ship. I said, "They didn't find anything."

"They said that? They didn't find the crash?"

"Oh, they found it. What was left of it. Which apparently wasn't much." And so I told Chas about the fate of the ship.

He was silent a minute, absorbing this news.

"So that's where we're at," I said. "Help is at least several days away. The Mi'hani will be after us soon because without me they don't know where the site is. But neither do we. Not exactly."

"Actually," said Chas, and held up a square object. In the darkness, I took it to be a handheld.

"You..."

"Yeah," he said, and I could hear his grin. "It's all here."

Something like hope kindled in my chest. I hadn't realized how lost I'd felt without those coordinates.

"I could kiss you right now." My tone darkened as I added, "But it won't do us a great deal of good."

"Kissing me?"

That struck me dumb. Then I realized what I'd said and grimaced in humor. "No. The handheld."

Chas shrugged. "So we don't turn it on."

I looked at him as if he were daft.

Chas pointed up at the stars. "The mountains themselves run east and west, so finding our direction is easy enough. We can use landmarks to judge how close we are. There's the dip you showed me on the map, the tail where the mountain range trails south. We know our site is about twenty miles east of that. That'll be the challenging part, because the mountains are pockmarked with caves, and we can probably spend a week or more just searching those."

"Right," I said impatiently.

"What we need is a pointer. There's a star, a bright star that looks red, that sets at dusk this time of year. It goes down just over the site and gives us, basically, our longitude. That will drastically narrow our search."

And reduce our search time from possible weeks to maybe a few days, without needing to turn the handheld on even once, if we could help it. Yes. All right. Especially with the Mi'hani busy searching the bogus coordinates I'd given them, we might just stand a chance of finding it.

Then I frowned. "How do you know that?"

"Know what?"

Something in Chas' tone—too casual?—pinged my brain. "Star navigation on a Lost Planet."

"I studied the map before we left," he said. "You damn well drilled it into me."

I shook my head. "We didn't do stars." *I* hadn't done the stars.

"I did extra credit."

Something knocked on the door in my skull. I stared at Chas. He'd blended in with the rest of the night, a deeper shadow blotting out the stars. He'd helped set up camp—had known where to make camp—and dispensed the food and water. These were all things I would expect from an intelligent man and a quick study. But...he'd done things all *too* easily.

Quite suddenly, I asked, "How did you land the ship?"

Because we had landed—not crashed, as it seemed at the time. We'd lodged snugly in the crook of the spire's branches, a very lucky thing. It was much more likely we would have ended up on the ground or smashed and twisted against the trunk of one of the spires—truly crashed. But we hadn't ended up safe in the branches by luck, had we?

Chas' silence said more to me than any explanation. A shadow moved in the deeper gloom. Gravel crunched under his knee.

"I'm a vanguard," he admitted softly.

The vanguard. Of course. Experts in athletics, endurance, survival, xenobiology, geology, ballistics. Piloting. Navigation. Firearms.

Sita hadn't sent me with a research assistant. She'd sent me with a highly trained babysitter.

"Goddamn it," I snarled.

I was already on my feet. I kicked my plate. I felt the solid impact against the toe of my boot but didn't hear anything for a long moment, and then I heard a distant metallic ping.

"Dr. Wells?" Chas' voice was small.

"I take it you're not even a student. I take it that's all bullshit, too."

It all made sense now. Sita urging me to have an assistant—and then agreeing to give up trying to shove one on me, just before Chas showed up at my office. Chas, who seemed to be everywhere after that. Chas, who just happened to like rock climbing, whose student records didn't quite make sense. All of it was there, plain as day.

I strode from camp through the blackness. My hands gripped the hair at the top of my head.

Had Sita even told him to learn English? Oblitian?

This is my favorite of the languages. I fell in love with it while reading Words in the Wilderness.

That disarming grin.

I was a fool.

"This is why I work alone," I whispered, and I was alarmed to feel heat behind my eye sockets.

My fingers loosened. My hands slipped down to cup the back of my neck.

"Dr. Wells," Chas ventured again. He sounded shaken. "It's not true. Whatever you're thinking."

"Oh yeah?" I released my hands. "And what am I thinking?"

I'm a fool. I never learn.

He hesitated. "Anything except that I'm a paying university student who is your research assistant."

I said nothing.

"I am," he said. "I'm a student, I mean. I *was* a vanguard. I resigned three years ago to return to school, to learn the Lost languages, and...maybe...to study with you."

More lies? Well, that would make him the fool this time, not me.

"You don't believe me," he said. At my silence, he said, in perfectly clipped English, "I am telling you the God's honest truth. When Dean Tiwari offered me the position, it was to be your research assistant and nothing else."

The last of dusk had faded, leaving the deep black of full night and a spray of brilliant stars. I could just make out the shape of the stones surrounding us by the outline of solid blackness blotting out the stars. A white flash of light stuttered through the sky, followed by a snake of horizontal lightning. The electrical storms. Shielded in the spires, we hadn't seen them the first night. The light show played out in eerie silence, a spectacle of white and green and blue and red that had been playing for millenniums without an audience over an empty landscape.

I was tired. Tired and feeling too old for this kind of thing anymore.

I walked back in the direction I'd come and sat down on the lumpy ground. It might have been my imagination, but the living stones radiated warmth.

"We should probably get some sleep," Chas said from close by, so I knew I hadn't misjudged the location of camp. "They'll probably start a search early."

"You get some sleep," I said.

Hesitantly, he said, "I've unzipped the bag to make a pallet and put the blanket on top. I'll be on the right side."

"That's all right. I'll be out here." Despite my calm tone, I realized how petulant I sounded. The temperature had already dropped several degrees, and it would only get colder before morning. I stood. "How about I take the bag and sleep out here. You can take the tent and the blanket. I'm used to sleeping under the stars." In the following quiet, I realized Chas would be, too. "Or the other way around."

"I don't think that's a good idea," he said. Hastily, he added, "I mean, I'd feel safer if we were both in the tent. I mean, *I* would feel safer. For my own safety."

I scoffed. "Save it." I found the dispenser and spent a ration on tea, seeing as I didn't know when we'd find our next water source. I drank some and poured the rest into a canteen. Chas remained motionless.

I powered down the dispenser. My shoulder itched with Chas' awareness on me.

I said, "Better piss now. Or whatever else you need to do before bed. I don't want the tent shaking once I'm inside."

There was a moment of surprised quiet. Then he scraped to his feet and went a few feet to desecrate one of the standing stones while I tried not to listen and wondered, again, just how I'd gotten into this mess.

☆☆☆

I crawled into the tent first and lay out on the covers. Chas climbed in after me, and the tent did indeed shake. He tripped lightly on my leg.

"Ow. Sorry."

I grunted. It *was* nice to be in the tent. The walls gave an illusion of security, which I could use right then. It wasn't the flat, firm mattress of a Mi'hani prison cell, but Chas had actually done a nice job of making a bed. As I shifted onto my side, I realized he'd even given me the only pillow.

A peace offering.

As if to back that up, Chas whispered, "I'm sorry."

I didn't say anything. I was willing to let it rest because I had to. Not like I could afford to be a sulky bastard for the rest of the trip to my one ally on the planet. And...my one friend. Despite myself, and despite everything, I liked Chas. And Sita had just been trying to protect me. That was probably what stung the most—that I'd *needed* the protection. Granted, I would have been fine on my own if it hadn't been for the Mi'hani. Still. To think of all she'd gone through to coordinate Chas with me...and all Chas had gone through...I should have been flattered someone cared enough about me.

But I couldn't bring myself to forgiveness. Not yet. There was a big rock on my chest, and it wouldn't budge.

I wrinkled my brow. "What *did* happen to your leg?"

"Oh." Just the single soft word. I could almost hear his sheepish smile. "That's one of the first things we learn: how to jimmy braces so they heal faster."

I processed this. "How much faster?"

"A few hours. As in, it takes a few hours."

I stared at the black place where Chas was. "We traveled an entire day with your broken leg." An entire day of Chas using me as his crutch, his solid body pressed against mine through the hot afternoon, panting in my ear.

He had no response except the softest "hm," a little laugh. My mouth pursed, forming a suspicion. Then he shifted in the bedding and said, "Anyway, it doesn't work while walking. We could have sat somewhere for eight hours while it healed or we could have trudged along, away from the crash site and away from where the ships could find us."

I couldn't fault the logic.

"So why vanguard?" I said. "You're brilliant with languages. You could have gotten a scholarship to the university, if you'd wanted to start when you were younger."

"I know." No arrogance there, just a simple recognition of truth. A long pause followed that, long enough I thought Chas wasn't going to answer the question. Then he said, "I was really scrawny as a kid."

"You?"

He laughed. "Yeah. I read a lot of books, didn't go out much. I was the middle kid and kind of forgotten a lot. My older brother was my dad's favorite, good at everything—sports, school. My younger brother was Mom's pet, and he was always getting into trouble. But he was *good* at it. I was kind of the disappointment. I tried to stay out of trouble, but it always seemed to find me. I got used for target practice at school, and I wasn't even good at that. I got busted up a couple times and then said, 'Fuck that,' and learned how to run. I think that's what really pissed my dad off. I couldn't take a punch. Heh." A pause, and the slight sound of swallowing. "He pushed me around a lot. Not really physically, but verbally—which I guess sounds kind of wimpy, but it hurt. Nothing I did made him happy. So one day I said, 'Fuck it' again, and I left. Joined the military and became a vanguard. He wanted me to man up, so I manned up. And...I wanted to be like Dr. London Wells and go on adventures to uncharted planets. I think I must have read your memoir eight times cover to cover as a kid. It's pretty much what kept me alive. Or at least sane."

I had no idea what to say to this. My face burned.

"So when Dean Tiwari offered me to be your research assistant on this trip but asked me to keep quiet about it, I said yes."

The apology was in his voice again. This time, I almost cracked. The kid had won me with flattery, and he played the sympathy card well, too.

"What does your dad think now?"

"I don't know. I haven't talk to him since." The silence sounded like a shrug. "After I left, I realized I had nothing to prove to him. I proved it all to myself."

I felt an odd squeezing tenderness in my chest. I was thinking about my own dad, and how lucky I'd been that he'd approved of and encouraged me. How it ached to have lost that support.

In a low voice, I said, "You should probably tell him." What father wouldn't be proud of a son like Chas?

"Maybe. One day."

How quickly "one day" would come. One day would come, and go, and he'd be gone, and the opportunity to tell him would be gone. But I didn't share this with Chas. I was thinking about my own dad again.

The quiet that followed was a gentle one, but not a sleeping one.

"You never published another book," Chas said, and he must have turned in bed to face me, because his voice came from slightly closer. "Why?"

Well, there was a question. I considered telling him what I told everyone—that I just hadn't wanted to. Instead, I found myself saying, "I had a really different experience than you growing up. I was the younger of two kids. My older sister is Victoria. I think we were closer than other kids because of our parents. They didn't ignore us, per se, but they were both busy researchers. We entertained ourselves. We read, and we ran around in sim, and Vic learned Nahuatl. And I learned every language I came across. My parents caught on...not quite as quickly as they could have. But quickly enough. I was nine, and I could read and speak in something like 300 languages."

Chas let out a low whistle.

I shook my head. "I don't think I grasped what I could do, then. I knew I had a special ability, which, at that age, meant I could do something my sister couldn't. I might have bragged to everyone, except I was a little sneak. People came to the university from all different backgrounds, and they'd use their native language like a code, and I could understand them all." I paused, remembering some of the secrets I'd been privy to—and probably shouldn't have, at the age of eight. "And then it was my parents. They forbade me to tell anyone and insisted I go through my education normally."

"They were trying to protect you."

"Yeah. They were. They wanted me to develop normally, and they didn't want me to become the center of interplanetary attention. But for a long time, I thought they just didn't want me to be special. I kind of saw their reasoning, though. I kept a lid on it through university. Slogged through the classes. I'm not a genius; I just know all languages. I'm grateful now for the experience. What I got was an education, and also a full dose of humility, watching other students do better than me at almost every other subject.

"I was twenty-two when I decided I'd had enough. Kind of like you, I decided I wanted to prove myself. I grew up reading the stories of Allan Quatermain, a Late English adventurer, and I wanted to do what he had—go on impossible quests to unknown lands. And I wanted to make a name for myself in a way that had nothing to do with my ability—yet had *everything* to do with my ability. By exploring the Lost Planets, I put effort into something that anyone could have done, had they wanted. But only I could be the one to translate the languages.

"And I did. And I published a book about it. And suddenly I had everything I'd wanted: I had the attention and the recognition. People knew my name. I'd contributed to science and the humanities. And...I hated it. My parents were right. I had journalists crawling up my ass, my time wasn't my own. I wasn't my own. I actually went on my next quest to escape the media attention, but of course when I got back, everyone wanted to know if I'd write a memoir about it."

"Oh. Wow."

"So that's my long way of saying, 'I didn't want to.'"

"That's intense," Chas said. "I'm sorry it was like that. But I'm glad you did. Write the memoir, I mean. I wasn't kidding when I said it saved my life."

"Yeah," I muttered. "Me too."

The blackness in the tent had taken on a character of its own. Our body heat warmed the small space. Although I couldn't see the sky in here, there was still something about sleeping on a planet that was so different from sleeping on the station. A different quality to the silence and to the air and to the surface I slept on top of—especially the surface I slept on top of, which currently knobbed against my spine. A slithering aliveness moved under the surface of planets that was different from the mechanical buzz of a ship or space station. And with no ceiling or walls, I could fly apart in every direction.

But there were walls, here in the tent. And the warmth of bodies. And an aliveness near me that was different again from the aliveness of the planet. A sound of breath different from the breath of the breeze outside.

Quietly, Chas said, "London?"

His whisper sent a frisson up my spine. It closed the distance between us, made it into a bedroom, and here we were, under the same covers.

The tent really was a bad idea.

I swallowed hard, a wet sound in the utter quiet. "We should get some sleep."

For a few moments, we both just breathed.

"Good night," he whispered.

I closed my eyes, but it was a long time until I fell asleep. I really was glad Chas was alive and well. I listened to his breath even into the rhythm of sleep, and the sound of it made a pain in my chest.

"Night," I mouthed.

CHAPTER TWENTY-ONE

Things looked brighter in the morning. In the literal sense. The sun came up hard, illuminating the tent walls so it was like waking inside a paper lantern. I came to with a numb arm and a sore hip and about five kinks in my back, one for each of the round stones I lay atop.

Chas was gone. I heard soft scuffling sounds from outside and sat up, still disoriented and muzzy. I'd woken from an intense dream in which I was rescuing Chas, who hung from the lip of the ship's door. The impact of landing had thrown him out the threshold and he'd caught the doorway with the fingers of one hand. I gripped his arm in my hand, ready to pull him back in, when an angry pterodactyl swooped into sight—and I woke.

Chas crouched outside in an undershirt and his cargoes, fully grounded and uneaten. He looked up from fussing with the water purifier to see me peering out. He smiled, and suddenly, the sun didn't seem so bright by comparison.

I scowled. "What are you doing?"

He clicked the top of the water chamber shut and pressed the On button. "Purifying water."

I squinted at him and emerged from the tent. The clear blue sky had not a single cloud or sign of life.

I rubbed my eyes under my glasses, resettled those, and ran a hair through my hair. Judging by the amused glance Chas shot me, I might have made it worse.

"Sleep well?" he asked.

I made an unflattering sound. His pack lay open on the ground nearby. The food dispenser poked out from the mouth of the bag. By the wrapped packages of food piled next to the bag, I gathered he'd already used it to make rations and repacked it. I glanced up at the sky again.

"I made enough for a couple of days," Chas said. "I thought I'd get a move on before company arrived. I also double-checked our direction on the handheld. Once I'm done with the water, we should be good and free of technology for at least a day, and that's only because we just don't have enough space to store much water."

I surveyed his labors, noticing now that several of the stones had been cracked open like eggs, and weren't stones at all, but hollow, empty vessels. I was sure they hadn't been empty when Chas opened them, and had an uneasy feeling about the water now drizzling into the canteen. "How long have you been up?"

"A few hours," he said, and I couldn't quite put my finger on it, but there was something kind of evasive about his tone. He handed me the canteen. "I figured this might be our last solid night of rest, so I didn't want to wake you."

I accepted the canteen with a grunt of thanks.

"How was it, anyway?" Chas said, before I'd even got the mouth of the canteen to my lips. "The Mi'hani. How did they treat you?"

I paused with the bottle at my chin. "Professionally," I said, and took a drink. I made a face.

"Funny. That's the same look you made when you tried the absinthe."

Our gazes met. He flashed a white smile and went back to filling canteens.

I rolled our bedding tight and broke down the tent. It was well after dawn, the sun already well on its climb up into the sky. We really should have been out of here at first light, but I wasn't going to chastise Chas about that.

After breakfast, we didn't talk. By unspoken agreement, we traveled quietly, ears open for the sounds of distant engines, attention sharp for shadows from above. I enjoyed Chas moving beside me. Now that I knew it, the vanguard experience was obvious. Those lean limbs leaped and ducked behind rocks with a graceful efficiency that reminded me of Switch, the tiger. He met my eye once and grinned that crazy grin of his, and it was so like him that I grinned back.

We didn't sweat much, not on this dry planet, but I felt the water being sucked out of me by the parched pucker of my mouth and the exhaustion that dragged me back like an undertow. I rationed my water, taking small swallows to keep my palate moist.

We reached the foot of the mountains by early afternoon. Flat, chalky ground gave way to steep inclines strewn with pebbles. Twice, we saw ships in the sky—one coming, one going—and flattened to the ground, but we might as well have been mites hiding from a hunting hawk.

The white dusty ground turned to a pale-tan bedrock that tended to break off in pebbly chunks, hazardous footing if not for the webwork of pink tubes clinging to the ground like a net holding it in place. Chas guessed they might be related to the hollow stone things we'd slept on last night. I tried not to grab them with my hands, out of practicality more than delicate ecological sensibilities, because I didn't know how well they'd hold up to my weight—which was quite well, I discovered when I found myself dangling from a cliff by a handful of tough rubbery stem.

I swung my feet up onto a nearby ledge and got my legs under me again. The movement came to me naturally, an automatic response, my body remembering the old routine. Pain of death and injury had a way of focusing the attention in a way a safe, controlled climbing gym could not.

But I never looked down, because that way lay death.

Chas, on the other hand, stopped frequently to look behind at our progress and the growing vista. Quite stunning, by his reactions. "Incredible" was the word, as in, "Dr. Wells, this is incredible. You can see the entire Mi'hani camp" and "Look at that incredible horizon" and "You have to see this. You can see the forest we landed in from here. It's—"

"Incredible, I know," I said.

☆☆☆

A dry lightning storm blew in. No wave of damp air preceded it, just a crackling charge that made my hair stand on end and inspired me to power up the steep path, leaping rocks and short gaps that dropped away to nothingness.

Chas spotted a cave. "Cave" was an optimistic word for it. There was just enough room for us to huddle inside, if one of us wanted to sit on the other's lap. Chas crawled in first and I ducked in after him.

"Sorry," he said, and his elbow was in my face. His feet materialized in the place I wanted to sit. We were all shoulders and noses.

My forehead cracked against his. "Ow—quit moving."

"Sorry," he said again, and went still. I slid to a seat, and my shoulder nearly pressed against his. The roof of the cave angled so we both had to lean forward. We held still and tense—maybe me tenser than Chas, trying to maintain the centimeter of space between us. His breath was in my ear. I wanted to snap at him to...what, stop breathing?

"You know," Chas said. "It's okay if you want to relax your head back."

I bit my tongue.

Lightning crashed down outside our little pocket in deafening cracks that shook my nerves, the few I had left. Gradually, strain from the muscles in my neck traveled up. I had to move. But it wouldn't be out and it wouldn't be forward. Even if I'd wanted, my own body wouldn't allow it. A deep instinct for self-preservation locked every muscle against the danger.

So I leaned back in increments, easing the tension centimeter by centimeter until I'd settled back against Chas. I saved my head from his shoulder, until the last stubborn pain in my neck caused me to relax even that.

Chas didn't say a thing. His breath rose and fell beneath me—stiffly, I thought.

The darkness of the storm deepened into the night. The straight, hard spears of lightning gave way to thick whips of light, then fizzing nets that snapped across the sky.

We breathed into the quiet between cracks of thunder. Our huddle space smelled like ozone and sweat. The cold of night descended, but the three walls and ceiling of the cave cut the wind, and our body heat created a bubble of warmth.

CHAPTER TWENTY-TWO

The storm roiled till shortly before sunrise. I slept on and off hunched over my steepled knees. By the time the first light of day tinted the sky, I had a wicked ache in my neck and my legs were asleep in ways I hadn't imagined possible.

Chas fished rations from the pack, and we ate them in the chill, quiet dawn. I found a pair of painkillers in a small hidden pocket in my pants and swallowed them down with flat canteen water before the pressure in my skull could expand into something more urgent.

We left the cave soon after the sun appeared over the horizon and walked with the heat of it on one side and the cool air of night on the other. Lightning still snapped in the distance, deeper over the mountains. The air had never felt so alien as then, charged with chill and ozone. Smarter people would have stayed sheltered. We needed any headway we could get on the Mi'hani.

It was a grim, challenging climb, as stiff and exhausted as I was. The low gravity made for easier climbing in one sense, but I winded easier in this atmosphere and, tired, misjudged my movements, shooting too far past some footholds and too shy of others. More than once, I found myself my scratching for purchase with boot and fingertips.

Yet somewhere in the afternoon it occurred to me that our path up the mountain, as demanding as we found it, really was like a path, a narrow trail that switched back and forth. Almost like something created.

At last—thank every deity—we reached a proper cave. The sun tilted heavily in the western sky, throwing the cave mouth in shadow. I briefly consulted the handheld, but couldn't tell if this was a cave the Mi'hani had already searched. My memory of the Mi'hani map was already blurring with memories of Sita's maps. The shelf of rock outside the cave looked untouched. The only footprints were ours. Looking at the screen of the handheld, I was startled to realize how close we'd come to the actual site.

We stepped inside. After the glare of late afternoon sunlight on stone, my eyes took a minute to adjust. I couldn't place the smell of the place. Something old and beyond the ken of man, the bowels of an alien earth exhaling up through this vent. I suspected some geologic process or exotic, deep-rooted life-form that coiled in the darkness of the mountain.

I looked at Chas. He shrugged. It was quiet and dry in here, the ground covered in pebbles, but otherwise empty. I sank to the ground, and Chas lowered next to me.

"We should probably stay here," I said. "We've a better chance—"

Chas made a sharp motion with his hand. I stopped. I heard it, too. A rumble, barely perceptible but growing. It seemed to come from the stone itself.

Earthquake?

Chas and I exchanged a look of alarm. We dove toward the entrance of the cave just as the rumble separated into the beat of a thousand wings scratching at the air and cave walls.

The cloud descended.

I threw myself to the ground in a huddle. Tiny sharp claws scratched at my joined hands where they shielded the back of my skull. Wings tangled in my hair. Chas shouted wordlessly under the deafening screech. They weren't big, these creatures—but neither were piranhas.

I threw myself from the cave. The change in acoustics told me I'd made it out. I reached for my gun, but what would I shoot?

"Dr. Wells!"

Chas stood just inside the cave, waving his hands at me. The swarm had left him and was following me.

I threw down the gun, struggled briefly with the bag, and tossed that down after it. The swarm dispersed and coalesced again. Claws pricked my exposed back. I struggled to detach my flashlight, but couldn't get the catch. Instead, I grabbed the back of my shirt and hoisted it off, chucked it to the ground. My pants next, fingers scrabbling with the belt. Kicked off my shoes. I didn't know what possessed me save that, to my panicked brain, I didn't know what else it could be except some electronic I carried.

I hopped back. The swarm rippled and swooped away from me. Chas and I watched in fascination as it fell upon my clothes, made a tight spiral, and condensed around my shoes.

I must have been a sight to see, arms propped behind myself, legs akimbo, disheveled and half-naked in my boxers and undershirt. But when Chas met my eyes, there was no humor there, only wide-eyed surprise.

I crawled back into the storm on my belly and elbows. Thin white scratches scored the backs of my hands and arms, but none had broken the first layer of skin. I ducked my head against the tangling wings and grabbed a shoe.

I found it on the bottom like a pebble wedged in the tread, a tiny device. I pried it free with my pinky nail and crushed it between thumb and forefinger.

The swarm lifted. Chas ducked as it blew back into the cave. Our eyes met—he, kneeling on the ground with his hands over his head; me, on my belly before the wreckage of my clothes with a shoe in one hand and the crushed remains of a tiny machine in the other.

My ears rang in the sudden silence.

Then I was on my feet, dancing back into my pants. Chas scooped up the bag and swung it onto his shoulder. I didn't waste breath protesting. I was too busy yanking on my shirt.

Good-bye to the cave and its promise of stretched-out rest and fresh rations.

"I can't believe myself," I said furiously. "I can't believe I didn't think to check. They let me keep my boots. I'm an imbecile!"

Chas leaned into the cave to scan the ground where we'd been sitting, patted the bag at his back and the water pouch hooked at his waist, gave me a once-over. My shirttails flew free and one boot was hiked up over the pant leg, but I was accounted for. I holstered the gun. Chas turned and pushed on up the path.

"How far do you think they are?" Chas called over his shoulder. "To stay in tracking distance? What do you think—sound waves?"

"It's the only thing they'd be able to track up here with consistency." It would have had to been something too high to register—for our ears, anyway. The Turrian bat analogues had heard it loud and clear. I glanced up. No sign of a ship—yet. The only thing we could do was put distance between ourselves and the last place the device had been active. We'd been stationary there just long enough for them to get a read on the coordinates, if they'd been tracking us.

The path narrowed precariously. It had leveled out, at least, but every other step sent showers of pebbles falling over the sheer drop. I fixed my gaze on Chas' back and moved forward.

He stopped.

"What?" I asked.

"Dead end."

"No."

I slapped a hand to the cliff wall to steady myself. I'd come to take the trail up the mountain for granted. A dead end didn't register.

Chas turned aside so I could see over his shoulder at the place where our narrow shelf of rock dwindled into nothing.

"We must have passed another trail behind us," I said.

"No. Look. I think it continues up there."

I followed the point of his finger to a place about a hundred feet up where the cliff wall fell out of sight, recessed from view, which meant we were most likely looking at a shelf of rock like the one we stood on. I opened my mouth to protest, but the words clotted in my throat with the wad of dry spit there. We really had no choice.

"I'll go first," I said, with a quelling look at Chas that broached no argument. I fit the toe of my boot into the closest foothold and gave the wall a quick survey.

As climbs went, it was challenging, but not desperately so. It was pockmarked with some proper hand and footholds, along with some leaner fingerholds. Nice, uneven stone. Our only issue, besides being thousands of feet high and on the run from the Mi'hani who could show up at any time, was the threat of the rock crumbling under our weight. Of course the only way to test it was to bear weight.

I climbed, but didn't allow myself to think of it as one. I pretended I was always only one foot off the ground, and that each step was just my first step up. Between each move, I plastered myself to the wall, imagining I lay horizontal on the floor and the wall was the solid ground beneath me. My vestibular system rocked unsteadily and threatened to capsize. My hands grew sweat-slick. I swiped each over the front of my shirt to dry them.

"Shit," I breathed, and came to a stop.

"What?" Chas' voice came from not far below, rough with strain but solid—raw and human in this bare, vertical landscape.

I scanned the rock above me. I'd been so focused on taking each step, testing the strength of each handhold, I'd drifted from my original path and climbed myself into a dead end beneath an overhang.

"Oh shit," I said again. At the thought of backtracking, my stomach twisted around my lungs.

I peered to my right, where the cliff wall leaned out and bypassed the overhang. There was even a little foothold that looked like it could handle my full weight. Not far above was the top of the wall—within tantalizing reach, if I could just reach the foothold.

"What are we doing?" Chas said.

"Testing our skills. Fancy a challenge?"

He made a sound that might have been a laugh.

I flexed my fingers in their handholds to test their strength. Took a deep breath. Readied myself to release my legs, but stopped just short of it.

"Hey, Chas?"

"Yes?"

I swallowed. "I just want you to know...I'm really glad you're here."

He released a soft, surprised chuckle. "Yeah, me too. Not literally right here, though."

I breathed a soft laugh and closed my eyes. Then I opened them and released first one leg, then the other.

Dead hanging, they called it. An apt name. The world came to a stop as I hung there, dead weight hanging by nerve and a prayer. My arms quivered, and I was grateful, so grateful, for the hours I'd spent in the climbing gym. There I was, hanging from the rungs again, the mat a few feet below me, except it was really empty sky and a dry breeze, featherlight hands ready to claim me.

I turned my body. Rock scraped as I reached across the distance with my leg and brushed the edge of the foothold. With a heave of my abdominal muscles, I had one boot toe firmly on rock, then the other. I swiveled, released my hands—the world tilted and opened its jaws beneath me—slapped stone, and grabbed hold.

"Are you all right?"

I swallowed. "Yeah." Blood thundered in my ears. Dust had gotten into my mouth and coated my tongue and palate.

The lip of the cliff's edge was ten feet above. I wanted to reach up one hand and haul myself up. I wanted to lay here flat against the wall and give myself to the stone. I wanted to toss my breakfast.

"Take your time," Chas said.

I gave my head a little shake. I reached a hand up and took the next handhold. Stepped up and away, making room for Chas to follow the same path I had.

I heard the scratch of stone and Chas' grunt. A moment of silence. Then a booted foot landing on the foothold beneath me. Hands grabbed the wall.

I released a breath I didn't realize I'd been holding. Good. Just a few more feet from here.

I had the sudden recollection of standing on a boulder under an amber sky, peering up at the lip of a plateau. *Almost there.*

Chas strangled a yelp below me.

"What? What's wrong?"

Ragged breathing. The scratch of fingers on stone. Then: "My leg. It's giving."

My heart pounded against the wall. The edge of the cliff was two steps above, close enough for me to leap in this gravity. I'd had rope in my pack. That was gone now.

Chas gasped, shifted, went silent. A tiny avalanche of dust and pebbles rained down beneath him. "I'm fine for now," he said. "Holding on by my fingers. London. My ankle. There's something I didn't tell you about accelerating the healing brace."

"Don't talk," I said. I could make it to the top, reach an arm down—make a rope from my clothes—gods, anything.

More pebbles scratched and skittered down the wall below Chas. "All Father," he gasped. His voice changed, went small with panic. "Dr. Wells."

I looked down. Chas' desperate eyes met mine. The wall crumbled beneath his hands.

I swung an arm down, grabbed the top loop of the backpack just as his hold gave. My own feet were planted on solid stone, but at the sudden view of the grand vista below us—horizon and field stretching out and the plunging mountainside—vertigo grabbed me. I was standing still and yet pitching forward into open space, mountain heaving beneath me. My grip loosened.

A hand grabbed my wrist and hauled me up. Stone scraped my chest. The world dropped away from me. Then I was being dumped on solid ground at a pair of booted Mi'hani feet.

I rolled onto my back. A circle of guns surrounded me. I noted these but couldn't register the threat. I flipped over, darted for the cliff's edge. Nausea slammed up. "Chas!"

Someone grabbed the back of my shirt collar. I swung for a wild punch. The body dodged, hauled me back. Other men went to the edge and dropped to their knees. Someone shouted for rope.

Tense seconds passed, and then Chas emerged over the lip of the cliff, paler than I'd ever seen him. He scrabbled onto the ground and looked around at the party of men and women, a play of surprise and anger on his face. He rose on his knees and put his hands up.

"Let me go," I said, but the grip on my shirt stayed tight.

"Well, well, well," said a familiar voice. Mr. Myall stepped forward and looked us over with the mockery of a smile. "The famous London Wells—and entourage."

"Let me go," I said again, the panicky feeling rising.

"We've just gotten you back, why would—"

I puked.

The man holding me leaped back with a shout. There were mixed exclamations of surprise and amusement and disgust from all around. Myall barked a command.

I sagged on all fours, vaguely pleased to see I'd gotten some on Myall's shoes. "I told you to let me go," I said hoarsely, and wiped my lip as I looked up at him.

"Give him water," snapped Myall.

Murmurs of protest. No one wanted to give up their clean canteen. Finally one was thrust in my face from behind. It was the man who'd been holding my shirt collar, looking surly—probably not pleased I'd splattered his trousers. Good to know I wasn't the only one having a bad day.

I poured the water into my mouth, swished, spat, and drank. Drank more. I shook the canteen so the few drops left rattled, and handed it back.

Myall looked Chas and me over with obvious distaste, the smugness gone.

"Someone get him to his feet," he said. Pointing to my man, he said, "You—clean that shit off."

A broad hand gripped my arm. Nearby, Chas was also hauled to his feet.

Even puffed with anger, Myall was an inch shorter than me, I noticed with some surprise. "You'll take us to the site," he said. "Don't even try to tell me you don't know where it is." He clicked his fingers. "Search them."

I was treated to another rough and efficient pat down, and my wrists were cuffed. The atmosphere was tense. Two men and a woman stood in a loose circle with Myall, guns drawn. They looked harried and displeased.

Eight guards altogether. I was a little bit flattered.

"Nothing," said one of the men searching Chas. "Just water and rations."

This took an instant to register. I glanced behind to see Chas standing not far from the edge of the cliff where he'd been dumped, no bag straps on his shoulders. He met my gaze levelly.

One of the goons—not so bright—cried, "He was wearing a pack when we hauled him up!"

"You—!" Myall's face flushed red. He choked on the rest of his words and smothered his face with his hand.

Chas' other guard looked over the edge and didn't say a word.

The emotional shock hit me then. Or it might have just been the sheer exhaustion. I sagged into the hand gripping my arm.

Myall's eyes glinted in his pink face. "Give him more water. And a stimulant tab. I know you keep them, so don't look at each other."

Another canteen of water was produced, and a small yellow pill. Myall himself unwrapped a ration bar and stepped forward to feed it to me. I had the distinct feeling of a horse being fed and watered between races. I had the vague impulse to refuse.

Myall tossed the wrapper to the ground. "Hold tight to that other one, and get ready to toss him over the side at my order. If Mr. Wells gives us trouble, we'll send his friend off."

We set off up the trail, which was wide enough for two to stand shoulder to shoulder. Above us, the gray sky brooded, threatening another storm. We trudged on in an electric silence. I was held firmly, but not as roughly as Chas. They'd identified him as the troublemaker. The irony was, he'd been the last to look at the handheld, and of the two of us probably had the better idea of our destination. I held onto that kernel and walked on, docile.

The guards passed uncomfortable looks between themselves and up at the sky. Myall's own face was stony and set as he hiked forward. A man deterred neither by fate nor the threat of third-degree lightning burns.

Chas walked ahead of me, flanked to his left by a guard. He kept pace, but I noticed the limp in his gate. He favored his injured ankle. Just a small shove, administered in the right way, and he'd go pitching off the edge.

No denying the path was truly a path now. Some alien hand had carved a zigzagging trail up the mountainside. Testament to the tenacity of my curiosity, I wondered why a race of flying creatures would go through the trouble of cutting a trail up the mountain.

Just as I was wondering where our captors had landed their ship, we rounded a curve and I spotted the sleek plane atop the next rise.

Sure death, when we reached that. The doors would close. The threats would begin. I'd be forced to get very inventive—and watch Chas be thrown from the open doors when I failed to produce the research site.

A movement drew my gaze up. I swore I saw a pair of arms waving. When I looked, I saw nothing but an empty ledge. An instant later, a swarm of the cave-dwelling creatures took flight.

I stopped. Several sets of eyes turned my way.

"What?" Myall said. "What is it?"

I chucked my chin. "There."

"There what?" He scowled, followed my gaze.

"Your cave."

He gave me a darkly skeptical look.

"That's right," I said. "Right under your nose."

CHAPTER TWENTY-THREE

There really was a cave atop the ledge. Thank every god for that.

The pilot confirmed it and also affirmed that there was no access to it from this end of the trail save a climb up three hundred feet of cliff face. I had the sudden memory of Sita's voice telling me there would be no climbing. Flat terrain all the way. An easy job.

Right.

The horizon had turned black and snapped with electrical activity. The hairs on my arms swept up. Maybe I'd overplayed my hand. At this rate, they'd save the coordinates, pack Chas and me into the plane, and outrun the storm to return at a later time without us.

But wonders never ceased. One of the guards produced a length of rope and a self-locking device from her pack and hooked up for a climb. She scaled the wall with a practiced precision, setting cams every few feet as she went. At the top, she secured the line and sent it back down, a crude harness attached to the end. Another guard tested its strength.

"You and you, escort him up," Myall said. "The rest of you back to the ship with that one. If the storm comes closer, return to camp and put him in confinement, then return to this location when it's clear. Otherwise wait for my orders."

"Wait," I said, and as all gazes turned to me, found myself without words. I couldn't let them separate Chas and me. "We need him. Without the map, I won't be able to navigate the tunnels. But my associate learned the tunnels. I'm useless to you without him."

"Then maybe I should send you back to camp, is that what you're saying?"

I must have paled.

"The great London Wells, who always works alone..." he said, now eyeing Chas.

In the distance, lightning snapped over the horizon. That seemed to decide it for him.

He clicked his fingers. "You—you up first. Then we'll send Dr. London's *associate* up. Keep your weapon trained on him. Keep it on stun. If he twitches, shoot him. Then you're next, and Wells."

The guard went up, disembarked at the top, and readied his weapon while the harness was lowered for Chas. My heart sat sick at the bottom of my throat while they hauled him up, that gun trained on him. He remained limp and passive while the first guard pulled him over the edge and unhooked him. She pushed him to a kneel and left him like that with his hands cuffed behind his back.

Right. Good. Just like that, Chas. Docile as a lamb.

The next guard went up, and then it was my turn. My feet hadn't even left the ground and already I felt queasy. The female guard pulled me up with an astonishing strength. The world did a little roll. She grunted her annoyance when I leaned over, catching myself against the ground as she wrestled with the harness at my waist.

In moments, Myall had appeared over the edge. My skin buzzed with the oncoming electrical storm. The ground here was the same stone as everywhere else, but something about this ledge felt different, more expansive. I looked up. We hadn't reached the top of the mountain, but from here the mountainside tilted sharply and receded in a peak not far above us. Something about that last stretch of mountainside struck me, and the significance of it hit me an instant later: No path was carved into it. We'd reached the end of the trail.

Myall sent one of the guards to enter the cave first. He ducked through the low opening and disappeared, only to reappear a moment later and wave us in.

After the growing gloom outside, my eyes didn't take long to adjust to the darkness inside the cave. The light from the opening did not illuminate the entire space. Anything could be hidden in the darkness there. Solid walls. Tunnel openings. A swarm of waiting cave flyers.

The light flickered as Myall and the last guards ducked through.

There was a moment's pause as their eyes adjusted and they made the same observations I had.

"Well?" Myall said.

I made a silent prayer. *Chas, play this one up.*

"This way," Chas said, and I could have kissed him for the sound of his voice, confident and deep. He and his escort moved off, straight into the deepest of the shadows. Myall lifted his weapon and powered it to strong stun. He and the guards turned on flashlights at their shoulders.

They didn't light much. The cave was staggeringly large, with a wall that twisted sharply, so we never got a clear view of what lay beyond the next turn.

The opening of the cave became a slash of light in the distance, then disappeared.

"My patience wears thin," Myall said, and I heard the sound of a guard's grip squeezing tighter on his weapon. "There's nothing here."

"It's a large cave," Chas said, with such a casual matter-of-factness I could have laughed. "I can't remember exactly off the top of my head without the handheld, but the tunnel should be close."

We turned another curve, and as if by magic, the wall opened to a short stretch of blackness. For an instant I didn't recognize what it was, and then Chas' guard stepped closer, and his light illuminated the first several feet of a tunnel. The hairs on my neck raised.

Chas didn't look up. Didn't exchange a look with me. Didn't spare Myall a glance. Just walked into the tunnel with his escort at his side.

My guard exchanged looks with another. Guns clacked softly as several pairs of hands readjusted their grips. Myall's face looked set and hard. The light of one of the flashlights caught it at an angle, casting sharp light across his features, deepening his scowl and making a jack-o'-lantern maw out of his frown.

And I was thinking, *Oh please, let this lead somewhere.*

Chas walked on, seemingly unfazed.

The tunnel narrowed to single-file width. Chas took the lead with a gun muzzle at the small of his back. The ground tilted as we headed downward slowly but steadily. There were no cross tunnels, only the single narrow hall of stone spiraling down.

I had gotten my wish. This tunnel most certainly led somewhere, and it seemed to be the heart of the mountain.

Regarding the walls and flat ground, I thought of the zigzagging path up the mountainside, roughly hewn but not natural. Some intelligent hand had deliberately carved this path, as it had carved the path to the top of the mountain. For what purpose? I hadn't thought there were actual tunnels in these mountains. They were something I'd made up. Hadn't I?

The path went on. If we wanted to get out of here, we would have to turn about face and single-file our way back up. I wouldn't risk a fistfight in these close confines, much less a gun going off. The mass of the earth bore down on us, waiting for the right vibration to send it crashing down.

The guard's hand on my arm tightened.

Chas, you crazy bastard, where are you taking us?

Of course, he had no idea, himself. Or did he know something he hadn't told me? I didn't put it past him now. He seemed so sure of himself, I had to remind myself I was the one who had volunteered him for this role.

The air grew thick, clammy. A chill sweat settled on my neck. I cast a surprised look at the stone wall, which looked as dry as it ever had. I wanted to touch the wall to be sure, but didn't dare. A twitch would set these men off.

The path straightened but continued its downward trend. My knees should have ached, but the low gravity mitigated the strain of descent. Chas' guard flashed a look over his shoulder—just a quick glance that traveled past my shoulder to Myall, who walked somewhere near the tail of our procession.

The air was definitely damp now. It made sense Turris, which had little discernible surface water yet supported life, would have some kind of underground rivers for its deep-rooted organisms to tap into.

We had more to worry about down here than a handful of guards—and everything to worry about if one of those guns misfired.

Drowning in a mountain. Having my mind pillaged by the Mi'hani sounded almost pleasant in comparison.

☆☆☆

Chas stopped. We'd come to a place where the tunnel narrowed and turned, so I didn't see him until I nearly walked into his guard, who came to a halt behind him. He glanced over his shoulder, and for the first time since before we entered the tunnels, he met my eye.

That was my only warning before he whirled. The gun of the guard in front of me clattered against the wall. Panic shot up my spine, but no shot went off.

Chas raised a kick at the guard's head, but the tunnel was narrow and he was badly balanced with his hands tied behind his back. The guard caught his leg.

The power-slide of a gun ratcheted behind me. I ducked and kicked my leg behind in a low sweep. My foot hit the ankle of the guard behind me, but without enough force to do anything. He kicked the leg out, upending me. I plunged into the guard in front of me. He and Chas tumbled, and I went with them.

I landed on legs and a backside. A foot was hooking toward my face. I recoiled. Chas' next kick landed against the downed guard's head with a solid *thock*, close enough I felt the wind of impact.

Chas had a grim, wild expression. I struggled back from tangle of bodies, more afraid of him in that moment than the guards.

At a movement from the corner of my eye, I kneed the guard looming over me.

The guard beneath me moved, but that was Chas struggling his trapped leg free of the man's weight. Ahead, past Chas, a cone of light sprayed upward. It took me an instant to understand what I was seeing. The downed guard's flashlight had flown past Chas and dropped to the ground during their fall. The light didn't reach us here but glowed in the space ahead of us, illuminating—

A chamber. Ahead of us the tunnel opened into a chamber.

Chas braced his legs against the ground and heaved toward the room. The guards behind us scuffled and shouted. The one I'd kicked tackled forward.

I'd watched a few dirty fights in basement boxing clubs in Old London. I sat up to meet his dive head-on. Quite literally. Bone and cartilage connected with the crown of my skull. Laws of physics. Two objects in motion. His nose collapsed in a crunch.

He howled.

A shot went off. The sound cracked my ears and ripped through the tunnel.

The idiots.

I kicked and flopped my way over the body of the man beneath me, who had gone completely still.

Pebbles rained down on me. Myall was shouting. The ground rumbled. A new kind of panic went through me, and I kicked toward the chamber. My feet landed on muscle and bone. I didn't care, except it didn't give me good traction.

Rock peeled from the wall. That was just the incentive I needed. I threw myself forward, piling into Chas.

With a roar, the tunnel collapsed.

I pressed my face into the shield of Chas' chest as rock spat down. The ground rattled with the impact of stones falling, and I waited for the world to come down on us.

The rumbling slowed and then stopped.

I became aware of Chas' heartbeat, pounding fast against my forehead. A strong heartbeat. Alive. His breath blew harsh against the back of my neck.

A shiver went through me, and I rolled away.

I opened my eyes. Dim light illuminated a ceiling that vaulted upward, tall after the claustrophobic tunnel. No passage remained where we'd come from. It was now a wall of tumbled stone so close to where I lay that my arm pressed against one of the rocks. The avalanche that would have buried me if I'd landed just a couple of feet closer.

Chas scraped to a sitting position. "You all right? Dr. Wells?"

"Stunned."

He half snorted, half laughed, and then coughed.

I turned. "Are you? All right?"

"Yeah," he said between coughs. The air was gritty with dust. When at last he'd had it out, he said, "Shit," in a low, awed voice.

"You are the craziest bastard I know." Giddiness skirled through me. I had no right to be smiling, here on my back, my bound hands like a rock beneath my lower spine. Tears leaked from the corners of my eyes.

My laugh died to silence.

At length, Chas said, "Do you think any of them survived?"

I swallowed dryly. I looked again at the wall of stone that had been the tunnel.

Myall would have gutted me. A rockslide was a better death than he'd have given me. But the others...

I sat up. My wrists ached. A raw scrape on my left hand stung. I was surprised I hadn't dislocated my shoulder launching into the room.

I tugged gently at my bonds. They were as solid as ever.

The single flashlight beam continued to flare. A fine white snow of rock particles floated through its beam. Its light bounced off the walls, illuminating the whole of the chamber dimly. The room was bigger than I'd expected, but small enough to see all four walls. Four walls, and no door. Or rather, no door anymore.

I swallowed and my gorge rose up to meet it. "Chas."

"Yep," he said, sounding too brisk. "One problem at a time. Do you have anything sharp?"

To slit our wrists? We were at a dead end.

That meant no inflow of air. We'd suffocate before we starved.

I suddenly couldn't get my breath. No wonder I'd been giddy. Another wave went through me.

I willed my heart to stop pounding so hard. *You're burning up all of your oxygen, you imbecile.*

Chas exhaled forcefully behind me in a sigh that was not impatient, but was a sound one step from terror.

"What do you have in mind?" I asked.

Chas exhaled again, this time tinged in laughter. Hysteria. "Jimmy our cuffs. Dig our way out."

"Oh, fuck. Chas." I scooted around to face him. In the gloom, we stared at each other.

He smiled terribly. "If I kill you first, I'll have more oxygen."

I closed my eyes and might have laughed but felt ill instead. I breathed it down. "You are one sick bastard."

Cold sweat prickled on my brow. Our breathing was loud in the quiet that followed. An utter quiet, like a tomb, except for the occasional tiny avalanche of pebbles still falling into place.

I rolled my eyes upward. Maybe it was human nature to look heavenward in supplication, as if to find some message of hope in the clouds or pray for divine intervention. My gaze slid up the smooth expanse of the chamber's far wall, which was lit dramatically by the flashlight. Little juts of rock made long shadows up its length. My gaze tracked up the height to the seam where wall met ceiling and found an optical illusion that made me blink. I looked harder.

"Chas," I said, and pushed to my feet, using the wall to brace myself. I scraped my back but didn't care. "Chas. Look."

He rolled to his knees and got his feet under him.

The wall across from us didn't meet the ceiling. There was a gap of at least four feet, black with darkness.

My heart squeezed painfully with hope, though I tried not to feel it. "What do you think?" I said. "Is that a shelf of rock, or do you think there's an outlet?"

"I don't know. But it's part of the design. Look how straight the ledge is."

"There's a knife in my boot," I said. "You might be able to get it free."

We sat. Chas turned to fiddle with my boot lace with his fingers, which looked like a strange, leggy creature in the odd shadows of the flashlight.

Off came the boot, and I talked Chas through separating the knife from the sole. My own hands had gotten the dense numbness of cut circulation.

Unfolded, the blade gleamed thin and sharp. Chas looked over his shoulder at me.

"Think you could jimmy the lock?" I said.

He handled the knife, feeling the shape of it. He nodded.

"Right," I said, and turned my back to his. We pressed shoulder to shoulder. His fingers played over my bonds, mapping them, locating the lock. He held the knife by the blunt of the blade and worked its tip into the lock by feel. He hissed, tensed. Sucked on his thumb.

I didn't say a word. Didn't move a muscle.

At last he got it in and twitched and tugged until the locking mechanism snapped open.

I leaned clear of the blade and shook my hands free. I gasped as my nerves went up in flames.

"Give me a minute," I said, as I couldn't do more than twitch my fingers. "Are you badly cut?"

"I'm fine."

I flexed my fingers and turned to see to Chas' bonds. Blood had congealed in runs and smears over his thumb. It'd gotten onto the blade. I was surprised his grip hadn't slipped on it.

With fingers still thick with numbness, I used the hem of my shirt to dry his skin. The cut had stopped actively bleeding and didn't look deep. He'd keep his thumb. A relief, considering our only escape might well be at the top of that wall. I wiped the blade.

I didn't know how Chas had managed it. Even with full use of my hands and by the beam of the flashlight, I couldn't spring the lock. He talked me through it with an infinite patience I did not share.

At last it clicked open.

Chas leaned over his hands a minute, then shook them and looked up. So far we hadn't begun puffing like beached fish, so I had hope for a tunnel up there that led somewhere.

At the least, we wouldn't die with our wrists bound. And we had the knife.

"How's your ankle?"

"Still weak," Chas said. "But I'll climb with my teeth if I have to."

He bared said teeth in a ferocious grin, and I felt a sudden and equally ferocious surge of attraction.

"That'd be a feat," I said, almost breathless from that wave. "We won't try that today. How would you like to fly?"

Chas raised his eyebrows. I knelt and laced my fingers together.

"Your turn," I said. Earlier, Chas had thrown me up a wall the same way.

"You're pretending to help, but I know this is payback."

"I'm rescuing you. Steady."

His hand braced against my shoulder as he fitted his good foot onto my joined hands.

"Ready?" I said, and at the answering squeeze of his hand, I heaved him up.

He soared. A little gratifying. It looked like all those push-ups had helped restore some of my old strength.

Though maybe not enough. Chas nearly fell short of the edge. He caught it with his fingers and scrabbled for a foothold. After a scuffling minute, he hauled himself up and disappeared over the edge.

A pebble pinged against the ground. Dust drifted down in the light of the flashlight.

"Chas?"

Then the most beautiful words: "I think we're good."

My knees went weak.

"I'd ask you to throw the flashlight up, but let's not risk it."

"I'd appreciate that." I affixed the light to the shoulder of my collar so its beam shone upward. The wall was smooth, not made for climbing, although once upon a time there must have been a ladder of some kind, because I found grooves to one side of it. They were widely spaced, almost too wide for climbing. The kind of challenge I used to enjoy.

I shook my head. Since when had I stopped existing? Did I really plan on thinking of myself in past terms for the rest of my life?

Chas peered over the edge.

"Watch yourself," I said, as I edged my foot into the first groove, and he drew back. I splayed my hands against the wall, preparing to make the leap to the next one.

And stopped.

I was exhausted. My nerves were shot. Every muscle and half of my bones ached. The sour dregs that were a consequence of my last climb still clung to my gums.

"Dr. Wells?"

I rested my head against the stone wall. Millenniums ago, alien intelligences had cut and smoothed the stone by some unknown means—perhaps by hand, a flake at a time—so that I could lean here against its cold surface. What had this room been used for? Besides the walls themselves, the room was barren, not even a powder of rotted organic material to show where there had been furniture, or storage containers, or even a ladder to climb to the ledge above. Maybe these things had never existed. Maybe we stood in the far reaches of an underground hall that had never been completed. A long narrow tunnel that led into the heart of the mountain to this room—why?

"Dr. Wells?"

"Mr. Chambers," I said, with emphasis. "If I toss you the light, do you think you'd be able to catch it?"

He considered my question, surprised.

"That way you can do what vanguards do best: scout ahead. Get a sense of where the tunnel, or whatever that is, leads."

"All right, but I don't understand why we wouldn't do it together."

"I'm really not as young as you anymore. I'm tired. I just climbed a mountain and hiked down its center at gunpoint. I'm not even sure my heart's returned to my chest after that tunnel collapse."

"It sounds like you're on a roll. One more short climb should be easy."

"I need to catch my breath."

"Catch it up here. Then we'll go slow. I can't hobble very fast anyway right now."

"Chas. I can't." The desperation crept into my voice. I was long past caring. "Just go on up the tunnel and see if there's an outlet. We should be back down by the base of the mountains again."

He stared at me. I could just see his fingers folded over the edge. He must have been lying on his stomach, which gave his words a conversational feel. "You know it makes absolutely no sense for me to go on by myself. I should drop down there and give you a leg up."

"Don't even think about it."

"Don't think I won't. Come on. Just get yourself halfway and I'll pull you the rest of the way up. This can't be more than fifteen feet. I don't even know why we're having this discussion." He extended a hand down.

He was right. I didn't, either. Only, I was done with this expedition. I was done with running and climbing and shooting and carnivorous stalks of asparagus and water cracked out of the carapaces of alien plant mites the size of my head. I was done with the Mi'hani. Just...done.

"I'm coming down," Chas said, and began to withdraw from view.

"No," I said. "Stay right there. I'm coming up."

I sprang toward the first handhold and caught it. The wall tipped backward but I ignored the falling sensation, crammed my toe into the hold, and leaped again. A hand gripped my arm and Chas heaved me, chest scraping, over the ledge. I let out a cry as the flashlight grated against stone and nearly popped from its perch on my shoulder.

I rolled onto my back. The ground twirled beneath me, a ballerina at practice. The flashlight—still attached and working—beamed light over my face, making my eyelids glow red.

"Dr. Wells."

I suppressed a groan.

"Are you all right?"

"I will be," I said, without opening my eyes.

Undeterred by my warning tone, he said, "Good. Because you have to see this."

Something in his voice caught my attention. I sat up. The shadows in the wide chamber shifted as the flashlight moved with me. I unclipped the light and held it up.

Chas knelt a couple feet away. He chucked his chin. "Look."

There, on the wall, shadows resolved themselves into carved crevices. They continued on in a straight row, exact in execution. Inscriptions. Words.

I let out a low exclamation and went to touch them. Each carved segment was as thick as my forefinger, almost sharp-edged with precision, beveled to soft roundness at its greatest depth. I smoothed my hand over the surface, feeling the texture of the Turrian script under my palm.

"Mountain," muttered Chas. "Electricity, colors. Lightning?"

I stood back. "Within the mountain under which lightning strikes—like an angry god attacking the rock—the ancestors' voices live—are shielded, protected—in memory. But that could be stone."

"I think I just got a chill," Chas said.

I nodded, and then I sat. I stretched out on my back, arms tucked behind my head, and let out a long exhalation.

I laughed.

We'd made it. Somehow, we'd arrived at the very place we wanted to be.

Chapter Twenty-Four

We followed the script down the hall. My heart pounded not with fear but in that familiar way when I was onto a trail. A hall like this had taken many workers to carve, and not just unskilled laborers—skilled craftsmen to carve the words, priests or scribes to dictate. Supervisors and engineers. A lot of people, more than one long, narrow tunnel could have permitted. In short, this hall had to lead to another entrance.

Chas held the flashlight while I read. The words flowed in a liturgical cant, never repeating exactly but flowing in the poetic way of Turrian. Beautiful, but with no practical meaning. Gods, mountains, lightning, dreams, power, stone—the words went around and around, almost in spirals, an organic symmetry. It recalled me to a chant. How had this sounded spoken aloud?

The flashlight wavered. Chas held the flashlight in one hand rather than clipping it on his clothes so he could keep the beam steady. But his hand wasn't what had faltered.

The light flickered again.

Cripes.

"Turn it off," I said.

Chas did, plunging us into darkness.

I had never been in darkness this complete. The beginning of the universe waited in darkness like this—gods slept in tombs of stone under mountains.

I backed my shoulder against the wall to reassure myself reality was still intact. I stilled my own breathing and listened. Nothing.

"Chas?"

"I'm here."

I closed my eyes and let out a breath. Then I opened them, which of course made no difference. I had the incredible impulse to reach out and call him to me, to grasp his hand. But he was right there, just a few feet away. He wasn't going to disappear in the blackness.

"We should follow the wall as far as it takes us," I said. "We'll save the light for if we come across any openings or branches."

"That sounds reasonable to me," Chas said. "Want me to take the opposite wall?"

"A good idea," I said, although I didn't like the idea of being separated from him that far.

"All right. Why are we whispering?"

"I don't know," I groused. "The gods are sleeping. We don't want to wake them."

With Chas at the opposite wall, we edged along the hall. So far, we hadn't run into any fauna down here, although my primitive brain told me the darkness drew predators.

"Check," I said. Chas echoed, a few feet behind me. I slowed.

I tried walking for a while with my eyes closed, but I never could get more than a few steps without popping them open, even though my rational mind knew it wouldn't change a thing. My mind kept trying to make shapes out, eyes straining for single photons. Strange possibilities formed out of the Stygian depths. Sightless leviathans. Alien presences.

I'd read too many nineteenth-century adventure novels. I'd lived too many nineteenth-century adventure novels.

"What if there's another cliff?" Chas said.

I stopped.

"Well, as I'm walking slightly ahead of you, I guess you'll have warning," I said, but after that I tested the ground before taking each step. "Speaking of which, how's your ankle?"

"It hurts, but I'm not going to stop."

I couldn't fault the sentiment.

My imagination got wilder with the shapes it wanted to make out of void. I almost felt like I was reaching out of myself to mold impossible dream shapes out of the black clay. The world was a sandbox around me. I began to see gradients in the darkness, maybe the way the void began to separate itself before the birth of the universe. False dawn limned the air in front of me. A hazy hope of light.

"Do you see that?" Chas asked.

Now that Chas had identified it, too, I could make it properly. It appeared like an icy presence waiting in the recesses of the earth, a wraith deadlier than any winged threat because it had no body and was as old as the bones of the planet.

In fact, I realized, this was sunlight—sunlight that had bounced down corridors to this hall which was so black, our eyes could discern even those few photons.

I sagged a shoulder against the wall and let out a long breath. Relief was a painful beat in my chest.

"Tell me you don't want to run for that," I said.

"I do." There was a note of irony in his voice. Then I realized what I'd said.

"Right. Well. Even if we both had a complete set of fully working legs, we can't."

"I know."

"Because we shouldn't run headlong through the dark. And if we turn on the flashlight—that's assuming it doesn't die—we won't be able to see that light anymore."

"I agree."

"So," I said. "Now that that's settled."

The hall grew lighter by degrees as we inched ourselves along. First, just enough to make out the deep shadow of my own arm materializing before me. That relieved me more than it should have. The dark did funny things to your sense of reality.

The hall opened around me. The light sketched out an impression of space and depth. Something moved across the chasm of charcoal darkness, and that startled me. But it was just Chas, slinking along like a wounded tiger.

At length, I could see well enough to walk without aid. I pulled my hand from the wall. Even Chas moved faster now.

He stopped.

We'd come to a place where the hall curved. We'd been going straight until now. Little by little, the light had been taking on a quality of its own—soft and blue-tinted. By it, I could just make out every line of Chas' body as he leaned heavily against the wall.

"I hate to say it," he said. "But that isn't sunlight."

My insides dipped, but the news didn't startle me. I'd begun to suspect as much.

I dropped my shoulder against the wall. Chas peered ahead. The hall took a curve to the right, and being at the left side, he had the better view of where it went.

"Plant life?" I said. Superstitions of ancient gods aside, there were really only so many things that produced light. The asparagus stalks had glowed faintly at night. Subterranean and deep sea creatures on Earth used similar phosphorescence in places otherwise untouched by sunlight—usually to lure prey, a good thing to recall since at least some of the Turris organisms were carnivorous in inclination, as we already knew.

I did not want to discover any new species on this trip—even if the scientific community would be generously inclined to name them after myself. Not the kind of posthumous honor I wanted to receive.

I had a single small knife. Chas had the dying flashlight. Between the two of us, we had a single healthy body—my two working legs and Chas' properly working head.

Or maybe not so properly working. At that moment, he edged forward.

"Chas!" I whispered fiercely.

"Hold on."

"Chas!"

He ignored me and kept going. "It's going to eat you" struck me as ludicrous, but I couldn't think of any other words, so I watched with dumb horror as the light lured him on.

He disappeared around the curve.

"Shit," I said, and sprang across the hall. I made it in three bounds. I grabbed Chas by the scruff of the shirt, but I misjudged the distance in the darkness and we tumbled into the wall.

Chas laughed, his face inches from mine. I still held a handful of his collar, splay-legged and gasping for breath.

"Look," he said.

The hall took a curve. The scrawl of Turrian prayers was visible again, a suggestion of letters in the delicate light.

At the end of the hall—for we had reached the end—was a horizontal line of luminescent blue that ran the edge where wall met ceiling.

"I don't think it's biological," Chas said. "I think it's built."

We approached cautiously, side by side. Chills passed in waves over my skin.

"Well, I'll be damned." I stopped at the end of the hall. We had reached a perpendicular cross tunnel. This new hall curved out of sight in either direction—which I could see because it was perfectly well lit with the strip of light. Like everything else about the hall, it had been carved with exactitude. The light strip was just about a hand's-width high, running along the top corner of the wall and bright enough to cast the hall in a dusky glow. It gave the concave letters of the Turrian inscription extra depth.

Every hair on my body stood on end.

Chas rubbed his arm briskly. "It's like static."

I brushed my palm over my forearm, not quite touching the skin but feeling the brush of hairs. "And here I thought it was just the creeps." I smoothed a hand over my hair, looking up at the softly glowing light. Then: "Chas. Give me your hand."

He gave one over. I touched a finger to his. A snap popped between them.

"Ow!" he hissed, recoiling. Then he laughed and shook his hand. "I'd always thought there was a spark between us."

"It's electricity," I said. "They're harnessing electricity from the storms above and pulling it down here, to power these lights." I stretched on tiptoe but couldn't quite reach the blue strip. "This is the first advanced technology we've ever discovered on a Lost Planet. Of course. They would have had to light the halls somehow. And there is no soot on the ceilings."

I touched my fingers to the wall, feeling the fine grain of it, like it'd been sanded to smoothness, but not to a shine. Soft, matte stone. Almost buttery. I followed the curve of it with my hands. Something told me if I walked this entire hall, it would lead me back here in a perfect circle.

"Dr. Wells?"

"London," I reminded him, absently.

"Do you mind if I record?"

"Hm?" I blinked and looked at him. "Oh. Oh, yeah. I suppose that would be appropriate, wouldn't it?"

"I think so," Chas said, with a smile. The red light in his eye blinked on.

"Right. So. We reached this hall through a tunnel accessed from the highest elevation of the mountains. What started off as a natural cave led to a structure decidedly not natural." I touched a hand to the wall, then crossed to the other side, where my fingers lit on the carved words. "Turrian. A prayer, which is typical to the Lost Planets. But here." I pointed up at the light strip. "This is not typical. A source of light. Artificial light. Still running, because if I'm correct, the race who built these halls harnessed the power of the electrical storms that plague these mountains. This is momentous. This is a first. And these walls are perfectly carved. I can run my hand over the surface, perfectly smooth. I haven't seen this exactness at any other site. Not a seam in the wall.

This was carved directly from the stone of the mountain. Ingenious engineering and architecture.

"All right. We follow the path. Nothing yet, but if I'm correct— Yes. Here. We've come across another hall like the one we just came from. Except this one has a light. Here's more of the same prayer. These halls are arranged like spokes on a wheel, originating from this one, radiating outward."

Which meant the mountain was filled with tunnels, just as I'd fabricated for Myall.

My pace quickened.

"Here's another one, also with a light strip, same prayer. I wonder if there was a light in our first hall but it was broken. Yes, look. Here's another dark hallway, but if you look close you can see the horizontal line where the light should be. Not all of the technology has survived. It's only been a few millenniums. I'm surprised any of this... Let's go back. Let's see where these other halls lead."

Nowhere, actually. They both dead ended in chambers like the one we'd been briefly trapped in, except these did not have doors leading out. Just solid blank walls.

"Maybe these were meant to be tombs," Chas said. "All those inscriptions about sleeping and memories."

"It makes sense," I said. Not an idea I'd wanted to voice. There was still time for them to become tombs in truth.

There were more hallways like these, spaced evenly along the central circular hall. I tried two more of them while Chas waited, resting his ankle. Both of them led to empty chambers. I didn't climb down into them, but from where I stood I could see no evidence that doorways had ever existed against the far walls.

I shook my head as I returned to Chas, and he visibly deflated. "More of the same," I said.

But we still had more to check, and at least one of them had to lead to an entrance. I doubted a work crew had walked single file through that tunnel to the top of the mountain. More likely, that had been for ventilation and emergency access.

I checked a fifth hall. Another dead end.

It became a horrible game. Round and round the wheel, only there was no way out. The hunger I'd forgotten came back as a fierce gnawing, and my bladder pained me until I defaced one of the chambers, with

Chas (hopefully) well out of earshot. I prayed we wouldn't need to use the room for anything. It'd be smelling like an Old London back alley.

I suddenly missed the fictitious England. I'd been tossed on my face once years ago into one of the sim's infamous rancid puddles. It hadn't actually hurt. With the sim's pain effect turned to Low, it'd been an exhilarating rush of flight and an equally exhilarating, though unpleasant, splashdown. Still, not an experience I'd ever wanted to repeat.

Now I'd have given anything to be lying on the cobblestones, blowing bubbles in the morning's sludge. I missed the whores' catcalls. Hell, I missed the monkey. Drusilla.

"Want me to check the next one?" Chas said. The red light was off in his eye. I hadn't noticed when he stopped recording. Even a desperate search for an exit out of an ancient alien tomb got ponderous, I guess.

I shook my head.

"There's got to be another outlet," I said.

Chas managed a thin smile. "We've got nothing but time."

Which was my exact fear.

We came to another hall. I didn't have the heart to go down it. I didn't have the heart to wait for Chas to go down it either, to hang around for him to limp back into view and shake his head.

"We've got to be missing something," I said.

"Like this?" Chas said, from just around the curve.

I hastened to join him, and stopped.

"Like that."

The hall was probably no wider than the others, but it was brighter, which gave it the illusion of space. Each of the walls had a light strip and a line of Turrian prayer, along with a border of geometric patterns that might have been decoration. Nothing especially grand, but it could have been the entrance hall of a palace, the way my heart sped up.

"What do you think?" Chas said. "How about we check this one out together?"

I agreed. If it led to another dead end, I'd need a broad shoulder to collapse on. If it led to an exit, I wouldn't be returning.

☆☆☆

As with the other halls, this one had no side tunnels. Just this single path and its monotonous Turrian prayer, curving ever upward, making it impossible to tell just how far we'd come and how far we had to go. I had the unsettling impression we were walking the same stretch of hallway over and over again in a loop. There was no dust on the ground to show us footprints, if we had. Not a single clue that time had passed inside these walls.

Our footsteps echoed. Easy to imagine they were someone else's. Something else's. A sound being released from the encasement of stone.

And wasn't it strange that other beings existed—several different kinds of beings that supposedly existed independently of each other—that had each developed written language?

And might it be possible that, somehow, there were no other beings at all? That all of these different races were connected not just to each other, but to humans?

That humans were a surviving race of a single species spanning the universe? Never mind these planets had supported sentient life-forms with vocabularies and grammar before Earth's primate prodigies had discovered fire.

There was something big, big, bigger here, in the solid mass of millenniums. I sensed it like a sleeping leviathan under ice. A presence that could roll over, yawn, and swallow us without waking.

I stopped.

"This is all Turrian."

"Yeah," Chas said, looking at me with slight surprise like maybe I'd come a little undone.

The sense we'd been missing something clicked. "This is all Turrian, but where is the alien script? It should be in a tunnel in these mountains. These halls run through them in every direction. Do they connect?"

Chas frowned. "They could."

Only because I was so sensitive to any change, I noticed a slight shift in the atmosphere. By the way Chas leaned forward, tensing as if to spring into action, he did too.

And then the cave-in came into view, a solid wall of rubble that effectively created a dead end.

I didn't say a thing. I simply put my hands into my pockets and rocked back on my heels, regarding the floor-to-ceiling wall of rubble blocking our way.

It was almost a joke by this point. A cruel bit of sport the sleeping gods were having with us.

"Well," I said at length. "We have about six more halls to check. Then we can call dibs on tombs."

"I need a rest," Chas said. He leaned against the wall and winced as he slid to the floor. He pulled up his pant cuff and squeezed his ankle.

I sank to the ground opposite. "What happened, anyway? You said something about the brace."

He flicked me a look of chagrin. "You can accelerate the healing, but the bone won't be as strong. It's usually enough."

But not enough to flee for your life up a mountain. I didn't have the wherewithal to scold him. I'd been in a prison cell planning to stage an escape with a shaving razor. All that seemed like buried history now. Dead and buried under seven feet of rock in a tunnel collapse behind us.

Chas worked his strong fingers over his ankle and up his leg. I had the sudden urge to have that hand on me, the comfort and anchor of human touch in this chill stone hall insulated from time.

I didn't realize I'd been staring until the hand stilled. Chas' gaze, spectral in the blue glow, met mine with mild surprise and question.

I squeezed my eyes and tilted my head back to look up at the ceiling.

Allan Quatermain would have something to say right about now, something gentle and profound about the nature of the human condition. I just wanted to curl into the stone.

"What do you think caused it?" Chas said.

I lifted my head. I eyed the wall of rubble.

He said, "There isn't much damage to the rest of the hall. Do you think it could have been an earthquake?"

I stood. "Odd for an earthquake," I agreed. A few fracture lines reached along the walls and ceiling, but otherwise the hall was untouched.

In fact, the stones looked like they'd been piled. No messy spill of rocks, no pebbles and dust.

I peered at the place where three of the rocks met, at the tiny gap between them. Through it, I could just make out a greenish light.

I touched the gap but couldn't tell if that was a tiny stream of air I felt, or my own nerves. I glanced at Chas. "Stand back?"

Chas rose to his feet. He watched with interest from a few feet away as I scanned the wall of rubble for the likeliest rock. I chose one near the top that abutted the hall's right wall. I wiggled and pulled.

"Here," said Chas, and joined me to grab the rock just beneath it. Together we pulled. The stones shifted and set stubbornly. I cursed and jerked at mine. They ground together, then turned.

We paused.

"Try now," Chas said.

I wiggled my stone. Braced myself. Pulled it free.

I reeled backward with the force. The other stones rumbled. Chas leaped backward. I caught and steadied him.

The rocks, set solidly in their positions for who knows how many thousands of years, slumped and shifted around the new, glowing green hole.

It took us a few minutes to disassemble the rest of the wall. More accurately, it took us a few minutes to remove a couple more stones, after which the wall disassembled itself and we found ourselves standing before a green-lit hall that curved sharply up and out of sight.

The walls here sported a third line of inscriptions, one that ran above the Turrian. I recognized them at a glance. They'd become very familiar to me.

But I hardly cared about these now. At the collapse of the wall, a tide of charged air rolled over us, fresh and sharp with the stink of ozone. *Fresh* being the operative word.

"We found it," I said.

"Your language."

"The entrance."

CHAPTER TWENTY-FIVE

We found it at the top of the hall. The threshold. At first all we saw was a rectangular area of black as if our world had simply ended; then the end of the world flashed a brief and vivid white, and I realized that it was night, and the electrical storm still raged, and this was the sky.

I loped ahead of Chas, but the smell and feel of fresh air had already told me what I needed to know: that this was real, it was here.

The architects had designed the entrance to look out at the sky. I couldn't see the surface of the planet from this vantage, just a shelf of rock and the clashing light show. It was beautiful, really stunning, but I stared at it without any real appreciation for the aesthetic appeal. It could have been gunmetal gray and raining. A breeze streamed over my face, and out there, there were no walls. That was all that mattered.

Chas nudged my shoulder with his. I looked at him. His face flashed in the lightning, and he was smiling. There was something almost enigmatic about it. He glanced back over his shoulder.

"Well?" he said. "I don't know about you, but..."

I turned and regarded the green-cast hallway. There it was, the script that had been haunting my thoughts and dreams. My nightmares, even. Right there in front of me, where it had been for several million years.

It wasn't that I was reluctant to translate it. It was just that this was the easy part. To think of all the trouble we'd come through to get here. All of the weeks, the months of preparation...

And then there was the fact that nowadays it was very rare for me to encounter a bit of writing and not know immediately what it meant. Very rarely could I experience what it was like for most people, who only knew a few languages, or even only one—who could look at this line of pictographs and only wonder what secrets it held.

Was this how Jason had felt, about to retrieve the golden fleece from the tree from which it hung? After making it past the dragon, it almost seemed wrong just to reach out and take it.

"Look." I crouched. "It's the scout bot." I turned the small metal body over. It looked largely intact, no gross structural damage, though its metal limbs flopped like a dead crab's. "I guess now we know why we stopped receiving transmissions. Lightning damage?"

Chas bent down to inspect the black singe mark on its side. "Looks like."

That was a little unexpected. Not quite a disappointment, but... I'd suspected tampering from the Mi'hani.

I looked up to see the wall above the bot's resting place. Two lines of text, Turrian and the alien script, and above that the line of decorative patterns. But in the bot's last transmission, the picture had shown only alien script.

Chas watched me expectantly. "What does it say?"

"I'm not *that* quick," I said. I stood and stepped back. The alien pictographs were carved with the same precision as the Turrian. It was possible it had been added later—hundreds or thousands or millions of years—but if it had, the other race had been careful to use exactly the same methods.

I must have been standing there for a while, because Chas prompted again, "Can you read it?"

I shot him a glance part amused, part annoyed.

"How long does it usually take you, anyway?" he said.

I shrugged. "Not long."

"Do you mind if I record?"

I gave him another look. "But I promise it won't look like much."

"I don't mind. Do your thing."

I did my thing. And it really didn't look like much. I stared at the symbols, first stationary and then walking up and down the hall, slowly. It looked as if the same five feet of symbols repeated themselves. That could pose a problem if there was not enough original text here for me to get a grasp on the language. But I thought I'd be all right. I knelt and looked up at them.

The language was completely different from Turrian, not just in appearance but in form, and it wasn't until I made that realization that the meaning began to emerge for me. The symbols themselves looked decorative, true, and that lent the misleading impression that the language itself was impressionistic. But it was solid and practical, not abstract. In that, it was like Basic. It had one intended meaning, no delicate shades of contextual meaning. That was about *all* it shared with Basic, but that was all right, because the rest came together for me after that.

I stood and trailed my hand through the air, tracing the flow of the words.

"Hail the furious gods. Their voices sleep inside the mountain you strike."

Chas' eyes tracked the wall. It was probably the Turrian he was rereading. "It's basically the same thing."

I nodded.

Chas glanced at me, but I didn't meet his gaze. I stared at the inscriptions, trying to absorb the fact that untold millions of years ago, some alien intelligence had not only gone through the trouble of filling an entire underground complex with this message, it had recorded it in two languages. Not that providing a message in more than one language was by any means unheard of. Humans did it all the time, back to the Rosetta Stone. But this was no political decree. I wasn't sure what this was.

I should take notes, pictures. It took me a moment to remember I was missing my equipment. Another moment to decide I didn't feel like it, anyway. What was the rush? It'd still all be waiting for me when the rescue team arrived, unless this part of the tunnel collapsed, in which case we'd have bigger troubles.

And then there were the four other halls to consider. We'd passed them on our way up to the entrance, four darkened side halls I hadn't paid any attention to at the time, my sole focus on the promise of escape. I'd want to get back to those and see where they led. But right now, I was tired.

I returned to the entrance and settled down against the wall a few feet in, close enough to look out but not so close I risked ending up like the scout bot. Chas sat against the opposite wall and stretched out his bad leg. The red light had gone out in his eye. Had I disappointed him? I'd warned him it wouldn't be much of a performance. I could have made more of an effort for him, though. In the past—for other languages, for other students and colleagues—I had. I enjoyed giving a running commentary, explaining the process as it unfolded. Not that I could ever find adequate words to describe it. How did you explain intuition? Right now, it just seemed impossible.

Actually, I was surprised I'd been able to crack that language at all, given the state I was in. My brain could have been one of the cold stones we'd toppled back there. When was the last time I'd rested? The room at the Mi'hani camp? No. The cave, cramped against Chas. Right. Watching the light show, just like I was now. My body felt like stone, too. Dense. I felt like I was exhaling more than inhaling, slow and shallow, like a tide receding, sinking into the mountain.

☆☆☆

When I woke, the sky was solid black. Yet the space around me glowed a steady soft green. I peered up and the reality of the hall came back to me. The hard stone behind my head, the chill electrified air, the stiff clothing and stiffer joints, the dull hunger. The impossible bleakness of the situation, which was matched only by our impossible escape—escapes—from death and imprisonment. And Chas, sitting across from me, alive and asleep with his hands laced on his lap.

I flexed my fingers and moved my toes in their boots. I was afraid of what my feet had become, stuck in those boots. Best not to remove them now and find out. I swallowed dryly.

I sat up in degrees. Chas' chin rested at his chest, but at the scuff of my movement, he opened his eyes. He looked at me, blinked, and stretched his mouth in a tired greeting.

"How are you doing?" I croaked.

Chas scrunched his eyes in an expression between a smile and a grimace. "I've woken in worse situations." He ran a hand over his head and rubbed it.

The stone was cold and hard beneath me. I was aware Chas' body, hard as it was, would have offered a softer sleep, and warmer. Not that I'd actually meant to sleep, if what I'd gotten could even be called that. More like I'd passed unconscious without the help of a blow to the head.

"How are *you* feeling?" Chas said.

"Alive." And feeling every bit of it. Would being alive ever stop hurting again?

At least right now it was just sore bones and a general all-body ache that would go away with a mattress—hell, even a pile of leaves—and a real night of rest.

"It's still night," Chas said, as if reading my mind. "Why don't you get some more sleep? I can stay awake. I don't need as much. And I don't mind if you use me as a headrest, if that stone's giving you a kink."

It was tempting, so tempting. I could visualize the image of myself leaning on Chas' shoulder too well—or better, curling up with my head in his lap. Like a child, or a dog. Mouth open. Dead to the world.

"I've got all the sleep I'm going to get for now, but thanks," I said.

I stood. I cracked my neck, my ankles, my hips. Then I sat down again, for lack of anything really better to do. It was too dark out to travel. It wasn't as if we were in a rush to go anywhere, except that we'd need to find a source of water and food soon.

"Here," Chas said. He scooted closer and unhooked something from his pants.

I'd forgotten about the canteens Chas still carried.

"No, you go on," I said to the water he proffered, never mind my tongue was so dry it wanted to stick to my palate.

Chas shrugged and took a short swig.

I fiddled in my pocket and found my last two pain tabs. Well, why the hell not? I placed them in my mouth and accepted the canteen from Chas. The water, which had tasted stale to me before, was sweet. I wiped a drop from my lip and licked it from my knuckle.

I glanced up to find Chas watching. His gaze met mine, and my insides did a flip as if I were dropping off the mountaintop again.

His attention veered away. He pulled something from his pocket. Two packages of rations.

I was so astounded, I forgot the odd beat of tension. "What other miracles are you hiding?"

He smiled and flicked me a sideways look. He popped open his package. "This is it. So enjoy."

We ate and shared the water, and I felt better for it. Something approaching human, anyway.

"So how do you think the hive is faring?" I asked. At Chas' blank look, I said, "That was the ant nests' leader we left back there."

His eyes widened.

"What *does* happen when you kill an ant queen, anyway?" I asked with honest curiosity.

"Aren't there other female eggs that develop?"

"Something like that." Hopefully, the heir of this nest would lead the hive off the planet. Out in the black of the night sky, I saw no moving points of light that would indicate ships. I doubted they'd already vacated the planet. Lying low until daylight, most likely.

"Think they've already sent a rescue team?" I asked. Chas and I exchanged a look and glanced behind us.

"The cave-in will stop them, if they even find the tunnel to begin with," Chas said. "They'll probably assume us all dead in the collapse. We hope they do, anyway."

"How *did* you find that tunnel?" I said. "How did you know it led somewhere?"

I half expected another revelation from him like learning he was a vanguard. But he just grinned and said, "I didn't." Then: "How did *you* know that cave was even there?"

I blinked. I looked out at the black sky. I remembered...something. An impression. A hunch.

"I didn't," I echoed. "There were some of those cave creatures. I guessed."

But there had been something else, too, hadn't there? I couldn't recall what.

"Some guess," Chas said.

I grunted.

A mountain wind caught in the crags of the threshold and whistled. It was the only sound.

"So," I said. "As our resident vanguard, how do you suggest we proceed?"

He glanced at me. "Well...I think we're safe where we are. This is probably the best shelter we'll find. It doesn't look like anything living has been in here, and unless the Mi'hani start scouring the mountainside, I don't think they'll find us here. But despite impressions, that was it for our rations. We should probably move back to the spires at daybreak, while we still have our strength. We at least know we can find food and water there." Then, I think to reassure me, he added, "I've been in worse situations."

Just then, I didn't want to know the details.

"So..." Chas said. "What now? What will you do when we get back, now that you've made the biggest discovery this century?"

I harrumphed. "Write an article about it. But that's after I take a shower and eat a month's worth of rations. And I'll only be able to do that after the dean is done cornering me in her office."

"You seem to have a close relationship..." There was something a little more than curiosity in Chas' voice, and I looked at him with surprise.

"Sita and I? She was one of my dad's closest friends. I suppose you could say she helped raise me."

"Really? She looks young. Younger than that, anyway."

I smiled. "She'd be happy to hear you say that."

He grinned back, and I couldn't say why, but my neck heated.

"So what will you write in your article?" he said. "What will you say about the connection between the Lost Planets?"

"That there is one. There's not much more to speculate right now. I mean, there's plenty to speculate, not a lot to go on. I'll have to translate the Anemoi and Beira texts now, but if they're anything like this or the rest of the Lost texts, they'll be virtually useless to us. The lights in here are definitely interesting. Engineering students will want to study them. The technology might tell us what the words can't."

"But you must be proud you have proof now for your theory that there is a connection."

"Sure," I said. "I'm thrilled."

I left to look at the inscriptions again, not studying them so much as absorbing the fact I was here. I'd made it. We'd gotten free of the Mi'hani, found our escape from the caves, located the alien script, and cracked the language. We'd even discovered previously unknown and totally unexpected advanced technology. This was my hour of triumph.

What would Sita have to say? She'd be surprised when I suggested getting a real research team out here, but this wasn't a project for one man. I could appreciate that now, thanks to her pushing. Like I'd told Chas, we'd need some engineering students. And architecture too, maybe. Who knew what secrets these halls held, which were not kept in words?

But then, who was I kidding? The fact was there was nothing here. I couldn't shake that feeling. Empty halls and chambers. Empty words.

I walked down the hall, back to the toppled blockade. Down the hall through which we'd come, the Turrian continued on without pause, but the alien script ended. What was special about this spot, right here? There was no door, unless you counted the barricade of stones, and no physical changes in the hallway to mark it as different from the rest of the hall, unless you considered the different hall light color. But why that, even? And why did the alien script end here?

I couldn't ignore them any longer: I returned to the four side halls. Each was a third of the width of the main hall, two on either side. They had no light strips of their own, but I'd taken the flashlight with me, and I didn't worry about using up the battery now. Time to see where each of these led.

I shone the flashlight into one, and I could see where the scout bot must have taken its photograph. There was no Turrian here and no decorations, only the alien script.

The hall led to a dead end. A true dead end. No empty chamber, no nothing. Just a wall.

I had identical results with the other three halls.

Well, that was...not quite a letdown, because I hadn't really been expecting anything. I switched off the flashlight and lowered to the ground near the corner, where light from the main hall was just enough to illuminate the walls and cast the prayer script into shadow.

Hallways that led nowhere. Empty stone chambers built in an array into a mountain, all eternally lit, illuminating...nothing. A prayer on repeat.

It was all so characteristic of Lost Planet ruins, and even managed to be more useless and random than others. I understood the temples on Anemoi. They had been built for the worship of the wind. Their very design worshiped the winds, and so did the words.

But this was...what was this? For all appearances, a complex of burial chambers.

Burial. Buried...

I stood and touched a word on the wall. Buried. *Safe from the crash of godly anger, may the past thoughts remain buried in stone.*

I stepped out into the main hall to check the words, but my memory was not deceiving me. The translations were different.

I checked the other three halls. They each had different translations.

Divine power pours down. Whispers out of time are preserved from it in memory.

Godly Lightning scourges this temple. May its stone shield the thoughts of the ancestors.

Lightning strikes the mountain. The word memory is found beneath it.

I opened my mouth to call Chas, and then closed it again.

This was something, though I couldn't say what. The design elements, the architecture, and the smoothness of the script all told me that both of these languages had been inscribed at the same time. This entire complex of hallways had been created as a whole—which meant whoever had carved the alien script had also carved the Turrian, and so would know the intended meaning of the prayers and how to accurately translate the text. Which meant they had deliberately installed these different interpretations of the prayer.

One translation in particular caught my attention. *Lightning strikes the mountain. The word memory is found beneath it.*

No mentions of divinity in this translation. The alien language was very clear on its distinction between godly might and the purely scientific phenomenon of charged particles connecting with the ground. It didn't exactly make for stirring poetry—which could be why this translation fell flat.

I left to linger in front of the main hall translation again. It itched at me, but I couldn't think of what *it* was.

And then my eyes fell on the alien word for "mountain." It looked like a mountain, with a broad base and a cleft peak like a stylized mountaintop. Beneath it was the Turrian word for stone and memory—this, a rectangular shape to symbolize a stone tablet. It fit under the base of the "mountain" as if intentionally creating a picture.

Word memory. I'd been reading it as word-memory, as in "a memory made of words"—just an attempt at poetry. But what if it was, rather, the word "memory"? *Lightning strikes the mountain. The word "memory" is found beneath it.*

The hairs on the back of my neck stood up, and this time, it wasn't the static.

No.

No, that couldn't be it.

But there it was: The word for "memory" beneath that for "mountain." And above that? A lightning bolt as decoration.

It could just be a coincidence. Albeit, a very eerie and appropriate one. I couldn't count the number of times I'd been typing and whole strings of words had lined up exactly beneath each other. It happened too often to be just a coincidence, but it was.

I ran my fingers through the carved letters as I thought. Their lines were the width of my fingertips, concave and smoothly polished. It was just an idle action, nothing I thought about until my index finger slipped into an unexpected hole and hit a switch.

At the feel of the little moving button, I leaped half out of my skin. It took an instant for my brain to register that no, nothing had bitten me.

But the floor rumbled under my feet.

CHAPTER TWENTY-SIX

No way. I hadn't escaped near death and made the discovery of my life just to be crushed in an earthquake.

Run! Run now!

But just as quickly as it had started, the trembling stopped. There followed a long, still silence, then the sound of running footsteps. Chas appeared at the top of the hall's incline, saw me, and caught himself against the wall.

I shook my head. "Not an earthquake." My heart, unconvinced of that, staggered in my chest, trying to take off without me. At least one part of me still had its survival instincts intact. I didn't think we had anything to worry about, though. In the aftermath of the scare, my adrenaline-shocked brain was already putting pieces together.

I waved Chas over. His gaze darted around the hall, but he came, his limp more pronounced than earlier. He carried the broken scout bot in one hand.

"This," I said and pointed at the symbol for "memory." The glow from the hall's light strips fell in just a way that it threw the concave letters into black shadow, but when I shone the lamp directly at them, it illuminated the small switch inside. Chas bent to peer at it. He met my gaze.

I said, "What do you want to bet that not all these dead ends are dead ends anymore?"

His eyes widened.

An unholy energy filled me. I tore off down the hall, which looked completely unharmed by the rumble. A few of the stones we'd piled next to the dismantled barricade had rolled to the ground. I leaped these.

When I reached the circular hall, some impulse steered me right, toward the side we hadn't finished exploring. The first hall I encountered led to a familiar dead end chamber. But at the second, I let out a cry.

At the sound of quick, unsteady footsteps, I yelled, "Don't run!"

The footsteps slowed just a little.

Chas jogged up, breathing heavily. He halted and went silent. Together we gazed at the open door against the far wall.

"Do you think it was there the entire time?" Chas said.

"No. Look."

I turned on the lamp and pointed it across the room. A flurry of dust particles swirled in its beam, suggesting some great disturbance had taken place.

"And look," I said, pointing down. Where in the first chamber there had been wide-apart handholds—the very ones we'd used to climb to freedom—there were three broad steps.

"You don't think it's another exit," Chas said.

"No, I don't think so." I turned to the Turrian inscription on the wall. "What's one way to translate this prayer? 'Inside this mountain that the divine lightning strikes, the memories of the ancestors are kept in stone.' These letters here indicate a reverent tone, which I took to mean it's a prayer, just like most of the other Lost Planet inscriptions. But even so. It sounds more like a message than a prayer, doesn't it?"

Chas reread the wall, his eyebrows drawn.

"The alien translation in the front hall is not the only version," I said. "I went back to check those four small side halls. Each of them offered a different interpretation. Which got me to wondering: What if the real meaning of this is not symbolic, but literal? None of the Lost Planet texts ever tells us anything—why? Why, for once, can't it actually mean something useful?"

"You think they've actually buried something here? Ancestors—their dead?"

"No," I said, despite my shiver. "I don't think so. I think it's words, maybe a historical document. A stele. A stone tablet."

Though when I looked at the door, my confidence slipped. The threshold gaped like a gate to the nether realms. *Here the ancestors sleep...*

I shivered again, this time from the cold. A draft breathed up from the door, chill with damp. My heart still hadn't slowed from my headlong dash through the halls. I was hungry again, and there was a cramp in my calf. I could only imagine how Chas felt on his injured ankle.

"We should wait for the university to get here," I said.

"Whatever you think is best."

I looked at him. "You don't think so?"

He stared down at the door with a look on his face I couldn't read in the half shadow. He looked up and said, "I kind of want to see what's there. Don't you?"

The door stood open like a breech into the mysteries.

"Hell," I said. "Yes, of course I do."

I crouched to inspect the steps leading down into the chamber, though on closer examination, my "steps" turned out to be three stone shelves jutting from the wall, staggered in width to create a kind of staircase.

"Seems solid enough," I said, venturing cautiously out onto the first one on hands and knees. In the past, I might have bounded down them like a mountain goat, flying in the low gravity, but we'd had too many close calls with crumbling rocks and I didn't fancy another fall.

Chas padded to the edge, knelt, and dropped six feet down to the second step, swift and graceful despite favoring his injured ankle.

"Well, you make that look easy," I said, and hopped down next to him. We took the third step in a similar fashion and then dropped to the ground. The damp chill congealed over the floor like an invisible mist, clinging to my skin and clothes.

"On second thought..."

"Is that light?" Chas asked, leaning forward.

"I think the devil left the light on," I joked, although the dense feeling in my gut was not humor.

We approached the glowing doorway and looked in. Or rather, down. Another set of shelf-cum-steps led a hundred feet or more down to a hallway. You could only see its threshold from here. Red light spilled from it onto the landing. It looked like a vision of Hell, albeit a cold and damp one.

The good news was, no need for a flashlight.

"What do you say?" Chas said.

"Intriguing."

That was one word for it, anyway. "Terrifying" was another.

"Do you think they actually have something buried down there? It's like this entire place was built as a maze, or a puzzle. Maybe to deter grave robbers. Don't you think?"

"A fair assumption," I said. "Are you sure you can make it down there?"

"It shouldn't be a problem. Coming back up—that's a different question." He grinned at me. "But I've got you to give me a hand, right?"

I snorted.

Caution and curiosity arm wrestled in the pit of my stomach. The only thing stronger than the visceral desire to cringe back to the entrance was the desire to know what lay down that hall.

"We could wait, like you said," Chas said.

"Meanwhile you'll continue to plague me with questions about what I think is down there," I said. "I'll have to suffer a week's worth or more of speculation. You won't leave it alone, until it's easier just to go down there and look."

"This is true," Chas said.

I crouched down. "So we might as well check it out now." I hopped down to the next step.

We descended slowly. It was easiest to sit at the edge of each step, stretch my legs down, and slide down to the next, but I quickly learned to kneel at the edge and jump down. The stone was rough and saturated with moisture, and it only took sitting on two steps to soak the seat of my pants and realize my error. By the time we neared the bottom, the rest of my clothes were heavy with damp from the air. Moisture beaded on my lip and forehead.

"Well, we wondered where all the water must be," Chas said.

"Right. In my pants."

Chas burst into laughter. I lost my footing, dove forward, and fell in a crouch at the bottom of the landing.

"I'm glad you thought that was funny," I groused, running my hands over the seat of my wet trousers.

Chas, breathless, only shook his head and wiped tears from his cheeks.

I stood. It was a hallway like any of the others. A light strip ran the length of each wall, these ones red. Beneath those, at shoulder height, the prayer continued in Turrian.

Perspiration clung to the walls. I ran my fingers over this and came away with drops on my fingers. They smelled like nothing, maybe a faint note of damp stone. I touched them to my tongue and tasted clear water.

"This must lead down to an underground river," Chas said. "Hold on." He pressed his ear to the wall and then to the floor. He nodded. "I hear it."

I took his word for it. I didn't fancy pressing my face to the cold, wet ground.

"Well. Shall we?" I said, with a grand wave of my hand. Chas, to my surprise, bobbed in a pretty curtsy before preceding me.

The hall led us down and down. We had to be well below ground level by now. At last it leveled out. The rumble of water came faint at first, something felt rather than heard. It grew steadily. I wiped moisture from my brow and lip. The chill of the damp ached in my bones.

The rush of water grew to a roar, until the hall ended abruptly and we stepped out into a soaring cavern.

I had the impression of spuming water and a haze of steam, as if we'd entered a godly bathroom during a shower. Only, the god had stepped away too long and the shower had run cold.

White light lit the cavern. For a moment—forgetting it was still night—I expected to look up and see an opening to the sky. But that was a desperate hope. Far above, patches of phosphorescence clung to the craggy ceiling like moss.

We stood at the top of a proper staircase, tall blocks cut from the stone. A broken pillar stood near the bottom step. Its partner had been obliterated. Countless years ago, water must have crashed through and now ran in a swift, shallow channel at the bottom of the steps.

Ahead of us, thick ropes dangled from the high ceiling, smooth and flesh-like in the mist. They reached blindly through the air. Adrenaline shot through my system, but the movement was just the wind of the gushing water blowing them.

How quickly we'd gone from not enough water to too much.

I pulled off my glasses and dried them with my shirt, or tried, considering how damp the cloth was. It was no use, anyway. As soon as I put them back on, they misted again. Of course I would make the discovery of my lifetime and not be able to see it.

"We won't die of thirst now," Chas shouted, conversationally.

"But we're at real risk of drowning." Considering the slick steps, I added, "Or simply breaking our necks."

"Nah. We won't hit the ground hard enough for that. It would take some real talent to break your neck in this gravity, from this height."

The kind of talent I had, in other words.

We descended to the bottom step. The swift channel at its base was only a few feet wide, an easy distance to jump even in normal gravity, but the damp made it treacherous. A slip or stumble could drop you into the rushing current and you'd be off across the room in a couple of seconds, sucked into the underground river system.

"I think we found our roots," Chas said. At my look of surprise, he added, "Not the roots of mankind. I mean, I think we found the roots of our friendly flora above."

I looked at the white vine hanging into the river. Its end jerked in the current.

Before I could say anything, Chas reached out to grab hold of it.

He let go and rubbed the moisture in his hand. Sniffed his palm. "Just water, I think. Condensation." He took hold again and gave it an experimental tug. He raised his eyebrows in inquiry at me.

"No," I said.

He smiled like I'd made a joke. "It's just a short jump." He wrapped both hands.

"Hold on." I took the vine from Chas. "Let me at least be there to catch you."

I swung across the river. Chas came next. The ground under our feet trembled with the power of the big river at the far side of the cavern.

We found a bit of high ground against the near wall of the cavern where we could see through the spray. Had the staircase originally led down to something? If so, the river had swept it away. Strange to see such evidence of natural forces at work on these built structures, when the halls above remained largely intact.

From the patterns cut by the frothing surface of the river below, I got an idea of where stones, or other large objects, lay beneath. They could have been tumbled rocks from the cavern walls, or they could have been the ruins of ancient architecture. Impossible to tell.

"We should come back after our rescue crew gets here," I said. "We could use a couple of raincoats and a good set of galoshes. Not to mention some safety equipment."

"Did I make you nervous with my vine-swinging?"

"I make myself nervous."

Even as I spoke, I made another sweep of the cavern with my eyes. And that's when I noticed it.

"Tell me what you make of that," I said, pointing. The mist congealed, obscuring visibility. Then it stretched away again like pulled cotton.

"It looks like a doorway," Chas said.

"Blast and damn." It was well across the cavern, past a broad span of floor covered in a sheen of moving water. The water had the gleam of ice, but you could see its fast flow by the smooth ripples in its surface.

I said, "I'll go ahead. You stay."

"No way. Uh-uh. We'll both go."

I gave him a look of long-suffering patience. "Your ankle."

"I'll go slow. You won't have to worry about me."

But I did. I hovered beside him as we descended and picked our way over that broad plane of moving water, thinking this was insanity. The thin skin of water moved even faster than I'd suspected, and the constant force of it had polished the stone floor to slickness. The water dimpled over holes and hollows. Chas grinned at me as I played a splashing game of hopscotch to avoid these.

"You try this with fogged glasses," I shot at him.

He shook his head and edged around a pothole with considerable more composure. "No thanks."

Water seeped into my socks. This close to the river, the air shook with its roar. I abandoned my blurred glasses and folded them onto the collar of my shirt, though it hardly improved visibility. The steam consumed us. Drops formed on my eyebrows and beard. I tasted dank stone.

From the outside, the fog had looked like a single entity. From inside, with the light from the ceiling glowing down through it, it consisted of billions of fine droplets swirling and writhing in elegant shapes.

I looked at Chas. Chas looked at me. Even through the fog and without my glasses, I could see the question and interest on his face, and almost a fear. I knew the kind, because it was pounding through my veins. My hand trembled with it.

I stepped through the doorway, into dryness and a great, hushed space. I found a corner of my shirt not as damp as the rest, wiped my glasses, and placed them on.

We stood in a hall. It might have been taken straight from the pages of a northern fairytale. Light from the cavern outside, diffused by the fog, illuminated walls as smooth and supple as ice, with the same semitransparent quality. They flanked a staircase that curved up and out of sight, flared at the bottom and narrowing on the way up, like a grand staircase and lending to the fairytale feeling. Cut out of the same gleaming material as the walls, they caught the light from the cavern and appeared to glow. I thought it was a trick of the stone until I stepped forward and realized they were, literally, glowing. All of it—the walls, the stairs, the ceiling—emitted a faint luminescence, like white marble softly backlit.

Chas stepped in behind me but didn't say anything. Neither of us did. I think for a while, I didn't breathe.

Chas moved, breaking the spell. He cupped a hand against the wall. The pearly light pooled in his palm and silvered his fingers. "I've never seen anything like it."

Walls and ceiling flowed smoothly, organically, not a right angle to be seen. They curved in a subtle but definite way toward the back of the hall so the attention flowed to the stairs, the only hard edges in the room.

I glanced at Chas. He stared, completely still, I approached the steps. It occurred to me then that all of the preceding hours, days, weeks—my whole life—might have been leading to this.

If so, they'd left me too wet and drained to be excited.

I peered up the stairs and said, "It's a doorway. I think."

Difficult to tell from here because the threshold at the top of the stairs had no door, only the arching frame open to a space beyond.

Chas peered over my shoulder.

"I think it is," he breathed.

I shook with a shiver and stepped up, hand instinctively lifting for a rail. There was none.

"Watch your step," I said.

The steps looked slick, cut out of the same softly glowing stone as the rest of the hall. It was not ice. By some trick of architecture or ventilation, the air in the stairwell felt dry. A muffled rumble vibrated low in the bones of my legs, but that was the only reminder of the powerful presence of water outside this chamber.

I went slowly to give Chas time to climb, and because I was in no hurry to see what lay beyond the doorway. A very fine etching edged its frame, something I didn't see till I stood in front of it on the landing. Alien flora, I realized with a pang of surprise.

Chas caught my eye and smiled. The low light from the stone darkened his skin, but the whites of his eyes glowed. He gestured a hand toward the door. An invitation: *After you.*

"Ladies first," I muttered, and caught the look of startled laughter on his face as I stepped past.

It's completely dark, was my first thought. Whatever the source of the stone walls' eerie glow, it was not in effect here—either by design or malfunction. We would have to jiggle some life into the batteries of the flashlight in order to explore further, or come back when properly outfitted, refreshed, and ready to hike through another warren of abandoned hallways.

Though I knew instantly—in my bones, and probably by the feel and smell of the air in here—that there were no more hallways. This was a dead end, a single room, and not too big at that. One door.

Trap, came my next thought.

Then my foot set down on the floor, and my retinas exploded with light.

Chapter Twenty-Seven

I dropped to my knees and threw my arms over my head. The afterimage of light seared across my eyelids.

Idiot!

I came to a stop after a short skid across the floor. Cold and delayed pain radiated up my legs. I'd gone down harder than I realized. Dodging pterodactyls and avalanches intensified your reactions.

The sunburst against my eyelids turned red, then dissolved to deep blue and black. No debris or fire struck my skin. Beyond the resounding impact of my bones against the stone and the thud of my heart in my ears, there had never been a sound.

I lifted my arms and looked up.

The walls had come alive with light. Not the even, ghostly luminescence of the hall just outside, but sharp, thin lines of vivid white.

Save for the shaking in my own arms, all was still and quiet. No explosion, except in my imagination.

I glanced back. Chas stood in the open doorway. He didn't look amused anymore, or even incredulous at my dive. He looked pale and spooked in the wash of white light.

I put a hand to the cold floor and stood. A reflection of the wall appeared in its polished surface. In that peculiar way of stone, it muted the light but enhanced the detail of what I looked at.

What I looked at were vertical lines of very small, very fine script.

I surged to my feet. Chas' eyes popped as I whirled on him and pulled him inside.

"Look," I said, and pressed his palm to the wall. Fine, brilliant text framed our hands and made our fingertips glow red. Up close, you could see them as symbols, symbols I'd never seen before. A new language.

Chas took a beat to catch his breath and recover from the surprise, and then he swore.

I pulled away. Chas smoothed his hand over the wall, taking it in—the script, the height of the wall, the whole of the room. Every bit was covered in light, top to bottom. Every inch covered in text.

Chas laughed as I pressed both hands to the wall and jogged the room's perimeter.

"What do they say?" he asked when I panted to a stop.

I shook my head and stepped back. Hard to tell where one sentence ended and the next began, it was so densely packed and continuous. I picked a line at random and followed it to the floor.

"I don't know," I said. Bits of the text leaped out at me, snatches of meaning that just as quickly disintegrated. "It don't think it says anything. I think they're random words."

"What?"

"It could be another puzzle." I smoothed a hand over my forehead, pushing back my hair, pressing against a headache that had just sprung up. Another bloody puzzle.

"Want me to take a recording of it?" Chas said. "You can analyze it later."

"You mean from the comfort of my office with a snifter of brandy and a pipe? Sounds nice."

Chas flashed me an uncertain smile before turning to make a slow tour of the room.

I must have been more exhausted than I realized because next thing I knew, I was opening my eyes at a surprised sound from Chas.

"What is this?" he said.

He kneeled in the center of the room to examine something on the floor. It was a glowing circle about the size of a dinner plate, the only decoration in the empty room besides the text.

I crouched beside him. I expected the circle to be a flat panel like the hallway light strips, only circular. It took me a moment to realize what I was looking at: a compartment, round like a hatbox, set into the ground and lit from inside.

The compartment was not empty. Inside was a black sphere.

"What is that?" Chas asked.

I reached a hand toward it. My fingers touched a hard transparent surface at floor level. I tapped at what appeared to be glass.

The sphere inside was about the size of my fist, made of stone that swallowed light. Chas blinked and moved his head like me, trying to make it out. A disconcerting, almost disturbing, optical illusion—what appeared as a flat black circle from any one vantage point, yet obviously took up space.

Something else suggested depth, what I took at first for another trick of the eyes. I leaned in, close enough to hear Chas stop his breath, but I wasn't imagining it. A fine filigree covered the sphere, barely visible in the compartment's bright light. Lines no thicker than strands of hair looped in a chaotic pattern.

Chas bent down. "Is that...?"

"Hidden," I said. "Words hidden in the mountain. A secret."

He peered closer and then threw a glance over his shoulder at the writing on the wall.

"Not the same," I said. I tapped the transparent barrier covering the compartment. It made a slight, solid sound, like knocking on solid marble. "This is meant to be opened. That's the key to understanding the script on this. I bet if I can hold it in my hand, I'd be able to read it."

I was still knocking at the barrier with the single-minded focus of prehistoric Man when, with a scraping sound, it slid away.

Chas stood next to the doorway, his hand against the wall. At my wide-eyed stare, he waggled his finger and said, "There's a switch."

I looked at the sphere. Being open lent it a subtle new depth, the symbols delicately touchable.

"Afraid it's booby-trapped?" Chas said.

I must have drawn back visibly, because he held up a hand and said, "Joking."

"No, it's a good point. It could be. But I really doubt they'd aim to kill the person who made it past all of the safeguards."

"I agree."

But still, we stared at it until Chas offered to pull it out for me, and I waved him off.

The sphere had a peculiar lack of temperature. Not chilly like the rest of the room, but not warm either. It simply didn't register against my temperature receptors as my fingers closed around it. Nothing happened, except the faint jolt of surprise at the feel of it.

I removed my glasses to look at it closely. But no matter how I turned it, I couldn't make out the fine writing. It resisted the eye, fading into the black of the stone any time I looked at it straight on.

"Blast it." I pressed the heel of my hand against a threatening headache. "I'll have to do this later." I paused. "I've never taken an artifact before." Pieces of rock, shells, and skeletons. Never what might have been the sole, entire sample of a language.

"If it helps," he said, "I don't think anyone will miss it."

"No," I agreed.

I bundled the sphere in my sturdy flannel long-sleeve, which I tied around my waist. I kept one hand on the knot of the shirt and another resting against the sphere as I followed Chas through the Ice Queen hall and the roaring cavern.

We walked back up the red-lit corridor. I hadn't realized it'd been at such a steep grade until then. We stopped frequently to rest and catch our breath. Neither of us pretended to be anything but exhausted, and there was no reason to hurry.

Come morning light, we would travel to the spires and wait for rescue there. I'd entertain myself examining the sphere in the sunlight. I could trace the symbols into the sand to see them flat, and maybe make sense of them that way.

At last we made it back to the stairwell, or what I thought was the stairwell, except there weren't any stairs.

I glanced behind with an odd jolt. Had we taken a wrong turn? Ended up at a dead end?

If so, the dead end had a dip in its stone floor exactly like the one in the stairwell. I remember because I'd tripped down the last step and landed on it on my hands and knees.

It took a moment for the fear to register, a slow thick fear, delayed by my confusion.

I looked at Chas. He stared up at where the door should be far above us.

"You have got to be kidding me," he said.

"So I'm not just imagining it."

"It could be a joint hallucination," Chas said. "We've spent long enough with each other to share brain waves."

"The question is, whose nightmare is this?"

I ran my hands over the wall where the steps had been. Unlike the other chamber, where the steps each receded into a slot and left a groove to place one's hands and feet, there was nothing here to climb. And even if there had been, the door had disappeared.

I stepped back. I stared. There was nothing. Just that wall going straight up like a mine shaft—one with no opening. The door hadn't opened until I'd triggered that switch back out in the main hall, so it made sense it could close again.

A deep sickness curdled in my gut.

"The excitement never ends," Chas said, touching the wall. "Do you think it was timed?"

"I don't know. Just my luck. Maybe there's another way out."

But if there was, it was several miles and a drowned, battered river trip away. Chas and I returned to the cavern and searched high and low, but came up with exactly nothing. As far as we could tell, there were only two ways in and out of the cavern: via the red-lit hall, and via the underground river.

The ancients had buried their secret well.

"Look at this," Chas said, when I'd swung back across the rivulet to the stairs. He crouched near the ruins at their base. "I think there might have been a switch here to operate the door. It would make sense they'd build some way of allowing themselves out."

Because of course that would be the sane thing.

"Here," he said, and showed me several broken pieces. "This edge, here. And here, this was hollow. I think another piece fit in here, and toggled on this part." He looked at me.

If it had ever been a switch, it was well past saving. I surveyed the rubble covering the ground. There were small ditches and piles where Chas had obviously been digging through to find the pieces he showed me. He'd gone through methodically, but there remained the hope of finding another buried underneath. Maybe just the right piece to fit into that groove he'd pointed out, and then I'd find a way to articulate it with the mechanisms inside the pillar...using my bare hands and spit...

I stood from my crouch. "I need to get out of here."

Chas gave me a wide-eyed look but didn't say anything as he set the pieces down and followed me back up the hall, away from the constant roar and blowing spray. I was cold enough to have stopped shivering, and I'd gotten used to seeing through the blur of my glasses. I couldn't remember what "dry" meant.

Back in the stair-less antechamber, my flannel lay on the ground with the sphere tied into it, forgotten. I sat down and put my head back against the wall. I almost couldn't feel my fear past the pain in my head.

"London. Take a look. Tell me what that looks like to you."

I peeled my eyes open.

Chas said, "I think there's another switch up there. Do you see?"

I twisted around to look up the height of the wall.

"No."

"There," he said. "In the little recess right next to where the door opened. Right there."

My heart made a sluggish attempt at an excited beat. But: "What the hell good would a switch do with no stairs leading to it?"

"If the Turrians were a flying race, they wouldn't need the stairs."

I pressed my forehead against the heel of my hand. "Then why the bloody hell bother with stairs in the first place?"

"If there was another race that didn't fly."

I pinched the bridge of my nose.

"The race who wrote your alien script," Chas said. "A flightless, space-faring race that visited Anemoi and Turris."

"And Beira."

"And Beira. And maybe others we just aren't aware of yet."

"And how does that get us out of this cave? I don't suppose you can fly."

A considering pause. "You did throw me pretty high earlier."

That was far too high to be throwing Chas, even in this low gravity, even with nothing to lose. I told him so, and let him hem and haw and puzzle over our dilemma, testing the walls for climbing potential and taking experimental leaps. I could have told him to save his energy.

At last, he lowered to the ground.

Now I knew how Allan Quatermain must have felt, discovering the treasure of King Solomon's mines only to become trapped in the mines with the treasure. But Quatermain was unnaturally lucky, and he was the main character of a book, so of course he'd escaped the impossible situation intact. For me it would be a slow death of starvation, and maybe hypothermia. If I were lucky, I'd freeze in my sleep.

Dread crept into me like the chill—slow and marrow-deep. It struck me as an insult that I should suffer a headache on top of it all.

"How are you doing?" Chas said. He sounded too calm. I opened my eyes but didn't honor that with a response.

"We won't die of thirst," he said. "And we won't run out of air anytime soon. We can easily survive a week without eating. Another week, not as easily. The university will be here before then. They have the location of the ruins. They'll be crawling all over this place."

I closed my eyes again. If that was what Chas needed to tell himself so he wouldn't go crazed with panic...

I took a deep, steadying breath.

I still had the knife. I could pull that out now, end this quickly instead of dragging it out over the course of days or weeks. No reason not to, except I was a stubborn bastard.

How long would I hold out hope before I pulled it out?

I rocked forward. Curled over my knees and gripped my hair.

I should be more afraid than this, a remote part of me thought. *I should not be this numb.*

No. I wasn't numb. I was terrified.

I began to shiver in earnest.

I heard the scrape of Chas standing, his soft footsteps, the pop of his knee as he lowered next to me.

Oh God, not now. Don't.

And yet I felt the magnetic pull. I wanted to turn and cling to him. Somehow that would make this all better, having a neck to bury my face into, a warm solid living body. And not just any body. Chas.

"Hey," he said.

I was obliged to look up. He held a water bottle out. Something about the gesture struck me, and I looked a question at him.

"It's not water," he said, confirming my suspicion. "It's unfiltered from the stalks."

Somehow it didn't surprise me he'd kept some. Poison in a canteen. It was exactly the kind of hair-brained thing we researchers did.

What did surprise me was the earnest, calm way he offered it to me. Was this a merciful death?

"I did a diagnostic on the toxin you found. It's mild, like alcohol. It'll warm you up. And calm you down." He tipped back the canteen and took a drink.

I twitched with the involuntary urge to stop him, but he was already pulling the canteen from his lips and wiping his mouth. He looked at me with too-bright eyes. Still very much alive, and too collected.

His words registered. *Calm you down.* He wasn't joking, and that made it all the more ludicrous.

He continued to hold out the canteen.

Bloody hell. Well, why not?

I took the bottle and took three long swigs with no mind toward whether that was too much. Chas accepted it back without a blink and replaced the cap.

The liquor dropped through me with a force more violent than alcohol, a hot rush that went straight to my groin. I shuddered to my bones and threw my arms around myself. Calm? I shot Chas a look, knowing a moment's fear that he'd poisoned me—somehow knowing that for all my hair-pulling and theatrics, I'd have never had the gall to put myself out of my own misery. His eyes were too keen as he watched me. I'd never seen that expression on his face.

And then, just as quick, a hot liquid tide of relaxation rolled through me. Instantly, every muscle fiber in my body went loose and I knew that everything would be okay, even if this drug carried me off out of my life. It reminded me of the rush of endorphins I got off the med kit. The headache was gone, swept away in the current. I drifted sideways, untethered.

Chas gave a small, short chuckle. He sounded even closer. I felt the warmth coming off him like a glow, like I suddenly had a sixth sense, which was to detect heat and life.

Another rush dropped through me, a ball of molten lead to my groin that exploded on impact. Every cell of my body burned with need. I'd only experienced something like this once before, when I visited a drug den in Old London. That had been in simulation. Somehow I'd expected the intense surreality of that experience to be an embellishment, a programmer's fantasy.

I wondered if I was in sim, dreaming this entire trip.

Chas' shoulder brushed mine. Then his arms were around me. I pulled back, a token resistance. But Chas' grip was strong.

"Body heat," he said.

Then, as if in a dream, I was being drawn down to my side with Chas behind me. There was a crinkle of plastic and a thin metallic blanket fell down over us, snapped open and drawn down by Chas. I found myself in a sudden cocoon of heat with him, the drug making even the hard ground into a feather mattress. My head rested on Chas' arm, and I didn't know how that happened, either, only that it felt too good to move away. He cupped my bicep and squeezed gently. I made an involuntary noise. The drug lapped through me hot and devastating and lazy. I could just melt away into the ocean of it.

"Sleep for a while," Chas said, rubbing my arm—rubbing heat into me, I realized. I wanted to tell him I was plenty hot now. But I slid out to sea with the next wave.

CHAPTER TWENTY-EIGHT

I slid into consciousness, hazy and on the brink of a dream. I lay alone beneath the blanket. Chas sat a few feet away, bent over something on the ground. A red light winked, once, twice, slowly. The cold air prickled with moisture, but I was warm. The stone floor, though not a body, pulled me into its embrace. I faded back out.

Chapter Twenty-Nine

I woke to a hot breath against my neck and Chas pulling me closer. Clearly, no longer alone under the blanket.

Chas slid his hand from my hip to my ribs, perilously close to my nipple. An immediate flush of blood and adrenaline and other hormones shot through my body, and my heart slugged, like someone had crossed all the wires in my alarm system before setting off the bomb. The reaction was startling in intensity.

Then I recognized the sedate, sonorous rhythm of his breath. Asleep, I realized. Asleep, snuggling close.

And I was achingly, undeniably erect.

My pulse came too hard and fast. Liquor must have still looped through my system. What was the half-life of this stuff? The drunkenness had sharpened, an edge of hunger to replace the drifting euphoria. It made my skin feverishly sensitive. The air of the room was cold against my face; under the blanket, Chas was a living furnace. His feet nested against my own. I didn't remember removing my shoes, but then, I didn't remember much of anything after Chas brought the blanket down over us.

Had we...?

My heart slammed again at the thought, but other than the shoes, it felt like I was fully dressed, and my body felt spent, but not in that way.

"London?" Chas' voice, sleepy and deep, tickled the hairs at the nape of my neck.

"Hey." I managed to sound steady.

"Oh. I'm sorry," Chas said. He lifted his hand from my side, and the air at my neck grew cool as he pulled away.

"No problem." I missed the contact. I was drunk enough to acknowledge that to myself, but not so far gone I'd say it to Chas.

"How are you feeling?" he asked.

"Just fine. Not dead yet, and three sheets to the wind."

"That was some pretty powerful stuff." He sounded slightly chagrined.

"It did the trick."

Whatever the trick was, it was doing it. In every vein of my body.

"Good," Chas said. "You were starting to scare me, Doc."

I twisted to give him a look. "*I* was scaring you? That's what scared you?"

"I've been in situations like this before. You have, too. Panicking doesn't change things, except for the worse."

My pulse pounded, this time in outrage, but the feeling bled out of me almost as quickly as it'd come, pulled away on an invisible current. What he said was true enough. And it was a small thing to be upset about, just then.

There was a charged silence. The heat stayed, but the arousal had dialed down. That was a bit of good news.

The red light from the hallway still filled the room. It was perfectly quiet. Not even the rumble of the underground river reached here.

"Hey," Chas said softly, close enough to send a shiver over my skin. "Things could be worse."

Sure they could.

"We've got each other."

I snorted.

We lapsed into more silence. I could sense him containing himself, making no contact although his heat simmered only a finger width away. He hadn't moved his feet, though. Those remained tucked against mine. I could feel the tendons of his toes against my sole.

It seemed petty not to say something. Also, I needed to distract myself. So I asked, "Do you have any regrets?"

"I don't regret coming on this trip. I don't even regret coming down here. We all have to die sometime; why not making a great discovery?"

There was one way to look at it.

Chas continued after a pause, in a quieter voice, "My regret is abandoning my family. I shouldn't have left them."

The pain was naked in his voice. I'd never heard anything like it from him before.

Because I felt compelled to attempt a meaningful response, I said, "But you wouldn't be the man you are now."

"No, I wouldn't," he agreed. I couldn't tell from his tone what was between the lines there, only that there was a lot of it.

Chas asked, "How about you? Did you leave anyone behind?"

"My mom and my sister. But they both expected this. They'll be sitting around saying, 'I told you so' to each other, since they won't be able to say it to me. I'm glad for that, at least."

"They'll miss you," Chas said. It wasn't a question.

"Yeah. I'm sure they will."

"Anyone else?" he asked. "Anyone...special?"

"What, like a mate? No." And before that could turn into a topic to drill deeper into, I asked, "What about you? Anyone special to miss you?"

"No."

Just that. A single word, but a loaded one.

The warmth of arousal returned.

"You're a good-looking guy," I said. "I'm surprised you don't have the ladies hanging all over you."

I meant it to be teasing—mostly—so his answer caught me off guard.

"What makes you think I'd want the ladies hanging all over me?" He said it in an altered voice, husky.

"You're shitting me," I said, twisting to look at him. Maybe the drug caused the exaggerated incredulity in my tone.

"Is it a problem?"

"No." Scratch that. "Yes."

"Why?" he asked, in clear challenge.

"Chas," I said, in what was meant to be a warning tone. It came out sounding considerably more desperate.

He narrowed his eyes, but there was the suggestion of a smile there now. "Are you afraid I might do something to you?"

"*Jesus*, Chas." Now I did sound desperate. "We're going to die down here."

"We could," he agreed. "So I'm going to ask you a very serious question. May I kiss you?"

It was like being plunged into a bath of scalding water. I gaped at Chas over my shoulder. He watched me with grave eyes. Their gaze traveled to my mouth.

"You're a good-looking guy, Doc. Even with your mouth hanging open."

I closed it.

"We can't," I said, although the words sounded hollow, automatic, a little scared.

"Why not?"

"You're my student. I'm your professor."

"Not technically. And what does it really matter?"

What, indeed?

"No one will ever know. None of your lady friends."

"Lady friends!"

His full mouth quirked. "Gentleman callers?"

"Now you're being a shit."

"Probably." His humor faded. He whispered, "Let me touch you?"

I swallowed. Need gripped me. I didn't know if it was mine, the drug, or Chas'. I rolled to my other side to face him and found his hand under the blanket. He squeezed back lightly.

"I don't even know if you like men," Chas admitted. "There was speculation, but no one really knew."

Another thing the students talked about? Didn't they have better things to think about, like what they were actually supposed to be studying?

"Taking a risk?" I said.

He licked his lips. "Would it be funny to say this feels bigger than any of the others I've taken?"

I wanted to be able to laugh, but my mouth was dry. The weight of Chas' hand in mine was solid, real. His calloused fingertips pressed against my palm. How many times had I lain in my rooms and imagined him as I fisted myself madly? A shameful number. All those desperate solo fantasies, and the less solo encounters with virtual men in sim, encounters that always left me emptier when they were over.

Gods, don't let me die without having fucked a real man in years.

Yawning loneliness stretched its jaws around me, hunger so sharp my eye sockets burned. I guided Chas' hand to my cheek.

His eyes unfocused. "I can feel your pulse." He moved his fingers to the beat of my neck. "It's fast."

"It should be. I'm intoxicated." Not just on liquor.

Chas ran the pad of his thumb lightly over my windpipe. I went still and closed my eyes.

"You're beautiful," Chas said. "I've wanted to know which way you gaze since I met you."

I made a sound in my throat like a laugh. That was mostly at myself, because my immediate thought was, *You. I gaze at you.* And wouldn't that have been romantic?

Chas pulled his hand away and I did almost protest this time. He replaced it a moment later, thumb moist from his mouth. He ran it down my windpipe, making a trail of wetness to my collarbone.

I shuddered.

Chas caught me, gripped my shoulder. He chuckled. It sounded just a little breathless.

Hero worship. I'd told myself it was just hero worship.

I suddenly didn't want to be cuddled or wooed or play this game any longer. I thumbed open my pants. I took his hand and closed it around my straining erection.

Chas had just started to laugh. The sound turned into a gasp. "*Fuck,* London."

I pushed into his grip. "Does this—answer—your question?"

His answer was a groan. Then he was grasping at my pants, pulling them down. I lifted my hips, wiggled, and kicked. Felt a brief blast of cool air as I kicked the pants out into the room. Chas still had a hold of my shaft, as if it were his job to never let it go. His hot hand squeezed. I saw sparks and almost came at once.

I gripped his wrist, and he stilled. I reached for his buttons. He didn't stop me. His eyes half closed. He looked like maybe he was praying.

My fingers were not steady with his buttons. I jerked the waistband over his narrow hips. In the same motion, I slid him under me and pushed up to straddle him.

His eyes flew open. Their hazel was a startling color in the red-tinted light of the room. I lowered my hips to his and drove against him.

It was coarse and dry, two bucks rutting. But no friction had been sweeter. It only seemed wrong to do it with clothes on. Suddenly I needed to see him, human animal and human animal, to be with him skin on skin.

I pulled my shirt over my head, and Chas his. He looked flushed after the rush of fabric. The nubs of his nipples stood dark against his brown skin. Tiny, tight curls of black hair dusted his chest.

His eyes closed as we resumed our pace. I watched him in wonder, partly because I didn't remember ever seeing such an open and desperate play of feelings on the face of a lover before. And partly because it was Chas, and I marveled to see those expressions on him, inspired by me. His plump mouth parted. I loved that mouth. I almost kissed it. I went for his neck instead, teething his tight skin, feeling the bite of his nails as his fingers curled against my ass.

A warning tingle of warmth flared in the base of my balls. I pulled back, but Chas' fingers clenched. That did it. I pressed my mouth against his throat and shouted into his skin.

The truly startling thing, the incredulous thing, was Chas bucking under me, gasping, splashing wet heat across my belly.

Chas went limp beneath me. The ground became hard beneath my elbows but I didn't move. Wave after wave of warmth rolled over me, the drug extending the aftershocks of the orgasm, like the waves following a tsunami. We heaved for breath against each other, chests rising in unsteady counterpoint until finally I pushed myself up. My elbows stung from scraping them raw against the stone.

Chas' eyes were closed. Without my hands to pillow his head, it tilted back against the stone floor, exposing his throat and turning his face up like a man in rapture, which maybe he was. His belly glistened.

The pulse below his jaw throbbed. I kissed it and reached a hand across the floor.

"Hey," he said, eyes popping open at the touch of fabric against his stomach. "That's your shirt."

"It is," I said, as I mopped his stomach in long strokes. I folded the shirt in half and caught a rivulet of fluid spilling down his flank.

He watched me clean him and then myself. "That's going to dry stiff."

"I imagine it will," I said, and tossed it into the corner. "But I guess that won't be a problem. Not like I'll need it. As long as I'm in here, I've got you and this clever blanket we're under."

He gazed at me with an odd, glazed expression. It might have just hit him, too, that we would be under here together for a long time.

A long, long time.

Poor Chas. He hadn't signed up for this. Roped into this fool's errand by Sita.

And poor Sita, back at the university, thinking she'd secured my safety, soon to realize she'd sent not one, but two of us, to our doom.

This was the one I wouldn't come home from.

I lowered to my side and tucked the blanket around us, settled his head on my arm. I brushed my knuckles against his temple and he closed his eyes again. I had the urge to kiss his lashes. I didn't.

The sentimentality often came after sex. I'd almost forgotten that. The sentimentality, and the tide of sleep. I pressed my brow against

Chas' temple and hugged an arm across his chest. He laid his hand on top and squeezed once. Warm together, we slept once more.

☆☆☆

I woke with my head pillowed on Chas' arm. I wasn't sure how or when that switch had happened, but I lay there for a while, absorbing the experience. Hunger made a knot in my throat, and the floor was unforgivingly hard, but there was something very comfortable about lying here with Chas. Soon the panic would press in on me, but for right now, I was at peace.

I recognized immediately the little signs he'd woken—the change in breathing pattern, the minute change in muscle tension. Then he opened those amazing hazel eyes. He smiled at me. It was not a smile I'd seen, exactly, on his face before, although I'd seen something like it. It was his happy smile, but a little softer. And something else. Wistful, maybe. We were close enough to kiss, but neither of us moved in for it. I was too busy appreciating the piece of art that was his face.

I brushed the side of his face with my fingers, enjoying the short beard. I was conscious of the tenderness of the gesture and turned it into another, sweeping my hand down and giving Chas' neck a rough massaging squeeze. I dropped my hand back to my side.

I looked up at the ceiling. Cold reality rushed back to me. Literally cold: I was suddenly aware of the chill against my face. The awareness of thirst hit me hard, and the awareness that the thirst wasn't a problem I needed to worry about. Bleakness came with that thought.

"Why is it?" Chas asked gently.

"Hm?"

His eyebrows creased. He didn't respond right away, taking a moment to think about it. "Was there ever anyone? A partner?"

Although my head remained on Chas' arm, I felt several feet away from him. Then I relaxed. What the hell?

"Not for eight years," I said. "And I swore there never would be again."

Chas didn't ask the question, though it was in his eyes. That was one thing I liked about Chas. One of the many things.

"I was seventeen when I had my first relationship," I said, then added, "First committed relationship. Gilroy Stevens. I thought for sure we'd get married, screw convention, have book babies. He was a historian, and a damn good writer. Then he moved to Earth, and that was that."

Funny I could talk about it like it was someone else's life now. In a way, it was.

Chas' expression didn't change, like he was waiting for more.

"That was the prelude," I agreed. "Chapter one was Felix Mata."

His eyebrows drew together. "Dr. Mata? The guest lecturer?"

"The one and only. My mentor in graduate school. I was twenty. He was thirty-three."

Awareness dawned. "You were his student."

A simple sentence for a relationship that had been more complicated. How could I describe what I'd had with Felix? It embarrassed me to think about it. The spell he'd had over me. Just stepping into the room he could turn me on, and not just physically. He'd turned me on mentally, his intellect and suave personality. He could be a prick, sure, and that'd turned me on, too. Confident. Always confident—and not in a disgustingly arrogant way. Just...sure of himself, and he carried himself that way. In the classroom. In the bedroom. That had been his true genius: he'd perfected the art of confidence, and it was key to his every success.

"I was his tool," I said. "I was infatuated with him, and he used that."

I sat up. I realized my mistake as the thin blanket slipped from my shoulders and I dove upward into cold air. A shock, and then I tucked the blanket down over my lap.

"It was a lot of stupidity on my part," I said. "I think I wanted to impress him. Who the fuck knows. I told him a lot of things I shouldn't have. Pillow talk." I threw an ironic glance at Chas. "I told him about my language ability, the first person outside my family. I was really excited. He had just found the language records on Kandam, and I thought, I might have a crack at that. He thought so too, and invited me to join the research team. To have those files in front of me, all of those alien words." I framed my hands around an imaginary page. "They were so beautiful and like nothing I'd ever seen. It took me three weeks. Three weeks. And then finally, one day, it just clicked. Like that. I cracked the language for him."

I looked at Chas. "And then he published the results. My work. My translation. His name on the manuscript."

"No way. He did not."

"He did."

Chas pushed up on his elbow. "He didn't credit you at all?"

"Oh, right. He mentioned me in the acknowledgments. 'Thanks for the help in preparing this manuscript.'"

Chas swore. "You could take him to court. Do you have proof? Notes to show you worked on the translation?"

The fire in his eyes went a small way toward soothing the old hurt.

"I was a graduate student at the time. A nobody. And it's water under the bridge now. Everyone has to know, anyway."

Chas' mouth pressed into a grim line. "You loved him, and he betrayed you."

I laughed, but it was true. "Yeah, he did that. I was twenty-two. That's when I decided to go on my first expedition. It was revenge, plain and simple. I was determined to discover more languages and decipher them. I didn't want to just discredit him. I wanted to bury him. Felix Mata never had another Lost language to his name. My career exploded." I glanced at Chas with a lift of my eyebrow. "I told you how I felt about the public attention after that. It turns out I liked the credit but the publicity, not so much. That was something Felix took smoothly. He always did clean up nice for a camera." I tucked the blanket closer around my waist. "A few years later, I tried at another relationship. By then I was a little older, a little wiser, and firmly enough established I thought I didn't have to worry about anyone stealing my career. I kept my work and my romantic life separate. It turned out he was a journalist. He was writing a biography of me."

"No."

"Yes."

"And so you swore off relationships after that."

Actually, I'd threatened the man with epic legal action first—and then I'd sworn off relationships.

"It certainly keeps things less complicated," I said, and lowered back down next to him. I meant it to be light, but the truth was, another relationship like that would have destroyed me. It all sounded so mild when put into words, a series of bad decisions. The thing was, I'd always loved with my whole heart. I never could do things halfheartedly. I put my entire being into the things I was passionate about.

"Tough luck in love," I said, and dredged a smile. "Made up for by really good luck in life. Up until now." I glanced at the cave ceiling.

I was aware of the intensity of Chas' attention and the slight change in muscle tension as he drew toward me. I turned just in time for my mouth to connect with his in an unintended kiss. It took me a moment to recover, and then I gave myself into it.

All of those lonely years, numb and removed. I'd been missing this—this perfect, beautiful bond with another human being. All the successes in my career meant nothing next to this. Nothing more important than this moment of connection.

Chas pulled away from the kiss. His confusion and question were in the way he drew back and held the sides of my face. I didn't meet his gaze, but bent my head and buried it against his shoulder. I was aware of the hot liquid on my face. A sob bubbled up in me and I held it down, because if I gave into that, I was done for. I wanted to die with at least some of my dignity intact. So I heaved a shuddering sigh and rested there while Chas rubbed my shoulder lightly.

And the thought came to me: at least I wasn't going to die alone. Thank the gods for that.

I hooked my arm around Chas and pulled him close. We held each other, just breathing together, hearts beating against each other's chests. I could live for this. This was something to hold onto, to hold on for, something I didn't want to give up. I wanted to live for this.

I shuddered again, blinked hot tears from my eyes. Over Chas' shoulder, I caught sight of the broken scout bot. Chas had carried that with him from above, which struck me as odd and slightly compulsive. What he'd been planning to do with that pile of singed metal...

The pile of singed metal blinked a yellow light once, laconically.

I shot up and sat very still, heart pounding. I could have just imagined it—fever dream, drug flashback, the hallucinations of a desperate man.

The light blinked again. No hallucination.

I practically leapt over Chas, exploding into the chill hall. I paused only long enough to jerk my pants on. My eyes didn't leave the bot.

I dropped to my knees next to it, flipping the machinery over until I sorted out where the head was. I switched the On button.

A thin whining noise keened in my ears, pitched almost too high to hear. Lights popped on, green and blue, and it powered to life in my hands. I thrust it out at arm's length, like a thing I'd just discovered was alive and might bite me.

"It's working," I said. "It's working."

It thrummed and spat and whined, and in a moment, I was able to spread my hands away from it and it hovered on its own, casting its head around, taking in its surroundings.

I fell back in awe, feeling something vast like a laugh inside me. Then I scrabbled forward to its control panel and input an order. A moment later the thing buzzed up to the hidden door far above. It took only a moment to find the button Chas had spotted and to press it.

I didn't breathe.

Then the stone rumbled, and I let out a shout of triumph, and Chas and I were scrabbling to gather our things as stairs erupted into existence.

Chas hopped across the hall, blanket in one hand, hitching his pants in the other. I caught him and danced a dizzy circle with him.

"It worked," I said. It was a miracle, an impossible stroke of luck. All because Chas had thought to carry that thing along, all because...

I went still. In my arms, Chas did too. A certain memory came back to me of a dream I had, involving Chas and a blinking light.

I pulled away. Chas looked happy—but not as overwhelmingly relieved as I was. There was something like amusement there.

"You knew," I said. "You fixed it."

Chas smiled. He kissed my startled mouth and said, "Let's go before it closes again."

EPILOGUE

I flipped through a book in my office. *Treatise on the Wealth, Power, and Resources of the British Empire, in Every Quarter of the World, Including the East Indies*. The sort of book had excited my dad, one of the many thrilling volumes on English progress and power that glutted the ceiling-high bookshelves he'd left behind.

I'd intended to go through the shelves and see what I could toss. It was probably time. After five years, this office was as much mine as it had been his.

Instead, here I sat among the stacks, reading the books I'd pulled out of the bottom shelves for consideration. Some of them were from my childhood, volumes I'd read right here in the office. Even if they weren't watermarked originals, they were the very same copies my dad and I had read. I flipped the pages slowly, as if I could find us between them.

I'd started with the bottom shelves because they were easier. I was better at controlling the vertigo now, and after the sheer cliff faces of Turris, the solid bookcase ladder was small fry. But after all the climbing on Turris, I'd pretty much had it with heights for now.

I'd had it with a lot of things. Chief among them, shellfish. And soup. After escaping the cave, we'd trekked back to the spire forest and subsisted exclusively on the flesh of spire ticks. We'd roasted them over dung from the insect giraffes. That had been Chas' idea. Tick flesh had tasted like mushy sour crab and disintegrated in the mouth without any of the lush chewy texture of decapod crustaceans. We'd also discovered the toxin in the tick body fluids could be mitigated by boiling. The creatures' flesh was mostly water, so in roasting them, we made a kind of runny crab bisque.

The university's rescue ship arrived after two days. I'd never been so glad to eat a salad.

The ship had made good time. For a few terrifying minutes, I thought it would miss us. But it landed in the vast plain where the Mi'hani had been, and was still there when Chas and I caught up to it.

The crew members hadn't looked quite as astonished as they could have at our bedraggled arrival at their door, although the eyes of one of the members lingered a moment on the bottom of my shirt, which—looking down—I remembered was stiff from cleaning up the product of our desperate shag.

There had been clean clothes on the ship. And a hot shower. And a bunk room that, miraculously, I did not need to share with anyone, where I spent much of the trip home viewing and reviewing the mysterious sphere with its script I was sure must be a language, but could not figure out.

Chas had left me alone in the room. At times, I heard his voice raised in conversation and brief laughter with the ship's crew, and didn't know how to categorize the feeling I got from that. Since our escape from the cave, it had been back to business between us. I'd made sure of that. To say I was mortified would be an understatement. Chas and I had talked little during those days waiting for the rescue team, mostly about practical matters. On the ship, we'd talked even less. Sitting alone in the bunk room of the ship, I had missed the camaraderie we'd come to share. But I couldn't figure out where we'd go from there.

We'd arrived at the university three days ago and parted for our apartments. I hadn't seen him since then.

I scowled as I realized I'd been reading the same paragraph over and over without comprehending. Maybe that was the beginning of a headache between my eyes. I'd been reading all morning.

A knock came on the doorframe.

I looked up. I didn't know what had possessed me to leave my office door open, except I couldn't stand having it closed. Maybe nervousness after my two near-misses at being trapped underground.

Chas stood there looking clean and neat, jaw and mouth smooth, hair buzzed down to the thin felt fuzz on his skull that I remembered from the first time we met. He even wore the same lean-fitting olive shirt. There was something different about him, though. Something about the way he held himself, and the look in his eye. Like he knew something. Or maybe it was my own knowledge of Chas that had changed, and Chas himself was the same he'd always been.

I realized I was staring. I closed the book and stood. "Chas," I said, voice neutral. "How are you?"

He gave a polite, slightly self-conscious smile. A good-natured smile. "Alive and home. Can't complain."

"No," I agreed. "I bet by now you've even introduced our new Turris cuisine to your food dispenser."

Chas grimaced with humor. "Nah. It's been really nice to eat lamb. And fried food."

I crossed my arms at my chest, self-conscious of how defensive that posture must look. But it was really the most comfortable way to hold my arms.

Never mind how fast my heart beat beneath them.

I regarded Chas. I didn't know what to say next. I didn't know what our relationship was at this point. Student, research partner, or... Well, no. Friends, if anything. But what kind? Not the kind to go shooting together on a weekend afternoon.

Chas' gaze floated past me to the stacks of books. "Cleaning out?"

I turned. "Not quite. I was thinking about it. I was considering pulling down the bookshelves, clearing out all the old furniture."

"Why? I mean, I really love it in here."

I shrugged. Honestly, the words had just popped out of my mouth. I hadn't considered it before. No, I liked it in here, too. It was home in a way even my apartment was not. My past was in here, and my present. It belonged to my dad, and myself, but also to my community of students and colleagues. It felt...warm.

"Maybe I'll keep it," I said. "I think I'm just looking for something to keep me busy now that I've returned. Mata's got my classes till the end of the semester." Mata had my classes, and I wasn't yet ready to work on the research manuscripts I'd promised Sita. I owed her the Anemoi findings, and now Turris. She'd be on my case about them soon enough. For now, though, she was pursuing legal action against the Mi'hani on charges of unlicensed excavation, poaching, and kidnapping. That would keep her busy for a while.

"How about the artifact?" Chas said. "Any luck with that?"

I shook my head.

Hesitated.

"I have something to show you, though," I said. Chas watched as I glanced down the hall and closed the office door. I took a key from my vest pocket and opened the locked drawer of my desk. My heart beat faster. Maybe I was making a mistake. But there were some mistakes even I couldn't help myself from making.

I pulled my bundled shirt from the drawer.

"Turn off the light," I said.

Chas looked quizzical, but obeyed.

Light from the hall found its way through the slats in the blinds, enough to make out Chas' form, but not enough to ruin my demonstration.

"All right?" he said.

"Here." I crouched to hold the bundle beneath my desk, where it was darkest.

I unwrapped the sphere from my shirt.

Chas was just looking over the edge of the desk as I did so, and the sudden light from the sphere illuminated his surprised expression. Over the artifact, thousands of tiny symbols, previously only barely visible on its surface, flared with white light.

"Holy Jove," he breathed.

I turned the sphere so he could see the seamless pattern of symbols over its entire surface.

"It's just like the walls," he said. "When did you discover it did that?"

"On the ship, in my room. It glowed through the shirt. It does it only in absolute dark—or near absolute."

"That's amazing," he said. "And you still haven't been able to decipher it?"

"No." I closed the shirt around it again and rose from my crouch.

"What does Dean Tiwari think?"

I placed it back in the drawer and turned the key. "She doesn't know about it yet." I crossed to the switch and flipped it. Blinked for a moment in the sudden light.

"But didn't you tell the dean about what you discovered?"

"Sure, just not all of it."

Chas didn't ask me why. Maybe he suspected I didn't have an answer for that question. Probably, I needed a little time for the sphere just to be mine. Mine, and because he'd been there with me, his.

Yes, he was definitely changed. I was too. It hung between us, the knowledge of what we'd shared—and not just in the cave.

He took a breath to speak, but I beat him to it.

"I don't think I ever said thank you. A proper thank you, for getting me out of several binds. If not for you, I'd likely be on Mi'hani right now without a thought in my head, or I'd be another artifact on Turris. So thank you."

"I think we pretty well saved each other."

"We make a good team," I said. I steeled myself. "That said, if there was anyone I'd choose to be trapped in a cave with, it'd be you. But I'd appreciate if whatever happened there stayed there."

Chas paled. He glanced away, and his Adam's apple shivered as he took a swallow. For a horrifying moment, I thought he blinked tears from his eyes. And— All right. Maybe I'd underestimated his emotional involvement. Or maybe that was just disappointment, a healthy blow to pride.

He met my gaze. His eyes were clear, no tears there. But I had unmistakably hurt him.

"I know you've had bad experiences in the past," he said. "I understand that. But I hoped you might want to try again, because that meant something to me."

I closed my eyes and took a deep breath. Alarmingly, I was the one whose eyes burned. I opened them. "You broke my trust."

His expression fell. "I know," he said. "And I'm so sorry. Honestly, I didn't know if the scout would work. That's one thing. I thought I could fix it, but I wasn't sure it hadn't taken some internal damage I couldn't see, and I wouldn't have been able to fix that. I should have said something though. If I'd known how you'd been treated in the past, I absolutely would have. Even without knowing that, it was wrong. I realize that."

I folded my arms. "Right."

"You're doing it right now," he said, with something between a smile and a grimace.

"What?"

"You put up walls. You look at me, like... And then the walls go up. The gods' honest truth was, I needed to know. Because I wanted to think you were looking at me like that."

"Gods, Chas." I sat and put my face in my hands. Into the silence, the old grandfather clock ticked off the seconds. How were we even having this conversation?

At last, I said, "You admire me. And as flattered as I am, I can't take advantage of you like that."

It sounded wooden, even to me. Chas' smile was grim. "Remember, I was the one taking advantage of you."

My face heated. "You did," I said. "But I'm—" I almost said *the adult here.* "—the professor here, your senior, and I'm back in my right mind, and I would be the one taking advantage of you."

He squinted his eyes at me. "That doesn't make sense. So if I were to quit the program, it'd be all right then."

"No!" There was real and immediate horror in my voice. "No, it still wouldn't be right."

Chas watched me steadily, awaiting the rest of the explanation. Damn graduate students for wanting an explanation to everything.

"I'm flattered by your attention, really I am—"

"One month," Chas said, holding up his finger. "Let's give it one month. No obligations. It will be good for both of us."

I shook my head.

"Then once. One night in a real bed, both of us clean from the shower. So I can taste you."

Gods.

I swallowed through the tightness in my throat. There was nothing I could do for the other tightness.

"Once," I said, because gods help me...

"Once," Chas said, and smiled.

About the Author

Christine lives with her writing partner in the wilds of urban Oregon, where they raise weeds, worms, and eyebrows.

Twitter: http://www.twitter.com/dansedesirable
Website: http://christinedanse.com
Email: christinedanse@gmail.com

Coming Soon from Christine Danse

Shaper

The Mi'hani War #1, in the London Wells universe

Excerpt

I woke in bed. A different one this time, in a dark room. I vaguely recalled kind hands and laughter around a table. I didn't try to pursue the memory. I let it go like a shy creature or a small child, having faith that it would eventually come around. The room was dark but a small lamp cast enough light to find my way to the door.

I found her in the living room. She sat on the couch with her arms around a pillow, gazing at a fish tank.

"I remember you now," I said.

Her gaze snapped to mine. I recognized those blue eyes now. There was something in them, a startled look, and something else.

"You do?" Careful, neutral in inflection. Too careful.

"You killed the police who were after me."

Run, Mom had said on the phone. *Don't come home. They've come for Daniel. Run.*

I'd run.

They cornered me at the end of the street. She fell out of the sky—from one of the balconies, likely—and they dropped to the ground, dead. Her face had been a terrible blank as her gaze met mine.

"I thought you were going to kill me, too," I said.

"I wasn't. I was there to help you."

"I realize that now," I said. If she'd wanted to kill me, she could have snuffed me a breath after the men. But at the time, I'd been irrational with terror. And I'd run from her and—

The memory stopped there, but I could sense the immensity of what came next, the jagged terrible shape just beneath the surface. My heart raced, skipping beats, my body reacting to a threat I couldn't remember.

"Come here," she said.

It was strange and also natural, her invitation. I sat down next to her and let her put her arms around me. Comfort from a familiar stranger. Her hands laced loosely at my abdomen. A shaper's hands.

Mine too, I realized as I gazed down at them. That came very close to the terrifying memory, and I closed them.

She offered simple comfort: a warm body, a hand stroking my hair. The easy affection of someone who worked with kids. Of course, I wasn't a kid anymore. Whatever I'd had left of my childhood—the naivety of a woman in her early twenties—was gone, although I couldn't remember where to.

Why did I allow her to put her arms around me? She had to be an assassin, a shaper who could kill another with a thought. I was a rabbit in the jaws of a wolf. Even other shapers feared those who could kill another with such ease, making it seem like nothing more had happened than a stroke or a fatal skip of the heart.

"I knew you before," I said.

Her hand paused. The words just came. I didn't know what came next, what revelation was supposed to follow that, but she held very still.

NINESTAR PRESS, LLC

www.ninestarpress.com

www.ingramcontent.com/pod-product-compliance
Lightning Source LLC
Chambersburg PA
CBHW020256200626
46816CB00001BA/326